To Mark Ehrman

© John Tottenham, 2025

This edition © Semiotext(e), 2025

All rights reserved. No part of this book may be reproduced, stored in a retrieval system, or transmitted by any means, electronic, mechanical, photo-copying, recording, or otherwise, without prior permission of the publisher.

Published by Semiotext(e)
PO BOX 629, South Pasadena, CA 91031
www.semiotexte.com

Cover illustration by Adam Roth as a homage to the cover of X's *Under the Big Black Sun* (1982)

Design: Hedi El Kholti
ISBN: 978-1-63590-249-5

10 9 8 7 6 5 4 3 2 1

Distributed by the MIT Press, Cambridge, MA.
Printed in the United States of America

Service

John Tottenham

semiotext(e)

Los Angeles 2016–2019

I

"Do you need a bag?" I asked, and received no response.

"D'you need a bag?" I asked again, and again received no response.

I tried again, a third time.

This time, the customer looked up from his texting.

"What?" he said.

"A bag," I said. "Do you need one?"

"What kind of bag?" asked the customer, a clean-cut young man with facial hair and neck tattoos.

"Do I have to describe the bag?" I said.

"Is it a paper bag?" he asked.

"Yes, it's a paper bag," I said, and handed him a brown paper bag.

He walked off, looking put out. Perhaps he had wanted me to bag the book for him.

"Hi Sean." From whom this greeting came, I had no idea. It is the fate of the terminal bookstore employee to frequently be addressed by people he doesn't know.

A forlorn figure shuffled up to the counter with an expectant look on his face that suggested I should be pleased to see him. I returned an unconvincing imitation of his smile, anticipating the twenty minutes of my time that this energy-draining vampire was certain to consume. It was inconceivable that he would leave any sooner than that. He was fresh and ready to twist my ear off. This might be his first social interaction of the day, but it was my umpteenth, and I was trapped.

"What's going on?" he asked.

"Nothing."

"What else is going on?"

"You mean apart from nothing?"

He just stood there, waiting for me to alleviate his boredom. Not content with killing his own time, he wanted to kill my time too.

"You ever have this dream where you're in a dark room and can't see what you're doing?" he said. "You turn on the light switch and it doesn't work, and you're just alone in the darkness. Then you wake up."

"'Tell a dream, lose a reader,' as Henry James wrote," I said.

"'Lose your dreams and you may lose your mind,' as the Rolling Stones said. But they were talking about a different type of dream."

It wasn't what he said that was so boring, it was the sound of his voice and the desperation palpably simmering just below the surface. The merciless drone was the sound of him charging his loneliness on my battery. I could feel my already slim reserves of energy being sapped, ounce by ounce. *I need to think, I cannot think in your presence.* But what was the alternative, to spend time with him outside the workplace? That would be even worse; better to endure him here.

"I don't have those kind of dreams," I said.

The pest stepped aside to make way for a long-haired, denim-clad woman who prompted her young daughter to hand me a children's book. The straining child could barely reach to the top of the counter and I had to stretch down to grab the book. The kid smiled up at me, almost begrudgingly it seemed—fully aware of her own cuteness but somehow recognizing me as an undeserving recipient of it. I knew the routine: another fake smile was being extorted from me. I couldn't very well refuse a child: I forced out a weak and partially toothless grin.

"Do you do gift wrapping?" asked the adorable little girl's mother.

I took a deep breath and responded in the affirmative.

The phone started ringing.

"Hi-i-i-i-i-i-iiiii …" A perky, high-pitched voice on the other end of the line almost punctured my eardrums. "How's your day going?"

"Never mind that," I said. "What do you need?"

"Can I ask you if you have a particular book in stock?"

"What is it?"

"*The Artist's Way.*"

The wailing of a child tore through the air.

I put the caller on hold and began to crudely wrap the children's book.

Another stack of books and a soiled credit card were placed on the counter. I rang the books up, sickened by the continual swiping of cards and punching in of numbers, the dead time entailed by credit card transactions.

The denim-clad woman pressed up against the counter. "Don't worry about it," she said.

"It's almost done."

"My child is hurt," she announced in a shrill tone of maternal authority.

I handed the partially wrapped children's book over to her.

The phone rang again. The caller whose book I hadn't looked for was on the other end of the line: "I called up five minutes ago …"

"Yes, I'm sorry. We got cut off. We're out of it."

Without a word, she hung up.

I felt another unflattering Yelp review coming on.

The forlorn pest returned, the stale fumes of perennial bachelordom wafting into my face as he leaned across the counter to destroy what was left of me with meaningless conversation.

"I don't know what to do with myself," he said. He found his own company oppressive but didn't seem to mind inflicting it upon others.

"Thanks for the information," I said.

"I'm going to get a coffee," he said, and walked back to the café at the other end of the store, only to be replaced by another pest.

"You know I knocked myself out writing a puff piece about you a few years ago," I said to Cyrus Fapper, since he insisted upon standing in front of me at the counter.

"You did? I never saw it. What for?" said Cyrus, a dandiacal middle-aged culture vulture who flaunted his many artistic passions widely and loudly on social media.

"Your publisher put me up to it. But it was never published and I was never paid for it."

"I have good news," announced Cyrus with unforgivable nonchalance. "I have a memoir coming out. So maybe we could use it then."

"Congratulations," I said with as much conviction as I could muster. "A memoir concerning what?"

"My childhood."

"Very nice."

"Prolix are publishing it," he casually added.

"How did you swing that?" I asked, rendered almost speechless with envy and disgust.

"I pitched it to them."

Why would anybody want to read Cyrus' memoirs? He'd never published a book before; he wasn't famous. Then the light flared up over my head: His mother was famous—she had been part of the '60s

Warhol circle, and Cyrus had been raised in the rarefied low-life environment of the fabled Factory scene that people never tire of reading about in these less decadently glamorous times. Brigid Polk had been one of his babysitters. So, naturally, his childhood memories would command great interest.

"Did you get an advance?"

"A very small one."

But really, who cared about an advance when you were being published by Prolix? The distinctive logo on its tasteful white spine was a stamp of quality that automatically invited respect and curiosity from reader and reviewer alike. What more could a first-time author want than to be published by such a distinguished independent press? And it's not as if Cyrus even needed an advance: he was supported by some sort of trust set up by his mother, who, while documenting her years as a slumming artist in several memoirs of her own, had made a small fortune on the real estate market.

"What are you buying that for?" I asked Cyrus as he placed a copy of *Glass of Anger*, a Brazilian novella, featuring strong sexual content, on the counter.

"Gil recommended it," he said, referring to the store's owner.

"He likes any slim translation with a whiff of perversity about it."

"It looks good."

"It's crap."

"Have you read it?"

"I flipped through it. It's one of those translations in which the lady parts are referred to as 'her sex.' I can't read that. Nobody ever uses that euphemism in English, so why does it appear so frequently in translations?"

"If it's an old translation it might make sense," said Cyrus.

"It's a recent one," I said. "No word has ever been found that I feel comfortable using to describe feminine genitalia; all the usual appellations trivialize, vulgarize or demonize it, but 'her sex' really takes the cake."

At sixty-three pages this recently published book was no more than a short story, but it was presented in the form of a novel; it was the sort of book that people who wanted to be thought of as "well-read" felt they were supposed to like, and it was presented with a classic red-on-black design with bold lettering. I had given it a chance, reading a few passages between ringing up customers. The words lay dead on the page but it was flying off the shelves, and not only owing to Gilbert's recommendation. Its popularity suggested that the words must sing for somebody. Maybe it was another case of bad writers for bad readers, and vice versa. Can there really be a correlation between writers that write badly and readers that read badly? This dynamic clearly applied to music, art and film, so why wouldn't it also apply to literature?

"Do yourself a favor, read this." I pointed Cyrus toward a copy of Barbara Pym's *Some Tame Gazelle*.

"Subtle ... unpretentious ... comforting ... elegant ... understated humor." Cyrus recited the copy on the back of the old paperback, and put it back down. "I don't think so," he said.

"It's only three dollars."

"Maybe next time."

"There won't be a next time. Her work is too accessible and enjoyable to be appreciated by the likes of you. I'm not giving you a discount on that shit," I said, as Cyrus tentatively poked the credit card machine with the edge of his card.

"Go on, man, stick it in," I said, aggressively.

"That's what she said," he said.

"I doubt it," I said.

"Now it says 'Please Remove,'" he said, apparently mystified by this simple command.

"She probably did say that," I said.

"Send me a copy of your piece," said Cyrus as I handed back his receipt.

"I'm sure you can get more prominent puffers than me," I said.

"I don't know about that," he insincerely responded as he walked out.

This well-connected nonentity and literary fringe-player was getting published. Unfortunately, I didn't have a prestigious art-damaged lineage to trade on. My father had been an accountant. *Intellectual* was a dirty word in the household I grew up in. There was no hope. I liked Cyrus better, if at all, when he was a failure.

A smiling stranger walked in and wanted a smile in return. But smiling is hard work and I have to ration them out if only to conserve energy. I can't return the greeting of everybody that walks in: that would be painful, unnatural, and exhausting.

"Do you have any like Borges?" he asked.

"Do we have anything similar to Borges?"

I pointed him to the fiction section a few yards away. Two minutes later, he returned with a copy of *Labyrinths*.

"D'you want a bag?"

"That would be amazing," he said.

"Hello, my friend, I'm looking for *The Trial* by Kafka," stated a potbellied middle-aged man attired in a horizontally striped T-shirt and tight pants.

"Fiction, under *K*."

"I exclusively buy books from shops like this and have been doing so for five years," he said upon his return with the book.

"Congratulations."

A skinny guy in a wifebeater and shorts, so as to better aerate his armpits and nether regions, wearing his sloppiness as a cloak of unhygienic arrogance, brashly munched on a slice of pizza as he browsed the metaphysics section.

He swaggered up to the counter and thrust a copy of *The Artist's Way* at me: "Have you read this?"

"What do you take me for?" I said.

And then, the pinnacle of my evening, the most dreaded question of all. Here it comes again …

A yellow-haired woman stands there, beaming hideously at me.

"How's your night going?"

I can't take it.

But I take it.

I groan the words out: "Great …"

But it's not enough. I can tell that she needs more. I can also tell that I'm entering an irony-free zone, a black hole of positivity.

The idiot, just humor her:

"How's yours?"

"Really well. Thanks for asking." Her tone is as aggressively bright as her dyed hair, while her fake gratitude is a patronizing concession to my distaste for the exchange and signals her victory.

And as if that's not enough, she has to add insult to injury:

"Have an amazing week," she says, with her hostile smile still in place, as she walks off.

Wrapping children's books for Silver Lake MILFs; a target for the malodorous and the tedious: this isn't really the end of the literary business I had in mind. If I wasn't already a misanthrope, this job would have turned me into one.

How did it come to this?

It is what happens when somebody nearing the end of their prime, who is unfit for daily toil, and has a morbid horror of anything involving effort, is forced, through a harsh diminishing of circumstances, to earn an honest living.

It's a long story, too sad to be told, and I am not inclined to tell it. Life is plotless. Plots are for graveyards.

* * *

I have decided to stop writing for a while.

* * *

The most important thing is to stop writing, now: to stop prioritizing this so-called work that has generated no income and that nobody will ever read. This futile, masochistic, self-indulgent pretense has interfered with everything; it has been carried out at the expense of love and work: real work, that is, the kind that is a visible manifestation of mental effort, not this endless supposed honing of my craft compounded by the preposterous conceit that the torturous process of giving shape to my thoughts might actually serve some sort of purpose, when it is merely an excuse to immerse myself in a morbidly self-reflective haze, of which there is seldom any visible manifestation.

* * *

As I was walking out, my downstairs neighbor was walking toward the house; he was returning from the gym, judging by his garb, and had a cell phone pressed to his ear.

"We should do something about that," he said, reluctantly disengaging himself from his cellular conversation—"I'll have to call you back"—and gesturing toward the Latino gentleman who was sprawled out on the street near the garden gate, an empty bottle of Olde English malt liquor by his side, dozing peacefully as the sun beat down on him. "He was there when I left, two hours ago."

"I just noticed him. I've been upstairs working all day," I lied. I found the presence of a recumbent drunkard on the other side of the railings comforting; it wouldn't have bothered me if he became a permanent fixture.

"We should call the police," said my neighbor, as if there were no other solution to such a grave problem.

"Maybe give him a kick, wake him up," I suggested.

My neighbor leaned down, getting as close to him as he could stand, and addressed the man in Spanish. "Muy borracho. Si no te mueves, voy llamar a la policía."

"Thanks, baby," the napper mumbled back.

"If he's still here in fifteen minutes, I'm calling them," said my neighbor as he walked through his gate.

At the end of the street I looked back and noted with relief that the man had risen unsteadily to his feet and was stumbling away. As I was doing so, a full-grown man hurtled by on an electronic scooter, almost knocking me over. "You little prick!" I yelled after him, but he had a headset on and was already two hundred yards ahead of me.

A young couple walked by, typical of the new demographic, the new contentment: the settlers who pay exorbitant rents and populate the expensive restaurants that open on a weekly basis. It used to be that most people one saw on the streets of this serene residential neighborhood—the oldest in the city, on the western edge of downtown—were so-called minorities. These days the majority of passersby are majorities, young Caucasians with all the essential accessories perfectly aligned: smartphones, coffee, dogs, each other—babies are optional, meanwhile the dog serves to signify an aspiring breeder. The males wear trucker caps or beanies, tight pants or shorts, and beards—those ubiquitous signifiers of redundancy. The girls are unattainable. And there are joggers, joggers everywhere, where nary a jogger was ere seen before. From whence had they sprung, this ever-expanding population of callow dullards? The hybridized bastard offspring of fifty years of youth culture, compressed by capitalism.

I continued on my merry way. Since the death of my last car, I had reverted to pedestrian status. One of the few positive effects of all the recent changes in the city was that it had become easier to exist without a car, especially on the so-called Eastside.

On the major artery, Sunset Boulevard, swarms of young people poured down the sidewalk. On a late Friday afternoon they were setting out to enjoy themselves. Formerly the province of working-class Latino families, it was now a pedestrian thoroughfare lined with new stores, new restaurants, new coffeehouses, and refurbished bars that catered exclusively to a clientele of perplexingly prosperous young Caucasians.

It didn't really matter what city it was. It could be any major city in this country, perhaps in the Western world—I wouldn't know, I haven't left town in years. At this point in the rising decline of civilization all cities are more or less interchangeable, with their revitalized downtowns and influx of inexplicably affluent young white people into "ethnic" neighborhoods initially rendered "inhabitable" by a vanguard of artists and other layabouts (shock troops for gentrification who moved in before the lemmings, now expendable), and the

Sunset corridor of Echo Park had become one such district. What had happened to this neighborhood had happened everywhere, and I knew that it would be worse for me elsewhere. A new life in a new town at my advanced age was out of the question.

The conveyor belt of youth culture had been firmly laid in place, with its mass-produced bohemian lifestyles and generic youth zones. The bar that served as a social hub for rogue police officers involved in the notorious Rampart Scandal (when cops behaved more disgracefully than the gang members they were supposed to be policing) was now a meat rack with a dance floor. On the next block a longstanding "dive bar" had been reinvented as a young person's "dive bar," albeit one at which prices were as high as those at a Beverly Hills hotel. A few doors down, a Mexican bar, famed for its history as the site of numerous shootings and stabbings as much as its five-dollar shot-and-a-beer specials, now sold fifteen-dollar cocktails poured by a mixologist with a waxed mustache. The Vietnamese lunch counter that went about its business in an unassuming manner for years was now a glossy new lunch counter that served fifteen-dollar bratwurst sandwiches. The Mexican supermarket was now a massive health food chain store. The pawn shops were gone, the dollar stores were closing. A pleasantly decaying block of cheap clothing stores and antique shops that used to seem timeless was in the process of being razed to make way for a massive retail outlet, the last of the dusty old storefronts replaced with boutique showroom glass.

As was my custom, I stopped in at the Mexican market, TeeJay's, on the next block from the bookstore, to buy some broccoli. Another echo of the old Echo Park was the bakery next to it, Chilpancingo, where upon my entrance the lady behind the counter held up four fingers, confirming my usual order of four tamales. These purchases would serve as my meals for the following day.

I arrived at my place of employment, a bookstore that was formerly a Salvadorean café.

"Would you like to read your latest piece of fan mail?" said Gilbert, my former friend, former colleague, and current boss, as he coolly pulled up the bookstore's Yelp page in order to confront me with an unflattering review the moment I entered the store to switch shifts with him.

Looking over Gilbert's shoulder, I read: "I'm new to Echo Park and was I really looking forward to visiting this book shop that I heard was cool. It's a small shop with a coffee house at the back and they have a cool mix of new and used books but the attitude of the man with gray hair was so not cool (i.e. had a badittude = bad attitude) ..."

This was as much as I could stomach. This line of work was difficult enough without being pilloried by dunces on an online forum—but that, nowadays, is the way of the world, and, sadly, business owners take the complaints of their customers seriously; and there had been reports of customers leaving in horror, shaken to the core, their assumptions regarding the time-honored proprieties deemed fundamental to the customer-retailer relationship cruelly shattered.

"Is it so hard to be nice to people?" said Gilbert as he picked up his jacket and walked off in reproachful silence.

"I'm not sure what I'm guilty of."

It was a long yelp, and I couldn't be bothered to read all of it.

"Where are you off to?" I asked, attempting to introduce a cordial note.

"A meeting," he said.

"Have fun," I said.

A few years ago Gilbert would have found these Yelp lambastings as farcical as I did, but now, in his managerial role, he took them seriously. He had become a different person since he had stopped drinking: sobriety had unleashed a previously suppressed ambition, and his sense of humor seemed to have been sacrificed in the process.

Gilbert was of medium height and medium weight, and had brown hair. He was one of the world's great tension exuders, a hard worker whose energy and commitment had the perhaps deliberate effect of highlighting the lack of those qualities in his colleagues. I was always aware of his critical gaze; I couldn't relax in his presence; I was consistently clumsy around him; he was ten years younger than me, and he reminded me of my father.

Fortunately, we were rarely in the store at the same time and only encountered each other when we switched shifts twice a week. It was a relief when Gilbert left to attend his nightly Alcoholics Anonymous meeting, and I was left to brood over the Yelp accusations.

"Gray hair": This was galling. I thought I still had a full head of luxuriant dark hair.

While pissing into the sink in the staff restroom, I inspected myself in the mirror. Although the overall impression was of dark-brown hair, up close the grays were clearly visible. Once again my attention was drawn to the deepening vertical lines around my mouth that dragged my face down like the creases in an old canvas tent being stretched into place, pulled taut into a gathering lumpiness around the chin. Other lines, from no discernible source, appeared like the crevices on the side of a mountain that was about to collapse in an avalanche of sourness. When I viewed myself in semiprofile I was shocked to discover that the thing which happens to aging men's necks, which I had so far been spared, was happening to my neck: it was becoming venous and scrawny; it was beginning to sag and the veins were popping out like cables from chin to collarbone.

The mask shrivels into a skull and misery gathers like dewlap under the chin. When I see myself in my mind's eye I imagine I still look as I did twenty years ago. Then I catch myself in the mirror and barely recognize what I see. The last traces of youth have faded. Time has made itself known. Nobody is spared, not even me. I held on for so long. And now it's gone.

Smarting from the Yelp critiques (which I only ever read when they were brought to my attention) and from Gilbert's dismissive attitude, I sat behind the counter with my head down, a sitting duck for whoever felt like shooting their mouth off at me, a dumping ground for the unloading of loneliness and desperation.

Behind the counter, I was prey not only to the endless mad parade of customers with their various annoying needs but to every unhinged and lonely person who wandered in off the street, driven out of their claustrophobic hovel in search of some poor helpless soul to unload their desperation on. There was a ceaseless torrent of such types, one after another, frequently overlapping. My indifference or irritability, unfortunately, was never enough to drive them away.

A captive audience, unfortunately,[1] I have no control over my interactions. People that I can avoid the rest of the time always know where they can find me and drain me of the precious few remaining drops of my by now inconsequential juices—three nights a week and especially on a Sunday, the hardest day of the week.

It's simply not an ideal venue for social intercourse. Between ringing up customers, answering the phone, and dealing with other book business, there's no room for abstraction and consequently no appetite for conversation. I recoil visibly and groan audibly when anybody I know walks in. At this point I would groan at the sight

---

1. Rather than me wasting my time inserting the word "unfortunately" into every statement, from now on the reader should just assume it is there.

of my own mother, risen from the dead, were she to walk through the door, so drained and discombobulated am I from the relentless barrage of humanity. I used to wonder what made booksellers so grumpy. Now I know.

"Everything good? You're doing good, right?"

Well, actually, no, not exactly, but …

What's the point? An honest answer isn't expected. But at least give me the option. There exists, however dimly, a remote possibility that I'm not "doing good," and this increasingly prevalent presumptuous preemptive strike seems designed to prevent one from saying how one actually is doing; it can be simply translated as "If you're not doing good, I don't want to hear about it." Then again, as somebody—I forget who—once wrote, "A bore is a man who when you ask him how he is, tells you."

"Some things are going well and some things aren't," I replied, settling for a compromise that would hopefully be sufficient to get rid of yet another bookstore pest.

As usual, there was no time to gather my thoughts between unwanted exchanges with people I had no desire to communicate with.

I looked up and groaned when Greg Roach ambled in. Greg had been the bassist in a brutalist pop ensemble way back in the 1990s. They didn't possess an ounce of originality but they toured extensively, released a few records, and built up a so-called cult following. In recent years, however, Greg's fortunes had declined to the point where he had been reduced to working in a coffeehouse. We were about the same age, so I took some consolation in his predicament. There weren't many people of my own age whose position in life I could relate to anymore. Most of my contemporaries had money, had property, had each other, so when I found somebody that was still in the trenches, although I might not otherwise relate to them or even like them, it had a tonic effect.

"You look like the Hollywood version of your former self," I remarked, struck by how unusually healthy and content Greg looked, and hoping to get rid of him by way of a compliment.

"I just got back from Japan," he volunteered.

"Eh? How did you manage that?"

"My girlfriend flew me out there."

"What?"

In that infuriatingly self-assured manner that people often adopt when their luck has suddenly changed, he acted as if it were a perfectly normal turn of events that he should suddenly be in a long-distance relationship with a twenty-three-year-old girl, more than half his age, who had reached out to him via email from the other side of the world and flown him over to Japan so that they could consummate their love. It turned out, conveniently, that she was rich.

This fucker was balding and overweight, but he had been in a band with a minor reputation twenty years ago, and his legend lived on, as even the most minor legends tend to do in the rock-and-roll firmament.

"Did she pay for everything?"

"Yes."

"Did that create any tension?"

"We got through it."

"Are you in love?"

"You make it sound like an accusation."

So she paid for everything, and they were in love. That was nice. My only consolation was that Asian girls had never gravitated toward me, a curious phenomenon that I remarked upon to him.

"Why are you so dour?" was Greg's curt and insensitive response. And with that he was out of the door; he had to be somewhere.

Now even the dour ones were calling me dour, and moving on. Now even those most entrenched in the trenches were digging themselves out, or being dug out, and moving on. Now I really felt alone.

I resumed browsing a copy of Alain de Botton's *The Art Of Travel*. The opening paragraph was an exquisitely crafted evocation of winter. It reminded me of my youth and made me crave the seasons. I missed weather so much that even looking at a photograph of snow or rain filled me with yearning and nostalgia.

Considering how much he had written—at least seven books— I assumed that de Botton must be older than me, but when I turned to the biography I was horrified to find that he was a year my junior. Disgusted, I closed the book, with no intention of opening it again.

A mild-mannered young regular wandered in and stood in front of the counter, smiling, awaiting some sort of acknowledgment.

"You look happy," I said.

"I think I am," he said.

"Well, keep it to yourself. It might be contagious."

He moved along to the coffee counter.

"Hey." Another smiling customer stood there.

"Yes." I stifled a snarl.

"What's this book about?"

"I don't know, I haven't read it." *Am I supposed to read every book in this store in order to save you the trouble? Why don't you open it yourself?*

The capacity to suffer fools gladly should be part of the job description. The main requirement is the ability to answer stupid questions with a straight face, and, if possible, with a smile.

If only I'd spent my youth playing bass in a middling cult band, which could have been achieved quite easily. But it had taken a long time to see these things clearly, to see anything clearly; and now, as always, it was too late.

Something had to be seriously the matter when I found myself envying people I used to pity. I was ten years behind my time. But at least I had failed deliberately, or so, none too convincingly, I attempted to convince myself.

It had been an odd trajectory, this lack of a trajectory. At an impressionable age I had made a commitment to unrepentant bohemianism, and I was now finding that it was a lonely stance, since nobody else had taken it.

This was no way for a middle-aged man to be carrying on.

But I carried on. Like this ...

The store closed at ten o'clock, and after I pulled down the shutters, toted up the receipts, and emptied the trash, I walked back along Sunset, through the Friday-night streets of irksome revelers.

I peered into a bar but it was packed: a grimthorped sty packed with kids who were learning how to drink, learning how to smoke, learning how to hold a cigarette properly, with music blasting so loudly that one couldn't hear oneself think, let alone engage in conversation. Ten years ago that bar was a hole in the wall with a curtain in the doorway, and it was off-limits to the white man. In those days a fresh-faced Caucasian on the Echo Park stretch of Sunset, especially after dark, was an aberration. This primarily Latino area had slowly, then suddenly, been transformed into a nightlife destination for the sort of young people who would formerly never have been caught dead in the neighborhood, and wouldn't have entered it for fear of actually being caught dead. If one went out to eat or drink in those seemingly simpler and sweeter days, one went to a bar or restaurant that was patronized by locals. But ordinary pleasures and consolations that used to be taken for granted, like coffee and beer, were now fetishized, and as the prospectors and profiteers moved in, the locals were driven out of their old haunts and almost every business was turned into a bleached and sanitized version of its former self.

When I got home I fished three envelopes out of the mailbox. One was a subscription offer from *The New York Review of Books*, the other two looked like they were from creditors. I dropped them all in the trash, fixed a drink, and sat on the sofa with one hand around a glass of liquor and the other on my crotch.

Half an hour later, having drifted off, I awoke and caught sight of my reflection in the window, merging with the gleaming towers of the downtown skyline, and saw a tired and beaten man gazing warily back at me: a man who had just pulled a shift at a low-paying job and walked home on a Friday night to drink alone; a middle-aged man sitting alone in a room, masturbating over a memory, fantasizing about women who had forgotten about him, and brooding over deliberately missed opportunities. A shadow of my former shadow, slowly becoming invisible, turning gray.

* * *

How the fuck did it come to this?

A modest career on the lower slopes and outer fringes of journalism dried up when the frontiers of the internet opened up to people who were prepared, free of charge, to perform the services that writers had formerly been paid for.

Slopes: they were more like ditches, which I never tried hard enough to dig myself out of, having mostly slept in them, and fringes frayed to the point of ragged nonexistence.

A freelance writer and copyeditor, I edited an art magazine that folded amid the death of paper journalism (online revenue not being enough to sustain it). I also wrote a column for the same magazine that addressed various art-world idiocies and other vital issues of the day, which gained an enthusiastic local readership. However, after the magazine went under I made no attempt to place my monthly musings elsewhere, and found I didn't have much to say anymore—it wasn't always as easy as it might seem to find new things to complain about with conviction.

I continued to work as a freelancer until there was no longer enough freelance work to go around and hustling for work itself became too much work.

This unsteady means of self-employment was supposed to keep me going until the time inevitably rolled around when I could live in style on the returns from my own literary exertions, which I was toiling away at but never getting very far with. I was disciplined enough to sit down to write on an almost daily basis but rarely disciplined enough to spend that time actually writing. I never finished anything and seldom showed what I did to anybody.

For all but the most talented, driven and shameless hacks it was a parlous time to be plying the scrivener's trade. The small income derived from freelance duties was augmented by the accumulation of substantial credit card debt that I defaulted on when I could no longer make the required minimum monthly payments. I was forced to let go of all my cards at once—they were all maxed out in any case, and I had drawn cash advances on as many of them as possible.

Bereft of credit and no longer able to scrape by as a freelance journalist or copyeditor, some form of gainful employment became an urgent necessity—that dreaded thing I had somehow succeeded in avoiding for so long: a steady job.

Fortuitously enough, around this time a friend was in the process of opening a bookstore/café. Although I had never worked in a bookstore before, or in any line of retail work, and despite being temperamentally unsuited for such employment, she hired me out of sympathy, and I brought my friend Gilbert—thirty-four years of age and a recovering alcoholic—on board.

In those purer days there wasn't a café on every street corner and not every single business had been transmogrified into a pallid, youth-accessible version of its former self. There was no bookstore in the neighborhood at the time and it seemed like a good time to open one, with an adjoining café. Somebody had the bright idea of naming the place Mute Books.

At first, the selection of both new and secondhand books was embarrassing in its lack of quality and variety, but it improved greatly due to Gilbert's tireless work, into which he poured the full force of his addictive personality.

Now that it had become a respectable store—not exactly a powerhouse of idealistic utilitarianism but a far cry from its charmingly shabby origins—it served more as a neighborhood hangout and tourist attraction, as has every exploitable space in the heart of what was named, in a major weekly periodical, "the second hippest neighborhood in the country." Not too many bibliophiles cross the threshold of this establishment. Mostly it attracts the sort of people who wouldn't usually enter a bookstore: gawkers, pleasure-seekers, and fun-loving family groups who descend upon it en masse, especially on weekends, with most people walking straight through, chatting loudly on cell phones as they do so (we get it: you're "on the go"), to the café at the other end of the store.

In my midforties, with the résumé of a much-younger man, I reentered the workforce as a bookstore employee.

It's an honorable profession, of course, being a middle-aged middleman in the service of education and enlightenment—deepening, broadening, comforting and corrupting people's minds with potentially dangerous wisdom—and it requires a certain amount of knowledge, but it's not the kind of knowledge that translates into money.

I signed on for a couple of shifts a week, expecting the position to last no longer than six months. Five years later, I'm still there.

* * *

Hour after hour, day after day, year after year, decade after decade, consumed by this precious illusion of service to the pen: priceless time that might somehow have been used to benefit others, to benefit myself, from which I might even have derived pleasure.

Yet nothing definite emerged from it, only a copious and chaotic abundance of glorified note making.

There was no glory in it. And what have I received in return for this self-serving—if that—satisfaction of having attempted to actualize myself? Poverty and solitude have been the chief rewards.

And what, actually, was I attempting to actualize? Did I have anything to say that was worth saying at all, that hadn't been said better before, that might have justified such a substantial investment of time and energy: this unflagging commitment to a lost cause, as if it were a sacred act and not a sickness born of vanity?

What would happen if I didn't do it? Nothing. Nobody would notice. It wouldn't make any difference to anybody.

And I would be greatly relieved by the removal of this most unnecessary burden.

* * *

And I ask again: How the fuck did it come to this?

The plan—such as it was, such as it wasn't—was to live as fully as possible until I turned thirty; my twenties were to be reserved exclusively for adventure and experimentation. Then, having accumulated a sufficiently rich treasury of knowledge and experience, to embark upon a lifelong stretch of literary immersion.

To some extent I succeeded in this, but having fallen into the practice of just living, I found it a hard habit to break, to the extent that by the time I turned forty I still hadn't done anything—to speak of, so to speak—with my life; and entering my midforties, emerging from the fog of youth into the relative clarity of middle age, I found myself in much the same position I'd been in fifteen years earlier, with only an abundance of worthless repetition to my credit.

Throughout those two decades, however, I couldn't entirely resist what I thought of as my calling: I made myself write but I never finished anything, other than remunerative work. I had it in me, that which had to come out, but out of contrariness, self-spite and furtive optimism, I stifled it. I was never sufficiently *invested* in myself, from a practical standpoint, to make the necessary provisions. I figured that when the time came there would still be enough time—as if the future would stretch out indefinitely in order to accommodate my creative inhibitions.

One might or might not be forgiven for optimistically assuming that time stands still when one isn't doing anything; but although it seems to, it doesn't.

Throughout those lost years what, if anything, did I produce? Notes, only notes, dusty piles of notes, palimpsests in progress, discarded drafts, abundant abandoned works: a lengthy treatise on prewar country blues lyrics, accompanied by hundreds of couplets that were noted down as I listened to them and which were subsequently classified and considered in an essay that ran twenty thousand words before I gave up on it, having tasted the bitter pangs of rejection from several agents. At least two years went into that—not long compared to some other projects (four years were once spent on a twenty-thousand-word novella that I didn't even attempt to get published). Then there was the aborted fifty-thousand-word novel concerning the misadventures of a young man staying at an old-time residential hotel in a small Texas town, and a discontinued novel of comparable length about an aging hack attempting to write a novel: not the most original idea but I had hoped to bring something new to the exhausted enterprise.

Why, in the name of Mercy, did I embrace, albeit half-heartedly, this literary racket? And why did I wait until now, until it was so late in the day, so late in the lifetime, to do the right thing and stop writing?

It really had been a lifetime in the service of literature: if I wasn't writing, I was reading, and these days, selling books, which sadly seemed to be the most useful of these activities.

Life was supposed to be composed of many chapters, and I had been writing, reading, rewriting and rereading the same one for years on end, until all the life had been written out of it. Repetition and incompletion were the two staples of my life in art.

As if anybody would be foolish enough to expect to be rewarded for a dedication to literature in this day and age. And yet, some people were ...

"So many had sacrificed themselves for art without even their names surviving. On the other hand, what mattered most was that all who had given themselves to their work had their real reward in having actualized themselves."

It was easy enough for John Berryman to say that, considering the security of his place in the pantheon. To put it another way: so many had focused so much time and energy into producing work for which the world had no use, and all they got out of it was frustration and bitterness.

Could there really be any satisfaction in having actualized oneself if nobody else benefited from or even noticed one's actualization?

Based upon my personal observations, I would have to answer emphatically in the negative.

And now I had a new dilemma facing me: what to do with my time now that I had stopped attempting to write.

* * *

What do I have to do today? I pondered in semiconsciousness, and rejoicing at the prospect of a day without the pretense of literary activity, drifted back to sleep. *Why should I get up at all?* I mumbled to myself as I switched fetal positions. There was nothing to get up for.

The only problem was that I automatically awoke at the same time every morning—at 6:50 a.m., to be precise, when the first dim light seeped through the faded curtains—and could no longer sleep beyond that hour. Which was fine: it was the perfect time to rise, if one had some form of paying work or self-appointed duty to execute. But if one had no such lofty tasks to perform, there didn't seem to be much point in getting up.

The mornings of prolonged and untired sleep that characterized my youth were no longer possible, but that didn't stop me from lying there, floating in and out of sapped slumber. One had to endure the boredom of existence, which allows the mind to settle, in order to figure out what it was all about. By which reckoning, such willful stultification was necessary to my development.

Eventually I just lay there idly pulling on my rod, multitasking: masturbating and dozing at the same time. Early-morning self-excitation was certain to have a draining effect. But I had nothing to do until five o'clock when I was due down at the store, so why not?

About two hours later than usual I got out of bed, immediately assailed by guilt and grogginess. I looked out of the window: some yellow-hatted workers were repairing something. But I couldn't look down on the street for very long: it was too bright.

I got out of the shower and sat on the sofa with a towel wrapped around myself, floating in a stupor, with no desire to get up again. The phone rang: a rare occurrence since it was usually turned off in the morning to facilitate literary endeavor. But since I wasn't writing anymore, I answered it. My friend Mitchell was on the other end of the line.

"Hey, man, what's up?"

"Nothing. I'm just sitting here in a stupor. What's going on?"

"Much the same, much the same. Here, listen. I got some more stuff."

"Oh yeah?"

"You said you wanted some."

"I'm taking a break."

"You told me to let you know if I got more, so I'm letting you know."

"I appreciate that, but I've stopped writing so I don't need any at the moment. I may never need it again."

"That's too bad."

"Yes, it's a sad day for the world of literature."

"It's sad for me because I have to make more phone calls to unload this stuff."

"I'd love to help you out but I only use it as a creative tool, and I've stopped writing."

"You're not writing those articles anymore?"

"I stopped doing that a few years ago. Thanks for noticing."

"So why'd you stop? I liked them."

"Because I don't care enough anymore to eulogize or satirize anything. What have you been working on?" I quickly changed the subject, then wished I hadn't.

Twenty minutes later Mitchell was still rambling on about his various projects. He was writing another script; he wasn't getting paid for it, and he was amazed that a biopic about Theodor Adorno's days in Los Angeles wasn't being snapped up by a major studio. Mitchell had been in town for twenty-five years—hailing from the East Coast—and he still couldn't get the Hollywood glitter out of his eyes. No amount of failure was enough to discourage him.

"You know Lyn Lamrock?" he asked.

"The actress?"

"Yeah. She's been calling me up. She's getting on a bit but she still looks good."

"I used to fantasize about her when I was a teenager."

"Me too, pal. Well, she's been calling me up. I met her at a party. She wants to hang out. Can you imagine …"

"I have to get out of here," I said, cutting him off midsentence. There was no other way to end a conversation with him.

"When we gonna hang out?"

"Soon, I hope. In the next few days. Call me up."

I stared down at the street and the street glared back at me. Going out would destroy me. How best then to lay waste to what remained of the day? Deprived of self-invented routine, I didn't know what to do with the time that was supposedly mine. Other than write, there wasn't anything I wanted to do, and if I didn't write, what else was there to do but read? Presumably, there were other ways to spend one's time beside writing and reading. I could go somewhere, I could do something. But I didn't want to go anywhere or do anything. There wasn't anywhere to go or anything to do, especially on a weekday morning. I had spent enough time going places and doing things when I was a younger man. Those days were gone. And I didn't like the look of it out there. It was eighty degrees in February. I was burnt out on the sun.

* * *

You don't need to have a death wish to live in Los Angeles, but it helps.

When I first arrived here, many years ago, longer ago than I care to remember, it was autumn and I lay on the roof of an apartment building, slowly moving into a diminishing puddle of late-afternoon sunlight, luxuriating in the subsiding rays until they were completely consumed by shadow.

The sun was sacred, in those days.

Hailing from an older culture, fraught with ancestral disquietude, where the emotional severity cuts into one's bones, one craves the numbing quality that can be found here in Southern California. It lures those of us whose nerves have crumbled in older, harsher places. It's a good place to close yourself down.

There is safety in numbness, in so denatured a place: a beguiling and illusory softness, a magical numbness. The exchange of grim reality for feckless heliolatry is initially refreshing, but the sun is vampiric: it sucks the life out of things and stifles significance, and in this seasonless time warp we don't notice that we are slowly dying.

The subtlety of the seasons makes time pass more quickly, less dramatically. It is easy to lead a frivolous existence here, to sleep through life and dream one's way into death. The sleep acts as both preservative and anesthetic. One can remain young for longer here because more value is placed upon youth. And so one enters this dream that seduces, desensitizes, and destroys what's left of one's soul, and when one dies here, the city is cited as the killer—a phenomenon that doesn't seem to exist to the same extent anywhere else.

And I'm grateful, deeply grateful, to be stuck here, sinking in LA-lienation, in geographical and cultural isolation, seldom jolted out of numbness in this seductively deadening place. It is perhaps a damning indictment of me as a person, but I feel in my element here, and I wouldn't want to live anywhere else; these days, I can hardly imagine living anywhere else.

I still need the numbness. All these years in this numbed-out comfort zone have rendered me unfit for anywhere more bracing. This, to my discredit, is where I belong. It doesn't feel real. That's the beauty of it. Because the place I came from was too real. The place I came from was different, very different.

I was drawn to this city because it was as far away as I could get from where I grew up, because it was the antithesis of where I grew up—warm and wide open rather than cold and confined—and it seems that a lot of other people came here for similar reasons.

Los Angeles is a place for people who don't fit in anywhere else, and Echo Park used to be a place for people who didn't fit in anywhere else in Los Angeles, until the digitally induced homogenization of reality had an unfortunate effect on the demographic. Witness this neighborhood.

* * *

"D'you have Patti Smith's new book?" … "Do you have any books on trolls?" … "Do you have *The Insomniac's Daughter*?" … "Do you have any Plato like *Dialogues* or anything?" … "Do you have a restroom?" … "Do you have a paperback copy of *Breakfast of Champions*?" … "Do you have a garbage can back there?" … "Do you have like a little paper bag or something?" … "Do you have a copy of *The Unbearable Lightness of Forgetting*?" … "Do you have books about bands?" … "Do you have any books about dragons?" … "Do you guys have any coloring books?" … "Do you have a Russian section?" … "Do you have *The Dentist's Brother*?" … "Do you have any Edie Sedgwick?" … "Do you have a recharger?" … "Do you have open mic nights?" … "Do you know anywhere I can buy smoothies?" … "Do I buy books or rent books or what?" … "Do you know the last name of the guy who wrote *The Insomniac's Dentist*?" … "Do you have anything else by Vonnegut?" … "Are there any good pizza places around here?" … "Do you mind tossing this for me?" … "Do you guys have a restroom?" … "Do you have a second?" … "This is a great place."

"Thanks."

Recognition, at last. Customers often assume I own the place, owing to my advanced age. In fact, I take orders from somebody ten years my junior, whom I recommended for a job when the store opened five years ago. Because he is reliable and ambitious, because he cares, he is now the manager (an irony that is not lost on him and the main reason I haven't been fired yet), whereas I'm still pulling one day and three night shifts a week, which utterly deplete me.

Although the business of selling, buying, pricing and shelving books is not exactly backbreaking labor, I have never in my life been so wrung out as I am at the end of these shifts.

Of course, I don't own the store, I am merely a humble servant in the service of literature. I could have run with it, like Gilbert, and invested my future in it by buying in as a partner, but I didn't feel like running with it: I don't run with things much, and I didn't have the money to buy in, and if I had I would have cashed out, as the original owner did—tiring quickly of the book business and making a permanent move to upstate New York with her family, leaving Gilbert in charge.

Gilbert used the bookstore as a crucible of personal enhancement, transforming himself—morally, professionally and financially—into a better person. He saw in it an opportunity for salvation, whereas I viewed it as a form of penance: a cruelly fitting form of punishment for not having done my own work—to be consigned to the role of minor cog in the relentless turnover of a commodity that I could dispatch a superior product of if I ever got around to it.

* * *

The days passed emptily. Now that I was attempting *not* to write, I didn't know what to do with my time. After a lifetime of attempting *to* write—never just "writing," always "attempting" to write—I was now attempting *not* to write, and I was finding it almost as difficult as my rigorously half-assed attempts at writing.

It wasn't my first attempt at *not* writing. I'd tried to cut it out before but had never lasted very long. What tended to get in the way was the deluded conviction that I had something to say, and that if I didn't say it nobody else would. Although even if this was the case it wasn't necessarily justification for saying it; whatever it was, it didn't necessarily need to be said; perhaps it would be better left unsaid. Either way, this time I hoped to have the strength to go the distance.

Although already agitated, I made a fourth cup of coffee. While it was brewing I picked up the latest issue of *The New Yorker*, which had arrived two weeks earlier. I only subjected myself to such a dependable source of irritation because I had been given a year's free subscription, of which this issue, thankfully, was the last.

Over the course of twenty-five years I had succeeded in finishing precisely one story in *The New Yorker*—it was written by V. S. Naipaul—and rarely had I managed to reach the end of one of the polite, lifeless poems they seemed to regard it as their duty to publish; but, ever the optimist, I flipped through the opening pages of advertisements depicting sullen models in absurd surroundings, and arrived at the week's fiction offering.

The short story, ostensibly about a failing marriage, shifted effortfully from an art-world setting, with just the right degree of condescension, to commentary on social media, and from there to the political spectrum. It could easily have existed without the political angle, but framing it in that context guaranteed that it would be taken seriously. The story was therefore relevant on at least three different levels: a calculated bombardment of relevance.

Purely in the interest of reveling in further irritation and time wasting, I looked the author up online. A brief search established that he was still in his midthirties and the recipient of various scholarships, grants and awards. His stories had appeared, among other places, in all the right places. An image search turned up various photographs of a bearded, bespectacled individual whose face seemed disinclined to conceal a deep appreciation of his own overeducated superiority. He resided in rural upstate New York with his wife (also a writer) and their child, and a dog, judging by a photograph of him with a dog at his feet. Both he and his wife taught at Cornell. He was twelve years younger than me, which wasn't particularly young anymore.

* * *

Standing outside a bookstore downtown, following the well-attended reading and Q&A for his new book, *The Death of the Novel*, Jackson Valvitcore lit a cigarette.

"I didn't know you smoked," I remarked.

"Only after readings."

"How's the book doing?" I asked, although I knew very well how it was doing, having personally sold numerous copies of it.

"Well …" He paused to reevaluate his recent fortunes. "Really well."

Indeed, why hold back? He took another drag on his cigarette, holding it between thumb and forefinger: a sure sign that somebody was doing "really well."

"A thousand copies in the last two weeks." He couldn't restrain himself. "Did you see the photograph of Kanye reading it?" he continued, grinning with pride and scorn. A carefully posed photograph of Kanye West reading *The Death of the Novel* had appeared in a French magazine.

That, I surmised, must be the advantage of having an abrasively declarative title that makes a major statement printed in huge lettering on the cover of a book. There was so much out there these days that the likelihood of a work of subtle originality getting lost in the shuffle was disconcertingly high.

"I saw you on Gruel Mucus' reading list," I said, referring to a heavily trawled arts blog where *The Death of the Novel* had received a glowing review.

Jackson took another thumb-and-forefinger drag. "Yeah, that was nice. Gruel Mucus ... that's funny. You don't like his work?"

"I decided not to like it years ago after reading *Lipstick Train*. I don't like the overearnest way in which he strives to make connections between all this unrelated stuff in order to flaunt his erudition. But I guess I'd like him if he liked me."

"We should hang out," said Jackson.

A young man approached us, or rather, approached Jackson. "Hey, I really enjoyed that, thanks," he said. Jackson thanked him for his thanks, a conversation sparked up between them on the subject of a mutual friend's new book, and I receded quietly from the picture.

* * *

Shouldn't art be the residue of life and not the main thing?

This novel thought entered my mind while I was brushing the coffee stains from my remaining teeth. I held on to it and as soon as I got out of the bathroom I wrote it down.

Unless writing was the means by which one earned one's livelihood, wasn't it more important to live? If one enjoyed writing, then write, but if it wasn't financially rewarding, or rewarding on any level beyond the dubious notion of actualizing oneself, and if nobody read what one wrote, then why engage in an act that nobody else benefited from or cared about? Even if one wrote professionally or out of a sense of purpose, wasn't it still more important to experience life than to describe and examine it?

There were perhaps a few uniquely gifted individuals out there whose work was edifying and entertaining enough that the prioritization of art over life, or the more exalted status of art *as* life, was justifiable.

If somebody had a singular vision, surely it was their duty to share it. Self-actualization could be an act of service to one's fellow man. But perhaps there were a lot of singular visions that weren't worth sharing; and it was doubtful for the vast majority of people that called themselves or thought of themselves, or were thought of, as artists that on their deathbeds they would look back and value their creative or professional achievements over love and the living of life.

On my deathbed, or in my last ditch, I suspected that my deepest regret would be that I had never done enough for others. But I hadn't done much for myself either, so it evened out.

But perhaps what one valued most on one's deathbed wasn't the most reliable index of worth. Anyway, I wasn't on my deathbed, I was sitting on the sofa, draped in a towel at eleven o'clock on a Wednesday morning, and it was consoling to consider the potential supremacy of life over art: it justified my decision not to write. But what about living?

* * *

"Good morning, sunshine," said the fetching young barista as I poured myself a coffee behind the café counter. Despite her comeliness I couldn't entertain prurient thoughts about her, or any of the girls in the kitchen: the malodorous waft of breakfast burritos always acted as a deterrent.

I walked to the other end of the store and dragged the dollar cart out onto the sidewalk, where it was already getting warm. I assumed my position behind the book counter, turned off the abrasive rap left on by the café girls, and selected something more relaxing from the bottomless Spotify trove: the two-hundred-song Bob Dylan mix I'd compiled. Within thirty seconds I was faced with a smiling young woman who bought three cardboard children's books, a scented candle, and a three-legged ceramic pig figurine.

"Do you wrap?" she asked.

"We do," I said, "but I'm afraid we're temporarily out of wrapping paper." There was a huge roll of it on the floor behind me, which fortunately she didn't notice. I hadn't taken a sip of coffee yet or done the crossword, I wasn't going to wrap books. I hid the roll of wrapping paper behind some boxes, placed a cushion on the otherwise uncomfortable stool, sat in front of the computer / cash register, and pulled up the online version of *The Los Angeles Times*. The lead story concerned the potential dismantling of the postal system. The world had gone mad. There didn't seem to be much use in pointing that out anymore—it was old news, but one was given fresh cause to be amazed by it on such a frequent basis that it was difficult not to continually bemoan the current state of things with renewed vigor.

A torn, greasy piece of plastic was handed over. It had obviously been in somebody's mouth. I endured the fifteen-second wait for the five-dollar transaction to go through, staring at the machine and avoiding eye contact with the customer.

There are seven or eight steps involved in completing a credit card transaction, and the entire procedure, from the moment of it being handed over to the printing of the receipt, takes approximately thirty seconds—often longer, if as is so often the case, the machine is malfunctioning. I handle roughly two hundred of these transactions a week, which amounts to at least an hour and a half a week—no less than seventy-five hours: three full days; nine full workdays a year—spent processing and handling these items of mercantile filth.

Still, I had more personal reasons for hating credit cards.

A man holding a cell phone walked up. "Who's playing the music?" he asked.

"Me."

"I was literally, this moment, texting a friend of mine to tell her about this song and it started playing."

"That is incredible. That has probably never happened before." For, indeed, it was a remarkable coincidence. "Nobody 'cept You" was a fairly obscure song: a "deep cut," as they say nowadays.

In order to prove the veracity of his statement, the customer passed me his cell phone to show me the text message.

"I believe you," I said. "I'm being sincere. This has probably never happened before. What are the odds? It's a great song. I don't know why he left it off *Planet Waves*. It would have been one of the best songs on the record."

"Because it was unfinished."

"But he could have finished it. He might have abandoned it because it sounded too much like another song on the record, maybe 'Something There Is About You.'"

This seemed a plausible explanation. For the same reason Dylan left other songs off other records: for example, excluding "Call Letter" from *Blood on the Tracks*, because it bore too much of a musical resemblance to "Meet Me in the Morning." I wondered if Dylan realized that there would always be aficionados to pick through his work and save him the trouble, and I wondered if he even cared. It must be a nice feeling: to be secure enough in one's legacy to know that there are numerous self-appointed executors who will take it upon themselves to devote themselves to sifting through it, as opposed to fearing that one's entire oeuvre will be lost when one dies.

And so the Dylan marathon continued throughout the day, seven hours of it, and I found myself marveling over many felicitous lines and couplets, turned out with such grace and seeming effortlessness: "Somebody got lucky but it was an accident"; "Take what you have gathered from coincidence."

But still the inevitable collapse occurred. The place filled up with the Sunday-afternoon crowd: the people one didn't have to deal with during the week, because they were working. This was their day of freedom, and they celebrated it by buying things, including books and cups of coffee.

On Sundays, I was always bound to succumb. By two o'clock any matutinal serenity had slumped into nausea and agitation, coinciding with the torrential influx of sad sacks, blockheads, time wasters, customers, lunatics, and visitors from the Inland Empire. The sunshine brought out all the fools, and it was always sunny here.

By midafternoon I was crawling around on my hands and knees in front of a wheelchair, picking books off the floor: soiled and useless books that arrived piled up in the seat of a wheelchair that was pushed through the door by a pallid, staggering, unshaven white-haired man in baggy stonewashed jeans and a moth-eaten T-shirt; books that toppled out of the wheelchair and spilled across the floor as soon as I touched them.

I looked into the man's moist gray eyes, and at the gray stubble on his gray face, as he held out a glossy mass-market paperback with an embossed cover. "You don't want this?" he pleaded.

"It doesn't sell."

"What about this?" He feebly proffered a battered Tom Clancy hardback without a dust jacket.

"It will go straight onto the dollar cart and it won't even sell there."

The man just stood there, dazed, holding on to the back of the wheelchair, oblivious to an incoming couple who were attempting to maneuver a baby carriage around him.

"Where else can I go?"

"Did you try Byron's Books?"

"I just came from there."

"So these are the rejects?"

"They took this many." He measured about a foot's worth of books between his hands. He had pushed a wheelchair overflowing with unwanted books three miles on a hot afternoon from one bookstore to another.

"It's all crap. I'll give you ten dollars," I said, picking out a grubby volume of Khalil Gibran and a relatively unsullied Book Club edition of Patrick White's *Voss* that probably wouldn't recoup the outlay. I went back behind the counter and handed him a ten-dollar bill from the register.

Four new paperbacks were placed in front of me: Patti Smith's highly overrated memoir *Just Kids*; a wildly popular volume of emo-poetry called *Milk and Honey*; Chris Kraus' *I Love Dick*, which had recently been turned into a television series; and Jarett Kobek's *I Hate the Internet*. I hadn't read any of these books but I had sold so many copies of each of them that I loathed them all on sight.

"D'you need a bag?" I asked the customer as I rang them up.

There was always a long pause before this question was answered. Nobody wanted to admit to wanting a bag now that it was deemed ecologically wasteful.

"If you've got one," he said after wasting five seconds of my time with pointless hesitation. "Is it a paper bag?" he added.

"No. I don't have one," I said. "But if you need one you can go to the store next door and get one from them."

"OK" (pron. *oh-kai*), he said, as if it were not OK.

"It's all right," I said, as I put his books in a brown paper bag. "I was joking. It was a joke. I wouldn't offer you one if I didn't have one, that would be cruel."

"OK," he said again, and walked off without saying thank you, as if he was questioning my sanity.

The humorlessness, the relentless fucking humorlessness.

One clown after another: humorless clowns, hirsute clowns, sad clowns, beautiful clowns, killer clowns.

I sat behind the counter, simmering as graciously as possible. I didn't want to provide a bag, and I didn't want to have to describe a bag. In this respect, bookselling and writing, the vocation I was attempting to give up, had a lot in common.

A young couple snuggled up to each other directly in front of me, purring and whispering as they made their purchase. *Go away, just go away,* I muttered to myself as I scanned the barcode of the Rilke collection that the young man was insisting on buying for his lady friend, overruling her unconvincing protestations.

"'If I die on top of the hill ...'" I looked up. The male half of the couple was now singing along to the latest Dylan selection. *Yeah, I get it, you're grooving on life. You know the song, congratulations. Now shut up and stop showing off. Your happiness is not infectious.* I ripped the receipt from the credit card machine and tossed it across the counter.

"Take it easy," said the boyfriend.

"Have a nice day," said the girlfriend.

"It's a little too late for that," I said.

Given that this was a bookstore, one might hope that it would attract a comparatively refined clientele, and perhaps it did, but this environment of constantly cornered overstimulation was still far too great a sensory overload for my fragile nervous system. How would I manage in the real world? I didn't want to ever have to find out.

This was the perilous point of the day, when irritation was in danger of overflow and explosion. On the verge of tipping over, I had to pull back and restrain myself from losing it: from facing that which was already lost and unloosening it.

The unmistakably idiotic sound of cell phone jabber within close range began to jar on my sensibilities. I walked around the counter and into the design section, where the source of this one-sided uproar could be found.

"Take that shit outside," I said.

A chubby man in skintight bicycling garb reluctantly removed his cellular device from his ear.

"This isn't a phone booth. I can hear you from the other end of the store."

"It's difficult to talk out there because of the traffic," he said.

"Well, keep it down then," I spluttered out.

No relief was gained as a result of this interaction. I lacked the necessary polish to smoothly voice an objection; it always came out sounding strained.

"Do you have a book called *The Artist's Way*?" a woman called out to me.

"Yes, it's right there," I called back, pointing to the metaphysics section in front of which she was standing.

"I can't find it," she called back.

"It's right there," I said, "where that guy is texting. Well, every single person in here is texting. In front of that guy in the pink cap on the bench who's texting. Never mind …" I walked back into the teeming Sunday-afternoon crowd of texters, cell phone squawkers, socializers, and, occasionally, people looking at books, and directed the woman to a stack of the book in question.

It can be difficult to look at people, not only for the obvious reasons but because nowadays they're usually on cell phones. Even the sight of somebody staring into a cell phone is repellant, and en masse the collective digital toxicity becomes overwhelming. I was the one person who had deliberately removed the texting feature from their cell phone service. I assumed that texting would mean inviting more chaos into my life than I could handle.

A bald, beaming clown face with an intricately groomed beard and mustache bobbed up in front of the counter and stood there staring at me, spittle hanging from his lips.

"Can I ask you something?" he said.

"You are asking me something …"

He leaned across the counter: "Do you guys have a restroom?" The hairy-mouthed smile of a man who clearly suffered from vagina envy widened and moistened hideously. "Do you have a toilet I can use?"

"I don't need to know what you're using it for," I said, turning away in horror, and pointing toward the back of the store.

Why did people need to seek directions to a restroom? Couldn't they figure it out for themselves? It was a small enough place, where did they expect to find it? I had never entered a store or public place and sought directions to the restroom. I didn't want to bother anybody or draw attention to my biological needs. I looked around until I found it myself. Its location was usually fairly obvious, and if it wasn't I'd still keep looking for it. This gentleman, however, was clearly of a different, less resourceful breed.

I returned to my reading and managed to get a few sentences in before I was interrupted by another helpless customer. But they were good sentences: "The true masters are those who relinquish their vocation," wrote George Steiner. But what if one had never embraced one's vocation? Never mind …

"Do you have anything by Richard Brautigan?"

"Yes, over there, under *B*," I said, resenting this intrusion upon my reading, and directing her toward the fiction section a few yards away.

She selected a copy of *Trout Fishing in America* and brought it back to the counter. "How much is it?" she asked.

Stop fucking pestering me. Can't you see that I'm trying to read? I pointed out the price, which was clearly marked on the back of the cover.

"Oh," she said, and walked off, leaving the book on the counter.

The store telephone rang: "Do you have any books for the children of transgender parents?" asked a shrill voice on the other end of the line.

"I didn't know any existed."

"Excuse me."

"I meant books on the subject, not the parents …"

The caller hung up on me.

It was all so dispiriting.

By the time "Knockin' on Heaven's Door" rolled around and the Dylan mix came to an end, I was undone. A big beaming blond woman stood in front of me with an immense grin plastered across her face. She expected to see that fake smile returned, but she wasn't going to get it.

"Hi!"

"Hello."

"I want to know if you've got a few books."

"What are they?"

"*The Draftsman's Daughter.*"

"What is it?"

"It's a book."

"I know that. What kind of a book?" I was going all out to be courteous. It was a matter of too many questions and too many faces, and they were blurring into each other, sharply.

My honest attempt at being patiently accommodating was doomed to failure.

"Forget it. I can tell I'm bothering you," she squeaked, and walked out huffily.

Out of sheer rage, I kicked a shelf, denting the spines of several James Crumley novels. It was all right, he could take it, he was a tough guy. Whereas I was too sensitive.

Then the music died and I grappled with the receiver in sweaty frustration for an hour. Gilbert came in at five o'clock to cover the night shift and fixed the problem in half a minute, grunting impatiently as he did so, like a foreman taking over from a peon, which was what our relationship had been reduced to.

"Ayayay," he said despairingly as I left.

* * *

I awoke on Monday morning with a punishing headache owing to the cocktails I'd consumed the night before, alone, while recovering from the atrabilious humor I'd succumbed to during the grueling shift. It was a day of vicious sunlight and the sound of construction from a roof across the street hammered into my already throbbing skull, yet I continued lying there, with earplugs stuffed into my ears, drooling into the pillow, drifting from dream to dream until I rose, without volition or desire. The effects of oversleeping were as deleterious as any drug, and if I stayed home I would only be prolonging and intensifying this condition. In the interest of waking up and moving on with the day it was practical to place myself in a different environment as soon as possible.

Grand Central Market was a network of lunch counters and produce stands occupying a cavernous block-wide hangar of a building with entrances on two parallel streets, Hill and Broadway. When I first came to town—and for a long time thereafter, and for a much longer time before—its state of utilitarian grace remained intact, but in recent years the old counters that mostly offered Mexican fare at almost ridiculously low prices had been replaced by businesses purveying every conceivable variety of cuisine—sushi, free-range burgers, gourmet toast—with everything priced beyond the means of the old clientele; and the vast produce section, which had been providing cheap groceries to locals for a century, had been reduced to a tiny island.

I stood at one of the counters and sipped a five-dollar cup of coffee. For a hundred years the market had reflected the local population, and it had now changed to reflect the new upscale downtown, or DTLA as it was now known: the residents of expensive lofts and workers at dot-com businesses and fashionable stores replacing the residential hotel dwellers and office workers of the pure old days. And there were a lot of people walking around taking photographs of each other, of themselves, and of their food. What used to make downtown so appealing was the complete absence of the types that it was now teeming with. Where had all the poor people gone, for whom this place had been such a long-standing resource? They had been pushed farther into the margins, and the margins kept expanding.

Even the buskers on Broadway looked prosperous. Urban renewal, of course, is usually viewed as a cause for celebration, but I rued the revitalization; I liked places that remained suspended in a state of perpetual decay, which for years had been the case with downtown LA, and from which it had only recently been given a vibrant and unsightly overhaul. For a long time downtown was a dream: a dream that I'd taken for granted. It was all over now, and I missed it.

But what was the alternative? Obviously, a new owner wasn't going to maintain an aesthetic of cozy squalor. People died or moved on, the old owners sold out, businesses changed hands, nothing ever stayed the same. It wasn't progress, it was just change, the way of the world more than a sign of the times. And the constant emphasis on this cherished substance known as authenticity was a self-serving fabrication, based on the limitations of one's own frames of reference and imagination.

I passed by on the opposite side of the street from Clifton's Cafeteria. The fate of this once-treasured refuge was too sad to contemplate. It had once been comforting to know that it would always be there with its indoor streams, grottos and fake redwood trees: a timeless sanctuary for downtown dwellers, workers and scufflers, where one could get a good cheap meal in uniquely enchanting surroundings and escape the madness outside for as long as one wanted. But after seventy-five years as a family-run business it had been bought by the sort of developers who delight in giving facelifts to venerable old downtown haunts in the name of preservation. The new signage tastelessly drew attention to itself: "Living History, Cabinet of Curiosities."

A flaneur in autopia, with nowhere left to flan. Waves of that familiar doomed feeling I often experienced when I made the mistake of going out during the day washed through me. Much of it, I realized, was connected with money, and the long-engrained self-defeating but intractable perception that I was incapable of earning it: a perception that I had done little to discourage. Bookstore work was all I was fit for in this day and age, and I was barely fit for that. I told myself that the same fate would have applied to numerous other artists if they hadn't pursued their vocations. It was impossible to imagine those people having regular jobs. But there was one big difference: they *had* pursued their vocations, and I hadn't. My crucial deficiency was that I still *hadn't* got around to doing the work that I believed it was my inviolable duty to do.

The desire to enjoy an afternoon drink behind the swinging doors of an old bar was frustrated by the fact that there wasn't anywhere, not a single place, that hadn't undergone an uninviting transformation. The King Edward, the Golden Groper, Jack's. The same neon signs continued to shine outside these old haunts, but the interiors were not so much shadows of their former selves (it was their shadows that had been so consoling) as blatantly bland versions of their former shadowy selves.

All but one place. Down an alley, through a side entrance into an old, partly residential hotel, the Sterling, and into the Secret Bar, the one last perforation into the sacred anomie of the past. It was a very ordinary bar. The only thing it had going for it was that it had nothing going for it: it hadn't changed—and nowadays that was enough. It was the only remaining undespoiled "dive bar" downtown ("dive bar" having become a condescending term for a regular bar that by virtue of its normalcy has become a novelty).

I ordered a Presbyterian from the apathetic Asian bartender and settled into a booth.

The bar was completely empty. The jukebox had been set to play selections at random. A song by Bob McGilt—another sickeningly self-congratulatory love song, typical of his oeuvre—came on.

The familiar niggling thought that I should have been a musician was reawakened. If I'd been in a successful band in my youth, even for six months, it would have provided a foundation of rock-and-roll notoriety that could have been traded on for the rest of my life, and parlayed into subsequent activity in any other field of the arts. A ready-made audience would have been guaranteed, consisting of older people unable to let go of their youth and younger people who accepted that anything from that bygone golden era was superior to what they were now obliged to put up with. I would always be known as an early member of that hallowed band; and it could easily have been accomplished. Bob McGilt had been a friend at the time and he had invited me to join his nascent band because he liked the way I looked and seemed to find my company tolerable. Using the flimsy excuse that I didn't play an instrument, I begged off, not realizing at the time that anybody with even the most rudimentary grasp of rhythm and melody could master the bass guitar. McGilt and his band then went on to "great things" and we lost touch with each other. On our few subsequent encounters, he had been conspicuously ill at ease in my company. We didn't seem to have anything to say to each other anymore.

I could easily have learned to play the bass in two weeks. It would have set me up for life, and the musician's existence of constant travel, pliant women, and facile adoration would have agreed with me. It wasn't as if I had anything better to do. It would have been a sensible investment in my future. I didn't realize it at the time, but there were very few things I did realize at the time.

I should have been a musician. But it would have been too easy.

The McGilt song had a certain appeal: I couldn't deny it, much as I wanted to. He knew what he was doing; he'd been doing it for a long time, and he was adored for it. Overadored, perhaps. Yes, definitely, overadored.

I was going to order another drink but the bartender had disappeared. As I walked out, two alley cats were feasting on the remains of a cheese sandwich donated by a security guard who sat playing video games on his cell phone in a parked car, adjacent to the construction site of yet another new corporate monolith behind the hotel.

When I got home I found several familiar-looking envelopes from credit card companies and debt collectors in the mailbox. I placed them in the bulging trash bag filled with such dreary communications that was stuffed into the cupboard below the kitchen sink. I never opened the letters and I never picked up the phone if I didn't recognize the number. I just ignored these tedious importunings and hoped my oppressors would eventually give up and fade away.

Exhausted from contact with reality, I had to lie down. Wandering aimlessly around downtown, a reversion to my misspent younger days, had not been a fulfilling way to spend the afternoon. As I drifted off, I realized that I would have been much happier staying at home writing, even if nothing ever came of it: it was simply a more pleasant way to spend time.

* * *

I poured myself a coffee behind the café counter, walked to the other end of the room, and switched over with Julie, the charmingly mousy, frowzy, fiftyish blond who pulled three daytime shifts a week. I placed the filthy torn cushion on the stool and headed straight online.

"He would sit in the ditch at the edge of the road for hours. He'd just sit there and pick grass."

Immersed in the long, sad decline of Jackson C. Frank,[2] I sat at the counter, resenting any intrusion upon my reading. Having priced and shelved all the books on the new-arrivals cart, I sat at the counter browsing a biography of this famously obscure singer-songwriter that had arrived in a recent book buy. I had immediately started leafing through it, beginning, of course, with the photo section, which charted the singer's physical decline from scarred but handsome youth to ruinously bloated and blinded middle age. Under such interruptible conditions, I scoured it for the most tragic passages, which were not in short supply—for here was a rare case of the biographer having no need to reinforce the calamitous aspects of his subject's life in order to create a wrenching trajectory— considering the recurrent bad luck that befell Frank throughout his relatively short life: burn victim, mental illness, homelessness, blindness, relieved only by a brief interval of prosperity, productivity and acclaim that accompanied the release of his one precociously brilliant album in 1965, which included his most famous song, "Blues Run the Game."

When he was in his early twenties, Frank had already written the songs upon which his reputation rests. Townes Van Zandt did most of his best work before he turned thirty. Both died in their early to midfifties: a decade I floundered upon the brink of, looking down into it as if it were a pit that would swallow up the remains of hope and promise.

---

2. A literary figure would be more suitable in this connection. Frank Stanford or Breece D'J Pancake would have worked well, but I don't have the time or energy to change it now. A singer-songwriter will have to do, although this contrivance risks upsetting the evenness of tone that I should be striving toward.

So many people whose work I enjoyed died in their fifties and early sixties. Up until fairly recently that seemed like a reasonable life expectancy. Now it didn't seem anything like ripe old age, and the worst part of it was that I hadn't created anything that would outlive me.

A lot of these troubadours who were coming to mind as a result of the evening's reading, many of Jackson C. Frank's cohorts and contemporaries, hadn't even made it to forty, or in some cases thirty: Nick Drake, Sandy Denny, Tim Hardin, Tim Buckley. They had led fast lives, whereas I had lived a slow death.

Disturbed by this roll call of the deceased, I went online and checked the dates of some singer-songwriters with greater longevity. The findings were not encouraging. Mickey Newbury died at the age of sixty-two, with his years of peak creativity long behind him; John Fahey died at sixty-one, John Martyn at sixty. At the time of their passing they had seemed at the end of their careers, but they were little more than a decade older than I was.

Of course, I had no business comparing myself to singer-song-writers (it was enough of a stretch to compare myself to other writers): musicians always blossomed early, and all these people had led richer and rougher lives than I had.

I should have been a singer-songwriter. Never mind—always mind—that I couldn't carry a tune. But it was too late for that now.

It was pleasant sitting there on a peaceful Monday night, in a terminally subjunctive mood ("An old man working alone at night in a dusty shop is always a sign of emotional malaise and a tortured relationship with the past," as I had read somewhere). Not many customers came in, and those that did weren't much trouble.

"Is this the sequel to *Moby-Dick*?" asked a smiling customer, holding up a copy of *I Love Dick*.

"Are you a comedian?" I rejoined. In black T-shirt and porkpie hat, he looked like one.

"No. But humor's a good thing. Life can be tough," he said.

"I didn't say you were funny," I said. "I just asked if you were a comedian."

"That's a good one," he said. "You're the comedian. You know, if I were to cast somebody who works in a bookstore, I'd cast you."

"I hope you'll forgive me for not taking that as a compliment."

"You look smart," he said, trying, no doubt, to put a positive spin on this disheartening observation.

"Yeah, see how far it's got me."

Yes, it was pleasant sitting there. I was able to relax and read, and so engrossed did I become in Jackson C. Frank's travails that I took the book home with me and continued reading it in bed, reveling in vicarious morbid empathy.

As soon as I closed my eyes I realized, with a clarity that seldom penetrates the numbed-out haze I prefer to exist in, that I was going to die in the not-unforeseeable future and that all this procrastination was counterfeit immortality, a dragging out of the mortal condition, under the illusion that doing nothing prolongs life.

I opened my eyes and it was still there: death with a capital *D*, followed by capitals *EAT* and *H*, a pure and natural fact. I lay there, no longer turning things over in my mind, but facing them: facing fear, facing fact. It was blurry before. But now I could see it: the End.

It occurred to me that I had always taken too much comfort in the premature deaths of great men, with whom I had nothing in common: to know that they had died made it easier to accept that one would also die. By giving of themselves, they had enriched the lives of others. Whereas, if one hadn't, one could fancifully relate to those who had but couldn't credibly compare oneself to them. And it wasn't as if death was going to wait until I got around to doing something to make its move. It makes no distinction between the active and the inactive, the fertile and the barren.

There's not much point romanticizing death when you're old. When you're young, yes, it can be fun; from afar it can be viewed romantically, but at this late stage it was too close and cold for comfort.

I awoke at dawn with my defenses down: a forty-eight-year-old man with a cum rag under his pillow, gripped by a fresher, starker fear, unleavened by any obfuscating impressions, and accompanied by those awful early-morning sounds—the shunting of trucks and isolated traffic noises that herald the start of another city day.

At that early hour, I was acutely conscious of my body as a mechanism that must eventually fall apart, of my heartbeat as a clock that was winding down. There was no way out of or around the awareness that my time might not be long: a fact that when seen clearly, obscures everything else, that no amount of empire-building or legacy-leaving can change.

Since I was having such an "Aubade" moment I got out of bed, entered the graying light of the other room, turned on the computer, and checked Philip Larkin's dates. Much as I thought, he died in his early sixties. And he hardly wrote during his last decade. When faced with the inevitable, apparently, he was not resigned to his fate; he destroyed his diaries and required heavy sedation in the hospital.

Robert Lowell died at the age of sixty, Richard Hugo at the age of fifty-nine.

That gave me ten years. But I wasn't a poet either, so I couldn't really compare myself to those figures; I wasn't really anything in particular, just a humble aspiring prose stylist, and I hadn't even started yet.

Youthful melancholy was so much more pleasant.

* * *

With the help of a little white pill, as the sun was rising, I put the death awakening to sleep. I woke up later than planned, with a Jackson C. Frank song, "Marlene," playing in my head, and the knowledge that I had to finish a sustained work of prose before I croaked. This experiment with not writing wasn't working out. There wasn't anything else I felt compelled to do.

It had always been the right time to do the work I believed it was my special duty to discharge, and I had always postponed it, playing a perverse and perilous game with myself, which I had taken too far: putting off the crucial matter of embracing my calling for as long as possible. The phrase "there is still time" carried less and less weight, and that worn-out maxim, "Whatever doesn't kill you makes you stronger," only applied until you reached a certain age.

The past now outweighed the future and I was at least ten years behind my time—make that fifteen—but I still wasn't ready to grow old, because I hadn't done anything yet. I had a lot of catching up to do.

Time wasn't on my side anymore. We had once been on friendly terms, but time was now the enemy—private enemy number one—and I had to fight it, or work with it. That which remained had to be spent wisely. I had to finish something while there was still time. Get all this stale stuff out of my system. Give it one last push. What else did I have to do?

I turned the phone off and turned on Freedom, the internet blocker that deactivates the temptation of online distraction for any speci-fied amount of time. Ideally, this time reserved for writing should be like air travel, when one is granted immunity from the demands of reality until one touches down at one's destination, or in this case, when one lays down one's pen and reopens the lines of communication, throughout which time other concerns should not be allowed to intrude.

But something was missing.

Three hours later I had only a few clumsy sentences to show for myself. The initial spark of urgency had soon been snuffed out by self-consciousness, which was what usually happened without the stimulus of medication coursing through my system. It was foolish to imagine I could ever manage without it.

In order to think clearly I found it useful to dull my senses a little. The medication was used purely as a creative tool, of course, in very moderate doses. It enabled me to sit in one place for three hours without entirely succumbing to restlessness and distraction, and it relaxed the critical faculties so that I wasn't continually censoring myself. It made the practice of writing a lot more pleasant.

There was nothing else for it. I was going to have to call Mitchell up.

Fortunately, he still had the pills.

He sounded rushed. "What time? I have to be at the Chateau at seven. I'm meeting Lyn."

"Who?"

"Lyn *Lamrock*," he said, placing heavy emphasis on her last name, clearly vexed that I'd already forgotten the identity of the minor celebrity he was courting.

"How about in half an hour?" I suggested.

"OK. I won't be able to hang out," he said.

That was a relief.

I had never heard Mitchell sound so excited about a date before, or known him to date a woman of his own age. He had always seemed enviably indifferent to the pleasures of the flesh: a sex camel, reliant upon occasional therapeutic contact with young women; and he had always been resolutely opposed to the notion of a mature relationship. As he had often said, "A woman will always come between you and your drugs."

Fortunately, he lived in the neighborhood. I took a DASH bus, fifty cents a ride, up Echo Park Avenue on a sweltering February afternoon, to Mitchell's longtime bachelor pad with its fetid clutter and dusty shelves lined with unproduced screenplays. Mitchell always implied that he was paid for writing and rewriting screenplays, but since he was always so vague about it, and since nothing he wrote ever saw the light of day, it seemed reasonable to assume he was a remittance man. He maintained close ties with various aging relatives, who were probably willing to support his Hollywood aspirations until they paid off.

I bought three hundred dollars' worth from him, which, with my modest, maintenance-level intake, would keep me in good stead for a month's worth of literary endeavor … and ever … end ever. I took enough to satisfy my needs, seldom more. I wasn't wired for excess, and in that, I realized, I was lucky.

* * *

The golden glow crawls into my system. As the gently pulsating warmth stimulates the associative flow, confidence builds and moments of potentially derailing distraction and indecision are calmly endured. A few lines fall into place, almost effortlessly at first. I feel in harmony with the world and something resembling love toward everything in it. But my world is very small and there is very little in it. For the time being, it has been reduced to this desk, these words, and some music playing softly in the background; and in this state of withdrawal, with no outside interference, these precious elements are magnified.

The plan, in my own anesthetized way, is to adhere to Laurence Sterne's dictum of alternating between states of inebriation and clearheadedness while communing with the muse: "once drunk, and once sober:———Drunk—that their counsels might not want vigour;———and sober—that they might not want discretion," as stated in his eighteenthth-century postmodern classic, *Tristram Shandy*.

In this manner, three hours passed smoothly. The initial sensation of well-being gradually dissolved into serene torpor. Occasional spurts of activity punctuated the haze, until the haze descended completely, my head drooped, and my eyes began to close. By the time Freedom turned off, an embryonic paragraph had emerged. It wasn't much but it was more than I would have achieved without the stuff, and the experience had been painless.

* * *

"You had two reviews yesterday," said Gilbert, as I stepped behind the counter.

"Only two? Both favorable, I take it," I said, feebly attempting to add a touch of levity to an inevitably dismal exchange.

"Perhaps you would like to see them?" he suggested in a grinding whisper.

"That's all right."

"I think you should see them," he said even more softly. The angrier Gilbert became, the more softly he spoke. He remained with his back to me as he pulled up the store's Yelp page on the computer, forcing me to the tribunal of humiliation:

"This busy bookstore and cafe in an Eastside neighborhood isn't your typical book and coffee shop. It attracts a hip clientele and there are plenty of unusual titles on the shelves. But I still expected a welcoming local bookstore, and was given much sass from an older male cashier with a disrespectful, can't be bothered attitude who was rude to me and my daughter (who was being very well behaved btw). I will not be returning as I can find the books I want for cheaper on Amazon. I left feeling slightly violated. There are also some street people who hang out around this bookstore panhandling, and on at least one occasion one of them has come into the store as well and been kind of distracting / disruptive while I was browsing."

"Why is it so difficult for you to be polite to the customers?" said Gilbert, virtually whispering.

"She left feeling violated. What more could she ask for?" I said, rising helplessly to my own defense. "I am polite to them. What do they expect? This is an independent bookstore, it's not McDonalds."

Without speaking, Gilbert scrolled down to the next Yelp review:

"I know this place *isn't* a fast food restaurant but I do expect some service. I heard this place was awesome but it really fell short of my expectations. I would really love to write a great review for this book store for I love to support local bookstores. But I had a really bad experience. The man behind the counter was extremely rude. He sneered at me and threw the receipt at me. The service can be summed up in two words: Non-exisistant."

"There's never any reason for sneering," said Gilbert, sneeringly.

"There's something about me that rubs some people the wrong way," I said weakly.

This none-too-convincing explanation exemplified the clumsiness I invariably fell into around Gilbert. Everything I said to him came out sounding weak and wrong. Our awkward chemistry owed much to the shift in dynamic between us over the last five years: his transformation from alcoholic wreck to sober business owner, while I remained steadfast in penurious shiftlessness.

"There have been some very difficult customers in here recently," I said. "We should start our own Yelp page to complain about them. And how about a velvet rope at the door? This open-door policy isn't working."

"I don't like to hear people saying they're never going to set foot in the store again because of the attitude of the staff," said Gilbert, unamused.

"It doesn't matter how polite I am. I put on my soft voice; I talk to them as if they were children. I don't know how I can do any better. If I go any further in adopting some pose of fake smiling warmth, that will really scare them off."

Gilbert picked a bag filled with clothes from the floor.

"What's that?" I asked.

"Yoga," he said plainly. As he walked off, I remembered one of our first meetings, seven or eight years earlier, when he had sloppily accosted me in a bar, and loudly berated me, with alcohol-sodden breath, for being old. "You're old," he had wailed in horror, as if aging was the most deplorable and undignified thing anybody could do. And I was still comparatively young then.

Oh, to be forty again.

And so the shift began—a bad start to the evening, and it was likely to get worse with Gilbert still lurking around, killing time before he had to leave for his yoga class, making for a dynamic that reminded me of my adolescence: the atmospheric plunge that occurred when my father returned home from work every night at seven thirty, disrupting my solitary idyll of musical and literary appreciation, and hailing that most solemn of ceremonials, the family dinner.

In a pitiful attempt to look busy I did some shelving.

While I was attempting to transfer an armload of unsalable books to the filthy, dusty dollar cart on the sidewalk, a tall, bald customer stopped midstride in the aisle and stood in front of me texting. "Can you stop fucking texting and move the fuck along," I muttered viciously, more in the interest of heightening my own frustration than any form of communication, and not expecting to be heard. The customer moved along but when he reached the doorway he turned around and fixed me with a stare. He was shaven headed and covered with tattoos, and obviously worked out.

"You should apologize," he said.

"What for?"

"Because you told me to stop texting."

"I'm sick of having to navigate an obstacle course of texters to get around this fucking place."

"All you had to do was tap me on the shoulder."

"I didn't want to tap you on the shoulder."

"You should apologize."

"All right. I'm sorry."

Disappointed with myself for having apologized, I returned to my position behind the counter.

"How are you doing?" said Aaron, as he wandered in. I viewed him peripherally as I continued doing the crossword puzzle in front of the computer. He was short, bespectacled, bearded, an accomplished draftsman who often sat at one of the tables in the café and drew comic strips that documented his social, romantic, and financial frustrations.

He leaned across the counter and whispered: "I tried to have sex with that girl."

"Eh?"

But we were interrupted.

"Do you have blank books?" asked a painfully thin, well-heeled woman of a certain age.

"There might be some over there," I said, pointing to the erratically stocked notebook shelf. "Or over there," I added, "on the table"—referring to the table in the middle of the room that contained a treasury of postcards, notebooks, and such dreaded knickknacks as candles, incense, and ceramic pig figurines.

"I went over there the other night," Aaron continued, leaning over the counter, talking quickly and quietly. "I gave her a long speech and I basically told her 'I'm a creep, and all this sexy talk we do over the phone and instant messaging or text or whatever, I can't follow through on any of that. That's all fantasy. When it actually comes down to it I just want you to jack me off while I play with your tits, that's pretty much it. I'm a very underwhelming lover. I can't get it up in person, I just can't.' But you know what, I just have to say that so the expectations are so low that if I perform at all, then I'm better than what I told her. She's very literary and that's cool. She wants to tell me about how she organizes her books, and she paints."

"She's an artist?"

"I don't know. Where d'you draw the line? Who is and who isn't? I suppose you're an artist if you say you're an artist. That's the way it goes, nowadays. Everybody wants to be thought of as an artist," said Aaron.

"Artists that can't draw or paint, writers that have no command of language, singers that have no voice of their own. The internet provides the means to support such illusions," I said.

"D'you own this store?" asked the painfully thin woman, when she came back a minute later with a lined notebook. Her eyes glistened spitefully.

"Sort of," I said. I could see where this was going. My skin was beginning to crawl. Something about me had rubbed her the wrong way. I was used to this dynamic and felt a certain hopelessness. I was on the verge of being yelped.

"Would you like a bag?" I asked in my softest, most ingratiating voice, knowing that this woman expected nothing less.

"Wow," said Aaron, after she walked out. "Wow. That look she gave you was pure evil."

"I know," I said. "As you are my witness, I did nothing to offend her. I handled her with kid gloves, but it makes no difference, they detect something in me that rubs them the wrong way."

"What's she even doing here?" said Aaron. "It makes no sense to me. If I walked into a scene that was radically different to what I'm used to, I'm not going to impose myself upon it. You don't just show up and start acting like an obnoxious bitch, you find a way to blend in. She looked like she came from Brentwood."

"Yes, she had that look," I said. "A skeletal, hard-eyed, angry, aging anorexic from Brentwood or somewhere. People like that really do exist."

"Excuse me."

A full-grown man in shorts, T-shirt and a backward baseball cap was standing there.

"D'you know where the toilet paper is?"

"What?"

"Do you have any toilet paper for the bathroom?"

"Use your hand," I sideways muttered to Aaron.

"Excuse me?" said the childishly attired customer.

"I said, 'I don't understand.'"

"What don't you understand? There isn't any toilet paper in the bathroom."

"OK, calm down. I'll get it for you."

I walked to the other end of the store, removed an industrial-sized roll of toilet paper from the cupboard in the alcove, and handed it to him as he entered the restroom. Then I returned to my station and continued with the crossword, only to have my nerves rattled by a high-velocity rumbling emanating from the fiction section.

I stood up and saw that somebody was sitting on a footstool, directly in front of the fiction shelves, with no concern that he was blocking the way of customers who might actually want to look at books, and he was speaking so loudly, forcefully and speedily that his speech was outpacing thought itself and entering a realm beyond that of language. At first I assumed that he was mad, but he was wearing a headset and a miniature microphone hung around his neck.

But perhaps those accessories were just props used in order to facilitate make-believe conversations. With so many people walking around wearing headsets, yapping into the air, and more authentic lunatics around than ever, talking to themselves in the time-honored manner of genuine insanity, which was soothing by comparison, it was becoming impossible to differentiate between the sane and the insane—and there was something about the sound of a loudly broadcast one-sided phone conversation that was even more of an affliction to the ears than the incessant drone of banal chatter. It used to be that if one needed to make a phone call when one was out in public, one used a pay phone, which took place in a private booth, ensuring that one's conversation wasn't heard by others, but the technology of self-absorption had turned the public sphere into one giant phone booth.

"How much is this book?" asked a customer.

"Sixteen ninety-five. I'll give you half off if you tell that guy on the cell phone to take it outside."

"Done," he said, and without much difficulty the man was cast out, yapping incontinently to himself as he slowly left the store.

"Can I trouble you for a bag, please?" asked a grinning customer.

I reached under the counter and handed over a brown paper bag, without putting his books into it.

"Service is extra, I guess," said the customer, still grinning.

That interaction reaggravated me. It didn't take much.

I returned to browsing a biography of a celebrated twentieth-century American novelist that had been left on the counter: "The 21-year-old man who walked out of a publisher's office that morning had no career, no money, no prospects, and nothing to fall back on other than a ruined confidence in his own abilities." How, I wondered, could one fall back on ruined confidence? The author in question had already enjoyed a spectacular academic career at the best university in the country. The period referred to was a very brief interval between academic success and literary glory, possibly the only few months of his entire life during which he experienced even the slightest taste of professional rejection. But it was always in the biographer's best interest to heighten the tragic, even when the tragic was greatly eclipsed by triumph—because if they didn't, then they didn't have a story. But what did I know? We all had our own battles.

The night started to drag. That was when I began to enjoy it. Sometimes toward the end of the night shift the place calmed down to the extent that I could settle into the pure zone of reading and listening. I savored that dead-end feeling, and sometimes enjoyed talking with the other lost souls who washed up in a bookstore/café at ten o'clock on a Monday night.

I looked up. Standing in front of the book counter was a grinning young man with a loudly weak voice.

I couldn't bring myself to return his grating greeting.

"Tired?" he asked, with sickeningly fake concern.

"What do you want?"

"Where can I put this?" He held up a poster for a reading series at a nearby venue.

"Over there."

"Do you have any tape?"

I handed him some tape and continued reading.

A minute later I looked up and he was standing there again, returning the tape: "Well, thank you so much, I hope your night gets better."

"Piss off," I wanted to say, but I said nothing; I just took it. A lame duck target, I was expected to absorb the abuse owing to my position behind a counter.

Some people didn't get it: they didn't realize this wasn't Knott's Berry Farm, that they weren't going to receive obsequious service with a simpering smile. Some people didn't seem to understand the nature of a bookstore, and what should be asked of a bookseller.

* * *

There's something sad and distasteful about these stray hairs that fall onto the desk. And these days they are usually gray.

I hold a curly, wiry gray hair to the morning light, then I put it in my pocket, from where it will fall to the floor when I next remove my handkerchief. There is no mistaking the hard evidence of age. I might as well think of myself as a fifty-year-old and gradually ease into that horror.

Am I an old young person or a young old person? The former, I fear. I have been young for too long, longer than anyone else; but in terms of staleness, I am old beyond my years. As you can probably imagine,[3] this would all be a lot easier to take if I were ten years younger. But I said the same thing ten years ago. And ten years before that.

Age is just a number: yes, and that number is unsettling.

How did I get this old? Considering how long it took to get started, how little I've achieved, and how lowly my station in life is, I should be at least ten years younger. Turning fifty is almost unthinkable, it cannot be fathomed; it is the last horizon. When one turns thirty, one is looking at forty; when one turns forty, one is looking at fifty, which is disconcerting enough; but when one turns fifty, one is just gazing into the abyss. A great divide has been crossed, on the other side of which is another zone—one without return or returns, one in which proof of failure has finally been furnished, with a date stamped on it.

"After forty, every change becomes a hateful symbol of time's passing,"[4] Samuel Johnson wrote. At forty one can still be a late bloomer; at fifty it is all over. Nobody achieves first-time success after the age of fifty: if you're fifty and you're not a success, then you're a failure. No other age carries such weight; it is, at least, a sort of halfway funeral, and one is attending it alone.

But at least I still had a year and a half to contemplate that dreaded milestone. Forty-eight was the last age with even the slightest residual glow of youth about it. At forty-nine one is conspicuously knocking on the door of fifty. The widest psychological age gap, from what I've observed, lies between forty-five and fifty; it is much wider than the difference between forty and forty-five, or any other lustrum.*

---

3. Should I address the reader directly? No, that urge should be resisted. Dear reader, you will not be addressed directly.

4 Quotations from other authors should be avoided, especially when they make my own lines pale by comparison.

I refuse to age beyond forty-eight. At this age I will remain. Forever forty-eight.

* * *

"Hi, I like your shirt," said a young woman carrying a clipboard. "D'you have a second to talk about human rights?"

"No."

"All right, have a good day."

I strolled past the canvasser and into the health food market in order to purchase some spinach and immediately encountered an old friend, Bill.[5] He was accompanied by his "better half," as he called her—his girlfriend or wife or whatever she was—and catching sight of me he grabbed her from behind and aggressively rubbed her belly. My first thought was that he was simulating the act of love, but the penny dropped when he said, "Can you keep a secret?"

"Three months," she said, beaming.

"Yes, I noticed you looked different," I remarked.

"You mean fat?" she laughed.

"No, you have a glow about you." And she did: a rosy, waxy bloom that resembled plastic fruit.

"Congratulations," I said. I didn't know what else to say.

"Are you down at Mute today?" asked Bill.

"This evening," I said.

"I'll pay you a visit later."

"Don't," I said. "It's not a suitable venue for social intercourse."

---

5. I can't spend hours coming up with a name for a character, especially one that isn't going to appear again in this book. Bill will have to do.

This tiresome exchange needed to end so that I could get home and put the hours in. The pretense of taking an interest in each other's life based upon a brief period of time, many years ago, when we had both been in the same place—a place that many people pass through, putting in their compulsory flirtation with bohemia, before moving on to lives of familial responsibility—had been endured; five minutes of my time had been invested, and it wasn't as if he really wanted to talk to me anyway.

Back in his bachelor days, Bill and I had been close, but as his career as a screenwriter took off, we drifted apart. The only time I ever heard from him anymore was when he needed to complain about his relationship to somebody.

I didn't understand people who took having children for granted, as if it was natural or something, and formed these cozy little units at such an early age, or at any age. Then I realized: they weren't young. In fact, in their late thirties / early forties, they would be considered, by the world at large, to be old parents.

Well, the race had to be perpetuated and I certainly wasn't going to be much help in that department.

Next, my progress was impeded by my ex-girlfriend's best friend, Klarisa Dicsuonted. She was slowly moving through the produce section, selecting only the very finest vegetables for the delectation of her family, and smiling to herself as she did so as if warmly anticipating the rapture of their evening meal.

The reverberations from the last relationship I endured, two years earlier, were still capable of provoking fierce partisan enmity among the wounded party's inner circle, so in order to spare Klarisa the embarrassment of acknowledging somebody who had treated her best friend so badly, I put a hold on my need for spinach and retreated to the cereal aisle, where I tried to make the best use of my time by studying the ingredients listed on a box of high-end Norwegian muesli.

For the last two years I had somehow managed to avoid my ex-"girlfriend" but I hadn't been so fortunate when it came to her friends, and they still viewed me with contempt. The relationship in question ended when my "girlfriend," Louise, found another woman's bloodied tampon in my kitchen trash can. Naturally, I tried to come up with an explanation but I didn't have a ready-made excuse at hand and my faltering attempts to justify the presence of this offensive item were not received kindly. It didn't help matters when it emerged, thanks to another of her friends, that the tampon belonged to a girl who was Louise's junior by twenty years, but it did have the salutary effect of ending a strenuous yearlong relationship, for the first eleven months of which I'd attempted, for reasons that elude me now, to walk the line.

I thought Klarisa had left but she was standing in the checkout line one aisle over. The bitch shield was instantly deployed: she stared straight past me as if I didn't exist. It would be beneath her dignity to acknowledge the sort of scum that carried on with girls half his age behind his girlfriend's back, especially after she and her husband had initially been so thrilled to welcome me, as part of a new couple, into their recently bought Eagle Rock house to share their vegetarian Thanksgiving dinner.

I just wanted to get in and out of the supermarket as quickly as possible, but too often it was a nerve-stretching obstacle course of awkward evasions and intempestive absquatulations.

It was all so dispiriting.

* * *

Twenty thousand words. I have written 20,000 words. I have never gone this far in my brilliant noncareer as a failed prose stylist. This is sufficient cause for celebration. But who will celebrate it? To announce that one is writing a novel is to set oneself up for ridicule and failure. There's no point talking about it until it's finished, preferably until it's published. It's sad, very sad, if one broadcasts that one is writing a novel, and it doesn't get published.

Divided by 320 (roughly the amount of words on the page of a trade paperback), this amounts to 62 pages. In the unlikely event that I ever finish this thing, the ideal word count would be 75,000, about 250 pages. That's the sweet spot, and by that projection I'm one-quarter in.

At the grindingly precious rate at which I don't exactly exert myself, there's a lot of work to be done (if the amount of time I "put in" were commensurate with actual product, I would have amassed a substantial body of work by now, several groaning shelves' worth—if not of a Jamesian or Dostoevskian amplitude, then at least in the Flaubertian range), and even once that seemingly unattainable goal has been achieved, a lot of revision will be necessary. I imagine that I would be delighted if I could finish this thing in the next year and see it published by the time I turn fifty. But that is asking a lot of myself, and of others.

If I don't finish this thing or if I do finish it and it doesn't see the light of day, it's going to have been a massive waste of time. The time for mistakes and experimentation is over. If I don't know how to do it by now, then it's too late. All other options have been erased. The multiple works I once envisioned are a long-forgotten fantasy. Now it's all about this one thing. There's no time left for anything else. No process, all product. It's too late not to continue.

* * *

Twenty boxes of books were stacked in front of and behind the counter, almost blocking ingress.

"Where did these come from?" I asked Gilbert.

"They're all from the Ben Selvin estate. His girlfriend brought them in."

"That was quick. His corpse is still warm and his books have already been sold off. Is this everything?"

"Everything she didn't hang on to."

I enjoyed these sorting sessions with Gilbert, when some semblance of our old friendship was apparent; as we picked through boxes full of books we were on equal footing in a relatively relaxed atmosphere.

"It looks like there's still a lot of good stuff," I remarked, spotting several Philip K. Dick hardcovers at the top of one box. "Some of these are signed," I added, as I cracked open a pristine first edition of *Confessions of a Crap Artist*.

"How did he die?" I asked Gilbert.

"Some sort of cancer. He was only fifty-two."

"Fuck," I groaned. I didn't want to sound as if I related too directly to the fate of this deceased acquaintance who had passed on two weeks earlier—a local bookman who had amassed a substantial library of arcane books throughout a lifetime of involvement in various aspects of the book trade.

"How much did you give her?"

"Five thousand," he said. It was one of the biggest book buys the store had ever made.

"Why didn't she sell them online?"

"She didn't want to bother with all that."

Five thousand dollars: What could one get for that? A month-long vacation. Depending on the sentimental, fetishistic or intellectual value that one placed on literature, it might be worth it.

Noting a copy of *4 Dada Suicides*, I dug deeper into another box, unearthing a rich lode of surrealist literature.

"There's virtually a complete set of Atlas Press here."

"I know," said Gilbert. "That was Ben's main area of expertise."

Ben and I had enjoyed many conversations over the years. He was an affable and knowledgeable sort, a true bibliophile who cared deeply about books, their form and their content—one of a dying breed, now dead himself, before his so-called time.

And this is what it came down to: all the time and care that went into amassing this unique library—material artifacts of love and knowledge dispersed at a pittance—ended up as a profitable haul for a used bookstore.

A literary life in twenty boxes: I began to put a price on it.

Helen, an acquaintance, marched up to the counter wearing a big smile. She leaned over and shoved her cell phone in my face: a baby photograph was displayed on the screen.

"Do you know who that is?"

"No. Should I?" To the untrained eye, newborn babes all look the same; any familial resemblance is impossible to detect.

"It's Joe's son," she announced, with surrogate maternal pride.

I knew that our mutual friend had married but had no idea that spawning was on the agenda. The marriage had been something of a surprise in itself. During the time of our friendship Joe had been a charismatically gawky flaneur, and the author of numerous autobiographical sketches that described, even romanticized, an existence of genteel poverty and dignified otiosity. I had optimistically assumed that he was that rare individual who was committed to a life of bachelordom. He didn't have much luck with the ladies and he was defiantly disparaging whenever the subject of relationships came up; he had certainly never expressed any desire to settle down or to become a dad. Then he moved to Portland, of all places, and for the first time in the ten years I'd known him, he acquired a girlfriend. By all accounts, his paramour was quite "a catch."

And that was the last I heard of him. The once-lengthy emails, concerned with his many literary and musical passions, became shorter and more infrequent, before drying up completely. The next thing I heard, Joe was engaged.

The cell phone photograph of the happy couple pulled up by Helen confirmed reports of his fiancée's comeliness. He had *done very well* for himself. Now, naturally, there was a baby on the way, and they had bought a house to raise a family in, despite Joe's never having had any steady source of income that I was aware of. He had always led a very modest existence and resided in small apartments.

But there comes a time when the quirks and misbehavior of youth come to an end and adult responsibilities must be assumed. When we're in our twenties we're all ostensibly in the same position, but once we're in our thirties and forties the pressure is on, and even the most idiosyncratic and uncompromising characters are liable to buckle under the pressure of convention and readjust their priorities. Everything must be done in the right order, and although predictable it can still come as a shock when some people suddenly turn their lives around—sober up, straighten out, settle down. Inevitably, the time to show their hand arrives: to reveal what they've been holding, or withholding, all along.

Maybe that's what Joe always wanted: the same thing everybody else supposedly wants. One couldn't really blame him: the rewards for a life of unrepentant bohemianism are not very tempting—solitude and poverty would be fairly easy to resist, I imagined, if an attractive alternative were to present itself.

How he got by had always been something of a mystery; and perhaps his wife had the money, which would add up, romantically and economically. These lifestyle transformations were often financially motivated, and men were just as likely as women to do the "sensible" thing at the right time—to hold out for as long as they could but still eventually capitulate.

Well, good for him. Maybe his defiance had been a form of defense; maybe he had merely resigned himself to the solitary life because he thought he couldn't do any better. But to turn one's life around so completely, to go from being a diehard bachelor to a family man overnight at the first opportunity: Wouldn't that suggest it had all been a phase, a game, that he had merely been biding his time? Plus, it made me feel more alone in the stance I'd adopted.

"Oh," I said.

"Are you going to be flying up for the party?" asked Helen.

"What party?"

"They're celebrating the new addition to the family"

"That's nice. Are you going?"

"Yes, *we're* going. Why not?"

Why not, indeed? As far as I could make out, neither she nor her artist boyfriend had any source of working income. She was "a photographer."

Of course I'm not going to be flying up for the party. I don't have the money or the time. I don't fly around the country going to parties. But I couldn't tell her that. She was so free from financial worry that it would never occur to her that others didn't enjoy the same freedom—she probably thought I worked in a bookstore purely for the fun of it—and any allusion to her privileged position might make her uncomfortable.

"Anyone here yet?"

I was leaning against the counter, facing a cart crammed with used books that were waiting to be shelved, when the evening's featured reader, Teddy Morbid, strolled in, wearing black jeans and a black T-shirt that showed off his muscular tattooed arms. He used to be in a punk band, now he was a writer, by virtue of the fact that he had written a book chronicling his misadventures as a heroin addict and his road to recovery. Now he meditated and worked out a lot. The book was called *Wasted* and there was a blurry photograph of a guitar and a syringe on the cover.

On the back cover there was a photograph of the author with dyed-black hair, earrings, and tattooed shoulders. His expression suggested that he had weathered the storms of drug addiction and emerged with newfound dignity. Now, with the wisdom of a survivor who learned the hard way that drugs aren't cool, he had to tell everybody about it, and in the telling of his supposedly cautionary tale, with its irresistible tales of excess, the drug lifestyle would inadvertently be romanticized.

"Jim should be coming down," said Teddy, proudly referring to his patron and publisher, Jimmy Dripp—the renowned actor of screen and screen—not merely by first name but by the diminutive that was only used by his best pals.

I had already had the pleasure of engaging, as a listener, in several conversations with Teddy, all of which centered exclusively on himself and his literary enterprises. Not once had he ever inquired as to what I might do other than sell books.

That seemed to be the way it went with a lot of these addicts. At first, it was all about gratifying their urges and destroying everything else; then, once the addiction "spiraled" out of control, it was all about denial of that gratification and intolerance of anything that opposed the new regime of abnegation.

Sometimes, in the interest of self-improvement, and with what was obviously great effort on their part, the addict would attempt to take an interest in a person from whom they had nothing to gain, but that didn't happen often.

Then, if they were even remotely famous and capable of putting pen to paper, or paying somebody else to do it for them, the sordid but ultimately triumphant story of excess and recovery, with the addict as hero, was documented.

I would like to have offered a more vehement condemnation of the drug-memoir epidemic but I couldn't take it out on Teddy, not on his night of glory, when he was going to be sharing his junkie war stories with an adoring public on the patio of the bookstore, but I could at least be mildly critical of his patron, who was guilty, among other things, by association.

"How did you get Dripp to publish you?"

"Jim's a friend, we go way back."

"Yes, of course. But he can't act, can he? Honestly, has he ever once appeared in a decent movie?"

"Have you seen *Dead Woman*?"

"That may be the one exception. It was good despite him, and it wasn't that good. And that was twenty years ago. He appears in franchises. He never inhabits a role, he airbrushes his characters with a sheen of cuteness. Plus, he expects to have this bad boy reputation when he's done nothing to earn it. He cultivates the company of other celebrity bad boys and basks in the reflected glory—"Hunter," "Keith," "Iggy," you … all of whom are flattered to be patronized by a famous actor."

"You're just jealous of him," said Teddy, rising in stout defense of his friend.

"Yes, of course I'm jealous of him. What other reason could a man have for not liking Jimmy Dripp?"

"He's a good person. You should like him, he reads," said Teddy.

Which, after all, is all I was: a seller and reader of books.

"Is he going to publish anything other than drug memoirs?"

"He's publishing some Kerouac letters that have never been seen before," said Teddy, putting me in my place.

"Taking a chance on fresh young talent, eh? That's laudable."

"He's publishing my first book," said Teddy.

"Yeah, but you're already known … as a musician. There's nothing further to say on the subject of drugs. Every nickel has been chipped out of that rock."

I leaned back in order to relish the full malice of this pronouncement.

"It's a literary tradition," said Teddy, patiently, as if he were giving a history lesson to a recalcitrant student. "There's a book from the eighteenth century called *Confessions of an English Opium Addict*."

"It's from the nineteenth century, actually: Thomas De Quincey. I haven't read it, although I did enjoy his *Recollections of the Lake Poets*. That wouldn't interest you though. It's not about drugs."

"The thing is that there's a long history of writing about drugs and as long as people take drugs, people are going to write about it."

"Well, it's run its course. Heroin memoirs are as played out and predictable as Marvel movies at this point."

"In my book, remember …"

The arrogant swine took it for granted that I'd read his book, which, of course, I hadn't. I wasn't about to read some sloppily written drug memoir by an aging punk rock singer when I'd barely penetrated Henry James, but I threw him a bone.

"Yeah, it's good."

"Thank you," he said, with condescending mock courtesy. He had already had so much smoke blown up his ass by his celebrity friends that a fire alarm went off every time he broke wind; the insincere endorsement of a lowly bookseller wasn't going to mean much to him.

"The drug memoir is a shortcut to credibility for people who have nothing to say. It's too easy. You have a built-in readership of people who crave vicarious depravity on the cheap," I said.

Teddy was a good sport to put up with my good-natured teasing. I escorted him through the store to the patio where I had reluctantly set up the microphone, the PA system, and rows of chairs for his reading.

"Let me know if I can be of any further use to you," I said, and returned to my duty of pricing and shelving used books.

There were too many events of this nature at the bookstore for my liking. Owing to Gilbert's checkered past, the place was frequented by his twelve-step buddies, most of whom were recovering drug addicts, also known as "musicians," making for a sort of rock-and-roll bookstore, augmented by continually blasting music and prime location on a thoroughfare of flourishing nightlife.

"How are you? Are you doing good?" said Alicia, an evening-shift-barista, as she walked around the counter.

"No." That was all I could manage, one word, a simple negative.

"Why not?" she said, and put her arm around me, squeezing me into her ample bosom.

"I'm doleful."

"What does that mean?"

With the arm that wasn't tentatively clasping her waist, I googled the word. When it appeared on the online dictionary she took a photograph of the synonyms with her cell phone: "mournful, woeful, sorrowful, sad, unhappy, depressed, dismal, gloomy, morose, melancholy, miserable, forlorn, wretched, woebegone, despondent, grief-stricken; more."

"Are you all of those things, Sean?" she asked.

"With the possible exception of 'grief-stricken,' yes."

She then pointed her cell phone at me and I smiled for it.

"Is that going on Instaflam?"

"Maybe."

My arm remained around her waist. I didn't want to offend her by removing it.

"Did you have a lot of hair when you were young?" she asked, rubbing my head.

"I still do, don't I?"

"Yes, that's why I ask."

"There's no danger of my ever going bald, is there?"

"None at all. If you did you could wear a fish cap …"

"What's that?"

A customer appeared at the counter and I removed my arms from Alicia's waist. Another copy of *White Fragility* was sold. While making the transaction the late middle-aged white lady sang along to "Under My Thumb" (live 1969, *Get Yer Ya-Ya's Out* outtake), and walked off humming it.

"Goodnight, Sean," Alicia said as she walked down the steps, and I returned to my reading.

After ten o'clock only the lost and the insane wandered in.

"You see this book," said a windblown old man, waving a copy of *Designs from Pre-Columbian Mexico* at me. "I found a copy of it at my local library, at the rack, you know, when you walk in. I got it for a dollar. They influence my art. I produce small paintings. Lately I've been giving them to waitresses."

A few drops of spittle flew out of his busily working mouth and landed on the counter, missing my thumb by an inch.

"Much better than cash," I said, moving my hand out of the way.

"This one waitress tapes them to her bedroom mirror. She must have so many of them by now that she can barely see herself."

I don't care, I don't care, I don't care ...

"I don't care," I said.

"What?" he said.

"Maybe it's a very small mirror," I said.

"She is very slim and tall," he blathered on, unbidden, sprinkling the keyboard with saliva as he did so.

The conundrum of whether or not to draw the sprayer's attention to his freely spurted ejecta presented itself. Perhaps he hoped that I hadn't noticed it, perhaps he didn't give a shit. The latter hypothesis seemed more likely.

"She's sixty-two years old but she has a great figure," he continued. "I go there for happy hour. You can get a really good craft beer for three dollars, and I get to stare at her."

"That's great," I said. "Maybe you should propose to her."

"She's married," he said.

In order to avoid further sialoquence I came out from behind the counter and did some shelving.

At ten thirty, half an hour before closing time, I congratulated Teddy on the reading, which, shockingly, he seemed satisfied with. About fifteen of his friends had shown up (not a mean figure: others, of greater renown, had drawn less); three copies of *Wasted* had been sold, and the author read for four times longer than necessary (once they have a few people in front of them, most readers can't stop themselves from rattling on, despite the fact that their material is completely unsuited for oratorial purposes and they're getting no response whatsoever from the audience). I didn't have the heart to ask him what happened to Dripp.

What a waste of everybody's time, especially mine. He lived to tell the tale, but nobody was listening.

I was left alone on the patio, frazzled and clammy, dismantling the PA system and disposing of the half-empty coffee cups left by Teddy's AA buddies. I returned the tables and chairs to their accustomed positions, replaced the soap and toilet paper in the restroom, and took out the trash. Such are the responsibilities of a humble bookseller.

Teddy returned home to his family. Nobody would want to read about his current life: sobriety, monogamy and physical fitness don't make for stimulating reading. Heroicize your addictions, if that's all you've got. But what about somebody who doesn't have an addiction to excuse *his* wasted life?

* * *

I rise early, eager to dull my senses.

Descending shafts of light, like those that illuminated praying saints in medieval manuscripts, stream down through the grimy, faded lace curtains in the bathroom window and land in a shimmering cascade on the stained tile floor in front of the toilet. These beams of swirling motes, perfectly aligned, irradiate the dust that otherwise remains unseen, so much dust: a mesmerizing manifestation that is only visible in the early mornings, upon getting out of the shower.

There is abundant dust in the world, and sleep is a beautiful thing, magical in its power to erase the mood of the day before, renew one's vigor, and allow for a fresh start, before things have time to get sullied, before time sullies things.

When I reenter the bathroom a few minutes later to hang up the towel, the funnel of light has vanished. Within an hour I have taken the pill that summons me to my task; and a delightful hour it has been, knowing that solitude and sedation await me.

In the interest of forming sentences that will probably never be read, all lines of communication are down. Freedom is turned on, the phone is turned off, and the little yellow pill dissolves cozily into my system. With no possibility of interruption, and my nervous system sufficiently subdued, a climate conducive to the discharging of duty has been created.

I wash the pill down with a deep draft of water and wait for it to settle. The first tinge of pleasure is felt in the gut, from where it spreads out, generating an overall sense of well-being that keeps me in one place. For a few hours, awash in chemical warmth and positive intent, plunging into multilayered streams of abstraction, I feel receptive and giving. I don't want to do anything else.

* * *

"The first run of five thousand copies is almost sold out," said Jackson Valvitcore, attempting, I assumed, not to sound too pleased with himself. But maybe he really wasn't pleased with himself. Maybe I was wrong to assume that somebody would naturally be ecstatic when their novel became a runaway success. Perhaps success could be an anticlimactic and deflating experience.

Settled comfortably in a torn red-Naugahyde booth in the Secret Bar, Jackson sipped the cocktail I had bought him. He had written to me earlier in the week, suggesting a get-together, and I had written back, saying "I would love to hang out, but you're doing a little too well at the moment for me to be entirely comfortable in your presence. Maybe after all the fuss has died down a bit." He seemed to find this amusing, perhaps not realizing that I was being honest.

On the other side of the room, in the only other occupied booth, three Korean men sat silently together, staring downward. My first thought was that they were having a prayer meeting, before I realized they were staring at their cell phones.

"You must find all this attention gratifying," I said to Jackson.

"It doesn't make any difference. It just makes me angrier. I don't have time for anything anymore. I'm writing emails all day."

"To whom?"

"I have an agent now and he's going to make me rich," he laughed, still reeling with apparent disbelief from the impact of success. "They're selling it to Germany and France. I could give you figures if you want but they might upset you."

"Not at all. I like to see my friends doing well. Go on."

"Seventy thousand to France, forty thousand to Germany"

"It's not that astronomical."

"There are other countries, and they're trying to sell another book of mine."

I knocked back the last of my cocktail and cast a glance over at Jackson's glass: it was still three-quarters full. At the speed he drank, it would take him half an hour to sip down the rest of it. After making some quick calculations based on rate of alcohol consumption offset by dwindling available funds and chances of Jackson buying the next round, I figured that I would have finished one more cocktail by the time he finished his current one. By no means was I a fast drinker, but Jackson was a very slow drinker and a very fast writer. For the last five years he had written at least one book a year, not all of which had been published, and he still thought he wasn't getting enough done. He was, and always would be, ten years younger than me, and he never seemed to have to work for a living, so naturally he had more time and energy than I had.

"You've written another book?" I asked upon my return from the bar with another Presbyterian.

"No, it's something I wrote four years ago, a 150,000-word novel called *Fuck Fame*. It's a good title, isn't it? The depressing thing is that these publishers have no taste, they're just factories, they just need new product to move. Nobody would touch it when I shopped it around. They're only interested in it because of *The Death*."

He had good reason to be pleased with the success of *The Death of the Novel*. He had written a provocative book that said something, and because he believed in it he had launched his own press and published it himself.

"One thing I've learned as a published author is that it's all about the title," he said.

"Yes, I've learned the same thing from my work as a bookseller," I said.

I wasn't excessively tormented by his good fortune, and maybe there was something in it for me. Several other titles, mostly by friends of his, were slated for imminent release on an imprint that was bound to receive exposure owing to the success of its first publication.

I wondered if I should mention that I was writing a novel. He hadn't asked me what I was up to, but I could easily throw it into the conversation: *Yeah, I'm writing a novel.* But I stopped myself. It would feel wrong as soon as I said it. It was probably better not to bring it up at this point. No, I wouldn't mention it.

Half an hour later, after taking his last sip, Jackson cut our evening short: he had to rise early in order to catch a flight to New York in the morning.

* * *

A low-flying police helicopter churns the blue sky above where I sit, scrambling the desired ambience as I strive to form scentences. Even with the internet turned off, opportunities for distraction are still plentiful—just like old times, in my once-screenless existence, back in the pure old predigital days.

Maybe it would be easier to enter the region of pure art if I wasn't always getting up to do the things that supposedly make it possible for me to get anything done at all.

Throughout a three-hour session I listen to at least three records, which means getting up to flip or change a disc six times. The process of selecting a record, removing it from its sleeve, and placing it on the turntable lends itself to distraction. I drink three mugs of coffee every morning. After making coffee or changing a record I wash my hands compulsively, and there are the unavoidable calls of nature. Altogether, this means that any potential stretch of free-flowing immersion is broken at least eight times during a three-hour session, often for more than five minutes at a time, which adds up to about half an hour of not writing, not to mention all the time that is spent dwelling on things other than the task at hand. If an hour's worth of actual work emerges from a three-hour session, that's a good morning.

It is a great triumph to resist, if only for a few minutes, the trifling distractions that account for the majority of my time, and allow myself to "get lost" in "the work." (Twenty minutes have elapsed between writing the last sentence and the next one.) I can't stop running a steady stream of lamentation and exhortation as I proceed, as if commentating on a sports event at which I never let myself get ahead, goading myself only into stasis.

Essentially, it's not really about writing, it's about entering a zone in which writing is sometimes possible. In which respect, writing is like sleeping: always necessary, occasionally refreshing, frequently insufficient—and in the end, nothing much comes of it, only insomnia that is alleviated by medication, and a lot of strange dreams.

Having sat in front of it for so long without touching the keys, the screen faded to black. When I bestirred myself from abstraction and reopened my eyes the reflection on the computer screen looked old and bitter; the impression of a life well lived was not visible on my features.

I looked ancient and enfeebled. I had never seen such bags beneath my bloodshot eyes. Although thin-lipped and walnut-creased, mine was still a young man's face—an aging young man's face—with the lines of age carved into incongruously youthful features; an unwillingness to let go of youth was visible in my physiognomy.

My hair was graying and my teeth were like the world: yellow, white, brown, and black—composed of about the same percentage of each, with the whitish ones fortunately at the front, and the most discolored, missing and crumbling teeth—jagged islands in a sea of pain—situated toward the back. Of those that remained, most were beyond repair or needed extensive work that I couldn't afford (teeth are the most reliable signifier and stigmatizer of social standing: wealthy people do not have bad teeth).

Soon I would be joining the ranks of the invisible. Time had caught up with me; it had me by the scruff of my sagging neck, but

I struggled with its grip because I still hadn't delivered what should have been delivered long ago.

In a moment of weakness, I checked my phone. It contained one voicemail, from Mitchell: "We're having a small party on Friday night ..." Things were moving fast between him and Lyn Lamrock; Mitchell had switched to the oppressive first-person plural with shameless ease—that heartless "we" that excludes you and often heralds a negation of the newly shackled party's former way of life: coupledom as dissociation, marriage as self-divorce.

When we first met I had felt an immediate affinity with Mitchell because his teeth were in worse shape than mine (unlike mine, however, his most blighted teeth were prominently placed in the front of his mouth), only to soon find out that rotten teeth were not a firm foundation for enduring friendship. In any event, it wasn't long after we met that he had implants put in—a costly operation that was no doubt paid for by his family.

I also took consolation in Mitchell's company because he was one of the few men I knew that seemed committed to bachelordom: a rare quality, and one, it turned out, when put to the least rigorous of tests, that he didn't actually possess. I never ceased to despair over the inevitable. But I probably wouldn't be attending his party. I worked that night.

I prepared my fourth cup of coffee and returned to the desk. What was the point? I had read a thousand novels but I had no idea how to write one. I hadn't taken an English class since I was seventeen; I didn't know any of the tricks. I was unable to create or recreate dialogue, which seemed to require a degree of audacity and deception on the part of the author that I lacked. The process of continually finding new ways to state "he said" and "she said" seemed a cruel obstacle to the writing of prose, as did creating a plot and inventing characters. Why strive to do something that didn't come naturally? The results were bound to be wanting. So what was I going to do instead, just live? I had already failed at that.

Catching sight of my reflection on the computer screen again, I still looked old, bitter and weak. I knew that I was old and bitter, but was I weak? Yes, I probably was, because I had never committed myself to anything or anyone, and that is generally, and perhaps justifiably, regarded as a major source of weakness.

Since conception had always been inconceivable to me (I strongly suspected that I was mercifully infertile, no proof having ever been offered to the contrary), it had to be my duty, despite my status as a genetic dead end, to create something other than human life—i.e., art. If one didn't provide for one's posterity genetically, surely one ought to leave some other sort of legacy.

But what if one did neither? That was a good question, and one that I didn't want to provide an empirical answer to.

How unthinkably empty my life would be without all the books I'd read and the music I'd listened to, which have provided the backdrop, often the substance, to every day of my existence.

If it was at all within one's power, one hoped to provide a similar service by making one's own contribution, not to merely lurch along in a closed world of imaginary activity.

But what if it wasn't within one's power?

Then one was going to do it anyway, even if it was a poorly executed conceit.

That was the problem: there was enough crap out there already and one didn't want to add to it.

Then there was the pressing matter of what to write.

Yes, give it one last push. But of what and onto what? To write in a thinly disguised autobiographical manner and document the life of a middle-aged bookseller with frustrated artistic aspirations?

No, I could never stoop that low.

If I must insist on going through with this, at least address something relevant and contemporary. Write a novel about the fallout from gentrification. That will give it some credibility.

That disturbing reflection on the empty screen must somehow be covered—with words.

* * *

As I entered the bookstore, I noticed a woman, Cindy, with whom I was on cordial terms, working at one of the tables. She possessed a rare, delicate, glass-like beauty, and I had always been charmed by her. She looked up from her laptop and made a hand signal at me, consisting of outstretched thumb, forefinger and little finger, and I walked over.

"What does that mean?" I asked her.

"You should know," she said. "You were probably sixteen years old when everybody was doing it."

With that remark a barrier was instantly erected, and it was the only thing that was going to get erected between us.

"I'm probably younger than you," I said weakly, at a loss for a better quip.

"When I was out last night I got carded," she said. "The bouncer at the Satellite refused to believe I was over twenty-one."

Gazing into her soft hazel eyes, I could see how this might have happened.

"Wasn't that Ghanian guitarist playing there last night? He's playing there tonight too. I was thinking about going," I said, although I had no intention of going: it was too expensive, as was everything nowadays. Going out to eat and drink cost twice as much as it did ten years ago, and I had less money now than I had then.

"You'd better not go," she said. "Then you'd have to like something."

"What's that?" I said, hoping I'd misheard her.

"Well, you hate everything, don't you?"

"Actually, no …" Not that old insult yet again. The urge to blow my top had to be resisted. This inconsiderate, ill-considered and oft-voiced accusation elicited a scowl that risked turning into a growl of anger and petty despair. In the heat of the moment I had to restrain myself and strive for evenness of tone. No matter how gravely warranted, a splenetic outburst had to be avoided; too many battles had already been lost as a result of losing my temper.

"Nothing burns me up more than that shallow, erroneous, unfounded, insupportable and ignorant observation," I said, while being careful not to raise my voice, and aided in this effort by awareness of others within earshot. "You can't have any idea of the vast sweeping range of my erudition. I have consumed entire genres and studied every root and branch of subjects that you're not even aware of. It's inexcusably rude to make such facile assumptions about somebody you barely know."

"OK, I'm sorry," she said, laughing uneasily. "Obviously I was wrong."

"It's particularly irritating to be insulted in this flippant manner because I would have achieved a lot more *myself* if I hadn't been so busy absorbing other people's work," I continued, unable to stop myself, while succeeding in keeping my voice down. "As a result of liking some things so intensely, there are other things I dislike intensely. It's called discrimination, good taste."

"I get it," she said. "I was wrong, OK?"

I walked off without apologizing or making any attempt to clear the air.

"Doesn't he get it? No one cares. Why doesn't he just give up?" As I stepped behind the counter, Gilbert waved a book at me: the unread and unbought novel of a mutual acquaintance, Franco McFraenular. To the horror of his friends and the complete indifference of the reading public, Franco kept self-publishing his own books, using the print-on-demand method, for which, in his case, there was no demand whatsoever.

"Sorry about that," I said, having taken pity on Franco and bought three copies from him on my previous shift, and put them on display. "If we put them up there somebody might buy them," I added.

"Who would buy this?" said Gilbert, who had removed the books from the display shelf. "It's butt-ugly as well as unreadable."

"Did you crack it?"

"It's sad," he said unfeelingly. "I don't want to look at it, or touch it, let alone read it."

He had a point. The hideously designed glossy cover adorned with a blurry, garish photograph and bleeding print ensured that Franco's latest book would probably never be opened, let alone read. There was a very real possibility that it wouldn't be read by a single person, regardless of how many of his friends he begged or bribed to contribute glowing reviews on the Amazon site.

"Don't buy any more books from Franco," said Gilbert as he left.

Cindy looked the other way as she walked by the counter on her way out of the store. It pleased me that I had succeeded in maintaining evenness of tone when responding to her idiotic, disrespectful and downright slanderous assertion, but she might not have appreciated this unprecedented achievement and would doubtless describe me to others as having lost my temper. I told myself that my commendably subdued indignation had been justifiable but there was something undeniably spiteful about dressing down a desirable but unattainable woman, especially when there was such an age chasm involved. I was conscious of that uneasy dynamic and would prefer to have avoided it, but it was too late now, the unflattering impression had already been made. It was pitiful but I craved to be understood.

"Well, I'll be sorry to see you go," I said.

"We're sorry to go," said Paul, a millionaire of my acquaintance. He hadn't been a millionaire when we'd met fifteen years earlier, but he had bought a house in the Echo Park hills, and now he and his wife were planning to relocate to Asheville, North Carolina, a liberal boomtown in the Smokies, where their child would receive a first-rate education.

"It's hard to leave this place," he continued. "We love it here and we have a great life but this neighborhood is unrecognizable from twenty years ago. You've been here a long time, you know how it is."

"Yes, there's a difference between somebody who moves to a neighborhood when they're a distinct minority, and those that follow once the territory has been settled. It used to be a safe haven against the types that now flood into it, and they're all younger than us, of course."

"Exactly," said Paul. "One doesn't want to pull rank, but we moved in because it was affordable and because we liked it. There's no lid on it anymore, it attracts one and all. When I moved here, twenty years ago, I was respectful of the place. These people don't give a shit. There are so many people who want to grab a slice of this. In a few years it'll be like Abbott Kinney in Venice, and we don't want to be here for that."

"It's all right if you've got a beautiful house in the hills," I remarked. "Then you live above all this. I don't suppose you'll have any trouble selling it."

Before Paul could respond we were interrupted by the moaning demands of a Latino beggar: "Gimme three dollars for a slice of pizza, man."

"Sorry man, I don't have it," said Paul, moving out of the way as the beggar shuffled further into the store to pester other patrons, and a young white woman sidled up to the counter to buy an Angela Davis book.

Paul pressed up against the counter again. "There have already been fifteen bids. We don't want to just take the highest one. We want to sell to somebody who will bring something to the neighborhood. We've put so much work into this place, we've done a good thing with this house, and we're not going to sell it to somebody who just wants a piece of the action so they can flip it in five years. We don't want to encourage greed."

Copies of *I Love Honey*, *Milk and Dick*, several postcards, and a three-legged ceramic pig figurine were banged down in front of me by a teenage girl with a stuffed wallet.

"Moving will be liberating," I said to Paul. "It'll open you up; you won't miss it here, although this place does have a tendency to suck people back in."

"It's a wonderful city with so much going on and all these overlapping circles," said Paul. "But it's time. I'm pushing fifty. We're moving to a small college town and we want to work with new collectives that don't cater to the most wealthy; we want to pool our resources. It's an alternative to the dog-eat-dog way of making money in order to buy property. Look at these people," he added, as a mongrelized mishmash of young people filed in through the door.

"It's worse than Westwood. I can't even walk down the street. I don't know how you can take it."

"I can't take it."

No sooner had Paul walked out than Aaron walked in—bespectacled, bearded, short and beshorted.

"There's nowhere for me to sit," he said, surveying the chaos.

"Let's find a place for you," I said. We walked back to the café section, where rows of laptops were propped up sentinel-style on shared tables, occupied by rapt typists, most of whom were spellbound by social media or writing screenplays.

"There's a spot here," I said, pointing to the only open seat.

"Not enough room. I need to draw."

He followed me back to the book counter, and once I'd assumed my position behind it, leaned across and whispered confidentially, "So I saw that girl the other night ..."

"The one with the underarm hair?"

"Yes, and I didn't have a pill."

"D'you need another one? I've only got those ones that get you red in the face. You want one of those?"

"Maybe. It was pathetic, she was like 'Do it, do it, do it,' and I was trying ..."

"Did you wear a rubber?"

"Yeah."

"That was your first mistake."

"And I'm allergic to latex too. When I was a kid all the adults would laugh at me when clowns started blowing balloons up at birthday parties and I'd have an allergy attack, and I didn't understand why it was so funny. They make me itch."

An older man, of bloated pallor, gray stubble and foul breath, handed over a volume of Vita Sackville-West's correspondence.

"There must be something else out there on Sackville-West," he said, sounding peeved. *I hope I never emit that mephitic stench*, I said to myself, and turned my head away.

"She was a gardener," I said, offering up all I knew about Vita Sackville-West in one sentence.

"I know," said the man who looked and smelled like death, and he walked off.

Aaron moved back in and leaned across the counter.

"We went out to dinner the other night, at that vegan place that just opened down the street," he said.

"How was it? It's always packed in there."

"Good," he said. "The problem is there's no playfulness. I try to make jokes and she doesn't understand them. I don't know what to do about that. It's a missing component, and you can't really say that to someone."

"Yeah, you can."

"You going to be here tomorrow night?"

"Yes, I'll bring you a pill."

I rarely needed those pills anymore and I still had an ample supply from a purchase two years earlier, so there was no reason not to share them with Aaron.

A young woman was walking around the store, screeching into a cell phone that she held in front of her, conducting a conversation with a man whose voice, reverberating with distortion, was almost as loud and annoying as hers.

I reined in my mounting irritation, hoping that she would shut up. But she didn't shut up, and when she sashayed into the proximity of one of the signs prohibiting cell phone conversation, I walked over.

"It should be fun…," she was saying, and stopped when I addressed her.

"It's bad enough having to listen to you but I have to listen to him too. Your voices are taking over the entire fucking store," I said, pointing to the notice directly behind her.

"I'm sorry I offended you," she said as she put the phone down. "I didn't know it was rude."

"It's just common sense, isn't it?" I said. "Supposing everybody in here was walking around squawking into a cell phone? It would be utter chaos. Not that it isn't already. There are signs posted all around the store. Not that anybody notices them. They're too busy engaging with their fucking cell phones."

And with those words I left her. Five minutes later, she walked out. "Nice friendly bookstore," she said as she passed the counter.

"Piss off," I retorted.

Maybe I shouldn't have waited until I lost my patience before confronting her. One puts up with it for so long, and by the time one says something one has already lost one's temper. I'd been in a fairly good mood when I entered. Now I was rattled. It hadn't taken long for them to unstring my nerves this time. But with any luck she wouldn't yelp me; she probably thought I owned the place.

In order to dump some empty boxes in the trash behind the store I had to pass through the patio, where a reading was getting started.

"It's awesome to be here, ladies and gentlemen," announced the emcee, a balding and bearded young man with dead eyes. "Our first reader is an incredible writer. She's part of our workshop, really special. She's a poet and a new mom."

A large woman took to the small stage.

"I'm reading off my phone because I don't want to waste paper," she said, and proceeded to orate: "Living is an art form ... every day is art, art is all we have ... I didn't ask to be alive."

What did they teach in this workshop, I wondered, "feelings"? I walked back to the counter and returned to browsing the *Times* online. It featured an interview with a celebrated young author whose new novel, which "tackled" identity politics and postcolonialism, was displayed in the new-releases section directly across from where I was sitting. The novel, *White Kisses*, had inspired a fierce seven-way bidding war among rival publishers, and commanded an advance in the high six-figure range. Out of curiosity, and the desire to be irritated, I took it down from the shelf and opened it.

Flipping through it, I saw page after page filled with a daunting array of names: Amy, Felix, Melissa, Rick and Layla—they sounded like annoying people. And one-word sentences. I hate one-word sentences. Hate. Them.

It was all so dispiriting.

"Oh my God, I love this one," squealed a floppy-hatted young woman to her floppy-hatted friends—a gaggle of young women who had filed in, squealing and giggling, a few minutes earlier. They wandered around loudly, picked up books, took photographs of each other pretending to read books, bent the spines of books, took photographs of photographs, pointed at things and said "Oh my God" a lot.

"Ooooh, this is good." They stood grouped together near the counter, declaiming selections from a volume of Twitter haikus, attempting to outgiggle each other until their combined uproar reached a nerve-scraping crescendo of exaggerated merriment. I cranked the music up in an attempt to drown them out and braced myself for the next eruption of oppressive giggling.

"Oh my God, oh my God, oh my God." Was it even humanly possible to giggle so loudly and for so long? Apparently. There was no escape from it. They didn't know when to stop, and why should they stop? They were young and they were having fun. Maybe they were getting off on the novelty of being in a bookstore, perhaps for the first time, and making a spectacle of their enjoyment, which was something that could potentially affect others in a positive way. But they seemed to be trying too hard and their careless, innocent giggling grated on my worn-out nerves. I wanted to yell at this gaggle of gigglers: *D'you often walk into businesses and stand around screaming at the top of your lungs?* But my exasperation would only be exposed as something mean and crudely expressed.

Eventually they left, their screaming fading as they walked out, dissolving into street noise. Naturally, they left the door open.

This place was turning into a communal phone booth and photo booth, and I felt like a cross between a toilet attendant, mental-health worker and zookeeper. As I begrudgingly closed the door, in order to contain the air conditioning, I picked a recent back issue of *The Paris Review* from the dollar cart on the sidewalk and leafed through the featured interview: "For me, writing is an investigation of being human, and of the different ways there are of being human," stated the prominent author.

There was no hope.

Upon reentering the bookstore, the first thing I saw was a nose-picker in the philosophy section, avidly probing his nostrils as he turned the pages of *The Society of the Spectacle*. I poked my head out onto the patio again. The reading seemed to be running smoothly. The audience consisted of a few tolerant friends, most of whom fiddled around on their cell phones and occasionally supplied forced laughter as the reader droned on, humorously and inexpressively, complaining about her love life and her childhood.

"As a woman …"

I closed the door again.

With its open-door policy for self-declared writers, this place was becoming ground zero for emo-lit. As long as people were expressing themselves, any mode of delivery was considered acceptable. It was more akin to public therapy, a triumph of feeling over craft, the literary equivalent of a twelve-step meeting.

I looked up from the slice of pizza I was queasily attempting to eat when a woman appeared in front of me at the counter. She was short of breath and appeared to be in discomfort.

"Do you have a bathroom I can use?" she asked breathlessly.

"Yes."

"Where is it?"

I jerked my head toward the rear of the store: "Obviously," I said, and returned to the pizza with even less appetite than before. Considering the state of my teeth, a hard, sharp slice of pizza was not the ideal form of sustenance, but I was tired of all the food in the café and there was a pizzeria on the next block where I received free slices, so it was a matter of convenience. I ate it very carefully, chewing gently on the left side of my mouth, as there weren't enough undamaged teeth left to masticate with on the right side.

The phone rang yet again. "Do you have *The Savage Detectives*?" asked the caller.

"Yes," I instantly replied after a lightning squint down the fiction aisle. So familiar had I become with the spines of certain books that I could identify them from a distance of fifty yards.

"How are you doing tonight?" asked a wary-voiced woman as she passed by, dragging a scrofulous dog behind her.

"Great," I said, vaguely recollecting that I hadn't been entirely capable of mastering my apoplectic humor when we last encountered each other, at this same place. "Seeing you always cheers me up," I added in an attempt to atone for any offense that might accidentally have been given before.

"You weren't too happy to see me the other night. Why are you so pleased to see me now?"

"Why wouldn't I be?"

"Because you're a curmudgeonly old man."

"I beg your pardon."

"You heard me," she said, addressing me by my surname, and walking off.

Being addressed by my last name always brought back memories of parental and pedagogic discipline. But what really stung was the reference to my senescence. If my station in life was commensurate with my age it wouldn't be so troubling, but I was still in the same position I was in twenty-five years ago. Most of my contemporaries had moved on and were now established in their professional, creative and familial lives, whereas I had turned a corner and hit a wall, with the contrary values of youth hammered into place: a callow negativism matured to a dubious vintage, with a voluptuous bouquet of regret and a lingering aftertaste of self-disgust. And I had a last name that easily lent itself, enunciatively, to stern rebuke.

Gloomy introspection was interrupted when three books were placed in front of me by a woman with a yoga mat under her arm: *I Love Hate*, *Just Milk* and *Dick and Honey*.

"How's your evening going?" she asked as she fished around in her bag for her purse, and then into her purse for a credit card, and then selected which card to use—the entire transaction adding up to a full minute of dead time.

Take your time. Take it, my time. I've got all the time in the world, obviously. I wouldn't be sitting here otherwise.

"Great," I said quietly.

"'Great,' she repeated, as if not satisfied with my utterance. "That's a very automated response."

"It was a very automated question," I said between gritted teeth as she snatched the receipt from my hand.

"Are you doing shit out back?" asked an incoming litterateur.

"Yes, a reading is taking place on the patio," I informed him.

It had been going on for hours. These punishers and poetasters never knew when to stop, despite the lack of enthusiasm shown by the audience. Even when they did eventually shut up, they would be standing around on the patio, yammering until closing time, when they would finally break up their learned assembly and proceed to some nearby watering hole where they could continue hugging and congratulating each other. Then I would be able to clean their trash up.

About an hour before closing, a rugged blond-haired man entered and removed a handful of books from a bag.

"What's all this crap?" I asked, glancing at the useless selection of self-help books, mass-market paperbacks and unpopular fiction.

"I got it off the donations cart at the library," he said with disarming honesty.

The man's robust and otherwise appealing appearance was of the kind that might be described as "movie-star good looks" were it not marred by numerous festering lesions that covered his sun-burned face and arms. A pair of headphones, held together with duct tape, dangled from his head.

I told him to put the books on the dollar cart and asked if he needed anything.

"Just a cup of coffee," he said.

I walked over to the café counter, poured a coffee, and brought it back to him at the front of the store.

"How are you doing tonight?" he asked. His eyes glimmered with a rueful vitality.

Tempted as I was to toss out a negative quip, I realized that his plight was infinitely more acute than mine, and found myself lost for words.

"Have a good night," he said hesitantly, smiling warmly as he put his headphones back on and returned to the street.

The publisher of the micro-press responsible for the reading came back inside to reclaim the unsold books, signaling that the night's entertainment was finally over. He stood at the counter, talking to a friend who had evidently enjoyed the reading:

"I'm like pretty hit or miss about poetry but that was really cool."

"What's supercool is that our books came back from the printer just in time for it," said the publisher.

"I thought the *Weekly* piece was cool," said the publisher's friend.

"He made it sound like really ..." I waited a good five seconds, assuming, imagining, somehow hoping that a new superlative was forming in the publisher's mind, but after those five seconds a word emerged. And the word was " ... cool."

This man's head, two feet away from mine on the other side of the counter, was blasting a direct line of arrogantly sloppy unintelligibility into my aching eardrums. "Stop saying Cool. For the love of Mercy, just stop saying it.[6] I am so sick of that word!"[7] I silently screamed.

The publisher of several books of abysmal poetry said the word "cool" again; this time he managed to jam it twice into the same sentence, with an "I was like 'Cool'" and another "supercool," although at one point he enlivened his meager repertoire of impoverished superlatives with an "awesome."

---

6. Exclamation points will not be used in this work.
7. On certain occasions, exclamation points will have to be used in this work.

His friend handed two of the publisher's books across the counter: they were the only copies that sold all night. This amounted to a twelve-dollar profit for the store, hardly worth the price of cleaning the patio afterwards.

"Cool," he said as I handed him his receipt.

I went out to the patio and began moving things around. As I lifted a heavy table, I felt a familiar sharp pain in my lower back and cried out in agony. The few lingering attendees realized that the fun was over and repaired to the alleyway to continue prattling. With bare hands I gingerly plucked paper cups, cigarette butts and wads of tissue off the ground and placed them in the already overflowing trash bag. As I removed the bag from the plastic container a jumble of pastry scraps, soiled napkins and coffee grounds spilled out and spattered my newly pressed trousers. I dragged the torn bag across the patio, leaving a slug trail of filth in its wake, and dropped it into the dumpster.

I remembered that it was the night of Mitchell's girlfriend's party. But I was already too drained from dealing with strangers to deal with friends. I couldn't look into another face or listen to another voice. In any event, it was up in the hills, miles away, and I didn't feel like spending twenty dollars on a Lyft. But it was comforting to know that Mitchell would be at home in a setting where bottom-feeders mingled freely with sharks. I assumed that his new girlfriend, Lyn Lamrock, had sensed the deep pleasure he took in being around celebrities and had reeled him in with the irresistible promise of her famous friends. Career advancement might even be in the offing. There was no going back now.

Such bitter thoughts circled my tired mind as I swept the restroom floor. Unable to find any hand soap, I refilled the dispenser with dishwashing liquid.

II

I don't know how to create the impression of time passing. But it passed, weeks passed by, during which nothing much happened.

I continued to write every morning. In two weeks I had written 3,182 words. If I maintained this breakneck pace, it would add up to 82,732 words within a year. But that estimate was perhaps unduly sanguine, as during that time I had written for three or four hours, five days a week, in my customary state of sluggish jangled urgency but with less distraction than usual and buoyed by the sensation of embarking upon something new: a quiet exhilaration I had felt many times before—that never lasted.

Think about it, I thought to myself: If I write 400 words a day, five days a week—discounting Sundays and one other day—I will have accumulated 104,000 words in a year: a 350-page novel (at an average of 300 words per page).

That was a wildly optimistic goal. It would be a massive achievement if I wrote 400 words in one day, let alone two days in a row.

Lately, there seemed to be a trend toward short books that contained groupings of discrete paragraphs, so as not to put too much strain on the reader. And the more one wrote, the more there was to get rid of. So it made sense to write less.

If I wrote 200 words a day, five days a week, 52,000 words would be accumulated in a year, which would amount to a very manageable 175-page novel. But I had never managed it or come remotely close. Then again, I had never deliberately set out to achieve that modest goal.

Realistically, the very least I ought to ask of myself is a 1,000 words a week, which seems to lie within the scope of even my waning capabilities—adding up to a grand total of about 40,000 words in a year.

But why place so much importance on the span of a year? If I pushed myself, couldn't I complete something in six months? Others had done it. Jackson wrote *The Death of the Novel* in two months.

But let's not get carried away.

Even at this early stage I'm beginning to find this process distasteful. But this squirming and stalling at the sound of one's own voice, this recoiling from the sight of one's words dying on the page, is what must be transcended if anything is to be accomplished. For once in my life I must press on and finish something, even if it should have been expunged from my system years ago and has subsequently grown irredeemably stale, even if it falls far short of my aim.

At my grindingly slow rate of production, I don't have time to write a lengthy book. Rather than straining after some goal that is simply not within reach, why not resign myself to what I am capable of doing? But what am I capable of doing?

* * *

Despite the precautions taken against it, distraction was always within reach. The bag full of empty bottles in the corner of the kitchen was beginning to bother me. I carried it outside and placed it against a lamp post on the sidewalk, so that a bottle-and-can collector would find it and take it down to the local recycling center. Then I dragged three overflowing trash cans onto the street while bitterly railing against my downstairs neighbor who, in the three years he had been living below me, had never once taken out the garbage.

A young couple and their dog were walking by. A couple and a dog occupy a lot of space. The woman carried a paper coffee cup and led a pointlessly large hairy beast on the end of a leash, while her equally hirsute partner, wearing jeans tighter than sausage linings, lagged, unleashed, a few steps behind, transfixed by the cell phone he held in front of him at eye level as if propelled forward by its sinister force.

"Stop fucking texting," I spat out softly, but not softly enough, as I heaved another trash can onto the sidewalk, fresh early-morning hate leaking out unchecked as the woman stopped, looked back in my direction with a quizzical expression and said something to her escort, who momentarily disengaged himself from his digital device and also looked back at me.

I went back inside.

On my way to the desk I stopped at the sofa, where I sat down and picked up a book from one of the towering stacks on the coffee table. The author was another one of those annoyingly admirable men whose lives seemed expressly designed to remind me that I hadn't lived fully enough or accomplished anything.

I finally sat down to write and registered a familiar sensation in my mouth: the splintering of a rotten tooth, caused by a sharp nut in my morning muesli. A tongue probing confirmed my apprehensions, and I placed the broken, blackened fragment on the desk beside me. Now I had even fewer teeth to masticate with, and it looked as if I might have to start taking the pills for their intended purpose, which seemed like a waste. (That was how it had started, with a prescription following an extraction; but it wasn't long before the dentist tired of my fake toothaches and other sources were sought out.)

I attempted, in a rigorously inattentive and painstakingly half-assed manner, to proceed with my task, but dental anguish and other distractions had thrown me out of the zone I had initially taken so much care to enter.

I needed to set my house in order.

One imagines one's life being chronicled after one is gone. But much as I have envisioned being posthumously canonized, I know that these funereal fantasies will remain unfulfilled. The mythic lift, the staggered decline, the biographical details nobody knows or cares about: it will all be lost. Nobody is sufficiently invested in my cause to tend to my legacy. Everybody else is too busy chronicling their own lives, and who in their right mind would want to unravel these interminable reams of disordered and mostly worthless prose?

Maybe, if I'd cultivated a friendship or two with legacy preservation in mind, something might be deemed salvageable. But I hadn't been cunning enough for that. It wasn't as if anybody was going to take the trouble to piece my story together after I was gone, as they would do for a successful author like Jackson Valvitcore. It was depressing to consider that my legacy would be considered a burden, not a gift, in the unlikely event that anyone were to consider it at all, and in the unlikelier event that I were to leave one. So I was going to have to do something about it myself, in advance, with time rapidly running out.

So, reluctantly and in vain, I take up my own vain cause.

Like so many other fools who will never deliver upon it, I am convinced that I have a major work in me.

It's all been said and done before, and said and done better. But I can't let that stop me. I have nothing new to offer. Maybe nobody does anymore, now that culture has cannibalized itself to death. The only remaining option is to speak honestly. But I'm not sure I'm capable of that.

I can feel my powers—such as they are, such as they were—withering. It's a shame that I didn't use them more when I was in full possession of them. But it's too late now to fret over repetition and hesitation. At this rate, if I'm lucky, I might produce a book before I die.

Maybe this is where I can finally begin, with the conviction that I have nothing to say. It's not the most original idea, but I'm running out of steam, running out of ideas, running out of time, and I can't allow having nothing to say to stop me from saying something. Although it isn't easy to suspend self-disbelief and succumb to the phenomenal arrogance of imagining anybody might take an interest in it.

Paragraph by paragraph, I anticipate my potential readers dropping away, wearied and irritated by this tiresome outpouring. But I must insist on pressing forward, if only to honor a life's work of discarded manuscripts. With so much unfinished, so much unbegun, nothing, no matter how worthless, can be thrown out anymore. I have to complete something, even if it is ignoble of sentiment and unsound of construction; even if it's not up to the standards of what I once threw out; even if it is the exact opposite of what I had once hoped to achieve—that I was probably never capable of achieving in the first place; even if it reflects badly upon me; even if it is crap. Unseemly as it is to be carrying on like this at my age, and tedious as it must be to others, I intend to force myself forward, and, for once in my life, finish something.

The very thought of it made me want to lie down.

I got up from the desk and stretched out on the sofa.

At three o'clock I switched the phone off, fixed myself a Presbyterian, pressed play on the CD player, and drew a bubble bath. I slid into the tub as it was filling up and once submerged increased the flow of hot water until it was almost boiling. Then, and only then, did I know something resembling contentment.

It is my duty as a novelist to describe my time in the bathtub, basking in the consolation of art and liquor—I should be summoning the sounds of cars rumbling by on the street outside, the strains of eerie violin sliding in, and the gurgling of water as it lapped against the overflow drain; I should be depicting the ant scurrying along the side of the bathtub, flirting with the spume-laced waterline, then darting back up to attempt egress through the deceptive crack at the bottom of the fake beige-veined marble tile; and I should be delineating the first exquisite sip of the Presbtyerian, rich with the promise of relaxation, as it eased down my throat, and how I abstracted myself from these material surroundings and lost myself in the soothing world of Barbara Pym's prose—not to merely state, drily and diaristically, that I enjoyed spending time in the bath, but to reproduce the experience with telling details and evocative little flourishes.

Show, don't tell; reveal, don't say: this credo is repeatedly impressed upon the budding writer. It is the established, critically approved method that enables the reader to experience the story through action rather than exposition. The use of adjectives is strongly discouraged. "Interrogate your story," they tell us—whoever they are, whatever that means; or as Chekhov's famously stringent injunction would have it, "Don't tell me the moon is shining; show me the glint of light on broken glass." Unfortunately, this is one of many technical feats that lie beyond my limited range.

I lay there, decompressing in watery repose, watching the ants running up and down the wall from ledge to showerhead, some-times encountering each other and stopping for a few seconds, as if exchanging information about the terrain and weather conditions, before continuing on their travels. A fat mosquito buzzed around my head, the book drooped in my hand. As I was drifting off I felt something ticklish on the end of my right toe. I opened my eyes and shook an ant away. It was time to get up and go to work.

* * *

A respectful hush usually graces one's entrance to a bookstore, where a low hum of conversation, at most, is to be expected. Not this one. It is the noisiest—and most inappropriately named—bookstore I have ever entered, and I have entered a lot of bookstores. The adjoining café could easily be identified as the source of unabated racket, but it too is noisier than any coffeehouse I have ever entered.

What's to blame for this relentless and progressively more insuf-ferable noise level is the store's prime location in a newly fashionable neighborhood that has taken off to the extent that a large part of the clientele consists of people who think a bookstore is some sort of novelty, just another place to make noise and take photographs in.

People raise their voices when they enter, as if to announce themselves and make their presence felt. They talk as they enter, they talk as they leave, and they talk too loudly as they try to impress each other. The area between the front door and the counter is a problem: there's just too much room there for people to assemble and make noise. It doesn't seem to occur to them that there are others within the radius of a hundred yards who don't want to be subjected to a barrage of mindless prattle.

"I'm fine without a bag," said a self-proclaimed "multidisciplinary artist" I'd seen around, as he handed over a credit card in payment for some unfathomable work of critical theory. He plucked the receipt from my hand and joined a chattering cluster of similar types close to the counter, some of whom I knew by sight.

Like a lot of people with no visible means of financial support, they were *artists*.

"I'm making ten short films right now," said the Renaissance dabbler to his friends.

"Literally?" said one, a photographer, whose work was popular on Instagram.

"Really?" said another, a performance artist, whose performances were rapturously received by a handful of friends.

"Cool" (pron. *coo-awl*), said another, a self-published poet, in what was altogether a fairly typical example of discourse among the culturally conversant of the city.

Sitting at the counter near the front door, I was forced into the role of unwilling eavesdropper, a lamb to weak-voiced slaughter— and laughter: ear-ripping laughter, hysterical shrieks, skin-crawling giggling that cuts into me like a knife through the butter my brain has been churned into in this madly overstimulating environment.

After a day spent in scholarly retreat, during which I spoke to no living soul, it was jarring to be thrust into this profane multitude. Several separate "like"-littered conversations merged into one crashing, clashing, thunderous din around the counter.

Can I get ten seconds of fucking peace! I whisper-yelled to myself as another carefree time consumer strolled in: Greg Roach, accompanied by an attractive Japanese girl who looked even younger than the twenty-three years Greg had quoted during our previous exchange. Greg was about to turn fifty. For him, everything was coming around just in time. Everything falls into place in a timely manner for some people. I was not one of those people.

"Sean, meet my fiancé, Shima," said Greg, making the introductions. Surprisingly, she didn't recoil from this possessive mode of address; in fact, it seemed to please her.

What the fuck is she doing with you? I said to myself. She excused herself to use the restroom and when I was left alone with Greg at the counter I posed a more delicately phrased version of this question to him.

"Yes, she's moving here. She's buying a house. We're going to live together. I'm going to ask her to marry me," he replied, as if it were perfectly natural for his wildest dreams to suddenly come true, and that he was merely claiming his rightful reward. Coming from somebody I had heard bitterly despairing of ever experiencing sex or love again, this swift transition to complacency was disconcerting.

"Are you still working at the coffeehouse?" I asked, very much hoping that he was at least still gainlessly employed.

"I quit."

"That's nice."

The abyss between one side of the counter and the other had never felt so wide, and I felt like throwing myself into it.

In order to get away from Greg I removed some second-hand fiction from the cart and carried it to the shelves. A shabbily attired young man was sprawled out on the long bench in the middle of the room, in front of the philosophy section, with his head in his girlfriend's lap, browsing a rock biography. I looked down and addressed him as I passed by: "This isn't a flophouse, pal, you've got to sit up."

"Is that a rule here?" he asked, looking up and gradually straightening himself out.

"Yeah, it's a rule."

A copy of Anthony Trollope's *Can You Forgive her* needed to be slotted into the far end of the fiction section, where it would doubtless languish for months, perhaps for years, before eventually being consigned to the graveyard of the dollar cart, where this extraordinarily prolific Victorian author would be joining his illustrious contemporaries, Thackeray, Gaskell, and even Dickens.

Trollope's rigorous writing regimen has often been documented. "Let their work be to them as is his common work to the common laborer," was the guidance he offered other writers. If they followed his example, he claimed "No gigantic efforts will then be necessary," although his method seemed a "gigantic effort" in itself: he kept a timepiece in front of him and forced himself to produce 250 words every fifteen minutes, putting in three hours and amassing 3,000 words every morning, before knocking off at eight thirty to leave for his day job at the postal service. In this manner, he wrote forty-nine thick novels in thirty-five years. Perhaps, if I diligently applied myself, I might eventually succeed in completing *one* of my own.

On the next shelf down, dwarfed by the spacious spines of David Foster Wallace's precociously vast oeuvre, stood a lone copy of Robert Walser's *Jakob von Gunten*.

It had been almost a quarter of a century since my first enchanted encounter with Walser. He appeared, at the time, to be the purest exponent of the Literature of Impoverished Solitude—a self-explanatory genre that had taken shape in my mind at an impressionable age. Knut Hamsun, Beckett, and Emmanuel Bove ranked among its foremost exemplars. The novels in this genre—*Hunger, Murphy,* and *My Friends,* among others—were always short and written self-consciously in the first person by melancholy urban loners. Some of Kafka's short stories also belonged, and Dostoyevsky's *Notes from Underground* was perhaps the bedrock.

Walser possessed irresistible biographical credentials: a scripturient and peripatetic literary man who always lived alone and eked out a frugal living by his pen, he wrote hundreds of uniquely charming sketches—feuilletons, as they were then called—for magazines, as well as a few novels. His was too finely honed a sensitivity for this world, and by the time he reached my age he was residing in a mental hospital.

He has subsequently become justifiably renowned; a new Walser translation seems to appear every few months. Despite which, he is still known for being obscure, and frequently heralded as such in contemporary testimonials; but to be known for being underrated is in itself a form of being rated, and to be known for being obscure is in itself a sort of fame.

True obscurity is to not be known at all.

There were talented people who were repelled by the coarser aspects of the business, who were too lazy or contrary to compete, or for other reasons best known to themselves chose not to put their work out there, or do it in the first place, and consequently adopted a stance of pretending not to care, while time slipped by. That way lay bitterness.

Often, this hapless elite were able to maintain confidence in their abilities precisely because they hadn't subjected their gifts to the scrutiny of others—owing to an inability, were they to reveal those gifts, to accept the rejection that might be dealt them by their perceived inferiors.

It was distressing to consider all the stuff that never saw the light of day, and most of the stuff that did, and one sympathized with the willfully obscure. But it's not as if the cream naturally rises to the top. It has to be pasteurized.

Gazing across the crowded room I noticed a woman standing at the counter and returned to my station.

"How much is this guy?"

The candle proffered by the woman was apparently a "guy."

"It's not a guy, it's a girl: candles are female."

She didn't laugh.

"Sixteen dollars," I said.

"I don't need a bag," said the customer.

I wasn't going to offer you one, I said under my breath.

A man walked in, holding his cell phone in front of his face, filming his entrance to the bookstore as if he were Christ entering Jerusalem.

Keep your head down. Don't look up or around. Just stare at the screen, look things up on the internet.

"Can I ask you if you have a particular book in stock?" asked a soft feminine voice when I answered the phone.

"What is it?"

"*The Power of Now* by Eckhart Tolle."

"Hold on, I'll check," I said in my soft voice. I returned to the crossword and after half a minute picked the phone up again.

"No, I'm afraid we're out of it," I said, with honey-tongued conviction.

"Thanks for checking." Her response was so polite that I almost felt guilty about not having checked.

Aaron, wearing gym pants and a begrimed Miles Davis T-shirt, walked up to the counter, lowered his voice in seething despair and said, "I can't take it anymore. I feel like I just walked into a Robert Crumb cartoon."

"How d'you think I feel?" I said.

"I know," he said sympathetically. "Do these people ever shut up?"

"Never. They're afraid to shut up, because if they do they'll have to hear themselves think, and all they'll hear will be silence. The less someone has to say, the more they say. No banality or triviality is off the table as far as subject matter is concerned. Were it not for stating the obvious in ready-made phrases, they would never speak. One almost never overhears intelligent conversation in public. Think about it: How often is one struck with the thought, *What a rich sonorous voice that man has; he is expressing himself so eloquently upon such a worthy subject?* Never. The emptier someone's mind, the louder and faster they talk, and the more reliant they are upon clichés as a means of communication. Because they have no thoughts to speak of, they never shut up. They fear the silence that will confirm their emptiness, and fill it with mindless gabble and amplified insincerity. If they gave themselves time to think, they'd never say anything; it would be too taxing on their meager resources. An empty head is necessary in order to endlessly keep talking; the emptiness serves as a sort of fuel. As well as ignorance, it takes a certain amount of arrogance to loudly conduct a private conversation in public. Most thoughtful and sensitive members of society, or even polite outcasts, don't shout in public; they keep their voices down, not wanting to inflict their utterances upon strangers. Some people never shut up. I can't talk for that long, ever."

A customer a few feet away looked up from his cell phone and threw me a wary glance.

"It sounds like you've given it a lot of thought," said Aaron.

"Unfortunately, I've been given ample cause to do so. People who say 'like,' 'awesome,' and 'oh my God' should just be lined up and shot. It's a reasonable solution."

"The world is falling apart and this is all you care about?" said Aaron.

"Yes, it's the most important thing."

As I was making my way from one end of the store to the other, stepping over small dogs and squeezing around large men in shorts with bulging backpacks, I was accosted by a generously proportioned brunette whom I didn't immediately recognize.

"Look," she said, pushing out her swollen belly.

"What?"

"I'm pregnant," she announced with a shrill combination of pride and desperation that explained her newfound corpulence, and looking closer into that puffier, ruddier face, I recognized Helen.

"What else is going on?" I said, declining to share her elation.

Now that Joe, the last man standing in her circle and hitherto the least likely of parents, had bitten the bachelor dust and entered the spawning pool, it made perfect sense that his remaining childless friends would follow suit. One didn't want to be left out. It was that time of life when hormonal urges meet social duress: a time of panic subsiding, ideally, into complacency; time to lock it down. It's a terminal state of closing time at the bar with everybody desperately pairing off with whoever happens to be around when "last call" is announced. Timing is of the essence. Only the weak survive.

Noticing a customer at the counter, I excused myself, while silently commending myself on having resisted the impulse to congratulate Helen on her highly unoriginal achievement.

The credit card machine was acting up again.

"Stick it in," I said.

"It won't work that way," said the customer.

"Slide it then."

"That's not working either."

"Do it more gently," I said, feeling like a skittish whore. I couldn't help thinking there were better uses for my time than instructing people how to use a credit card machine. But that was what I had reduced myself to, and in the process I realized that I had become a living cliché: the cantankerous bookseller. No book or movie that included a scene set in a bookstore was complete without such a stock "character."

"Do you trash things?" asked the customer.

"What? … all right."

I was too distracted to respond appropriately, and instantly annoyed with myself for taking his paper cup and throwing it across the floor into the proximity of the trash can, when I should have flung it back into his donut-bearded face. I vowed then to never again discard a customer's trash.

The ruggedly handsome homeless man walked in, grinning shyly.

"Have you read this?" he asked, taking a Philip K. Dick novel from the book cart between the door and the counter, where I was pricing used books.

"I'm incapable of reading anything futuristic," I said.

"It's not set in the future. We're living in a Philip K. Dick novel. He anticipated social media. It's all there in this book. He looked into the future and wrote about it."

"I like his early mainstream novels, the ones about traveling sales-men, used-car dealers, and record-store owners in '50s California. They all have great titles—*In Milton Lumky Territory*, *Puttering About in a Small Land*, *The Man Whose Teeth Were All Exactly Alike*. He wrote each of them in a few weeks while he was on speed, although perhaps he wrote on speed throughout his entire career …"

A young couple barged by us on their way out of the store.

"You're not getting your book?" shouted the girl.

"I can get it cheaper online," her male escort yelled back with inexcusable carelessness.

"I need ten dollars," said the blond homeless man.

"What for?" I foolishly asked. Who doesn't want ten dollars, when they don't have it?

"To feel better," he said, sounding tired, but with a smile of resignation. "I'll be all right tomorrow, when I go to the clinic and get back on the purple juice."

"D'you want a cup of coffee?"

"That would help."

As I walked back to the café counter to pour him a squirt of mud, it struck me that most of the homeless people in the neighborhood were more refined, more gracious, and simply better company than most of the colonizers. And they were usually better dressed.

"Thanks," he said as I handed him the coffee. "That'll take 25 percent of the pressure off."

I took a five-dollar bill out of the till, handed it to him, and rang it up as a payment for used books.

"Tony," he said, by way of introduction.

"Sean," I said.

"Well, you have a good evening," he said, as he walked out into it.

The phone rang again: "Do you have gluten-free bagels?"

I walked the forty yards from the book counter to the café, where I handed the phone over to the new barista, a handsome young man with his life ahead of him.

"Where are you from?" I asked when he handed back the phone.

"Billings, Montana."

"You're kidding. No, you're not kidding. Why would you kid about such a thing?"

"I can't help it, man. That's where I'm from. I'm not even from there, I'm from a smaller town but I went to college in Seattle. I guess I'm going to have to get used to people calling me a hick."

"I wasn't calling you anything of the sort, I swear. I'm genuinely impressed. I've driven around Montana a lot. I'm probably the only person who has vacationed in Butte five times, voluntarily, alone. Back when I used to travel. Well, one time I had female company."

"Why do you like Butte?"

"The entire downtown, otherwise known as Uptown Butte, or Butte on the Hill, is on the historic register, and it feels as if you're walking around in the early twentieth century. It has a unique atmosphere, with an abundance of red-brick architecture dropped into the Rockies, surrounded by scarred hills occupied by abandoned gallows-like mining scaffolding. What did you study at college?"

"I was in the writer's program, but I dropped out."

"Not dissimilar to Richard Hugo's trajectory," I remarked.

"You know Richard Hugo?" said the boy with excitement. "He's one of my favorite poets. 'Degrees of Gray in Philipsburg.'"

"'You walk these streets laid out by the insane.'"

"'The principal supporting business now is rage.'"

"Yes."

"Why did you drop out?"

"To focus on music."

"Is that why you moved here?"

"Yes."

"Oh dear."

"Do you have something against musicians?"

"Not really. I just regret not having become one myself."

(131)

"Why didn't you?"

"It would have been too easy."

"It's not too late."

"Oh, yes it is."

A red-haired girl in an old dress appeared at the café counter. On the one previous occasion we had met some sort of palpable connection seemed to exist between us, but a counter and cash register, compounded by constant interruption, had acted as an impediment to flirtation. The boy, however, didn't seem to be experiencing any such difficulty. While light conversation flowed between these two attractive young people, I leaned against the sink and studied the redhead's features. She had soulful, glittering eyes and full, sensuous lips. There was no doubt about it, she was beautiful. But the words "cool," "like," and "awesome" spilled with disturbing ease from that beautiful mouth ("I have to practice with my other band tonight"—"That's cool"). Her fluency in Panglossian utterances might prove to be an insurmountable obstacle to the furthering of our relations. But one could always make exceptions for special cases; maybe she could be spared from the firing squad.

"What do you do? I mean, when you're not working here?" asked the boy after the redhead, who didn't appear to have remembered or even noticed me, flashed him a devastatingly radiant smile before walking away.

"I'm supposed to be a writer."

"Poetry?"

"Fuck, no. Journalism. Well, I used to be a journalist, but that all dried up. It's a bit embarrassing really. I'm trying to write a novel."

"Why's that embarrassing? It's great, if you can pull it off."

"If …"

"What's it about, if you don't mind me asking?"

"Well, I have no grasp of plot, character or dialogue and my imagination dried up years ago, so I'm obliged to rely on personal experience rather more than I would prefer or approve of."

"A lot of great novels don't have a plot," he said. "Nobody really cares about it."

"I certainly don't. It just gets in the way of things."

"Writers only use it out of a sense of obligation, when they have no respect for their readers."

"True," I said. For these were consoling words.

"Didn't Beckett say that he had no desire to write?" said the boy.

"He might have *said* that but he licked the plate pretty clean when it came to the literature of nullity and negation. He didn't leave much for anybody else. I would be delighted to find a few scraps to call my own."

"How many words do you have?"

"About thirty-five thousand, but most of it will need to be thrown out."

"So it's just a single narrative voice?"

"More or less. Yes, unfortunately, yes."

"But you can use that to your advantage."

"Only if it's done properly. I'm not sure it is."

"Can I look at it?"

"No way. We've only just met."

"That's perfect. I won't be bringing any preconceptions to it."

"It's not in any kind of presentable form at present. It's just a lot of unruly strands that need to be untangled."

"You're going to have to show it to somebody at some point."

"That's what worries me. It's a bad sign that I can't bring myself to show it to anybody. Maybe I inherently realize it's crap. It wouldn't hurt to get a second opinion. I'll think about it," I said, without any intention of thinking about it, and returned to the counter.

"That was the best mix I've ever heard! I Shazamed literally every song. Do you know what Shazam is?"

"Yes."

A few hours earlier, without any concern for stylistic consistency, I had strung together a set of beautiful music that covered the waterfront from country blues to Krautrock to postpunk, downer folk, dub, soul and jazz. On the way out of the door a lively young fellow saw fit to express praise and gratitude, and I had to agree with him: it was probably the finest playlist ever assembled. Perhaps my time down there wasn't being entirely wasted: others were benefiting from my musical taste. That was something.

* * *

I looked over what I'd written the day before. At the end of yesterday's session I had been delighted with it: today it made me squirm. But the medication hadn't kicked in yet, and I needed that fuel for false hope in order to keep going and get anything done at all.

A squirrel runs down the telegraph pole outside the window, a stray dog limps across the sidewalk. And that is the extent of nature in these parts. Urgency fades into futility, and once again I find myself on the verge of giving up before I have even begun. Silence drills through me, birdsong flickers in the air, overlaid by the drone of traffic and tinnitus. If I could see myself sitting here, a benumbed idealist, a lazy perfectionist, sinking into the unseizable day, barely engaged in the simulation of activity, I don't know whether I'd laugh or cry ... or remain numb.

There are going to be days like this, of mysterious, inexplicable and unyielding dullness, from which nothing can be salvaged: drab, cheerless days when there is nothing in you that is worth releasing; days that should be abandoned but which you endure as if serving a self-imposed sentence.

And it is too late for such days when you have already served a lifetime's worth of them. And once again you ask yourself: Is it too early to give up?

It is difficult to unnumb myself when the prospect of numbing myself is what gets me out of bed in the morning.

Every morning, the same tired lament: "I should have risen earlier."

It was blurringly obvious that I should have risen earlier—at 7 a.m. to be precise, at which time I was fully awake. Yet I lay in bed until I was saturated with grogginess: a grogginess that was subsequently compounded by medication and overcaffeination; a grogginess that deprived me of the satisfaction of executing my task in a clearheaded manner.

By the time all the compulsive arrangements necessary to enter the required state have been made another tired mantra is echoing muddily through my mind: "I could be doing more."

No, it doesn't *write itself*, as some authors blithely claim: the "narrative" doesn't have a mind of its own, the characters don't take control. After two bedraggled hours no actual composition has taken place, and I am aching to be done with this masquerade.

It's just an excuse to sit here, under the influence of a modest stimulant, in a pleasantly medicated haze.

Yet I honor this stale ceremony, as if anything of value might be extracted from the refinement of futility, and force myself to sit in one place for another hour, mind slowly swirling, staring at the screen, until the internet blocker turns off, signaling that the session is over.

There is nothing to stop me from sitting here all afternoon. The need to fortify myself can easily be satisfied by rice cakes and yogurts. No urgent matters, other than the ones I continue to ignore, require my attention, but a craven urge to check the phone tugs at me.

The uneasiness that intensifies as the moment of contact with other people's reality approaches—voicemails, emails, anything that might disrupt the peace and quiet needed to do "the work"—is usually unwarranted.

On this occasion, three calls from an unknown number awaited me when I plugged back in. One message had been left:

"This is an important message. We are required to notify you that this is a communication from a debt collector … This is an attempt to collect a debt and any information will be used …"

What would happen if I responded to these calls? I had no idea: I had never responded to them.

Once freed from the self-imposed bondage of creation, I felt a great sense of relief, and a surge of energy that might have been useful during the preceding lifeless three hours.

How refreshing it would be at this time of day to trade badinage at a gathering of kindred souls—or even one kindred soul—with volleys of wit raining down on the table over a delicious repast with ample libations. But not in this town, not in this day and age.

I placed a Pyrex dish containing five fish sticks in the oven and steamed some broccoli.

A few hours later, after a short and unrefreshing nap, I dragged myself to the bar of self-judgment and subjected my recent efforts to fearless critical scrutiny. After a few pages my worst fears were confirmed: what was clear to the author, owing to his awareness of what he was attempting to do, was not polished enough to make sense to an innocent reader.

Maybe I lacked the skill necessary to realize my ideal. Maybe, as I had said to the boy, I couldn't bring myself to share the fruits of my solitary toil, or any portion thereof, because I suspected it would be found wanting. Maybe fear of confirming this sad fact was what was holding me back. Maybe it wouldn't hurt to get a second opinion. Maybe I should show the work to the boy. He had a precocious intelligence and a ready laugh. It would be preferable to get some feedback from somebody I barely knew, and surely the opinion of someone almost half my age couldn't be too crushing.

* * *

"I was just thinking about you."

"You were?"

"Yes, I was just shelving one of your books."

"Foster Garret wrote a novel?" remarked Melinda Waterform, a prominent local author whose career had recently taken off, as she surveyed the counter display.

It surprised me that she wasn't already aware of this. But if I didn't work in a bookstore, I wouldn't have been aware of it either; I wouldn't even know who Foster Garret was: a poet who wrote a novel.

"I don't really know his work but my friend Len Berner is very close to him," Melinda continued. "It's funny but we were at this party in New York and Len saw Foster and he said, 'I've got to ask him about something,' because Foster's a really good friend of Will Berwin and Will had written this piece …"

Naturally, I was supposed to automatically recognize these names that were being flung at me. The name-dropper, or flinger, always assumes that you know whom they're name-dropping and that you care as much as they do about the names they're dropping. But when the name-dropper is famous it is no longer regarded as name-dropping. I sometimes wondered if one of the principal lures of fame consisted in the promise of being able to mingle freely with the famous and drop names without being accused of name-dropping.

"What's Len Berner like?" I asked.

"He's great, really funny."

Much as I suspected. He looked like an asshole. But if he was nice to me, I'd probably like him.

I pointed Jackson's book, *The Death of the Novel*, out to Melinda, and voiced surprise when she said that she hadn't heard of it either.

"Well, I've been out of town for a few months."

"Where?"

"I just got back from a writer's retreat in Italy."

She didn't ask what I had been up to. It was naturally assumed that I wasn't up to anything—which wasn't too far from the truth.

"This job is driving me to drink," I said to the barista.

After running a lot of bureaucratic red tape the store had finally secured a costly beer-and-wine license. There was both good and bad in this development. It meant that a rowdier element would be frequenting the store owing to the availability of alcohol, but it also meant that I could drink on the job.

Retail was young person's work. It was acceptable when you were on your way up, but at my age it suggested that you were on your way down; it bespoke lack of ambition or plain defeat, especially in this town. Due to strategic improvidence, this was how I'd ended up. If indeed this was the end. Much of the time it certainly felt like it.

It wasn't that bad: it wouldn't be bad at all if I were twenty years younger. All I had to do was sell books, buy books, price books, shelve books, and deal with customers. I couldn't really complain. I could sit and read and listen to whatever music I wanted to listen to. There were certainly many worse fates.

Standing behind the counter, I sharpened a pencil with a razor blade, to a needlelike point, for the purpose of pricing books. But no matter how much one sharpened a pencil, among other things, it would soon wear out and dull again, and eventually there would be nothing left to sharpen.

A beautiful woman walked through the door, smiling directly at me. I smiled back at her. She walked up to the counter and fixed me with a seductive stare. I held her gaze, meeting the look of challenge in her eyes. Her sensuous lips opened, I felt a quiver inside, and she spoke.

"Do you guys have a restroom?" she said.

I sat down and skimmed an article on William Burroughs in a back issue of *The New Yorker* that had arrived in a bag of used books. The author stated that Burroughs was not a "wealthy heir," as depicted by Kerouac in *On the Road*, but the recipient of an allowance from his parents *only* until the age of fifty. The case of Burroughs is well known. Literary America's most notorious junkie was the scion of an immensely wealthy Midwestern family, heir to the Burroughs Adding Machine fortune.

The same went for numerous poètes maudits and underbelly chroniclers. Sam Beckett made many lengthy trips around Europe in his younger days. The wretched condition of his shoes is frequently mentioned by biographers, but how these travels were funded, outside of a few occasional stints as a private tutor, is never explained. Maybe he just couldn't be bothered to go to the cobbler's. It is said that he "borrowed" money—from his mother.

Travels are extensively cataloged but how they were funded is rarely addressed by biographers. It's as if they don't want to know. All too often the writer comes across as a magical being who is able to float freely around the world without financial encumbrances of any kind. And sometimes, as with Burroughs, Elizabeth Bishop, Ezra Pound, E. E. Cummings, and many others, this is the case. How these authors financed their freewheeling lifestyles isn't given much attention by biographers. Such troublesome practicalities are to be sidestepped as they might interfere with the hardship it is always in the biographer's best interest to heroicize. For example, we are often told that Faulkner was "broke," when he lived in a mansion and kept servants. A lot is made of how he wrote *As I Lay Dying* while working the night shift at a factory, but after that brief stint of actual work, while in his twenties, he supported himself by writing (painful as it must have been to crank out Hollywood scripts for a few years: a tragedy that is inexhaustibly lamented by his biographers, although it didn't put much of a dent in his daunting prolificity, and many of the screenplays were worthwhile). To always focus on tragedy, and to present triumphs as tragedies: that is always the biographer's underlying and overriding aim.

Inheritances, if they are mentioned at all, are always "small," although they always seem to allow their beneficiaries to live without having to resort to employment. Such was the case with Charles Baudelaire: while on the low end of the scale, Malcolm Lowry may not have enjoyed the most lavish lifestyle—residing in what is usually described as a "squatter's shack" outside Vancouver—but he never had to work a job; he was free to fully immerse himself in his work.

Leisure allows the writer the peace of mind to develop their gifts unfettered by financial exigencies. This is especially true of so-called "experimental writing," which is where phantom income truly comes into play—and play is often what it amounts to, for it is the domain of those fearless boundary pushers who can afford to experiment. Burroughs, Gertrude Stein, Harry Mathews: freedom from financial hardship afforded these heavy hitters the luxury of being able to commit themselves fully to breaking new ground. It is hard to imagine a working-class person indulging in experimental fiction—they simply don't have time; they're too grounded in the experiential to take off on such flights—B. S. Johnson being a notable exception. It isn't true of everybody and it doesn't detract from the quality of the work, but there are enough cases of the passive-income writer for it to be a significant and curiously neglected aspect of the literary lifestyle.

Even Charles Bukowski, a writer whose name resounds with skid row integrity, had money stashed away from the sale of his father's house. He inherited it when he was in his thirties and left it in the bank, untouched, never alluding to it—or the substantial NEA grant he later received—in his entertaining and frequently fictive accounts of hard living. This safety net facilitated the carefree attitude necessary to romanticize "living on the edge"—an interesting fact that has been glossed over by biographers, as if a cushion of financial security were a matter of minor importance, not a pivotal psychological key.

In the world of fine art, the case of Van Gogh, the prototypical poster boy for starving artists, comes to mind. Vincent may have had a hard life but he subsisted on handouts from his much put-upon brother, Theo, that allowed him to hone his craft without the aggravations of wage earning. It's hard to imagine him getting much painting done if he'd had to hold down a job, in which respect we are greatly indebted to his brother, a secret hero, as were many patrons.

The myth of the starving artist is just that: a myth, promoted by hagiographers intent upon dramatizing the plight of their subject. If you can live without having to work a job, you're doing fine.

Does freedom exist? Yes, it can be bought: people who have money are free. They can afford to do what they want when they want—and that is freedom, which, we are often told, is happiness.

As the wealthy often like to remind us, money doesn't make one happier, but it certainly does make life easier. It provides the security necessary to do things without getting distracted, of which thirst for knowledge is a by-product: it is something one can afford to satisfy when unharried by worldly concerns. If you're rich, you can afford to appreciate things, to have interests, to be amazed.

Indigence tightens the mind; it makes it harder to think of things outside oneself; it cripples curiosity, kills self-confidence, and constricts one's sense of wonder. The harrowing pathology of poverty incorporates bitterness and immorality. What is often called anxiety or depression frequently boils down to financial distress. And the poorer you become, the uglier the world gets.

The cure for poverty is also extremely unpleasant: it involves work.

Debt worries lingered in the back to front of my mind all afternoon. In order to put them to rest I went back online. Half a minute of research reinforced the comforting information that the statute of limitations on debt in California is limited to four years. It had been three and a half years since I defaulted on my credit cards.

I picked up the books that had been left strewn about the long bench by inconsiderate browsers and reshelved them. In order to accommodate a battered Tom Robbins paperback it was necessary to shift a couple of dusty Jean Rhys novels from the beginning of one shelf to the end of the one above it.

"I have a question: Does anybody know this book?" asked a customer who was holding up a copy of Baudrillard's *Seduction*. This man, probably attracted to the title and the photograph of a woman with long, flowing blond hair on the cover, hadn't even bothered to open the book, choosing instead to be enlightened by proxy.

"What do you mean by 'anybody,' what do you mean by 'know'?"

"I mean anybody in the store, what it's about."

"I don't know. I haven't read it. Do you want me to ask around? You can probably find out for yourself if you open it."

Having nothing further to add, I returned to shelving.

I suppose I could have been kinder, but I couldn't afford to be.

Being a good person sounds great … on paper.

Some former curmudgeons, later in life, make a conscious decision to become warm and encompassing individuals. As mortality becomes more tangible, they realize that it's a waste of rapidly diminishing time to be cagey and mean-spirited, and with an effort, no less laudable for being discernible, they summon long-buried reserves of warmth and generosity. They realize that it's time to be a good person, and strive toward that end until it comes naturally.

Such a position, however, requires financial (and sometimes connubial) well-being: a secure center from which geniality and generosity can flow outward. It can be a heroic feat and is probably very rewarding for all concerned.

Unfortunately, I was incapable of it on a practical level, as I would probably never be able to financially (or connubially) afford it. And keeping one's spirits up is hard work. It takes so much less effort to indulge ill humor.

Some further reshuffling a couple of shelves up was required owing to the high demand for the novels of Haruki Murakami, an author I would never read. He had been read enough, by other people, and I suspected that his popularity was a sign of mediocrity. He didn't need me, and I didn't need him.

An empty space at the other end of the *M* shelves marked the sale of more Cormac McCarthy books. The remaining volumes needed to be shifted sideways. Purely out of masochism, and to see what all the fuss was about, I once forced myself to wade through one of McCarthy's novels. It was heavy work: the author's straining brow was visible as he forced out his turgid prose, which combined the worst qualities of Faulkner and Hemingway—exhibitionistic prolixity and grueling masculinity—with no flow, no humor, and no feeling (the literary equivalent of NFL football: all effort, no rhythm, all stop and start) while continually tripping the reader up by inserting ill-fitting obscure words into his laborious sentences for no apparent purpose other than to flaunt his sesquipedalian proclivities. *I could do better than that*, I thought, but that would entail coming up with plot, character and dialogue, of which I'm incapable.

A customer looked up at me. "Do you work here?" he asked.
"What is it?"
"Do you guys have a restroom here?"
"Through the corridor."
"In the back?"
"There's only one corridor."

I moved the stepladder slightly to the left. Another popular contemporary author, Karl Ove Knausgaard, needed to be restocked.

By the same token that I didn't have to read a book to dislike it, there were some contemporary authors whose works I liked although I would never read them. I wasn't one of those people that imposed aesthetic boundaries upon themselves and circumscribed their tastes in an attempt to define themselves by their antipathies (i.e., *I only read books that are difficult enough to be worthy of my scrutiny*). I wanted to like everything, but one only had so much time, and writing should come before reading and living should come before writing, and at this point I had spent more time reading than writing and more time writing than living, and I balked at the prospect of an eight-hundred-page novel, and by now Knausgaard had written six of these. But there was something sympathetic about his craggy, soulful, mischievous features: he looked as if he knew he was getting away with murder but couldn't stop himself. I liked his face, which was more than I could say for a lot of authors.

From my perch on the stepladder I looked down and observed a fetching young woman perusing a familiar paperback with the title, *The Tentacles*, stamped in large purple letters on a black background. This steady-selling book of recent vintage, published by the estimable Prolix press, had a short, spectacular opening paragraph in which the author, Candy Burrows, described herself being ravaged on a concrete floor. I enjoyed watching women being held riveted as they read this lurid passage, then walking up to the counter to purchase the book, not realizing that following this paean to the pleasures of rough sex it descended into a tiring tangle of identity politics and gender issues in the form of autofiction, as such works were now being labeled. But I couldn't dislike it too much because on the one occasion I had met the author she had been warm and friendly, which was more than I could say for a lot of authors.

One couldn't go wrong with an opening like that. Reel the reader in with rough sex, then proceed to bore them to death with politics and theory. Remember: the opening paragraph need bear no relation to the rest of the work. It is merely a means of grabbing the reader's attention.

The woman was soon standing at the counter, ready to purchase a copy of *The Tentacles*. As I scanned the barcode, I was struck by how slim the book was. Picking up another copy from the excess stack behind the counter, I flipped through it and found it to be very easy on the eye, consisting of short paragraphs separated by longueur-lessening lacunae. With such an attractive structure and inviting brevity, it was a triumph of form if not content.

It was the struggle with form that had always held me back from delivering my urgent message to the world. "To write—was not that the joy and the privilege of one who had an urgent message for the world," as George Gissing had written. But I still couldn't figure out an appropriate form or framework—or, for that matter, an urgent message.

After five pages of puffery from all the right people—Samantha August, Kane Wostenbaum, Gordon Kim, Michelle Coffee, etc.—*The Tentacles* contained 153 pages. At thirty lines per page, with about ten words per line, that came out to an average of three hundred words per page, amounting to approximately forty-six thousand words in the entire book. That seemed like a realistic goal.

Another look at the author's bio revealed that Ms. Burrows was still in her thirties.

The main problem with contemporary authors was that they were nearly always younger than me. And I refused to read books by anybody that was younger than me, which ruled out most contemporary authors. (If I refused to read books by anybody that was younger than I am now when their book was written, that would rule out most books, and I would be confined to the books of authors who were past their prime.)

A young man appeared on the other side of the counter.

"Do you have a restroom I can use?" he asked politely.

"Go ahead," I said.

"Where is it?" he asked, still standing there.

"Where d'you think it is?" I shot back.

"Where do I think it is?" he repeated my words, dumbfoundedly.

"Yeah, where d'you think it is? It's a small enough store. If you take a brief glance around the room you'll probably be able to figure out where the restroom is located. It's one room with a book counter at one end and a café counter at the other end. Beyond the café counter is a short corridor and at the end of that short corridor is an alcove. Beyond that is the exit door. If you have even the slightest familiarity with the layout of commercial architecture you should be able to figure out that the restroom is located in the alcove next to the exit door. But why figure it out for yourself if you can ask me, right?"

"Wow," he said, as he turned around in the opposite direction and walked back out of the store.

"I thought you needed to piss!" I shouted back after him as he exited the store.

I returned to my light reading: a drug memoir written by a musician or a musical memoir written by a drug addict—it was hard to say which. Such fluff was all that I was capable of reading on these shifts. As usual, this latest addition to the ever-expanding category of rock-and-roll addiction memoirs didn't contain much on the subject of music, being an interminable celebratory bewailing of a few heroically misspent years of drug addiction during which, coincidentally, the author produced all his best work, and the return "journey" of recovery, during which he produced nothing worth listening to. The last image in the photo section was of the smiling author—a canonized survivor of massive pleasure and seventy-year-old first-time father—balancing a baby on his knee.

I put the book down. Wasn't that what you were supposed to do when you were young, get fucked up? It built character. It was an activity to which no special significance should be attached. These sobriety-embracing musicians wanted credit for doing more drugs than anybody else—years ago. In order to serve their dubious purposes, pleasure that was once embraced was now depicted as "a struggle."

Drugs were taken until they didn't work for you anymore: you had fun until it became stale, then you acted like a martyr about it by delivering morality lessons and casting yourself in the role of heroic survivor, and with these glorious lamentations of bygone excess you romanticized the condition and carelessly encouraged others to follow in your self-consciously staggering footsteps. It was impossible to write about drug taking without romanticizing it. You enjoyed your period of insensibility, and profited from it. Then you had to spoil the experience for others, with the help of a ghost writer.

I returned the book to the biography-and-memoir section: file under *H* in fiction.

I didn't have much to bring to the table in the form of excess. Unluckily for me as a writer, I had always been able to handle my drink and drugs. I could raid my cabinet of formative memories, discuss my molestation by a female history teacher at the age of ten, and make a strong case for being taken seriously through that. But I didn't want to write a "fictional memoir." It's all been done before, and the memoir section of a bookstore is an even sadder and dustier place than the poetry shelves.

As a compensatory last resort there was always the myth of posthumous glory. But to receive posthumous acclaim, one had to die first. If I killed myself, of course, it would completely validate the work. The only problem was that I hadn't done the work.

Yes, one had to have *done* something.

Maybe I could be a posthumous failure too ...

"Weren't you at the Jackson Valvitcore reading a few weeks ago?" A feminine voice prodded me out of my introspection.

"Yes ... He's a friend of mine," I said, realizing that acknowledging our longstanding friendship branded me as a potential name-dropper: a humble bookseller bragging about his connection with a rising literary star. But what was I supposed to do, pretend I didn't know Jackson anymore now that he was successful?

"It was a really good reading, wasn't it?" she said.

"It was all right," I said, restraining myself from making a belittling remark; we had only just met and maybe she didn't find backstabbing attractive.

She did look familiar, and I had noticed her earlier in the art section, poring over a Hans Bellmer monograph. Eventually she had walked up to the counter. She had a pale complexion, high cheek-bones, gull-gray eyes, and long, lustrous black hair. She was probably in her early thirties. Her name was Mona.

"Have you read any good books lately?" she asked with a feline smile. Her voice was soft and tentative, hinting perhaps at darker forces within. I stepped down from the counter so that we could meet on equal footing.

I smiled back in the hope that it made me look younger and less bitter. The layers of vertical and horizontal lines around my mouth disappeared into a rictus that, despite several visibly missing corner teeth, evinced a somewhat mitigating degree of leftover youthfulness.

"Barbara Pym," I said. "Spinster literature. I find it comforting."

"You read for comfort?"

"Not exclusively, far from it. I adhere to John Waters' dictum that one should never read purely for enjoyment."

"He said that?"

"Yes, in his recent collection of essays. I reviewed it," I said, seizing the rare opportunity to draw attention to how I had once done something other than work in a bookstore, and mentioned the periodical that my no-longer-recent review had appeared in.

She didn't seem particularly impressed. "You probably get a lot of reading done here," she said.

"Not really. Mostly trash, rock bios. It's hard to focus on anything more challenging amid all this chaos," I said, as she looked around the by now almost empty store. "Most of my reading takes place in the bathtub," I added, hoping to impress her with an interesting personal fact.

"Really?"

"I often read for two hours or longer in there, sipping a cocktail, with classical music playing softly in the next room. It gives me more pleasure than anything else."

"Anything?" she said, smiling again.

"Just about," I said.

"Doesn't the water get cold?" she asked.

"I adjust the taps with my toes and drain the existing water as I'm doing it." It always amazed me when people asked this question; the answer seemed so obvious, but maybe some people didn't read in the bath.

"Don't your hands get wrinkled?"

"No, because they're above the water level, holding the book."

"You don't get faint?" That long smile appeared again.

"Sometimes, when I finally emerge. Where do you read?"

"Usually in bed ..."

"Do you work here?" We were interrupted by a customer.

"What gives you that impression? Never mind. What do you need?"

"Do you have *City of Quartz*?"

"Under *D*, over there."

I reluctantly disengaged myself from Mona and led the helpless customer to the LA-and-California section, where I was interrupted by another customer who needed to be led to the graphic novel section, and by the time I got back to the counter, Mona was gone.

The first customer returned with a copy of *City of Quartz*.

"How much is this?" he asked. I opened the cover, revealing the price, clearly marked in pencil on the top right-hand corner of the first page.

"Oh," he said, and forked over a credit card.

Tony appeared in the doorway, his face a lunar surface of bloody eruptions, and I groaned, not wanting to deal with anybody, even somebody I liked.

"How's life treating you?" he asked as he walked up to the counter with a self-effacing smile.

"It's hard to say," I said. "I can't really complain to you, can I? You're always doing worse than me."

"That should make you feel better."

"Not really. You're not exactly the criterion by which I measure how well I'm doing."

He laughed generously.

"Did you make it out to the clinic and get your purple juice?" I asked.

"I didn't go. I was lifting cans and bottles to recycle and I had to guard my cart. I'm doing all right today. I got paid, so I got a jar of instant coffee."

I assumed the payment he referred to was government money.

"How d'you drink the coffee?" I inquired, curious about the cooking methods of the homeless.

"I just pour it in my cup and add water from the water fountain," he said.

"What did you do today?" I asked, since he continued standing there.

"Nothing."

"What do you mean, nothing?"

"That's what I do, nothing. Lie around and sleep."

"What do you make of all these young people?" I asked, referring to the clientele.

"Reminds me of what I might have come to," he said. "Do you want any of these?" he asked, holding up a plastic bag filled with mass-market paperbacks, more rejects from the weekly Edendale Library sale.

"Put them on the cart outside," I said.

"Well, you're looking good," he said.

"You too, pal."

"You have a good evening."

"So when are you going to show me your work in progress?" said the boy, as he stepped up behind the book counter. Despite the relentless demands made upon him as a barista, he exuded a cheerful energy. I didn't understand how he managed it, but he was about half my age. I didn't know exactly how old he was. I hadn't asked him because I didn't want to have to answer the same question.

"I don't know about that," I said.

"Are you in a rut?" he asked.

"What do you mean?" I knew that I was in a rut but I didn't like it when other people brought it up, and I would even argue, unconvincingly, that I wasn't in one:

"What are you talking about? I'm trying to write a novel."

"How's it coming along?"

"All my creative juices," I said drily, "are being poured into it."

"So you're almost done then?"

"Pouring it out at an average of a hundred words a day, at most."

"When are you going to let me take a look at it?"

"I appreciate your enthusiasm but it isn't in any kind of presentable shape at present."

"That's what you said last time. How about a couple of chapters?"

"Chapters?"

"You know what I mean."

"I don't know about that. I'm feeling more and more uneasy about it. It's an act ... a work ... of great narcissism and treachery."

"Aren't they all though?"

"There are degrees, and I may have exceeded the bounds of propriety. I've thrown a few people under the bus. I only hope they emerge unrecognizably disfigured."

"But it's a novel, right?"

"Yes, but ..."

"Don't worry, they'll love it."

"I doubt it. But I've resigned myself to it. Whenever I try to write in a positive vein it comes out sounding unconvincing and weak."

"Maybe that's a weakness in itself."

"Maybe."

"Can I be in it?"

"Why would you want to be?"

"Why not?"

"What could you bring to the proceedings?"

"Oh, I've got a lot."

"That device is a little too cute, isn't it? And it must have been used before, probably by a Spanish or South American author."

"But it would be different coming from you."

"It wouldn't work in the context of this book."

"Oh, come on, man."

"I guess I could use a positive presence. But you're going to have to bring something to the table."

With that, I wrote down his email address, and as soon as I got home, before I had time to change my mind, sent him a PDF containing the first thirty pages of the work in progress.

I put the kettle on and brewed myself a mug of laxative tea to ease the strain of medication-induced constipation. It tasted foul. But impotence and constipation were a small price to pay for the state of mind necessary for the creation of immortal works.

* * *

For almost twenty minutes I was on a roll, and I rolled into a rut.

I became too aware that I was making progress to continue making progress. The initial smoothly flowing stream was reduced to a turbulent trickle, and I was left seeking a more dispassionate mode.

I pulled an old notebook from the pile in front of me and flipped through it to discover what I had been doing exactly one year earlier:

"Long lie in," it read, then "Calls from other creditors ... I'd feel better about dying if I'd produced a body of work that people drew solace from."

I picked up a notebook from two years before that:

"Did everything in wrong order today ... Didn't make much progress, don't have much time left to make progress in."

A notebook from five years earlier revealed: "Long time getting started, too distracted ... Difficulty finishing article ... Just do what

I should have been doing all along … If it's all I'm capable of doing, just do it."

It struck me that these notebooks were the most repetitive documents ever committed to paper.

The clock in the upper-right corner of the screen notified me that I had been awake, so to speak, for three hours, during which time it was hard to say exactly what I had been doing. The customary hour or more—in this case, more—of compulsive preparation had been customarily misspent. At 10 a.m. I had turned on the internet blocker and made some furtive incursions into the sphere of activity.

At such an early hour I was easy prey to untoward invasions of the nervous system, and once distraction had been allowed to seep in, it often *surged* in. Turning off the telephone and the internet wasn't an entirely dependable safeguard: there was more than enough potential distraction in one's mind alone, and all too quickly the stillness of the occasion could degenerate into stagnation.

It's pointless to struggle over something I am never going to finish, and in the unlikely event that I do finish this thing, it probably won't be published, and in the highly unlikely event that it is published, it probably won't be read.

At this rate, in ten years' time, if I live that long, I might have completed something. And then I will be in my dotage. One book from a lifetime dedicated to literary endeavor isn't much to brag about.

The false modesty of claiming one's work to be substandard suggests that one was once capable of better, but is belied by the glaring fact that one has never proven it.

But, in all modesty, false or otherwise, the sad fact is that *one* did have it in *one* at one time but *one* didn't seize the moment, and *one*'s current work is inferior to what *one* likes to think *one* was once capable of producing.

I couldn't trust any fleeting confidence I might have in this work. My feelings about it changed from day to day, hour to hour. I still had trouble believing that my efforts were completely worthless. The only solution was to submit it to the scrutiny of a discerning reader.

I thought half an hour, at most, had passed, but when I looked at the clock, fifty-five minutes had been lost. I didn't know where that time had gone but it wouldn't be coming back.

Then another twenty minutes sped by. Then another half hour that I couldn't account for. It was another one of those days: every time I looked at the clock it was later than I thought.

Was time passing more quickly or was I slowing down? Sometimes time moved slowly, other times it flew by. These days it mostly flew by. And I was still only adhering to the first part of the "Write medicated, edit straight" dictum.

I would like to have kept going, but Freedom turned off and as soon as I went back online, no matter how briefly, the route back to my task was firmly blocked by the temptations offered by the internet.

It takes so long to get started, then it's time to stop. Like life. By the time one has figured out how to live, there isn't much time left to profit from what one has learned, and all I have learned is that I'll never learn.

I can stop whenever I want, of course, but it's too late for an early grave. I can't go on, but I will go on, because it's harder not to go on than it is to go on.

It would be nice if all this were building up to something. But it isn't.

*　*　*

Weeks passed, nothing much happened.

The first ant of summer crawled across the desk.

*　*　*

"You don't have a name."

"What d'you mean, I don't have a name?"

"In the book, the protagonist doesn't have a name," said the boy, placing a teasing emphasis on the word "protagonist."

"I was hoping you wouldn't notice that."

"It's a hard thing not to notice."

"I can't bring myself to name him. I'm terrible with names."

"The reader needs a name to hang the character on."

"But he seemed to be managing quite well without one."

"You must have thought of some names though."

"All right, how about Hangland?"

"I like it."

"I was considering using Sean for his first name but a lot of people seem to dislike that name and it's too phonetically close to my own name."

"Like Henry Chinaski for Charles Bukowski."

"Something like that."

"How about just using your real name?"

"No way. It's supposed to be a novel."

We had repaired to the Secret Bar after work so that we could discuss his evaluation of the excerpt I'd sent him. The boy had made detailed notes, which both touched and worried me.

"This place reminds me of a bar in Seattle," he said.

"It hasn't been turned into a self-conscious version of its former self yet. But give it time," I said.

He scrolled down his phone, consulting his notes.

"One thing I noticed," he said as tactfully as possible, "is that the tenses aren't always consistent."

"Some parts are written in the present tense, others in the past, one can alternate. It's all right as long as it reads smoothly," I said.

"There are a few times when it doesn't."

"It might be a bit all over the place now but it will be consistent in the final edit," I said reflexively. I could keep making excuses until the thing was finished. Then I would have to stand by it—an unnerving prospect that provided further impetus to drag *the process* out.

"Ideally, I'd like it to be entirely in the past tense," I added. "But, much as I dislike it, some parts work better in the present."

"The present tense draws too much attention to itself. It has an immediacy but it diminishes suspense," said the boy.

"You sound like you're quoting from a guide to creative writing," I said. "There is no suspense to this thing, that's not the point."

"You still need to keep the tenses straight."

"Are you suggesting I comb through fifty thousand words and switch all the verbs into the past tense? That sounds like a lot of work," I whined, somewhat irked that my efforts weren't being more rapturously received; he was, after all, the first person to have read the work. I thought he might be more easily impressed, but the boy clearly possessed finely honed critical faculties.

"The best stories start with 'Once upon a time …'"

"I know, I know. I don't like writing in the present tense, or reading it. It's *New Yorker*–style crap that unfortunately caught on. But much as I loathe it, it seems to be coming naturally in this case."

"They say *Bleak House* was the first novel written in the present tense."

"I have never finished a Dickens novel, and at this point I seriously doubt I ever will. I can't read long novels anymore. But I have finished at least ten novels by George Gissing."

A dark-haired girl who was sitting with a group of friends in a booth on the other side of the room kept looking over in our direction.

"She's checking you out," I said to the boy.

"I have a girlfriend in Seattle," he said.

"How long d'you think that's going to last now that you've moved to the big city?"

"It keeps things simple," he said.

"I would have thought it complicated matters. Resisting temptation is hard work."

"It's easier than tense straightening," said the boy. "What do you do for female company?"

"Avoid it mostly, at present. I see an older woman once every few weeks. We take comfort in each other's decaying bodies."

"How old?"

"Younger than me, older than you."

"'The bitter promiscuity of the failed romantic.'"

"You know me too well. Who wrote that?"

"Huysmans. Have you read *Against Nature*?"

"Read it? I was weaned on it."

"Do you ever think about settling down, Sean?"

"Settle down? I am settled down. I don't need anyone else to complicate it. The last one just about destroyed me. I'm too old to marry, too young to settle down. As for you, if you're under the age of thirty, you have no business being in a serious relationship, especially a long-distance one. It is your moral responsibility to be out there banging everything in sight. There's plenty of time for the soul-destroying boredom of relationships later."

"I like getting to know someone," he said.

"That's an interesting angle. I've never thought of it that way before. But you must know her well enough by now."

"Maybe too well," he said, ruefully.

"Don't be a traitor to your youth and beauty," I said.

More cocktails were ordered. The dark-haired girl kept looking over, and the boy looked back at her.

"Writers always complain about how hard their work is," said the boy, brushing his overflowing locks from his unfurrowed brow.

"Well, it's not like music, is it?" I responded, with automatic bitterness. "Every night when you hit the stage you're having a great time and being adored for it, and you have the company of your bandmates. As a writer, on a good morning, in utter solitude, you're lucky to squeeze out a few lines that nobody's ever going to read."

"You've got to put it out there, man. Don't hide your gold under a bushel."

"It's not 'gold,' it's 'light.'"

"Either way, it's weighing you down."

I was taking advice from somebody who was young enough to be my son. It could be worse, I mused, as the warming sips of bourbon coursed through my system and pacified my mind … It could be a lot worse. Since my life hadn't changed in twenty-five years, I was an honorary member of his generation. Maybe I should be grateful for that.

"I have this friend in Billings," the boy was saying. "He's a great writer, he wrote these stories that are as good as anything I've ever read, but he doesn't do anything with them."

"Why not?"

"He doesn't feel the need to. He's not ambitious."

"That's not necessarily laudable. It's one thing to not do the work, that's immoral; but to do the work and not put it out there, that's selfish. If one has the ability to provoke, console or inspire, it's one's duty to make a contribution."

"I sometimes wonder if there's a lot of great work out there that's never going to be read because people don't put it out there," said the boy. "I've known a few people like that, like Richard—people who are so sure of themselves that they don't need the validation."

"Yes, I've known a few such cases in my time. Such cases definitely exist. They're out there," I said, and cleared my throat.

"You talk a lot about duty, Sean. It's my duty to have sex with as many women as possible and it's your duty to put out creatively."

"There are people out there who write very well and have something to say but find the business of putting themselves out there distasteful, especially in this day and age."

"Anyone in particular?" said the boy.

"I wasn't referring to myself, just artists in general."

"Sure," said the boy.

"And think of all the women you're depriving. You'll regret that later, all the ones that got away."

"There aren't that many," he said.

"Ambition itself is an acknowledgment of insufficiency," I added, dredging up a half-remembered quote that I'd forgotten the author of and claiming it for myself.

"Another thing."

"Yes?"

"Well, there is something else."

"What?" I responded, snappishly.

"The lack of female characters."

"Right." I grunted, experiencing a sinking feeling, as if I'd been found out. "I'm incapable of creating them. I have to work within my limitations, and I'm very limited. Anyway, how can a man write with any real perception about the lives of women? It requires an insight and audacity I don't possess."

"Tolstoy and Flaubert did it," said the boy. "They wrote novels from an exclusively feminine perspective."

"Well, I can't do it."

"Have you ever tried?"

"No. It seems presumptuous."

"Maybe you should give it a shot."

"I guess it is a failing," I said. "Everybody else seems to be able to do it."

"Henry James did it, and he was a virgin."

"Who knows for certain," I said. "Whenever Iris Murdoch writes from the perspective of an embittered middle-aged man with frustrated artistic aspirations, she nails it."

"You ought to know," said the boy. "Why don't you just take a woman from real life. What about that handsome woman who's always visiting you at the store?"

"Handsome? Is that how you'd describe her? You're talking about Mona, right?"

"That serious woman who always wears pants."

"Yes, Mona. I suppose I could develop that. But doesn't the term 'handsome woman' imply age and masculinity?"

"Maybe."

* * *

This tense straightening is tough. Yes, this tense straightening was tough, devilishly hard work: reverting exclusively to the more unassuming preterite, rewriting sentences I would have written differently had I used the past tense to begin with, combing through over forty-five thousand words, switching every "is" to "was," every "has" to "had," and every "lose" to "lost."

But it has to be done. Yes, it had to be done.

* * *

"I can't fuck her every day, I'm not twenty-five anymore. She doesn't understand I don't have those appetites anymore. I don't think she really does either, but she thinks if I'm not fucking her three times a day that I don't love her or something."

I'd never seen Mitchell so distraught over a woman; I'd never seen him distraught over a woman at all. His relationship with Lyn Lamrock, the woman he had been complaining about since I had walked in half an hour earlier, was already heading south.

"You've only been *together* for a few months," I said. "You can get out of this any time you want."

I resented having to walk over to Mitchell's bachelor pad on a sweltering morning. It meant breaking my precious flow and not putting the required hours into my writing. But he needed the money up front in order to procure the necessary medication, and the dealer—or in this case, the go-between—always calls the shots.

"She's always complaining that I don't eat her out enough," he moaned.

"What do you do to her?"

"She does yoga twice a day, spends half her time on Facebook. She's forty-eight, for fuck's sake," he groaned with frantic displeasure.

"Middle-age crazy or young crazy, it's all impossible," I chimed in.

"What if they're not crazy?"

"They're the worst of all, because they can't handle your insanity, and wouldn't be with you in the first place."

That was a good line, but Mitchell didn't stop to savor or even acknowledge it. I wrote it down in my notebook. The visit had at least triggered a memorable utterance that I could use later.

"It's time to let go of vanity and embrace decay," I said.

"I'm not embracing anybody else's decay," said Mitchell. "They can embrace mine. I don't even want to be in a relationship. I'm not afraid of dying alone."

"I see you've been posting a lot of photographs proclaiming your love for her online."

"Ach. That's her idea. I just do it to shut her up, otherwise I'd never hear the end of it. Makes me wince every time I do it."

"Why are you going through with it then? Why not just end it? What's holding you up?"

"I'm working on it," he said unconvincingly.

"What about the meds?"

"I'll put the call in today," he said, and continued moaning; he was in such an advanced state of distress that he couldn't talk about anything else. "She expects me over at her place this afternoon. She wants me to work there. I can't write with her interrupting me all the time, demanding affection. She's suffocating me with affection. I can't write around her, I can't even read around her. She won't leave me alone."

I handed over the cash.

"I should have the stuff in a few days," said Mitchell. "We'll have a drink, celebrate my independence."

"Good luck with that," I said in a gesture of solidarity, and walked out of his hot, dirty apartment onto the hot, dirty street.

* * *

Why waste time on this? It's too mean-spirited. It won't make the final cut, if there is a final cut.

These scraps of vanity and mangled ambition, these words dying on the page.

* * *

"The first run sold out. We printed up another run of twenty thousand copies, and half of them are already accounted for with advance orders. They're giving the French edition a massive push. They're rushing the German translation in order to have it ready by the beginning of the year. I'm going to Europe next month. I met the director of Vintage Books in New York. He came up to me and told me he loved my book. It's been optioned and they want to hire me as a TV writer. I figure, why not, that's the way it's going. Yes, I am writing a new book. I've written thirteen thousand words in the last four days."

That was more than I'd written in the last three months. Then again, Jackson always wrote quickly and a lot of revision would probably be necessary (or so I assumed; it didn't occur to me that some writers didn't need to do a lot of editing). And he was still ten years younger than me.

As I stood at the counter of the Secret Bar, ordering two more cocktails, I began to roughly calculate how much I had in the bank and if I would have to siphon funds out of my PayPal account in order to cover my expenses for the next month.

"We had dinner at the vegan place ... one of these Groupon things." I looked around to see two hirsute young men standing next to me, ordering drinks for themselves and their dates—two young women who were taking off their coats and settling into a booth. These were the sort of people I came to the Secret to get away from. It was troubling to see how comfortable they were making themselves.

"My imprint has three new books coming out," said Jackson, when I returned with our cocktails, "but they're all by men. It looks bad that we don't have any female authors. The next book should be by a woman ..."

"I'm *attempting* to write a novel." This surprisingly blurted-out statement sounded like an admission of guilt rather than a declaration of positive intent—and why did I always qualify any statement of this sort, even to myself, by saying that I was *attempting* to write instead of that I *was* writing?

"Really? What's it about?"

"If I *attempt* to describe it, it'll sound idiotic. I don't have any grasp of plot, character or dialogue, and my imagination dried up years ago. So, unfortunately, I have had to draw from firsthand experience rather more than I'd prefer or approve of."

"How far in are you?"

"About fifty thousand words."

"I'm committed to publishing female authors next year. I would make an exception for you though, or I could introduce you to my agent, if you want to make some money out of it. But it sounds like it wouldn't be ready until the year after next. Do you have a title?"

"A provisional one: *Positively Negative Street*. What do you think?" I looked over to check Jackson's reaction, as one does with someone whose opinion one respects.

"I don't like it," said Jackson with a forthrightness I would never have adopted with him.

"Why not?"

"It's too Dylanesque, and it's not provocative enough."

He was right about that. It was a good title but it couldn't exist were it not for the Dylan allusion that sparked it. Maybe it could be thrown into the text somewhere.

The two young couples were now commandeering the digital jukebox, sniggering as they played Steely Dan, Chicago, and other selections that they doubtless thought to be ironic.

"What's your first line?" asked Jackson. "That's also important."

I cleared my throat: "'I have decided to stop writing for a while.'"

"Ha. That's good."

Jackson's compliment inspired me to open up. "I excel, if anything, at the negative. I've tried writing in a positive, life-affirming vein but it doesn't feel or sound right. I can complain about anything. It's my gift to the world, not that the world's interested. I can't help it. What's the title of your new book?" I asked, quickly changing the subject for fear that I was exhausting his capacity as a listener.

"I was thinking about calling it *Damaged Goods*," he said.

"After the Gang of Four song?"

"I've never heard of that," he said. "But I suppose there would have to be a song with that title somewhere. I think it will strike a chord."

"You must have heard it," I said.

"Whatever," he said. "These are exciting times. Everything is off-kilter, there are too many conflicting forces at work. Something's got to break. A major earthquake, a plague, riots. I don't know what, but something's going to happen. These young people—my generation, I suppose—they're not equipped to deal with catastrophe; they're soft; they've never seen the sky on fire. It's not going to affect me though. I'm going to be fine. It's crazy, I am literally going to be entering the 1 percent. All right, maybe not the 1 percent but definitely the 2 percent. I'm going to have to get a money manager. I might have to buy property."

I was secretly buoyed by Jackson's friendly curiosity about my so-called novel, and the prospect of being published on his emerging but already successful small press energized me as he inexhaustibly held forth. Occasionally I would stem the tide of his eloquence with an aside while he took a few breaths and gathered more steam. Mostly, I looked forward to getting up and writing the following morning and hoped that a hangover and lack of sleep wouldn't get in the way of my undertakings.

"This place is cool. There are no hipsters here," said one incoming beardo to another as Jackson and I walked out.

* * *

It took twenty years (what with all the years it took to get started) to come up with those forty-five thousand words.

Now I have to come up with another forty-five-thousand words. And that might take another twenty years.

* * *

I spent the day sitting in the store, browsing a biography of Swinburne; when I got home I lay in the bath rereading a David Goodis novel. In the morning I got up and tried to write. But first, I went online.

Scrolling down *The Eastside* blog—the main site for neighborhood news—an article immediately grabbed my attention: "A modernist mansion in the ever more upscale Edendale Heights neighborhood of the rapidly gentrifying Silver Lake area has been purchased for $4 million by the phenomenally creative rock star and maverick Renaissance man, Bob McGilt ..." McGilt, my old friend, who, twenty-five years ago, had invited me to join his band, whose offer I had rejected on the flimsy grounds that I didn't play an instrument—the same charmed McGilt who had subsequently gone on to "great things."

Why, out of all places, did he have to move here? He would never have done so ten, fifteen years ago. There wasn't enough going on at the time. Now there was more than enough art, music, literature, and so on being produced here to put it on the same level as any other urban cultural mecca. An argument could even be made, if one cared to make such arguments, that although there was still plenty "going on" in McGilt's native New York, its glory days were in the past, whereas LA was the most vital American city of the present day. Proof of this cultural power shift could be found in the fact that LA—a place of disaffection, dislocation and reinvention—inspired so much animosity, suspicion and resentment, otherwise known as envy, from the denizens of other cities (New Yorkers and San Franciscans, in particular, seemed to regard it as their civic duty to hate LA and everything it apparently stood for), although, curiously, the hostility was never reciprocated: a sure sign of empire envy.

Now Bob McGilt had moved here, close to my neighborhood, and I didn't relish the idea of running into him: it could be very awkward for both parties, especially me. Not that there was much likelihood of that happening given the different circles we moved in: the difference being that I had spent my life going around in circles while his circles kept expanding. Over the last quarter of a century McGilt had met thousands of people, and been adored by thousands more; he had probably completely forgotten me, which was fine, but I was continually reminded of him because he was famous.

As well as being a writer—he had written a book of short stories, published on the strength of his reputation as a musician—McGilt was a reader, and Mute was one of two bookstores within the compass of his newly acquired mansion. That worried me. There was always something to distract and distress me online, and this was especially distracting, especially distressing. It was unlikely that I'd get any writing done on this particular morning.

Comparisons are odious. Nevertheless, I continue to make them and let them trouble me. In the twenty-five years since I'd last seen him, McGilt had put out numerous records, appeared in films, written books, had gallery exhibitions, opened a vegetarian restaurant, and raised a family. He seemed intent upon proving there was nothing he couldn't do, and he had rarely disappointed the legions of adoring fans who viewed him as a beacon of integrity in a benighted day and age. He was only a couple of years older than me—and here I was, with so much unfinished, so much unbegun, numerous abortive stabs, slabs of obliterated text, and abandoned palimpsests later, still struggling with my first work of extended Pose Friction, with no end in sight.

I stared at the screen, recognizing the difference between intention and implementation, fearing that I was seeing only the ideal but not the actuality of what I was doing. I had serious concerns that what I had produced so far was a load of crap.

Something could be well written and not necessarily be readable. Likewise, something could be written badly and yet be a pleasure to read. One had to make one's idiosyncrasies palatable. The easiest way to do this was to stop writing and communicate through a different medium entirely, preferably music.

Everybody listens to music, but not many people read anymore. (This tense straightening is infinitely tedious.) Reading requires more mental effort than any other art. Music is a soundtrack, a stimulus, a driving force toward other things; watching a movie is an entirely passive act, something to do when one is too tired, bored, or lazy to do anything else; looking at a painting makes very little demand upon one's time or mental energy. Writing is the highest form of art, the others are shortcuts.

The self-conscious novel is a lower form of literature, but it's all I'm capable of: a tired exercise in good old-fashioned modernism. It would be preferable to master-build a cathedral of prose in which the hand of the creator were invisible, surely the highest form of prose fiction, but this is all I'm capable of: Pose Friction.

It's too late to stop now. This thing keeps expanding, on a sprawling plateau of perennial midproject doldrums, and it can be pleasant sitting here, stroking the keys in anticipation. There's nothing else I would rather be doing. That's the sad part … one of the saddest parts.

There is, there was, in fact, one thing I would rather be doing.

The rumbling of a truck, a car accelerating from the intersection, the back door slamming downstairs, the yelling of a passing lunatic on the sidewalk ... the gurgling of water in the excess drain, the audible silence, otherwise known as tinnitus. I lay there, immersed, unable to immerse myself, in the pleasures of balneation.

Over the quarter of a century since I had last seen him, McGilt had been through a steady succession of creative, spiritual, and domestic transformations: he had done everything at the right time, in the right order, from his well-publicized "struggles" with drug addiction in his twenties—a period of irresponsible heroics, with one eye on posterity—to the predictable switch to sober family man at the appropriate time, the obvious time, in his thirties; and now, in his early fifties, he had become an artist overappreciated in his lifetime; he exuded the satisfaction of somebody who had done his work and was now at peace with himself; he could now relax and bask in the satisfaction of his achievements—but he kept rising to new challenges, the bastard. Some consolation, however, could be taken in his physical decline. On the evidence of recent photographs, he had put on weight, although his trademark slicked-back jet-black hair was still intact. A very vain man in his time—it was still his time—he had probably had a hair transplant by now; he could certainly afford it.

Once such a heady level of renown had been achieved one could write one's own ticket (or was it a free pass?), and the opportunities were limitless. To be loved and appreciated for who you are and what you do while you're alive, and to be honored and remembered after death: What could be better? If that was fame, I didn't see anything gauche about it. I would have enjoyed it too much: that couldn't be allowed. I had steered a different course, a deliberately difficult course, making things as hard for myself as possible, or so I told myself. Watching, listening, reading, waiting ...

A single sharp tinkle of ice cracking in the cocktail glass on the bath mat broke up my reverie. A car with a flat tire rattled by. The CD shuffled from string quartet to piano sonata. I opened my eyes and saw the dirt-caked shower curtain and a strand of dental floss draped over a disposable razor on the edge of the tub. The foam had evaporated, swirling and striating into sudsy islands woven by dissolving bubble bath. I pulled the plug out between my toes and lay there while the lukewarm water drained out.

* * *

I stepped out to behold a crimson-streaked sky that would soon be adorning ten thousand Instagram posts, and walked down the sleepy residential streets, suffused with a soft and forgiving evening light, to the main drag. It felt like the end here, both sanctuary and termination: a soft place of harsh realities where a sun that once meant something barely brushed against the world.

Despite my occasional complaints, I wouldn't want to live anywhere else. 'Twas ever thus. It was where I had wanted to end up, and where I would remain. Despite all the turds and all the transmogrification, it still beat the alternatives.

This street that lay under a now gloriously bloody-clouded sunset, and stretched another twenty miles to the ocean, had somehow been named Sunset. How did such a nomenclatural caprice occur? I racked my mind, came up with no answers, and decided to look it up when I got to the store. It would give me something useful to do down there.

The Indian summer evening was blighted only by the citizenry. The older one got, the more young people there were to be irritated by. But could this current crop be any worse than my generation, in our prime, had appeared to our elders?

Yes, they could. Back in the pure old days, *they* didn't know what to do with *us*; the powers that be hadn't yet learned how to process the strange and sudden cultural upheavals of rebellious young people. The accelerating and unifying effect of the internet was undoubtedly to blame. Under its sovereignty, nothing was secret or sacred anymore. This lot had been given everything they could possibly want: all the stimulation, all the information, all the directions and connections were laid out for them at the flick of a switch, and it was impossible to resist. Kept in a constant state of distraction, with every imaginable convenience at their fingertips, the rebellious instinct was efficiently suppressed. I felt sorry for them. They felt sorry for me. A climate of sorrow reigned.

I walked past coffeehouses, brewpubs, vegan restaurants. Two new businesses had appeared overnight (it had been almost two weeks since I had last taken this route): a bloated neon-lit parody of a tonsorial parlor, and a bicycle emporium that could be mistaken for an Apple store were it not for a few bicycles carefully positioned in an otherwise clinically empty room that exuded an intimidating ambience of tasteful extortion.

I stopped at Teejay's to buy my usual order of broccoli. The door was locked and there was brown paper neatly placed over the windows. I peered through a crack: the shelves were empty. The last cheap grocery store in the neighborhood was no more.

Entering the bookstore, I smiled guiltily at Gilbert behind the counter (it was the only way I could smile at him). He was ready with a new Yelp review to confront me with: "I asked the man behind the counter for directions to the bathroom and he lost his temper ..."

The odds were good that one of the people who had recently asked to use the restroom would lodge a complaint.

"I'm not a toilet attendant," I said.

Gilbert lowered his voice. "Sean, you know you're wasting your time here."

"I'm only in it for the money," I said.

"You should be writing," he said, attempting, as usual, to be reasonable.

"I am."

"You should move to New York."

"Are you trying to get rid of me?"

"People care about literature there."

"I can't start over in a new city. I'm too old for that. And it's too expensive."

"You should apply for grants."

"I haven't done enough."

"You should get all your old columns together; they would make a good collection," said Gilbert as he left.

"Thanks," I said.

It was a shame that our friendship had deteriorated to the point of nonexistence. At one time Gilbert had respected me as a jobbing journo and was pleased to work beside me at the store, assuming that mine was only a temporary position. These days, I respected him for having radically turned his life around, while he barely tolerated me for having become such a weight on the store.

I stood behind the counter and surveyed the kingdom I'd be ruling over for the next seven hours. It was business as usual: All the tables and chairs in the café were occupied and groups of caffeinating customers were spilling into the aisles, where they stood around, loudly chatting. A sun-dried woman, wearing shorts and a T-shirt, covered with sweat and dirt, was walking around picking books up, flipping through them, and putting them back where they didn't belong. A young man was sitting cross-legged and barefoot on the floor in the design section; his backpack was laid out beside him, as were his shoes. The long bench in front of the philosophy section was occupied by a number of young people, staring deeply into their cell phones.

They swarmed around the counter, pressing in from all sides; they wandered in off the street, through the oft-bottlenecked doorway, and started, or continued, yelling at the top of their lungs as if straining to make themselves heard in a crowded bar, with no concern for my bedeviled presence, a few feet away, a captive non-audience, trapped in a vortex of verbigeration.

Desperate eyes, desperate chatter. This place, a bookstore of all places, had become a magnet for the cliché-spewing masses. Groups of clucking people stood around loudly batting their gums, from which issued endlessly churning streams of prosaic pleniloquence.

I cranked the music up to drown out the clamor but it only caused the waves of amplified insipid conversation to crash down harder, and there was no way to avoid it at the counter: the squealing and cackling, the chaffering of sciolists, the scraping of chairs, the dropping of books, the convergence of so many different sounds and conversations at different pitches from different parts of the room. A noisy parent was disciplining a noisy child; a dog owner was barking at a barking dog ("Down ... down ..."). So many voices crying out ... to be smothered.

It wasn't just the volume, it was the tone of the voices and the content—when one had the misfortune of being able to make it out—spilling out of mouths that refused to remain shut that was so maddening. As if silence had to be filled, and what it had to be filled with ...

"Oooh, a bookstore!" ... "Oh my God!" ... "Where are the beatniks?" ... "I wouldn't call this Silver Lake." ... "I was like cool." ...

"There's a new dispensary over here." … "Yo. That is a cool book." … "Nick and Linda are having their baby shower on the 19th." … "John Waters wrote a book?" … "Love it." … "We put in an offer on a house today." … "Supercool." … "It's like postapocalyptic, kind of." … "Oh wow." … "They had two after-parties, they had an after-party and an after-after-party. I went to both." … "That's so cool." …

The predictability, the grating insincerity, the static washing over static.

Desperate eyes, desperate chatter, desperate smiles.

Every time I looked up, somebody was smiling at me. They were attempting to smile me to death, to murder me with smiles. I wasn't physically or mentally capable of smiling or even nodding at everybody that walked in.

Keep your head down, it's the only way. Keep your head down and don't look up when a customer appears. If you look into every face, they will destroy you.

Between interactions, I checked *The Eastside* blog for information about the Teejay's closure:

"On Monday, a man who said he owned the building stood in the doorway of Teejay's Market as a worker changed the locks. The landlord said the market owners had been behind on their rent for several months when they closed without notice. … 'We are open to suggestion,' said the landlord, who did not want to provide his name." At the bottom of the brief and inconclusive article the comments section included various observations from around the neighborhood: "I bought salsa at Teejay's maybe 3 times. I won't miss it. I'm pretty sure the homeless in the area were stealing their shopping carts." … "The times I went, it was filthy, inside and out, they lost customers, because their operation wasn't properly taken care. About the shopping carts, after they got them back from the homeless they never washed them. I hope there is a nice Gym in our community."

The fact remained that I would now have to buy vegetables at the health food supermarket across the road, where they cost twice as much. Teejay's had been serving the community for longer than I had been part of it, and many others would be forced into the same predicament.

There was a sudden savage screaming from the café area. The sun-dried woman was going berserk, throwing chairs around, smashing a coffee cup on the floor, venting rage against her lot in life.

Keeping my head down, I looked up the origin of the street outside: Sunset Boulevard, a one-time cattle trail; it used to be called Bellevue Street, with one small section called Marchessault Street, after Mayor Damien Marchessault. It began in what is now Hollywood, where a fine view of the sunset over the Pacific was afforded.

The café personnel ushered the still-screaming sun-dried woman out of the back door. I turned the music up to drown out the voices but it just made them louder. Then I turned it down, and it made no difference. In a futile attempt to control the atmosphere, I put on a John Fahey album, but the languid precision of his guitar playing, which served as a perfect aid to spiritual abstraction in a quieter place, was buried beneath all the nattering, clattering, shattering—and in this place, in this condition, even the most beautiful music was lost on me. And soon the evening's entertainment would be starting up on the patio.

Another mentally ill freelance bookseller, sporting a Virgin Mary trucker cap and a Miss Brazil T-shirt, walked in with five books, one of which was a biography of Frank Zappa bearing a signature that looked as if it had been written by a five-year-old practicing his cursive.

"It's worth $2,000," he said.

"The book was published ten years after Zappa died," I said. "It's not exactly common practice for the subject to sign their own biography, especially after they're dead. Put it on eBay if it's so valuable."

"I'll take $75 for these four," he said, referring to a travel guide to Indonesia, a book on child care, an Erle Stanley Gardner novel, and a battered copy of *The Bridges of Madison County*.

He wouldn't budge, just stood there, with the books on the counter between us.

"I'm not running a fucking charity," I said.

"I didn't ask for your pity, man," he said, sounding aggrieved.

"Yeah, but you received it without asking. It's a gift. I'll give you five dollars just to get rid of you."

He accepted the cash and left, satisfied with the payment.

"And she's like 'Whu-uh' and I'm like 'Whu-uh-uh,'" shouted a grown man as he walked by the counter with a cell phone pressed to his ear—speech at the speed of thoughtlessness, language degenerating into gibberish as increasingly more impoverished means of communication are resorted to.

A young man stood on the other side of the counter. I looked at him, thinking: "The feckless young puppy, he's had it too easy"; and he looked back at me, thinking: "He's passed it, poor old fucker, he missed the boat."

"I have a question," he said.

"I'm not answering any more questions," I said.

"You're not answering any more questions?"

"That's another question. Do you want me to repeat that statement? D'you realize how many questions I've already answered tonight, from people who could easily have figured the answers out themselves? I've met my quota."

He shook his head in disbelief and walked out. He would probably yelp me. I didn't even care anymore.

Spray me with spittle, bombard me with idiotic questions, kill me with fake smiles. Finish off what's left of me.

I put on some free jazz: the sonic equivalent of the ambience in this place. Melinda Waterform's monumentally ineffectual and universally praised new novel, *The Habit of Absence*, was slapped down on the counter in front of me, followed by a copy of *The Death of the Novel* by Jackson Valvitcore.

It was all so dispiriting.

But what were the alternatives? I had to make money, and this was all I was good for anymore.

Tim, a scruffy young regular, shuffled in with a rucksack full of books.

"We're tapped out," I told him. "I've bought five loads of books already tonight. We don't have any more cash. Look at that cart." Both sides of it were crammed with used books.

"I'm telling you, Sean, it's good stuff," said Tim as he started removing his bounty, one by one, from the rucksack. "This'll sell, Joseph Campbell."

"D'you know how sick I am of people telling me how valuable their crap is? Every time you tell me how valuable one of your worthless books is, I'm knocking a dollar off what I would have paid you."

"It's good stuff," he said as he pulled out a jacketless Modern Library edition of *Winesburg, Ohio*.

"That's another dollar I'm knocking off."

"Come on, Sean, you've got to help me out, I'm broke," he said, giving me his most lovable smile, confident that his needs would be met.

"I'm sorry about that but I'd be a lot more sympathetic to your plight if I didn't have to deal with it personally. Now get out of my sight," I said, and handed him thirty dollars.

"How about a drink token?" he asked.

"I don't have any left. The folk singers took them all." The screeching of somebody passionately expressing themselves on the patio resounded through the store. They were giving it their all, and it was more than enough. I turned off the free jazz and put John Fahey on again.

"What d'you need?" I asked Tim.

"A macchiato."

"Tell them I authorized it."

Out of my peripheral vision a dumpster-sized shape hovered. I looked up from the screen. A full-figured woman opened her mouth: "We're in the neighborhood and we were wondering if you'd like to make a donation."

"To what?"

"We're raising funds for …"

"What have you got?"

"Well, we have a taxpayer ID number."

"How am I supposed to know if you're legitimate?"

"Forget it, you seem to be having some sort of …"

"Speak for yourself."

"Are you playing the music?" asked a slim woman with large, intelligent eyes and brown hair, as she made her way out of the store.

"Yes," I said, lighting up.

"Who was that last instrumental by?"

"Fahey … John Fahey."

"I thought so," she said. "I've really been getting into him recently. Thank you."

And with that, my mood immediately improved. There were, after all, some nice people in this world.

* * *

A man was sleeping soundly on the steps leading to the downstairs apartment, flopped out beneath a blanket, with several strips of cardboard for a mattress. I took keen pleasure in imagining my neighbor's outrage upon returning home to find a snoring bum flagrantly blocking his entryway.

There was a single official-looking envelope in the mailbox. The return address was a lawyer's office: Drago Lark LLP in Sacramento. Despite a strict policy of ignoring letters of this nature, a combination of curiosity, fatalism and obligation triumphed over firmly held principles, and I opened it.

"This communication is from a debt collector," it began. So far, so good. Hundreds of letters from debt collectors had landed in my mailbox during the three and a half years since I defaulted on eight or nine separate accounts. Lately the phone calls and letters had been tapering off to the point that I rarely thought about my creditors anymore. The pressure of debt wasn't as heavy as I'd initially feared, and this I had been led to expect when I had sought the counsel of my fellow defaulters. Several friends of mine had already been down this potentially ruinous path and assured me that if one didn't engage with one's persecutors there was nothing they could do about it—that all one had to do was ignore the letters and phone calls, and the problem would simply disappear. This approach seemed to have worked for everyone I knew who had been in a similar position. So I ignored the calls, didn't listen to the messages, and stuffed the letters into the bulging trash bag below the kitchen sink.

The notice continued: "We have been retained by xxxxSPV 1 LLC the owner of the above-referenced account, to collect from you the entire balance on an account you held with xxxxbank, N.A. xxxxSPV 1 LLC is the owner of the account and has the authority to collect on the account. The outstanding balance on your account is $20,264.83."

This was not a letter from the credit card company I defaulted on all those years ago, but from the latest in a long line of debt-collection companies. Credit card companies eventually despair of collecting debt from defaulters and sell the debt, at a pittance, to collection agencies who themselves give up on collecting the debt and sell it at increasingly deflated prices to other debt collectors. According to the statute of limitations in California, they are allowed to pester you for four years—and for me that time was almost up.

"If, after 30 days from receipt of this letter, you have neither disputed the above-referenced debt nor requested information regarding the original creditor, we will assume the debt is valid. This office will be entitled to file a lawsuit against you for the collection of this debt and pursue any and all legal remedies available by law to collect the debt."

This letter seemed to be from a lawyer representing a debt-collection company. I didn't care to parse the legalese. For all I knew, I had already received numerous documents containing the same threats, and no action had been taken. I wasn't going to rummage through that bulging trash bag containing almost four years worth of dunning letters in order to work out some sort of paper trail. The notice covered two pages. I didn't feel up to reading all of it. I decided to forget about it.

* * *

When awash in chemical warmth, it was possible to beguile myself into imagining I was doing something worthwhile. Under this beneficent influence, minor achievements could seem like major triumphs; even a few rough-hewn sentences or an embryonic paragraph could seem substantial, and there was a temptation to dream of glory.

One imagines publication and a readership, that the literary world will be set alight with the results of all this work, only to find at the end of the day—day after day for more years on end than one would care to reflect upon the tedious annihilation of—that what *one* has done makes no difference to anybody, that *one* will be lucky if *one* can get one's friends to read it. Even if *one* does pull off the impossible and finish this thing, *one* may find that finishing it is *one's* only achievement, and a private triumph at that; and if it isn't published, all this time, care and energy will only be fuel for further resentment.

* * *

"It's got to be face time every morning. Fuck, man, I'm trying to make it work but I have to write. I can't look at a book, I can't do any research while we're having face time. I'm obsessed with the Frankfurt school at the moment, but I can't talk about that with her. She's into angels, elves and flower remedies."

"What are you working on?" I asked, and looked down at the carpet, which was filthy.

"I'm rewriting the Adorno script. Some people are interested in it."

"Who?"

"Some friends of Lyn's."

Of course, there had to be an upside. Mitchell's well-connected girlfriend had arranged for some work to be thrown his way, which could result in the realization of his greatest dream: a produced screenplay.

"Anyway, she'll be back from Paris next week," said Mitchell.

"Do you miss her?" I asked, stupidly.

"Mostly, I dread her," said Mitchell. "She wants me to give up my apartment and move in with her."

"Why would you want to do that?"

"If I'm going to make a change I might as well do it with a celluloid cult heroine. What I'm hoping is that I can get some writing done if I move in with her."

"I thought you said you couldn't write with her around," I said.

"If I move in with her it might be different," he said, flimsily. "I'll have my own office."

"Well, I would urge caution," I said.

"It's the face time I can't hack," he groaned. "First thing in the morning, when I'm barely awake, I have to stare into her face for forty-five fucking minutes and listen to her talk about her day, and she wants me to talk about my day. I have nothing to say. Am I doing this because I'm a whore or because I'm afraid of dying alone?" he asked himself in genuine bafflement. It seemed that opposing forces were tearing him apart, to the extent that he was carelessly dropping his usual guard and revealing his opportunistic inner machinations.

"I thought you said you weren't afraid of dying alone," I gently reminded him. "You could have another twenty years or more."

Mitchell threw the pill jar across his cluttered coffee table in frustration, and I eagerly grabbed it.

* * *

It is hard to believe that I have been sitting here for two and a half hours.

I claim, to myself, that I write for three hours every morning. What that usually means is that I sit here for three hours, abandoning myself to useless gnawings and vacillations, and fighting the urge to lie down.

If I got paid by the hour, I'd be earning a decent living. If I got paid by the word, I'd be a pauper. Unfortunately, I don't get paid at all for my services to literature. But if sitting at a desk in a morbidly self-reflective haze were the equivalent of actual work, I'd be a multimillionaire.

Leaning forward, pressed up against the edge of the desk with arms folded, as if in a coffin, head hanging down and eyes closed, hovering in languid tension. There doesn't seem to be any way around or out of a morning like this.

Maybe the morning can be redeemed by going out in a blaze of glory in the final half hour.

No, that isn't going to happen.

In twenty minutes the internet will unblock: the familiar waves of relief and regret will roll in, and I will be faced with various encumbrances and obligations. Since I don't have anything to eat at home, I will have to fortify myself on the way to the store, but where: From the deli bar at the health food supermarket that replaced the Mexican supermarket or at the twelve-dollar-burrito stand that replaced the five-dollar-burrito stand, or on a fifteen-dollar falafel plate at the new Middle Eastern place that recently took over when the gourmet hot dog stand quickly went out of business at what was once the quaint old lunch counter?

The need to eat gets in the way of everything. As does the *need* to write.

There is never enough time, because too much of it is already lost. Too much time is spent reminding myself of what I have to do in the near future, and ruing the squandering of the recent past, even as I continue to squander the present. It feels as if I don't have time to do anything, so I do nothing but tell myself what to do … and don't do it.

Five minutes until the end of Freedom. I exit Full Screen mode because the popping sound it makes when the document page suddenly shrinks on the screen sends a jolt through my system.

One minute left. Nothing can be salvaged now. It's all over, for the moment, for at least another day.

Thus did the morning dwindle down to nothing worth remembering or saving.

Again I had squandered the all-important time that was mine, when time was/is running … out.

Now that the session was over, I finally felt capable of producing something.

* * *

As I stepped behind the counter Gilbert handed me a note.

"You have a love letter," he said with a calmness that failed to mask the raging tempest within.

It was written in capital letters on a folded scrap of paper and addressed to "Asshole." It read: "Dear Asshole, Thanks for making my visit to your store on Monday night so crappy. I was going to buy books because I like to support independent stores but I am going to spend my money at a less pretentious place instead. You—curly haired, craggy faced old asshole—were super unprofessional and super unfriendly. When I asked a simple question about a book I was looking for you refused to answer it. I'm sorry I interrupted your browsing online. Won't be coming back." It was, of course, unsigned.

"Are you sure it's meant for me?"

"It happened last night," said Gilbert, coldly. "I'm getting tired of apologizing for you. Have you read your latest Yelp reviews?"

"No, I can't bring myself to."

"One other thing," he said as he gathered his iPhone, bottled water and pack of American Spirits from the counter. "D'you realize the phone was off all last night?"

"Yes, I noticed that it didn't ring all night, now that you happen to mention it." I had, in fact, turned it off. "What are you doing this evening?" I quickly added.

"Meditation," he said, with something less than enthusiasm, and walked off.

The evening was off to a wretched start. A group of young women marched through the door, texting and squawking at the top of their lungs.

One of them interrupted her texting to point out a book to her friends: "She is the coolest woman who has ever existed, Kelley Gimlet."

"Who?" asked one of her friends.

"Chthonic Truth," chirped her well-informed friend.

They planted themselves by the counter and kept up their relentless squawk. I retreated to the philosophy section. But there were more young people sitting on the long bench, photographing each other and giggling, having the time of their lives. Meanwhile, in front of the fiction shelves, a shrill young weasel was whining loudly into his cell phone in an attempt to prove that he had stuff going on: "You're going to have a hard time attracting actresses with this script ..."

Suddenly, out of nowhere, a silence.

The hissing waves of tinnitus were broken after a few seconds by somebody shrieking "Oh my God!" at the other end of the store, followed by another "Oh ... My ... God!" from closer range. Sirens wailed, babies barked, dogs screamed, skateboards clattered on the sidewalk. The young women photographed themselves striking pensive poses while pretending to study learned books, and giggled, then danced in vulgar parody to the soul mix I was playing, and giggled some more.

I went back online and checked *The Eastside*. The headline read: "Hillside property sets record-breaking price: Echo Park house sells for $2.3 million." The house had been sold to an actor who made his name in franchise thrillers. It took a moment for this news to sink in. That was Paul's house. This was his contribution against the gentrification he had railed against so vehemently. Apparently, he hadn't thought his position through as scrupulously as he had indicated earlier. It seemed that now that he had everything he wanted, it wasn't necessary for him to think anymore. He had checked out. He couldn't see beyond his own bullshit. He was in a comfortable enough position that he didn't need to.

In occasional pockets of silence, I struggled to find a clear thought ... and gave up.

Aaron walked in, raised his eyebrows in my direction, and stood expectantly at the counter, waiting for me to engage with him.

"This place is turning into a fucking zoo," he said.

"You ever go to the zoo and find your favorite animal asleep?" I said. "Well, it's one of those nights. I have nothing left to give. They've taken it all out of me."

"It's too hot at my place," he said. "The dogs are barking. I can't handle the dogs. These people, they just let their dogs bark. I want to blow their fucking brains out."

"The dogs or their owners?"

"Both."

"I know. It's a jagged, neurotic sound. You can't think or write with a dog barking nearby," I said, out of sympathy with a fellow misocynist.

"They just leave them out there all fucking day. The guy next door puts his dog in the garden when he goes to work in the morning, and it's just out there barking all day, and when he gets home the dog shuts up. They don't have to put up with it themselves, they just inflict it on their neighbors."

"If a person was standing in a yard shouting that loudly, nobody would put up with it for five minutes, the police would be called, but we're supposed to put up with the barking and find them adorable. If we don't, we're hateful," I said.

"It pierces through the sound waves and hits a psychic nerve," said Aaron. "It's like a bomb going off, it's like a tear in the atmosphere. And I'm just trying to think. There's two dogs on my staircase, and if it's not one it's another."

"You live up a staircase?"

"You know where the Holloway is? My apartment is at the very top of the staircase behind it."

"I'd be curious to view the squalor you reside in," I said.

"It's horrible. It's just slob guys, just fucking pigs."

"But you're all going to grow out of that."

"I guess."

"Did you see the girl with the underarm hair again?"

"We hung out the other night. She let me do something I don't usually get to do."

"What's that?"

"I don't want anyone to hear me," he whispered.

"I can't hear you. I'm already virtually deaf and it's loud in here."

"All these people can hear me." He motioned toward several chatting couples.

"They don't care, they're having their own conversations. Listen … Blowjobs!" I shouted out. Nobody turned around. "See. They don't give a shit. So what happened? Did you take the pill?"

"Yes, and she let me … She let me …" He made a jabbing gesture with his hand.

"Are you into that?"

"Yeah, well, I don't usually get to do it. I just said, 'I need that,' and she obliged. I didn't even have to ask her. It was a nice surprise."

Aaron moved out of the way as a customer placed copies of *I Hate Honey*, *Just Dick* and *Milk and Kids* on the counter in front of me.

"Can I have a bag? It's a gift to my mother-in-law."

I don't give a fuck who it's for, I said to myself.

"Thank you, brother."

Aaron moved back in. "As you were saying …," I said.

"That helped my soul out."

"I'll bet it did."

"It was uplifting. It really was. I don't ask for much, you know, I don't need much, and then this," he looked down in horror at his cell phone. "She just texted me again. It's a long text. I can't deal with it."

The never-ending procession filed by, life passed me by. People going this way and that. I sat there, glazing over, digging my tongue into a newly reopened cavity until the nerve quaked, mapping out and navigating the ever-changing terrain inside my mouth—the new stalagmites and stalactites created by erosion and breakage.

"Have you read it yet?" asked an eager young regular, wielding a copy of Melinda Waterform's *The Habit of Absence*, as if it would be a perfectly natural act for me to read this nauseatingly ubiquitous bestseller.

"Of course not, and I have no intention of doing so."

"How can you dismiss something you haven't read?" he naively protested.

"Very easily and with complete confidence. Because I've seen the people that do read it."

"Well, it's very popular."

"Precisely. Judging by its popularity, and the looks of the people that buy it, I require no further proof of its mind-numbing mediocrity."

"So any book that's popular is crap?"

"If something's popular, it's usually crap, yes. If the average reader enjoys it, then it's average. The same applies to movies and music. There are occasional exceptions to this rule but they are rare. Why would you want to read something that everybody else is reading?"

"Maybe because it might say something about the times we live in and open up stimulating discussion," said the voice of youthful reason. "It's important to keep up with contemporary culture."

"There's something to be said for that," I conceded. "But I get more than enough of it through osmosis in my current position."

"Recommend something to me then," he pleasantly suggested.

I pulled a copy of Jane Bowles' *Two Serious Ladies* from the stacks and handed it to him. "Don't be put off by the cover," I said, referring to the hideous and sloppily executed double portrait on the cover. I could never understand why publishers placed portraits on their dust jackets. It was an insult to the reader's imagination that French publishers classily eschewed with their monochromatic, purely text-based covers that allowed the work within to speak for itself.

A man of about my age was walking out of the door but stopped when he saw me behind the counter. He was bald and overweight, with sympathetic, watery eyes—a longtime journalist; twenty years ago he had edited my work at the *LA Weekly*. We had been on the same path but due to commitment, perseverance and talent he had now advanced to the point that I never saw him anymore.

"How's it going?" he asked.

"Your book's selling well," I told him, avoiding the question and referring to a recently published collection of his articles.

"What are you up to?" he asked. "I haven't seen your byline in a while. Are you still writing?"

How could I tell an honest career journalist that I was writing a novel? It sounded shameful and discreditable, an admission of guilt. What was the point of broadcasting it? I would never finish it. But what else could I say?

"I'm trying to write a novel," I said.

"I'm glad to hear it. That's exactly what you should be doing. What's it about?"

I mumbled around evasively: "I'm not really equipped for the task. I have no grasp of plot, character or dialogue, and my imagination dried up years ago, so I'm obliged to draw on personal experience more than I'd prefer. I've had to throw a few people under the bus. Hopefully, they will emerge unrecognizably dis-figured. I'm concerned it might offend some people."

"It's important to be offensive nowadays," he said. "A lot of great art is offensive and they're trying to take that away. And you know who's trying to take it away from us: the Left, the same people who claim to be protecting our civil liberties."

"That's a good point," I said. We were interrupted by a customer, which allowed him to make his exit, and as soon as I could I wrote his words down in my notebook.

After I had counted out the drawer and emptied the trash, and the boy had finished washing the dishes, we walked across the street to the nearest bar. A deejay was blasting music from the halcyon punk and postpunk era—vicarious nostalgia for today's youth, who hadn't found anything better to replace it with.

"Dumb up the volume, because if you turn it down the quality of conversation will have to rise," I said to the boy as we claimed two barstools.

"At least he's playing good music," he said, as "Mannequin" by Wire came on.

We ordered two overpriced beers and the boy brought out his cell phone.

"You keep reinforcing the same points," he said, quoting directly from his notes.

"I know. It's all I can do."

"It seems . . ."—how could he put this gently—"a bit too self-aware."

"I know, I'm painfully aware of the self-awareness."

"And calculated."

"Maybe I can inject the spontaneity later. Your presence isn't exactly helping matters. This meta stuff dates it—it's anachronistic, modern, as in the 1970s. It will annoy some readers."

"Don't worry about it. You can blame me."

"What am I supposed to do, place a caveat at the beginning stating that it was your idea? It'll have my name on it."

"Put it in one of your footnotes. If you want to talk about meta …"

"You're getting a lot of dialogue but you don't have much of a personality. It's hard work getting a personality across. I don't know how to create an individual voice. I don't want you to sound too much like me."

"All you have to do is transcribe our conversations."

"It's not that simple. In any case, I've invented most of them."

"What about the sex scenes?"

"Since when was the deejay elevated to the status of priest?" I said, deliberately changing the subject. "This guy isn't even spinning records. He's playing music off a laptop. I've been doing that at the store for the last seven hours. I get no credit for it."

"You said you were going to include sex scenes," said the boy, raising his voice in order to be heard over the chorus of "Chinese Rocks."

"I don't remember that. I said I'd develop the Mona character!" I shouted back.

"You haven't done that!"

"It's getting too long. I'm cutting passages out, a lot of them. I'm not introducing any new themes, scenes or characters. You're the last one."

"There aren't enough female characters. You can't get away with that anymore. If you don't add a sympathetic female character, it's going to be labeled as sexist. You should at least have one sex scene. What about that woman you see once a week?"

"It was never once a week, biweekly at most, and these days it's more like once a month, if that."

"Why don't you include her? It will brighten things up."

"I very much doubt it will have a brightening effect. Maybe I could switch one of the male characters to a female one. But given the existing male characters it will be unflattering and it *will* be considered 'sexist.' Everything is sexist these days. You can't talk about sex honestly without being accused of sexism and you can't talk about race without being accused of being a racist. It's the fault of your generation. It's too loud in here. I'm exhausted!"

"You need to add some female interest or the interaction between us is going to come off as homoerotic."

"There's nothing homoerotic about it."

"I know that, but the reader won't. They'll think it's weird that you always call me 'the boy.' Can't you give me a name?"

"No. It amuses me. I'm leaving it in."

"But you have to have a sex scene."

"I've got something lying around from a few years ago, maybe I can just insert that. I'm burnt out on it. It just keeps expanding and becoming more unruly. It's already taken up far too much time, and there's still so much more to do."

"Maybe you should send it to somebody."

"But who?"

"What about Prolix? They publish 'challenging work by bold new voices.' You need to spend as much time putting it out there as you do putting it in there, working on it."

"I don't put *any* time into putting it out there. I don't know any agents. I haven't got the first idea about how to go about the business side of it. Prolix would be perfect, but they're probably out of my league."

"Hey, I know you."

As I was returning from the restroom a man sitting alone at the other end of the bar hailed me. I didn't recognize him.

"Nelson," he said, reaching out a hand.

"Yes, of course," I said, looking into his face and through the lined, papery skin, recognizing the features of the vaguely remembered person of whom he spoke. Many years ago, when I first arrived in town, we'd been habitués of the same coffeehouse, the Opal.

He was dressed elegantly and his long, thinning gray hair was neatly combed back. Alone at the end of the bar, he took measured sips from a bottle of light beer.

"You went out with Gloria, didn't you?" he said, referring to a barista at the Opal with whom I'd been romantically involved at the time. "How's she doing? You still see her?"

"She got fat," I said, and immediately regretted having made such a churlish remark, which Nelson didn't seem to find funny or informative. "She's doing well," I added, "married, two kids."

"That's good," he said.

"You know," he said, at the conclusion of the five minutes it took to condense the last quarter century of our lives, "when you reach our age things mean more, you have to be careful about how you spend your time, there's only so much of it left." He spoke as he drank, slowly and carefully, deliberately pacing himself in accordance with the needs of the body.

He was older than me, he had to be in his late fifties, and he assumed we were the same age. That was unsettling. But I was as close in age to a sixty-year-old as I was to a forty-year-old. Yes, it was time to let go of youth.

"We both dated baristas in the same coffeehouse years ago," I explained to the boy upon rejoining him, while being careful not to mention exactly how many years ago. "At the time it was the only coffeehouse on this side of town. He seems to be aging in a dignified manner, unlike myself."

"That's exactly the sort of thing you shouldn't be including in the book," said the boy. "You've already spent too much time comparing yourself to other people and mourning the passage of time. You need to stop reinforcing the same points."

"Yeah, maybe. I never claimed to be versatile."

"I'll drive you home."

"Thanks."

* * *

A cobweb in the window wavered in a light breeze, gently rocking a long-dead fly. Striving toward silence and stillness through a dusty, tangled web of thought, I could feel my precious few remaining drops of energy fading into a fog of mixed metaphors. What was the use of trying when I didn't have it in me? And I wasn't even trying. I couldn't hold on to a thought, or entertain a thought worth having; my vital forces—such as they are, such as they were—were clearly, unclearly, in decline. Was this really a useful investment of the little time I had left? And even if I had more time, wouldn't it still be a waste?

It had taken so long to do what I should have been doing all along, a lifetime to finally get around to doing something that was perhaps ultimately worthless. Give it one last shot. Then what, attempt to live? That might prove to be an even more strenuous undertaking.

It would have been gratifying, at this late stage, if my "work" was behind me and I was sopping up the gravy, but I hadn't started on the meat and potatoes yet, and in the unlikely event that I ever did finish this thing, no room will have been saved for dessert; there won't be much time left to enjoy the fruits of my labor, and there probably won't be any fruits. But I shouldn't be thinking about fruit or gravy, only meat and labor.

More than anything, I needed time. Having already wasted a lot of it, I now needed more of it, to use productively. But, unfortunately, that's not the way it works.

Because I had been leading the same existence for so long and hadn't done much, the illusion of youth and futurity was perpetuated, when, in fact, I was past my prime and barely getting started.

It had always seemed that I was just getting started, and I always had the feeling that I'd left it too late. I felt it when I was thirty-eight, even when I was twenty-eight. I would probably still be feeling that way if I made it to fifty-eight.

I wouldn't mind the slowness if it meant eventually getting somewhere. Were I to receive news of my impending death, my chief concern would be that I hadn't done the work yet, that I still hadn't finished *this thing*.

It was tragic (for me) at the end of the day, to consider that my greatest contribution to literature had been made as a bookseller: this life of trade, this trade-off life—a life dedicated to literature, which hasn't taken me beyond this desk, this bathtub, this bookstore.

These "sessions" were becoming progressively less productive, but I kept going.

Should I attempt to work through this blockage or take a break? Yes, take a break. That would surely be for the best.

* * *

The beer-and-wine license didn't make much difference. There were already enough drinking establishments in the neighborhood. Nobody really wanted to drink in a bookstore.

Stop saying "cool." For the love of Mercy, please stop saying "cool"! There are other superlatives, I spluttered to myself.

Two feet from my aching eardrums, a young woman loudly recited execrable poetry from a copy of *I Love Milk* to her coarsely hirsute boyfriend. "I love this *so* much," she gushed, with heavy self-congratulatory emphasis. "This is *so* cool."

What had I done to deserve the cruel fate of being subjected to such drivel?

My punishment for not having done my own work was to sell other people's work, and to endure the accompanying mortifications.

I looked across the room. Despite this being a bookstore, there were more people staring into cell phones than looking at books.

"Should I buy this?" asked a customer with whom I was acquainted, brandishing a copy of Moby's autobiography.

"I wouldn't read that if you put a gun to my head," I said.

"What about this?" he asked, holding up a copy of William Burroughs' *The Job*.

"Certainly not. It's the book that commemorates the novelty of the one time in his life that Burroughs held a job."

"Actually, it's a collection of interviews, it's great. You'd like it," he said, and handed it over the counter to me.

"I must have been confusing it with something else."

"*Exterminator!*, perhaps," he said.

Dogs barked, one-sided cell phone conversations squalled, children yelled, full-grown adults screamed, and an infant attempted to scale the cash register. I had to remind myself that this was still, technically at least, a bookstore.

Rising and falling and rising again, the crescendoes of babble from every direction reached an unbearable pitch as two flocks of young women merged into each other and immediately started, and didn't stop, greeting each other with shrieks of joy—"Oh my God! I haven't seen you in like forever! ... Oh my God!"—and kept up an incessant cocktailparty–like clamor by the front door, their voices operating on me as instruments of torture.

In order to avoid being spattered by this noisily splashing fountain of burbling inanities, I walked back to the café counter to grab a bottle of water.

"They're killing me up there today," I said to the boy, who was cleaning the espresso machine.

"What's the matter, pal, you don't like hard work?"

"Not much, no."

"You know, I was thinking," said the boy, "that maybe there's a little too much complaining in your book."

"Why don't you just say 'definitely' and 'a lot' instead of 'maybe' and 'a little.' That's what people mean when they say those words."

"All right then, definitely a lot of complaining," he said, and laughed.

"How would you like it if you were working in a record store at my age? I'm advertising the fact that I've failed at my vocation," I said. A line was already forming at the book counter, and I pushed my way back, treading over slumped texters and shouldering through chatty groups.

A young man with a beard and a baseball cap was standing at the counter.

"Can you look something up for me?"

"Aren't you the same person that just asked for ... ?"

"What? ... No."

There had been another cherubic young beardo in a plaid shirt up there a few minutes earlier. They were all beginning to blur into each other. How many faces must I stare into over the course of a day? There has to be a limit. I must have exceeded my quota hours ago.

Somebody was standing on the other side of the counter, singing along to "Gloria" (by Them) in a carefree manner (is there any other way to sing in public?). I looked up. The bearded singer was wearing a scarf and shades, and he was accompanied by a highly attractive young woman.

"Thanks, man," he said, as I rang up five or six books about Eastern religion.

"Thanks, man," he said again as I passed him the receipt.

"Thanks, man," he said yet again as I put the books in a bag for him.

Can you please stop thanking me, I said to myself. This over-thanking was an excessive reinforcement of the consumer-cashier dynamic, and it was getting embarrassing.

"Can we go to Best Buy now?" his girlfriend asked him.

"G-l-o-r-i-a-aaah," he started singing again, and broke off to say another "Thanks, man" when, to my great relief, they left, folding into each other as they walked out of the store.

"You know who that was?" said a young man who had been standing near the counter throughout the transaction.

"No. Should I?"

"That was Nut Wilkson," said the young man.

I had heard the name: he was a surfer turned actor; but I knew nothing of his attainments.

"He seemed like a nice guy," said the young man.

"Yes," I muttered. Much as I suspected, his brotherly gratitude had been an acknowledgment of his overrewarded position: humility as an expression of guilt, or pity. But at least it showed a measure of self-awareness.

Out of the black chaos a hand reached out to me. It held a crumpled paper cup.

"Do me a solid and trash this, will you?"

I didn't like the tone of this person's voice, and I didn't like his face either. Looking up from the computer, I saw a middle-aged man in a tank top, so as to flaunt his heavily decorated arms, where, amid a profusion of rose vines, bones and tombstones, the skull-like features of a man with short jet-black hair and sweeping sideburns was discernible: an unmistakable impression of a young Bob McGilt as rendered by a professional tattoo artist. McGilt inspired such love in his fans that they paid to have his features etched indelibly onto their bodies. There was no getting away from the bastard. His presence was nauseatingly inescapable.

"No, I won't do you 'a solid.' It sounds disgusting," I answered. "Are you suggesting that I shit in your hand? Trash it yourself. There's a can on the street outside."

This place had turned into a cross between a nursery, a dog pound, a lunatic asylum, a homeless shelter and a nightclub, and my duties included those of toilet attendant, roadie and trash collector.

Poisoned by the screen, deafened by the noise, maddened by the multitudes. I couldn't swipe another card, hold another book, look into another face, google another name.

Can I get ten seconds of fucking peace?

Apparently not ... .

"Hi. I'm looking for a book."

"Where are you looking?"

"Well ..."

"I don't see you looking anywhere. You're asking me to look for it. This is a tiny store. The sections are clearly marked. It's not as if you're entering a cavernous, labyrinthine bookstore like the Strand or

Powell's, where one might be excused for seeking directions if one was incurious enough not to browse. It's a small storefront with a few hundred square feet covering the area between the front door and the back door."

The guy was about half my age. I saw myself through his eyes, and I didn't like what I saw. I had turned into one of those people I used to fear, one of those sour and angry old booksellers or record-store clerks who intimidated me as a youth.

III

My forty-ninth birthday passed without incident. I didn't bring it to anyone's attention. The lamentable occasion was acknowledged by a few friends (fewer each year, it seemed) but my age was not alluded to, as is usually the case as a man grows older … as a man grows old.

Removing a long gray hair with a toothpick from the gap around the G key in order to prevent it from slipping into the interior of the keyboard, I realized that despite it having taken me three hours to polish a short paragraph, I was going to have to throw it out.

That extra hour in bed was to blame. I had woken up, fully rested, at seven thirty, turned over on my side, and awoke again half an hour later, having only delayed and intensified the turbulent flight into grogginess. A further half hour of smothering my head in the pillow doomed the morning to a befuddled blur.

Prioritizing every morning (these "precious and guarded mornings," as Emerson called them) toward this end, when so little comes of them, seems pointless, especially when practical matters require my urgent attention; yet in the hope of finally finishing something, as much as I still have it in me, with the hope of eventually moving on to living, if I still have it in me, I press on.

It has to be more than a way to spend my days.

But I wouldn't know what else to do with my days.

This so-called "process" of pulling it apart and putting it back together could be dragged out for years. I just don't have the time anymore. In biting my tongue until the time came to tell my story, I bit off more than I could chew.

And the penalty for having left it too late, my crowning tragedy, is to never finish anything.

When one medicates, one gets too attached to *the process*: one keeps piling it on, sifting through it, and refining it—it never ends.

The only way to finish *this thing* is to stop medicating and give it a ruthless edit.

Is there any point sitting here when I don't have it in me?

And this morning I definitely didn't, I don't, have it in me.

The morning is shot.

A blur, a befuddled blur.

To move on from this simulation of industry to not trying at all. That, at least, would be some sort of progress.

It is harder to sit here doing nothing than it is to actually do something. If it came easily I probably wouldn't do it at all. Without the challenge, there wouldn't be much point. It's all about submergence, the process of working through it.

Either way, get it over with, finish it, before my so-called muse suffers the fate of all organic *process* and dries up ... before it has even blossomed. Even if it falls miserably short of the standards that I once unrealistically imagined I was capable of meeting.

Just get it over with.

The only way out of or into *this thing* is to speed *the process* up. If I write two thousand words a week, with two weeks off, that will amount to one hundred thousand words in a year.

Then give it a good old-fashioned unmedicated edit. If I rewrite a thousand words a day, that will amount to about a hundred days' work. Therefore, realistically, in a year and a half *this thing* can be done and dusted. It will never be finished unless a commitment of this kind is made. Then what? Wait for the bidding war to heat up? It doesn't matter. Just get it over with. It doesn't matter. Timeisoftheessence. Speed it up. Speed it up and strip it down.

* * *

I looked out of the window and noticed the garden gate was open, indicating that the mail might have been delivered. My three hours were not quite up, Freedom was still on, but I yielded to the lure of distraction.

There was a single yellow envelope in the mailbox. It was marked "Urgent—Legal Matter."

I opened it.

"My name is Dan Tact and I am a consumer debt attorney at Lightman, Hack & Associates. I help California residents that have been sued for unpaid debt. Public court records indicate that you are named as a defendant in a lawsuit filed by xxxxSPV 1 LLC.

"IF YOU DO NOTHING," it continued, "xxxxSPV 1 LLC may obtain a default judgment against you. If this occurs, xxxxSPV 1 LLC may have the ability to garnish your non-exempt wages, bank accounts and personal property."

This, I assumed, was the latest in a long line of empty threats. Nevertheless, I felt obliged to check the credibility of these legal implications. When Freedom turned off a few minutes later I visited the LA Court website and tapped the accompanying case number into the designated window.

There it was, my name: Sean Hangland. A summons had been issued, a collection-case complaint had been filed, the case file had been forwarded to records for filing. At the bottom of this stream of confusing information was notice of a court hearing, at the Chatsworth Courthouse—in three years' time. It sounded like more elaborate stalling.

Stirred but not shaken, I had an uneasy enough feeling to do some online research, and typed in "collections-case summons three years' time."

Seven hours later, my eyes were aching from staring at the screen. What I had learned from an entire day's intensive research at numerous online credit card debt forums was that the distant court date was a fiendish ploy designed to lull the defendant into a false sense of security while the debt-collectors went to work on them. I was being sued by a debt collection company that had bought my debt from the original credit card account for a fraction of the original sum, and soon I would be served papers. When that happened, I would have to file a written response. If I failed to file a written response and send a copy of it to the court within a month of the papers being served, the debt collectors would be entitled to file a default judgment against me, which would permit them to put a levy on my bank account and garnish my wages. The prospect of having my meager hand-to-mouth income reduced even further froze my blood.

I wouldn't even have known there was a court case against me if I hadn't been apprised of it by the office of a consumer debt attorney who was doubtless hoping I would be lost and confused enough to call them up. The debt in question, I assumed, was the one for $20,264.83 that I'd been notified about several months earlier, but I couldn't be sure of that: I had other debts. I pulled the bulging trash bag of unopened dunning letters out from under the kitchen sink and near the top of the crumpled heap retrieved the letter I'd opened and subsequently ignored a few months earlier: the plaintiff was the same xxxxSPV 1 LLC, and the attorney was the same Drago Lark, so presumably this was the debt in question.

Another thing I learned from combing through the online out-pouring of debtor misery was that although the statute of limitations on unpaid debt in California was four years, if during that time a lawsuit was taken out against one by one's creditors, the SOL was extended until the time of the court case, which also helped to explain the distant date.

Indeed, I was lost and confused.

Exhausted and unstrung, with big numbers and nightmarish scenarios threshing through my head, I decided to take a little white pill and try to sleep on it.

* * *

A short high-pitched noise kept interfering with my semislumber. I peered through the gap in the curtains. An enormous equipment truck was repeatedly backing up on the street below. Occasionally, one was rudely reminded that one lived in the entertainment capital of the world. Another movie, or perhaps a commercial—what was the difference?—was being filmed in the neighborhood. A retired cop, in uniform, sat in a folding chair on the corner. Hairy men in shorts were busily running around: gaffers, grips, engineers—proud and vital cogs in the dream machinery. All these people, all this money, all this energy was needed in order to churn out another piece of Hollywood fluff. All these movies looked the same, and even those that claimed to be different or subversive were enforcing the same values. If one was motivated by familial loyalty any kind of criminality was permissible: drug dealing, robbery, murder—no problem, providing it was for the sake of *the family*. Film was a medium that could reveal reality and unreality in all its complicated beauty, yet it was almost exclusively used as an insidious propaganda machine for cranking out the elevation of family values.

I turned over on my side and pushed the wax earplugs in deeper. What was the point of getting out of bed? As soon as I got up I'd only start chastising myself for not having risen earlier. The truck kept beeping, unnecessarily. It wasn't as if the trucks didn't already make enough noise, and the street was blocked off.

I lay there, beclouding my higher faculties to the best of my abilities, while not entirely succeeding in dispelling fears about the lawsuit. The prospect of numbed-out literary endeavor was the one thing capable of getting me out of bed in the morning, and eventually, having rendered myself wholly unfit for the task, I dragged myself to the desk and half-heartedly attempted to drag my pen across the page: serving out a sentence, from which no sentences were served.

Medication compounded the existing grogginess and weighed me down further. Through a thick fog, the lawsuit weighed heavily on my mind. The awareness that further research was required kept gnawing at me until I had to admit I was too worried about it to focus on anything else.

Much as I hated to face it—much as I had succeeded in avoiding facing it for almost five years—the fact had to be faced: after all this time *they* had caught up with me, and I had to deal with *them*.

It was a daunting proposition; paying up was out of the question. Even a settlement for half as much as I owed was way beyond my means. And if I didn't pay them: the devastating possibility of garnished wages and a frozen bank account.

As soon as Freedom clicked off, I went online, found the number of a local consumer debt attorney at random, and called it. I explained my situation to him and was surprised by how helpful he was.

"Deny you owe them anything, then start negotiations."

"But I owe them money."

"All you need to do is file a written response and challenge them. They will be forced to take you to court. The court date will be in a year's time. They won't show up. My fee is $1,500. That covers everything except the filing fee, and I might be able to get that waived."

"What if they do show up for the court case?"

"They won't."

"Hypothetically ..."

"The $1,500 covers everything, including the court case. I have won hundreds of cases like this. I can email you a contract and we can get started this afternoon."

This sounded hopeful. I called another random lawyer.

"I don't deal with debt. I'm a bankruptcy lawyer. I recommend that you file for bankruptcy. It will cost you $1,800. Your debt will then disappear. What could be simpler? You have nothing to lose. Your credit's already shot. You can start building credit up again, and in a few years you'll have good credit."

This also sounded promising. What did I care about credit anyway?

Next I contacted Lightman, Hack & Associates, the law firm that had notified me about the court case to begin with. I spoke with a lawyer named Curt Sands in Phoenix, which was their closest branch. His businesslike manner inspired confidence.

"I can handle it. I'm used to dealing with Drago Lark."

"How much should I offer them?"

"About half of what you owe them. That should satisfy them."

"What if they don't accept it?"

"They will. I settle ten cases like this a day. I charge $500 for a debt under $10,000; $1,000 for anything over $10,000."

"How soon should I act?"

"Have the papers been served yet?"

"No."

"Then you've still got plenty of time. After papers are served, you have thirty days to file a response or come to a settlement."

"How long does it take them to serve papers?"

"They might act quickly, they might take a few months, rarely any longer than that. They'll come to your door. They are supposed to hand them to you in person but if you're not home they'll often just leave them on your porch. Keep an eye on your court case online ..."

"So I don't have to act immediately?"

"Not unless you want to. I can turn it around in a couple of days. I need to call Drago Lark anyway."

This seemed very reasonable. I felt a keen sense of relief. No action could be taken against me until the papers were served; that hadn't happened yet and might take a few months. There was plenty of time to consider these options and raise the money.

Most importantly, I could return to my work.

* * *

The buzzing, the droning, the surging of traffic, the sizzling tinnitus, the shakiness and blurriness.

I sat down, washed down a little yellow pill, and waited for the discomfort to subside. The gentle numbing warmth slowly enfolded me, smoothing out the creaking and the creases; the tinnitus leveled out, and once again I found myself, incapable of losing myself, in a state unfit for discharging what I stubbornly, unrealistically and unconvincingly, still clung to the notion of being my duty—weighed down by the forces that were supposed to raise me, sinking into a lyre-back chair amid the flickerings and trillings of a summer morning.

After three and a half hours, a few sentences were squeezed out like rancid dregs from an almost empty bottle, long past its expiration date.

Then I stopped for lunch.

I can't go on not going on like this.

This morning routine isn't working out. I awake groggy, having received either too much or too little sleep, or a combination of the two—going to bed late, waking up early and lying in bed too long: a combination guaranteed to turn the morning into a bedraggled blur.

In direct contrast to Rimbaud's "deliberate derangement of the senses," I had engaged in a willful beclouding of the senses, using sleep as a narcotic, the cheapest drug on the market, and compounding it with a low-level "creative tool"—the efficacy of which had diminished, on account of never taking breaks from it.

I sit down to sink in a haze of abstraction out of which, occasionally, a lucid thought might emerge. Weighed down by medication and cranked by caffeine, a stifling sense of urgency is surrendered to. An urgency, moreover, that is misplaced, in that I should be applying it to resolving my debt situation.

Dragging, draining. It's a struggle to strike the keys, a struggle to get the words down, a struggle to keep my eyes open. This stuff sets up a wall that has to be worked through, and by the time I'm emerging from it my circadian rhythm dictates that it's lunchtime.

Afternoons, surely, would be more conducive to the execution of this ill-considered venture, at which time the medication won't exacerbate the grogginess as it does all too often in the mornings— and mornings can be dedicated to dealing with the debt problem; therefore, I'll be satisfied that I've put in the necessary time and be able to write with a clear conscience in the afternoons, with tea as a soothing alternative to nerve-jangling coffee.

An early lunch and a start no later than 2 p.m. should ensure that the required time is put in before going down to the store three early evenings a week, although my afternoon bath will have to be forfeited.

* * *

A steady silence pulsated in the air. A train whistled in the distance (the nearest railroad tracks were at least a mile away, but still, pleasingly, one could hear the trains, through all the other noise).

I marveled at the foamy atolls, peninsulas and archipelagos swaying and shifting in the water, much as I must have done during my almost completely forgotten childhood.

The overdue and overwrought first novel by a blossoming fifty-year-old talent: Who would be snapping that up? It was already an act of great treachery and narcissism. If it ended up being self-published, it would look petty and desperate; if it was published by a major press, it would look less petty and desperate. The only way to validate *this thing* was to somehow get it published by a reputable imprint. I should take Jackson up on his offer to put me in touch with his agent.

I sipped a scotch and soda (my rotting teeth couldn't handle the sugar content in the Presbyterians anymore) and placed the glass back on the floor beside a copy of Barbara Pym's *Jane and Prudence*. I looked down at the soap bubbles dissolving in my pubic hair and it occurred to me that it was something of an achievement even to have gotten as far as I had with *this thing*. Medication certainly provided precious fuel for false hope, but I had to possess some belief in the work itself to have proceeded as far as I had.

Toward what futile end, I knew not.

I would like to have continued lying there for another hour but the dying strains of Vaughan Williams signaled that it was time to get out and attend to the unfortunate business of earning a living.

* * *

There was an atmosphere of more than usual giddy turmoil behind the café counter as I walked in. The café girls and some of their friends were grouped around a cell phone, gasping and giggling.

"What the fuck's going on around here?" I was moved to ask as I clocked in.

"Oh my God!" one of them shrieked.

"Bob McGilt came in," another of them gushed.

"Is he still here?" I asked, suppressing rapidly rising panic.

"He left an hour ago."

"And you're still this excited?" I said, somewhat relieved.

The source of their pleasure was a photograph of one of the girls with McGilt's arm around her. It was now posted on social media and was receiving a lot of likes and comments: "OMG," "So jealous," "I would of died," etc.

"How was he?" I asked.

"He was *so* nice," one of them said. "I served him a cup of tea. My hands were shaking."

"Of course he was nice. Why wouldn't he be? People always act surprised when a celebrity isn't an asshole. It's not as if they have to struggle with much adversity in order to be nice. They enjoy wealth, fame, adulation; they're living out the dreams of lesser mortals, so why wouldn't they be nice? They get much more credit than they deserve for exhibiting the most ordinary virtues."

"They're not always nice," one of them said.

"Who pissed in your cornflakes?" said another.

"Do I sense a tiny amount of jealousy?" said another.

I couldn't very well broadcast that McGilt and I had once been friends. It would sound like utterly implausible name-dropping, and it would give my age away. These young people probably thought I was closer to forty than fifty.

"Maybe he'll become a regular," I said, shuddering at the prospect, and walked across the crowded room to my post behind the book counter.

"Did you hear …?" said my colleague and contemporary, the mousy Julie, as we switched shifts. Nobody was immune to the charm of such a mythical figure, for long the object of distant adoration, materializing before their eyes.

"Yes, I heard," I said.

I had just missed him. Next time, I might not be so lucky. He'd only been living locally for about a month and he'd already visited the store. If he'd been here once, he'd be back, and I was by no means convinced that I would have the strength to resist exhibiting a certain bitter, cringing animosity if such an encounter was to occur in my harassed and beleaguered work environment. It would be difficult, nigh impossible, to strike the right tone if a mutual acknowledgment of our contrasting fortunes was forced into stark relief. It was a potential situation that I felt incapable of handling graciously.

* * *

The fact that I wasn't facing the facts had to be faced.

Every few days I'd call a lawyer or two and discuss my case with them. In this manner, by having the details repeatedly, and sometimes contradictorily, impressed upon me, I formed an understanding of the position I was in and what I could do about it:

"Better to lowball, then they'll make a counteroffer." ... "Deny you owe them anything. Then start negotiations." ... "You could dispute the validity of the debt and find loopholes." ... "Explanation of financial hardship. Forget it." ... "Don't assume that while you're waiting to hear back from them they won't file a default judgment." ... "Be careful about making verbal admissions over the phone. Don't implicate yourself in any way." ... "Filing a lawsuit extends the statute of limitations. Once litigation is filed, the SOL stops. Which means that once four years elapse, the debt can still be collected on." ... "They can't freeze your bank account until a judgment is made." ... "Offer half, then review the settlement, we request financials, wait for their counter." ... "Don't make partial payments, it's better to pay a lump sum." ... "Before paying, we get all the details in writing, always get everything in writing." ... "If there's no money in your bank account, they'll garnish your wages. They may garnish your wages anyway. You're better off making a settlement. I charge $1,200 for the initial engagement fee, no additional charges after the settlement is approved."

The legalese was confusing and worrying: I didn't know what they were talking about much of the time, but some facts emerged. It wasn't worth disputing the debt. Out of the $20,000 I owed, the debt-collection company would be satisfied with half of that sum. I should open negotiations by proposing a payment of $4,000 or $5,000 and they would settle for $10,000. It would be a quick and easy job for an experienced consumer debt lawyer to make a settlement with a debt collector; it was something they did every day and for which they charged outrageous fees.

If I contacted Drago Lark directly I could dispense with the services of a lawyer and save at least a $1,000. I would have to steel myself for that.

All this debt settling was going to get me deeper into debt, if I was lucky enough to be able to secure a loan from anybody. I didn't have any more money in my bank account than was needed to cover the following month's expenses. How could I raise $10,000 in a couple of weeks? Kickstart a GoFundMe? Out of the question. I couldn't bring myself to make a public display of my financial embarrassment.

Securing a loan appeared to be the only practical solution. But from whom? Jackson bragged about his newly acquired wealth but I felt uneasy asking him for a beer, let alone a substantial loan. The nature of our friendship was such that I couldn't confide in him about my situation, and this was the case with all of my prosperous friends. It is considered the height of bad taste to discuss one's financial woes with people who are in a position to help. They find it boring. Talk about things they can relate to, like servant problems; pretend to take an interest in their real estate ventures. The only people one feels at all comfortable discussing one's material difficulties with are those similar unfortunates who are in no position to help.

Paying in installments was another possibility, but as the lawyers had told me, if one chose to do that, the statute of limitations would remain open, which would involve further complications.

I thought I was going to come to a decision and the only thing I decided upon was not to decide upon anything yet.

* * *

"You know what's a real pain in the ass? All this 'he said / she said' crap, having to sprinkle these asides throughout the dialogue. If I was describing this scene I'd say 'He smiled patronizingly,' or 'He raised his glass.' I feel obliged to do it, but it doesn't come naturally."

The boy shrugged. "It sets the mood," he said.

"I see. Well, I'm not cut out for it. Another thing: in books and movies there's this unnatural practice of always adding one's interlocutor's name to the end of every sentence of dialogue. It sounds artificial."

The boy laughed sardonically. "Writing is not a natural act, Sean."

"I never address people by their names, and I don't like it when I'm addressed by my name. It reminds me of being reprimanded at school or by my parents."

The boy grinned. "It's supposed to establish character, Sean. It creates familiarity."

"Selection of detail, fixing of emphasis, anecdotal specificity, it's all beyond me," I moaned, the liquor warming my words. "I lack all the qualities deemed necessary to write a novel."

"It's not lack of ability, it's lack of interest," said the boy, as he tossed down his drink. "If something doesn't come naturally, that doesn't mean you can't do it."

"It's all right for you. You spent four years at college, you learned all the tricks."

The boy slowly nodded. "Three years that completely turned me off the idea of writing. Will you come outside with me, I'd like to smoke."

We covered our glasses with napkins and walked through the lobby to the front of the Sterling hotel that housed the Secret Bar.

It was getting dark. A dog walker curbed his German shepherd, cooing encouragement as the senselessly huge beast squeezed out a turd on a patch of sod beneath a dead tree. A floundering wino hectored a neanderthal bouncer outside a nightclub on the opposite side of the street. Two stiletto-heeled girls, betraying the sacred mysteries of the flesh, noisily clacked their way along the temporary pedestrian wooden walkway under the adjoining building. Ubers disgorged pleasure-seekers. A fire truck screamed by and I covered my ears.

"I'm incapable of description," I said to the boy. "In order to describe something one has to care about it, and I don't care enough anymore. As John Updike said, 'Description expresses love.' If one doesn't care enough, then one's powers of description go to waste."

"You could do it if you wanted," said the boy, taking a deep drag of his cigarette.

"I don't want to, and I can't," I said with a fierce sigh.

"Why don't you ever use in medias res?" he asked in a suspicious, almost accusatory manner.

"What's that?"

"You know, you begin a section in the present, then you track back and bring the story up to date," he said, looking surprised.

"I'm not exactly a storyteller. I don't go in for these newfangled techniques."

"There's nothing modern about it. Milton used it in *Paradise Lost*," he said snappishly.

"I'm familiar with the practice," I admitted. "I just never saw much point to it."

"It brings the reader straight into the action. There are advantages to that. Just give it a try," said the boy, flicking his cigarette butt onto the pavement and crushing it beneath his boots.

A girl sitting in a booth with a male companion looked up at the boy as we reentered the bar.

"Well, what did you think of it?" I said as we sat back down, getting to the point I'd been building up to all evening, which the boy seemed to be avoiding: his appraisal of the last extract I'd sent him, in which I recounted a typical night spent with Summer, the woman with whom I had a biweekly arrangement. It was a sketch I'd written a few years earlier and was considering including in the book out of convenience and in order to satisfy the boy's—and therefore the potential reader's—demands for a sex scene. "Does it look too tacked on?"

The boy paused, and with his gaze fixed steadily on me, said, "Yes, maybe it does a bit."

"Enough with these empty qualifiers. 'A bit' means 'a lot.' It looks tacked on, doesn't it?"

He smiled understandingly: "You could still use it. But it *will* be considered sexist."

"If anybody even considers it."

"There's not much point mentioning your *biweekly* arrangement if you're not going to include the sex scenes with her."

"I know. But at least the reader will know that the protagonist has sex sometimes."

He grinned sympathetically: "All that stuff about telling her what to wear isn't going to do the *protagonist* any favors."

"You're right, and it's too drawn from real life. I've thrown too many people under the bus already, present company included. I want to avoid any more of that."

The boy nodded his head in agreement. "Why not just develop the romance with Mona?"

"It sounds like a lot of work, all that buildup. Can I just skip the courtship and cut straight to the act of love? Fuck it, that's what I'm going to do. "

"It's up to you," said the boy, draining his glass and setting it aside. "If you think you can make it work."

* * *

The building shook and car alarms wailed, but it wasn't the long-awaited earthquake, just another low-flying police helicopter rumbling overhead. Tinnitus hissed through the steady murmur of traffic, distant hammering, and other city sounds.

Looking out of the window, I noticed that my neighbor's car was parked on the wrong side of the road on a street-sweeping day. I considered notifying him about this in order to spare him an expensive ticket, and decided against it.

"When my horse is running good, I don't stop to give him sugar," stated William Faulkner. I washed down a little yellow pill, giving my horse sugar before the starting gate even opened.

After an hour of waiting to feel something—waiting to feel nothing—I wasn't feeling anything: no seepage of mild euphoria, however fleeting, no effect. Alert to any hint of sensation, all I felt was frustration at feeling nothing: the wrong kind of nothing.

This stuff didn't work so well on a full stomach. I already knew that. This afternoon routine wasn't going to work out. Nothing was working out.

Through the window, I watched with pleasure as a parking attendant slapped a ticket on the windshield of my neighbor's car.

I still hadn't started practicing the second part of Laurence Sterne's "once drunk" / "once sober" dictum: I had only been writing *and* editing when medicated; I quailed at the prospect of a stone-cold assessment of my endeavors. Since the afternoon anodyne was kicking in so subtly I combed through some recent passages with a clearer eye than usual and wondered if my reluctance to view *this thing* with a steady, sober gaze was an indication of its lack of quality.

Did it suffer from dreaded first-novel syndrome? First-time novelists threw in everything they had stored up until that point, which was usually thirty-odd years, but in this case was fifty—a lot of buildup to what might well amount to middle-aged juvenilia; metafiction of the lowest order; stillborn prose whelped in a confusion of tinnitus and hesitation. Weren't first novels always deeply flawed? Then again, *Journey to the End of the Night, City of Night,* and *The Night of the Hunter* were all pretty good.

But in the same way that I wasn't sure if I was seeing what others saw when I looked at my reflection in the mirror, when I re-read my work I couldn't be certain if what I was looking at was only the idealized version of what I was hoping to produce—that which vividly existed in my head but not on paper.

There was no proof that it possessed any life beyond that insular sphere. What was alive to me could be dead on the page to someone else. Success lay in redressing the imbalance between how it existed in my mind and how it would appear to others.

It would have helped if I could have stopped right there and given it a good unmedicated edit, but I couldn't bring myself to, and so ...

* * *

I woke up and went back to sleep, using superfluous slumber to smother the kind of disquieting concerns that strike before one has had the opportunity to numb oneself out: the concern that the Drago Lark debt was only one of many debts that I had accumulated when I defaulted on all my credit cards four years earlier; the concern that if (as they surely would, as that was the way they worked) these other creditors discovered that I was negotiating with Drago Lark, they would then make their own attempts to collect from me; the concern that I had no idea where I stood with any of these creditors, having never opened their mail; and the concern—the fact—that these companies must sometimes collect on their debts, because if they didn't they wouldn't be able to remain in business.

Did I have anything left that I could sell? I had already let go of innumerable priceless artifacts—material manifestations of love and knowledge—that had been reluctantly parted with in times of financial strife: blues 78s, punk 45s, rare books, comics and fanzines. There were still some treasures left, but there was a widening disparity between sentimental value and what they would fetch on eBay. It would take too long, involve too much work, and there was no guarantee of making any sales. The only solution was to borrow.

By the time I finally got out of bed, having resolved the night before to stop writing for a while and focus on paying my debts, these concerns were smothered in bleariness. Taking into consideration that it could still be weeks, perhaps even months, before the paper servers came knocking, there was no reason not to continue with my work. There was no need to respond to Drago Lark until papers were served. The lawyer, Sands, had been quite clear about that.

With this in mind, I sat down to write, two hours later than usual. It was impossible to enter a poetic state of grace while in this constant state of ragged nervous vulnerability, but in order to medicate I had to engage in at least some pretense of application. Now more than ever, the suspension of worldly cares was what I craved. Whether anything came out of it was another matter. If deprived of this enabling atmosphere, more than likely, nothing would get done at all. Such was the symbiotic relationship between the habit of writing and the habit of medicating that they had become inseparable: if I didn't write, I didn't medicate, and I wanted to medicate, so I wrote.

Sometimes it takes a while to get started. Sometimes I don't get started. Sometimes, too frequently, I find, it's just not there. Sometimes other things need to be straightened out before I can move on. Sometimes, wrung out from equivocation, I don't move on. Some days it hardly seems worth trying.

This was one of those days.

I was in no fit state to discharge my duty, yet I sat there, too distracted and despondent to craft a felicitous sentence, or to see much point in doing so, but not knowing what else to do. Another cup of coffee was only made in the interest of wasting the time it took to prepare it.

What if this unfortunate need to externalize myself actually bore fruit and it turned out that nobody was interested in the lavishly selfless gesture? Such an outcome was certainly within the realm of possibility.

Then this self-generated need will all have been for naught, beginning and ending with myself, not spurred by any momentum grounded in other people's reality.

Just get it over with, stick a fork in it, then stop writing and move on to doing something worthwhile with my time—something that may be of use to others. Give it one last shot.

There was only one solution: publish a book with an abrasively catchy title, print it in bold letters, with a striking two-color scheme (red on black is a reliable perennial, and purple on black is currently very popular), and somehow get it out there. There's no place for subtlety in this day and age. About 180 pages ought to do it. People want short novels these days: they find them more aesthetically pleasing as objects.

A shorter novel is twice as good. Just write a short book and slap a sharp, declarative title on it. Never mind the contents, it's merely a matter of coming up with a memorable title, a grabber.

Boredom, Failure, Frustration, Contempt: all the best one-word titles had been used. It would be better to take the *I Love Dick* / *I Hate the Internet* approach. Those titles were strokes of genius that accentuated and came close to eclipsing the contents. "Death," "hate" and "fuck" were all useful words, and the personal pronoun was imperative. But "I Love" and "I Hate" were now both attached to prominent contemporary works—both, moreover, by local authors.

Or simply place the word "American" or "The Last" in front of any other word, and you have what is considered a credible title.

Forget it.

It had to be something that would provoke and seduce the potential reader, something so good that it might redeem any weaknesses in the work itself.

* * *

It's no good to lie around worrying. It's better to get up and worry.

The plan, as usual, was to spend the morning in the service of truth and beauty, but I was still rattled from the night before, when I had to set up a reading at the bookstore. It involved connecting the PA system and arranging all the chairs on the patio, only to then be told by my boss (formerly my colleague, prior to that my friend) to straighten them out—and then I had to deal with the demands of the author.

"Are you going to introduce me?"

"We don't do that here."

This wasn't the response she had hoped for.

I looked across the patio at the rows of empty chairs I had begrudgingly lined up. Only two of them were occupied.

"Most bookstores do that. I've been on a book tour for two weeks," she said, as if I should know who she was.

"Your publisher paid for this tour?" I asked, politely suppressing my incredulity.

She replied in an affronted affirmative, as if it would be absurd to suggest otherwise.

"I've never been asked to perform such a service before," I said, softening my voice as I often do when dealing with difficult creative types. "But if you want me to, I will. You'll have to tell me what to say."

"No, that's all right," she said, in a manner that indicated it wasn't all right at all, and turned away from me to greet a new arrival, a friend of hers.

I walked back into the store. A burly man was standing around, sporting a Fall T-shirt, on which the face of Mark E. Smith rippled like a fun house mirror over the folds of the man's potbelly. In order to wash away the queasiness left by the bossy author on the patio, I complimented him on his taste.

"I have recordings of every Fall show before 1988," he stated, loudly.

"I saw them that year, saw them earlier too, on the *Nation's Saving Grace* tour," I said.

"Wow!" He was impressed, overly impressed, and he reeked of alcohol.

"It didn't mean much to me at the time," I said. "I was too young to appreciate it."

"He saw the Fall in 1985!" he yelled out to a friend of his, who was emerging from the restroom.

"Wow," said his friend.

"I do other things too," I said.

"That's pretty cool," he said. "I didn't see them until the early nineties."

"It's not the most notable quality I possess," I said. "It's not what I really want to be remembered for."

But maybe it was my most notable quality. Maybe the fact that I saw the Fall in 1985 was going to be inscribed on my tombstone. What else had I done other than devour other people's work—entire oeuvres, entire genres?

Eager to change the subject from one that revealed my age (how quickly adolescence had turned into obsolescence) to young acquaintances within earshot, I returned to the topic of the Fall archives:

"Every show, that's impossible. Maybe every show that was recorded."

"It's pretty comprehensive," he said. "I'll send you a list."

"Why d'you cut them off in 1988?" I asked. "To this day, there's not a single record that doesn't have at least a few great tracks on it." To prove this point, I played "Noel's Chemical Effluence," a neglected tour de force, while he stretched out on the long bench in front of the philosophy section, appearing to be lost in deep musical contemplation.

A copy of *I Hate Milk* was slapped down on the counter in front of me, the words staring impudently up at me in bold black lettering, with the author's name, as if of incidental interest, in much smaller print underneath. Another young girl in a hat that didn't suit her was standing in front of me. She slid open the slot on the back of her cell phone and removed a credit card from it.

"These Fall archives are a fantastic distraction in my battle with cancer," said the drunken Fall fan, returning to the counter. "They should bottle this stuff and use it instead of chemo." After a while he tired of talking at me, went out on to the patio, and started shouting at the reader.

After that nonevent, I dismantled the PA system and returned all the chairs to their usual places around the tables, while the author glared at me. By the end of her reading she had managed to command an audience of nine people.

And now I had been sitting here for two and a half hours, in the shade of many wanings, indelibly etherized, in a medicated and musical haze that was meant to be soothingly conducive to cerebral exertions, but too distracted about debt and work-related aggravations to focus on my so-called task. My nerves jangled, my mood jaded, the morning almost over.

When the anxiety subsided, I found that I missed it and wanted it back.

* * *

The need to make water became unbearable. I groped through the familiar darkness to the bathroom and released a fitful stream of urine into the sink. The spasmodic nature of the flow reminded me of something I once read about cancer. I returned to bed and, unable to fall back to sleep, opened my notebook and read a few recent entries pertaining to *the work*: "Postscript: summary, elegiac speech" … "Change names of King Edward and Clifton's" … "Avoid, as much as possible, sentences beginning with 'I'" … "Female interest as indicator of sensitivity" … "Candidates for linguistic cleansing."

Taken unawares at four in the morning, I realized with more clarity than usual that this exercise had been a massive, misguided waste of time, a clear-cut case of too much, too late, and that the medication was merely a means of blinding myself to the ultimate futility of the act. I also realized, having already put so much time into it, that it was too late to stop.

I bit off a fragment of a little white pill and resolved to cut down on medicating as I drifted back to sleep.

* * *

Upon entering the air-conditioned comfort of the store on a murderously hot Sunday morning, I had to step around an unkempt individual who was sitting on the floor, frantically rummaging through a pile of unwashed clothing and trinkets that were spilling out of a grubby duffel bag. When I returned from the café, having made myself a coffee and a bowl of granola, I recognized this haggard, scruffy individual as Seth, a likable musician and recovering addict, one of the Narcotics Anonymous crowd, who had been frequenting the store since it opened. Upon seeing me he got up from the floor.

"Hey, Sean, I've lost my phone. Can I borrow yours?"

He was barely recognizable, his face caved in at the cheeks and temples, skin yellow and shiny; he had assumed a different shape, with his bones coming to the surface. Just a few months ago, he had been clean and sharp; now he was physically ravaged and mentally unsound. Some people weren't survivors; even some survivors weren't survivors.

He yawped incoherently into the store telephone: "Hey, man, I need a cab to pick me up at Mute Books and take me downtown ... No, man, you don't understand"—the garbled instructions he issued were something no cab-company operator could possibly comprehend.

"You have the best job in the world, Sean," he said as he handed back the phone.

It occurred to me that he might be onto something. It also occurred to me that I was glad I didn't know him better, because if I did his predicament would sadden me more.

"Can you call me a Lyft, Sean? I'll give you five dollars."

"OK," I said, as I sterilized the telephone with hand sanitizer.

I pried open an incoming box and inhaled the familiar fragrance of fresh books. It contained twenty copies of Emgona Merage's new novel, which would sell out in no time, more copies of *White Fragility*, and a five-hundred-page biography of Morton Feldman, which I looked forward to skimming.

I dreaded the return of McGilt. I watched the door.

An unpardonable-looking individual stood on the other side of the counter.

"Tantra?" he said, breathlessly.

"What?"

"Tantra?"

"What?"

"Tantra?"

"One more time."

"Tantra?"

"What about it?"

"Do you have any books on Tantra?"

"Over there. Buddhism or gender—tough call."

I spat my granola out in frustration on the computer screen. Not one minute passed without some unreasonable demand being made upon me. I felt like a literary traffic officer, giving directions, pointing this way and that, and I was starting to say out loud the things I used to only mutter under my breath.

"I resent Laura Sweeney for wasting my time," said an avid young reader who had stopped at the counter, an easygoing sort, with whom I conversed on occasion.

"She would waste the time of any discriminating reader. She needs to be slapped around," I said.

A sudden silence, both awkward and pregnant, descended over our formerly warm conversation.

"Only if she wants it," he said solemnly, and walked away.

Fuck him if he can't take a joke, I said to myself, while worrying that I would now be branded as an old-fashioned sexist. Some subjects were now strictly off the table as light banter, especially with sensitive acquaintances of the newly tagged "woke" persuasion. If one considered anything fair game for a cheap laugh, one could easily be labeled as some sort of inexcusableist. It was reactive, of course, and it helped reinforce divisiveness in an increasingly inflexible climate.

I reached into my pocket and took out a yellow pill. It was a departure from my policy of only using medication as a creative tool, and a waste of the necessary stimulus to the composition of immortal works, but Sundays had become unbearable; the unending demands placed upon me were guaranteed to shatter any peace of mind I might start the day with, and the pill was there, in my pocket, so I washed it down. The barely perceptible glow would warm my heart for a few hours, and customers and acquaintances would get to experience me being in a cheerful, lighthearted mood.

"What are you looking so fucking happy about?" I asked a young regular, half my age, as he strolled in.

"Nothing," he said, grinning widely, as I again questioned the source of his well-being.

"You have the look of a well-fellated man," I remarked.

He grinned even more widely.

"Stop being so coy."

"I just want to enjoy it," he said.

It was remarkable to consider the beneficial effect that a night of love could have upon one's state of mind, and for me, it had been too long. The beneficial effect of the yellow pill was also something to marvel at, but with that there would be no afterglow. I told myself to enjoy it while it lasted, knowing that the plunge into rancorous nausea was inevitable.

I returned to the crossword. For about two hours nothing bothered me much, and I looked upon my fellow man with relative calmness, but by two o'clock the warm glow had worn off and the siren call of irritation had become irresistible, coinciding with the deluge of customers.

The tide of human debris washed through the door, past the counter: the coffeehouse playboys, the urban backpackers, the aspiring screenplay hacks, the arrogant breeders, the amateur fatalists, the beard strokers, the nose pickers, the three-legged-ceramic-pig figurine purchasers, the restroom seekers, the elitists in short-pants. It was, as usual, an unseasonably hot day and the shorts-and-sandals crowd were out in great number. Few people could survive warm weather with beauty or dignity intact, and most didn't bother trying, or see any point in trying.

I walked out into the yellow afternoon of ear-piercing sirens and crashing waves of traffic and placed some dusty, grangerized, unwanted books on the dollar cart. I was standing on the sidewalk, trying not to take it all in, when a lonely and unhinged regular, one of the worst, seized the opportunity to further scramble my mind.

"I was coming in to see you," said the pest.

Fuck.

"It's a beautiful day," he said.

"Yes, and there are a lot of ugly people out here to testify to that fact."

"I'm sleeping in my car but it's all right," he said.

"I came outside to get away from people," I said.

This statement made no impression on him whatsoever.

"It's a tragic year for music. Are you sad about [*insert name of most recently deceased popular musician here*]?" the pest continued.

"No."

"But it's sad, isn't it?"

"All right, it's sad," I said as I scooped a splayed copy of Trollope's *Can You Forgive Her?* from the sidewalk. "What do you want me to do about it? I never met him, I never listened to him, voluntarily. I never saw him perform. I have no special memories or associations. I respect his contribution but enough people are grieving already. There would be no room for my grief, even if I had any to offer. It's better to save it for somebody who isn't getting their fair share. [*Insert name of most recently deceased obscure musician here*] died yesterday."

"Who's that?"

"Never mind. It's only going to get worse. They've reached that age. We've reached that age."

Yes, time was precious and it was running out. Stars were dropping like flies, and I was drifting into the rarefied altitude from which they fell.

"Not all of them. [*Insert name of another recently deceased musician*] wasn't that old. You're not much younger than him," said the pest.

"What are you talking about? He was ten years older than me."

"How old are you then?"

"Forty-eight."

"You're the same age as me then."

"I would have thought you were older than me," I said, horrified that this decrepit specimen was the same age as me. Gray hairs sprouted from his wattled neck. Watching people deteriorate, that's what I was doing here—that and watching other people make progress, which was worse.

I urged the pest to view our respective reflections in the window of a parked car.

"Well, you've got your hair," he conceded.

"It's not just that. Look at my face, it retains a youthful vitality. You look worn out."

A woman walked out of the store. "Are you the worker?" she asked.

"I've never really thought of myself as being 'the worker' exactly but …"

"Well, there's a leak in the restroom."

"Good to know. Thanks."

The pest followed me inside.

"This is cool," he said. "Is this Howlin' Wolf?"

"No, it's Lightnin' Hopkins. It doesn't sound anything like Howlin' Wolf."

"Well, I don't know."

"Well, what's the point of trying to guess about something you don't know anything about? On the off chance you'll get it right and be applauded for it?"

"My father took me to see B. B. King when I was ten years old," said the pest.

Static, static, static ... *I don't care, I don't care, I don't care.*

To the smug indifference of its owner, a little dog was yapping. I resisted the urge to kick it, although I imagined doing so in some detail as I stepped around it.

"Where's the fucking mop?" I said to the boy as I barged into the kitchen.

"Fucked if I know," said the boy, who was up to his elbows in the kitchen sink.

"By the way, what did you think of my attempt at in media res?"

"It was good," he said,

"Thanks. But it doesn't really work, does it? It looks jarring considering that I hadn't used it before."

"You could rework some other passages that way."

"No way."

There was water, mixed with urine, all over the restroom floor. Since a mop couldn't be found, I attempted to sop it up with piles of wadded napkins while being careful not to soil my trousers.

Returning from the restroom to the counter, I noticed a sad-eyed young beauty sitting at a table. I had been curious about her for a while and wanted to talk to her, but she seemed distant and shy.

A harried-looking woman was standing at the counter, waiting to purchase a candle and a children's book.

"I'd like them both wrapped," she said.

"We're out of paper."

"What's that behind you?" she said, pointing at the giant roll of brown wrapping paper on the floor behind me. I'd forgotten to hide it.

A jittery young man with a tattooed face and madly swirling eyes elbowed up to the counter. "Hey, man. Let me use the phone, will ya?"

I couldn't be bothered to argue with him and handed it over. "Make it quick," I said.

"I will, man."

At this moment, the dreamy-eyed beauty approached the counter. After many months of gazing longingly at her, she finally looked at me and quietly asked: "Do you know what Oulipo is?"

Finally, a perfect opportunity to engage with her and impress her, but the harried woman was impatiently filling out a greeting card on the counter while I was gift wrapping, and the restroom was flooding.

Nevertheless—always the less—I attempted to answer: "It's a movement that originated in France; writers set up linguistic challenges for themselves. Perec, for example, wrote an entire novel without using the letter *c*, or was it *e*? I can't remember." I started spluttering—"google it."

"I'll do that," she said, looking slightly embarrassed on my behalf.

"Things were starting to look up for me until I got stabbed …" The speed-addled lout stood at the counter, spouting into the phone. The harried woman and a gleaming-pated man bearing an expensive photography book looked on with undisguised abhorrence. As I wrapped the candle, I gestured at the lout to move out of the way so that purchases could be made.

"Listen, buddy, come to California and I'll take care of ya …"

"OK, that's enough," I snapped. With grimy tattooed fingers he handed back the phone and wandered off with the attitude of somebody who was used to being asked to leave public places. I carefully placed the phone back on the counter.

"You don't have to wrap the book," said the harried woman. "Just put it in a bag. I'm in a hurry."

"How's it going?" asked an ex-employee as she walked in. I hadn't seen her since she quit over a year ago.

"I don't know, I can't answer that question." Fuck. Take a deep breath. It's not her fault. I was glad that her art career had taken off; I had always liked her anthropomorphized cat paintings. Bring it down a few notches.

"Do you find it depressing or comforting that I'm still working here?"

She hesitated for a moment. "Both," she replied.

I returned to the restroom to finish the cleanup process. By the time I had finished, the sad-eyed beauty had disappeared, as had the pest. There was a cluster of customers in front of the counter. Out of this unsettling crowd a sour-faced septuagenarian emerged to jostle for my attention. He fished a greeting card out of a small brown paper bag: "I bought this card here yesterday; it doesn't have a message on it," he whined.

"What?"

"It's supposed to have a message on it. It says so on the wrapper." He showed me a receipt for $4.82.

"Take another one then."

"That's rude," he immediately shot back.

"What's rude about it?"

"It's the way you said it."

I wasn't in the mood to swallow my pride; I had already swallowed so much of it that I felt like throwing up.

"Give me a yelping then."

"I'm active on Yelp."

"You seem like you would be."

"Don't worry, you'll be hearing from me."

"Excellent."

I walked off, realizing that somebody who was prepared to go to the trouble of returning to a store in order to exchange a $4.50 greeting card wouldn't hesitate to take the time to express his grievances to the powers that be, and that those powers that be would soon be contacting me, with smoke coming out of their ears.

An hour later, the phone rang for about the hundredth time that day. I recognized Gilbert's number.

"Mute Books. How can I provide you with excellent service this afternoon?" I answered with mock-obsequious breeziness.

"You know why I'm calling, don't you?" said Gilbert. It sounded as if a confession were being painfully extracted from him.

"No," I said.

"I just received an email from an unsatisfied customer." If he didn't release the apoplectic rage that was clearly roiling just below the surface of his unconvincingly calm exterior, he might do himself a serious injury. "How much more of this shit are we supposed to take?!" he said, raising his voice.

"I'm sorry," I said. "I don't know what his problem was. I told him to just exchange the card. I knock myself out being polite and they're still not satisfied. You can't win …"

"You told him to yelp you."

"Not exactly," I said.

"The readers complained last Monday," said Gilbert, sternly.

I had seen that one coming. "I did nothing."

"Exactly," said Gilbert. "You did nothing."

"She acted like royalty. I offered to give her an introduction. I even ejected a customer to appease her," I lied.

"I'm going to send you the email."

A few minutes later, the email arrived, in which the wounded party complained about discrimination against old people (that was rich) and described our interaction as "the second worst experience I've had in a store in the last 30 years." (I should like to know what the other one was and why I didn't eclipse it. I want to be an all-timer.)

A young man appeared at the counter. "I was wondering if you could recommend something …," he started to say.

"I don't have the energy," I said, cutting him off with a ferocity that belied that claim. "Do I have to read the fucking books for you too? It's not as if I'm going to be compensated for the service. You throw two dollars at a bartender for popping the top off a beer bottle. I give you a book that's going to change your life, and what do I get in return? Nothing."

"Maybe you're in the wrong profession," said the young man, smiling wryly beneath a dense profusion of facial hair.

"No shit," I said.

"I'll give you a $2.00 tip," he said amiably, as he walked off to join his girlfriend.

"What d'you need?" I said, shamefacedly backtracking.

This young man's impressive self-possession in the face of my flailing discomposure had a steadying effect. He ended up with a copy of *Ask the Dust*, a safe choice for a fledgling reader, and I declined the tip.

"Did you hear?" said the boy as he handed me a beer.

"What?"

[*insert name of another recently deceased popular musician here*] is dead."

"You're kidding?"

Why, when news of death was delivered, even when it seemed inevitable, did I always ask the bearer of sad tidings if they were kidding?

"This afternoon," he said.

The news must have broken in the last half hour: I hadn't been online in that long.

"He was eighty years old," I said, "and he just put a new record out."

"There's hope for you yet," said the boy.

I went back online and scrolled down the ephemeral archives of self-congratulatory desperation on Facebook. It was such a dependable source of irritation, how could one resist it, especially when one's defenses were down?

This timely death was the latest in the ongoing roll call of the deceased, usually musicians, whose passing inspired a mawkish chain reaction of YouTube links that nobody listened to, accompanied by despairing comments about how awful this particular year had been in its disproportionate claiming of beloved celebrity lives.

It would be great if he had lived forever, but the man was eighty years old. Judging by the response on social media, one would think he had been scythed down in his prime rather than having lived a long, lucky, healthy, prosperous and creative life, with immortality guaranteed.

Death was riding every day. As the '60s and '70s generation reached their sixties and seventies, naturally, they were checking out in greater numbers. The time of timely death had come and they were going to keep dropping. People who were raised on pop culture (a comparatively recent phenomenon) were not used to the artists they grew up with dying. But sadly, not shockingly, this was how it was going to be from now on. Nobody was going to buck the trend of mortality, and the unsurpassable '60s/'70s rock-and-roll era that was hardwired into the collective psyche would pass from memory into myth as those who created it and those who bore witness to it passed on; and one day there would be no remaining living links (just as there were no longer any living links with '20s and '30s blues or jazz).

Doomscrolling with a hate boner, onward and downward through the stream of loneliness, vanity, smugness and desperation—another tired political rant, another couple, another sunset, another dog, another photograph of a couple at sunset with their dog—I came across a photograph of Mitchell with his lady friend that served as his latest profile pic. Their eyes were closed and their torsos were bare, above the breast, as they lay side by side, wearing nothing but beatific expressions, the very picture of contentment. Under this photograph Mitchell had written: "I am so grateful for this woman's presence in my life." The comments section was filled with the usual chorus of syrupy untruisms: "What a beautiful couple," "You're a lucky man," "So happy for you," "Worth waiting for." The object of Mitchell's irrepressible adoration also chimed in: "Thank you, Sweatheart! You're my favorite person!"

What a coincidence: you're his favorite person too!

I entered a comment of my own—"Dry up"—but quickly deleted it. Irreverence and dissent were forbidden on a forum solely dedicated to good attitude and bad grammar. I hadn't heard from Mitchell in a while, and the dwindling medication supply was becoming a concern, so I didn't want to rock that boat.

Tony, the ruggedly handsome homeless man, appeared, seemingly out of nowhere, as he always did, and I groaned freely, as I always did, in the select society of those among whom I could freely groan—those usually being the people whose presence was the least groan-inducing, in whose company I could express myself without fear of causing offense.

"It's been a while," I said. "I was beginning to wonder what had become of you."

He offered me the remains of a supermarket strudel.

"No thanks. My teeth can't handle it. What's going on?"

"I lost my backpack on the bus," he said in his usual self-effacing and matter-of-fact way. "I think I was too stoned. I'm afraid someone will steal my identity."

"I would have thought you'd be happy to let go of it," I remarked. "Stoned on what?"

"Fentanyl."

"You like that stuff?"

"These days, yes, that's what I take."

He produced a tiny package of flaky whitish powder.

"How much does that go for?"

"Twenty dollars."

"How much of it do you take?"

"About that much."

"Every day?"

"Yup," Tony meekly admitted.

"That's $600 a month," I said, aghast. That was about twice my monthly medication outlay. "You could live on that, if you subsidized it with a part-time job."

"Yeah, I could. I'm cutting it out. I have to."

"I'll help you," I said. "Hand it over."

"No. That could kill you if you took it all at once. I'm quitting at the end of the month, on my son's birthday."

"What do you need?" I asked him.

He dithered, as usual, before stating his needs. "I could use a coffee," he said.

I walked back to the café and poured Tony his usual coffee with five spoonfuls of sugar. I didn't feel sorry for him anymore, and now that the element of pity was removed, I didn't like him as much either. He received over a $1,000 from the government every month, and the majority of it was spent on dope. Meanwhile, he puttered around bashfully, getting free stuff up and down the block, when he was out of his skull on fentanyl the entire time.

Pulling up the batch report, I learned that ninety sales had been made since I clocked in. That figure could at least be doubled with the addition of non-sales-related questions, bringing the grand total of draining interactions to about two hundred throughout the course of a seven-and-a-half-hour shift. If I were a bartender, being tipped at least a $1 every time I snapped the cap off a bottle of beer, I'd have made about $200 in gratuities on top of wages, possibly a lot more. But since I was merely a humble servant in the service of enlightenment, I made nothing in tips. And it requires a lot more knowledge to field endless idiotic questions about books than it does to pour a glass of beer. Clearly, I was in the wrong line of work.

* * *

"Don't they understand? It's over. It died years ago," said Jackson.

We were having a literary conversation, and I didn't feel strongly enough, or strong enough, to argue the point, especially with Jackson, who would seize any opportunity to tirelessly and rigorously defend his position on any subject.

"I mean, for example, when all those fools objected to Dylan winning the Nobel Prize," he added.

"I don't know," I said, disingenuously. "Who objected to it?"

"People who still believe in literature," said Jackson, disdainfully.

"Some people might have thought it unfair to poets," I said. "You could be the greatest poet on earth and be completely unknown. Nobody can tell you what constitutes a good poem whereas everybody recognizes a good song when they hear it. Ironically, to call an artist or a filmmaker a poet is to bestow the highest honor upon them—'Lou Reed is a poet,' 'Tarkovsky is a poet of the cinema,' et cetera. It suggests that somebody has transcended the limits of their form and reached another, higher level. But if one actually is a poet, one is nothing."

"Maybe that's how it should be," said Jackson.

"Maybe they should give a Nobel to Neil Young," I said.

"He's not much of a poet, let alone a songwriter."

"'Red means run, son, numbers add up to nothing,'" I quoted.

"I never got into Neil Young. I was always a Dylan fan," said Jackson.

"You can like both."

"I always thought of Neil Young as Dylan's retarded little brother."

"Fair enough."

The Secret had been virtually empty when we entered, just a few solitary topers chatting with the Korean barmaid, but it was quickly filling up. Young people were pouring in, and they all seemed to know each other. Some sort of birthday party was taking place, and by the looks of the celebrants there wouldn't be more than twenty-five candles on the cake. As I sat there, it occurred to me that the debt collectors could put a levy on my PayPal account, not that there was much in it, but that grim possibility caused my blood to freeze a little. I wanted to hang on to this worry until it could be temporarily alleviated, to salve it and stroke it away, but this was the wrong place and the wrong time.

"My new novel is held up at Viking," said Jackson. "It was supposed to have been edited two months ago. They were supposed to put it out this summer. I don't know what they're up to."

"How long is it?"

"120,000 words."

"Yeah, but it will be coming out, won't it? That's something to look forward to."

"We've been arguing about the title. They have a very weird way of doing things. They haven't even edited this book yet and they're already prepared to give me an advance for another one. All they want is three chapters and an outline. Then they give you an advance and a deadline. But I don't know how the book's going to end up at this point. What am I supposed to do? My life's falling apart. My hot-water heater doesn't work and my landlord hasn't been returning my calls. And this French girl is coming over to visit me next month. What am I going to do with her?"

"I'm sure you'll think of something," I said.

Throughout his tale of woe there was an unmistakeable glimmer in Jackson's eye; he was, in fact, incandescent with self-delight, even his skin was glowing.

"Give them three chapters and an outline then," I said. "If the finished work doesn't adhere to the original proposal, so what? I wish I had your problems. What about the other book you wrote before *The Death*?"

"*Fuck Fame*. Yes, it's coming out in two weeks. Viking finally got that together. I meant to bring you a copy. In France it's being translated as *Baise la célébrité*. Poetic, isn't it? Are you coming to the Hammer next Thursday?"

"The Hammer Museum?"

"Yes, that's where the launch is taking place. Seven o'clock next Thursday."

The Hammer was on the other side of town. And it was at rush hour, and I was working that night. Even successful people still expected their friends to go out of their way to attend their functions. "I'd like to. I'll see what I can manage. Are they sending you out on a book tour?"

"Only the East Coast and the West Coast," he said. "I'm doing the Strand in New York the Thursday after next."

I could hardly imagine anything more pleasurable than being sent out on an all-expenses-paid book tour. "That should be fun," I said.

"None of it matters," said Jackson with ferocity. "Nobody reads anymore!"

That was rich. I had to think about that one for a moment; I didn't want to find myself caught in another *esprit de l'escalier* predicament. Now that he was successful Jackson was in the luxurious position of being able to tragedize his triumphs. Not content to be a winner, he had to spoil the game for everyone else by claiming that it wasn't worth playing, while he continued to play it.

"People still read, pal. I'm on the front line. I see it with my own eyes, they're hungry for literature out there, they're hungry for your literature, they even read poetry. I work in a fucking bookstore and ..."

"Only half the people who buy my book will actually read it, and only 10 percent of the people who read it will actually get it," said Jackson, decisively.

"But you're entering a different tax bracket thanks to the few people who do still believe in this supposedly dead form. Surely that provides some consolation. And nothing seems to stop you from producing at a furious rate."

I hadn't completely discredited myself with that response, although it felt incomplete. But I said nothing further on the subject. I was still hoping Jackson might publish my book if I ever finished it, or even set me up with his agent, and I didn't want to risk offending him.

Having perhaps temporarily exhausted his fund of discourse, he finally threw me a bone: "What are you working on?"

"The same thing. Something vaguely resembling a novel," I said, with as much apathy as I could muster.

"I hope you'll forgive me but I've forgotten what it's about."

"I don't think I told you what it was about. I haven't told anybody. I'm afraid that it'll sound idiotic if I try to explain it. After years of struggling with form, I finally acknowledged that I had no grasp of plot, character or dialogue, and decided to write a novel. My imagination dried up years ago, so I'm obliged to draw on personal experience rather more than I'd prefer. I have to finish it and somehow get it published, and maybe even get a few people to read it. I doubt all these things will line up before I die."

"I'm sure they will."

That was very convincing and comforting. "Unfortunately, I have to get it out of my system and actualize myself before I die," I said, the desired apathy having slipped away.

"What do you mean by 'actualize myself'?" said Jackson, leerily.

"You know, to externalize yourself, to bring forth what is within, to get it out of your system and into other people's systems; to provoke, console and inspire, if it's within one's means. To return the favor, so to speak. Having been cheered and consoled by the bitter words of others, one hopes that one might be able to perform a similar service. Then, for some, I suppose, there are material rewards. I'm not expecting that. The rewards have been material in your case, this year."

"Yes," said Jackson thoughtfully. "I suppose that is what it comes down to, for some people."

The subject of my being published on Jackson's thriving imprint had not been broached. I had been hoping that particular strand of conversation from our last meeting would be picked up again and expanded upon, but he had now probably either forgotten about it or was deliberately avoiding it.

I stared balefully at the insipid beauties and arrogant young upstarts who were responsible for the frequent eruptions of squealing, giggling and yelling on the other side of the room, with constant brain-curdling ejaculations of "cool," like," "awesome" and "Oh my God!" The occupation was in full force and there was no escape. These young fools would be returning and bringing other young fools with them and those young fools would bring other young fools, and the old fools would have nowhere left to call their own. The Secret was out. There was no point trying to cling on to anything that was rooted in the past anymore: young people were desperate to latch on to anything that was supposedly "authentic," which meant squeezing the life out of it and spitting it out in some flavorless, diluted form.

"This has been the most disastrous year of my life. I'm falling apart," Jackson was saying.

"What are you on about? You've got everything you wanted: money, love, respect. You've achieved all your goals. You're a success."

"But the hot-water heater in my apartment is broken."

"But you can afford to move out. Weren't you thinking about buying property?"

"Yes, I suppose so," he conceded.

* * *

When can this caricature of creativity be curtailed?

Day after day I was passing life by out of obligation to this most unnecessary and self-indulgent task. Many sacrifices had been made in vain. But at least I had something to keep myself occupied. A sense of purpose was a luxury. What if I didn't have that? Many were those who did not.

I recognized the ideal of what I was working toward, but I seemed to be incapable of realizing it. Then why not just satisfy myself with what I imagine I'm capable of doing rather than attempting to further perfect it?

That seemed like a reasonable solution.

But wasn't that what I'd been doing all along: recognizing what I was capable of and settling for less—a long process of resigning myself to failure, basking in the glory of potential until potential was dead.

Because the day already felt lost, I was already calculating how to make the most of my time the following day. All I did was tell myself what to do … and not do it. I couldn't get involved in the subtle shaping and shifting of sentences with the pressure and suspense of a lawsuit hanging over me. The longer I postponed dealing with it the more hopeless and helpless I felt. Outside of indiscriminate contact with lawyers and the anonymous desperation of online forums, mine was too shabby a predicament to discuss. My tortuous history of debt and defaulting was something I had always kept to myself. The intimate details of one's sex life were always fair game for friendly conversation, but never the details of one's finances. Debt was a lonely condition.

It's hard to concentrate on the subtle intricacies of an epic work of Pose Friction when one's focus might be thrown at any moment by a thunderous knocking on the door. Such an urgent knocking from a hand so practiced at frightening people into motion will be impossible to ignore, and the knocking will probably continue for a long time. I could peek through the gap in the curtains but they might look up and see me; I could cower—but cowering can't save me now: they will just leave the papers on the porch, and the whole ghastly process will be set in motion.

A car door slamming, a gate unlatching, a voice on the street: every sound outside makes me quiver. I hold out my hand: it is shaking. I can only imagine how much I'll be shaking when the knocking starts. There will be no time to compose myself before I open the door, and I will face the harsh deliverer of my fate as a trembling wreck. I might as well face my fate, run to meet it, as I do in my dreams. I just want to appear as unflustered as possible when I open the door to find a jaded, gray-faced paper server standing there. It would be wise to only open the door a crack so he won't be able look up the stairs and see the shelves, loaded with books and records, which could be viewed as assets. What will I say when the papers are thrust into my shaking hands? It would probably be best to say nothing. I wished that they would just get it over with.

* * *

"Even the disclaimers have disclaimers."

"I know."

"It's too self-pitiful."

"I know. But if I remove all the self-pity there won't be much left," I said, alarmed to hear the words whistling out of my mouth in an unfamiliar way owing to friction between my tongue and a newly jagged tooth.

"It's too knowing."

"I know."

"You make yourself …"

"The protagonist," I corrected him.

"You make *him* sound superior to everyone else," said the boy, referring to the notes on his phone. "It's as if the other characters only exist to draw attention to *his* integrity."

"I know. I don't like it either. Such charges might be leveled," I said. This new fricative discord was something I would have to get used to.

"How can I put this?" said the boy. "There are too many scenes that serve the same purpose. You must know that."

"It's deliberate."

"That doesn't mean it works. You keep making the same points. It could be much shorter."

"That's what worries me about being published by a major press. They'll insist on chucking out at least a quarter of it."

"It's too experimental for a major press."

"It's only an experiment if it fails."

"Exactly."

"I realize that I'm speaking idealistically but since I haven't tasted the bitter pangs of rejection yet, I can still dream. I'm sure I'll end up settling for a lot less."

"Why mock Kelley Gimlet?" the boy cut in, sounding almost hurt. "I have a soft spot for Chthonic Truth."

"I'm sorry to hear that," I said, "but that's the price of fame: the small price one has to pay for being grossly overrewarded for one's dubious contributions is to be pilloried by the envious and the unrewarded."

"Why bother though?"

"Because it's good honest fun," I said, and experienced a familiar twinge of guilt. The mockery had served no valid purpose. I didn't even mean it, didn't really care. I made a mental note to delete it.

"All the portrayals are negative," the boy went on, reveling in a newfound ruthlessness. "It's not just women, it's across the board. Everyone's unlikable."

"I tried to make you likable, but you're not doing yourself any favors. I tried to make an effort. I didn't make an effort, but I tried to. Sorry if it didn't pan out."

"Why don't you use some of your other friends?"

"There's only so much room. Of course I have other friends. You know how it is with novels. One's circle is reduced to a handful of people who move the narrative along."

"But you don't get any idea about what I do."

"I state very clearly that you're a musician."

"You never mention my shows or my recordings."

"It's a novel, it's not a promotional vehicle for your musical career. Fuck, I drafted you in to offer encouragement and all you do is run it down."

"It's for your own good."

"I know. But you're not the ideal critic, you're younger than me and you're more jaded about literature than I am."

"You don't even give me a physical description."

"I said you were handsome. What more do you want?"

"How old are you, Sean?" said the boy, taking out his annoyance by blurting out a question that he knew I wouldn't want to answer. Obviously, he'd been wondering about it. People did wonder about such things.

"Well …"

"Come on. How old are you, forty?"

"I'm ageless. I wouldn't want to date myself."

"Thirty-nine?"

I laughed mirthlessly: "Keep going."

"Forty-two?" he said, not laughing. "Forty-four?"

It was inconceivable to young people that somebody in my position could be older than forty-five. That was the cut-off age.

"If a man has not done his best before the age of forty-five, then he is not very likely to do so afterwards," stated the artist Jules Pascin. It was a good point, and Pascin proved it by killing himself on the night of his forty-fifth birthday, slashing his wrists and smearing a bloody love message to his young girlfriend on the walls of his studio. I was now four years older than Pascin at the time of his death. But perhaps life was still worth living, even if the time of one's greatest potential had passed.

I changed the subject: "It's too much work putting in all the 'he said'/'she said' crap. From now on I'm going to write dialogue without any of the pointless flourishes."

"You're avoiding the question," he said.

"Look, I'm a bit distracted at the moment. I've got creditors on my back. They're putting the squeeze on me for a lot of credit card debt that I defaulted on."

"That's not good."

"I know."

I provided him with a brief outline of my predicament.

"Is there anything you can sell?" he asked.

"Well, yes, but I've already let go of a lot of precious things over the years and all that's left is a lot of books and records that it would be too painful to part with and probably wouldn't add up to the amount I owe even if I did manage to sell it all."

"You can't take it with you," said the boy, unhelpfully.

"If you started rationalizing your behavior according to what you can't do after you're dead, you'd be in a sorry state," I said.

"Don't worry, everything's going to be all right," said the boy, laughing.

"Unfortunately, your conviction about how all right everything is going to be is not directly proportionate to how all right it actually is. You might as well say 'I don't give a shit.' Just say you don't give a shit," I said, the consonants fizzling out between broken teeth as I spoke.

I couldn't help surmising that the boy was offended, or worse, bored, by the work I'd shown him.

A late-night email from Gilbert arrived. He was still perturbed about my exchange with the yelping old man, among other things:

"… You have an opportunity to make a difference in a customer's life, to change their day for better or worse. You could choose to be polite and friendly towards the customer and have them walk away in a better mood, or you can be distant and rude, and too often this is the course you choose to take. It reflects badly on the store and yourself, and puts the customer in a bad mood, just because you can't be bothered to rise above your self-indulgent ill humor and make a small effort to be gracious … And PLEASE get texting on your phone! I know you think you're taking some sort of heroic stand but your refusal to text is a huge inconvenience to everybody else at the store."

The first part of this heartfelt plea struck a poignant chord. I decided to make more of an effort to be gracious with the customers. But I had no intention of following through on the second request.

* * *

"Hey, I have a question."

A skinny, bronzed woman in a summer dress, flashing a big toothy smile, strode purposefully toward me.

"What?" Drained and disheveled, I turned around from my task of unloading several boxes of used art books and faced this woman with her absurd energy. "What do you need?"

"It's OK, no problem. I don't want to bother you. It's cool," she said, as she stormed out.

I carried the empty boxes out to the trash, running a gauntlet of the sloppily dressed and the sloppily expressed, spattered by the shrapnel from a crossfire of inanities as I made my way through the store. Yes, that's the way it is: there is a definite correlation between those who disregard the laws of sartorial decorum and those who think themselves above obeying the rules of grammar.

"This is a cool-ass bookstore." ... "We met a very cool guy in the park today. He's an anarchist and he bicycles everywhere." ... "I'm going to New York for a week, then I'm going to Paris." ... "Oh, dude. I so want to go to Paris." ... "My trans-studies teacher is so awesome!" ... "Oh, cool." ... "Kara Walker. I love Kara Walker!" ... "I'm going to basically pitch like a video." ... "I'm like uh-huh." ... "My cousin edited *Throw Momma off the Train.*" ... "That's so cool." ... "D'you like Eileen Myles? They're like my favorite poet." ... "I just did a reading at Evergreen College." ... "I love Evergreen." ... "It was super mellow." ... "All I know is ..." ... "A part of me is like you know." ... "And I was like you know I don't know." ... "Right now my biggest problem is ..." ... "Hayley and I..." ... "I was like 'I can't do this.'" ...

After a few hours all noise was transformed into feedback with music, voices, traffic and kitchen sounds of grinding coffee and crashing plates all merging into one ghastly oceanic racket that washed over me like broken glass continually being flushed down a toilet.

Groups of people tittered in unison as they hovered over books on the display table at the front of the store, intent upon conveying the impression that they were having a wonderful time, and making sure everybody knew about it. The sight and sound of other people trying too hard to enjoy themselves can be an awful thing to endure. *We get it: you have a personality, you're spirited. Now shut the fuck up.*

To laugh quietly to oneself in public is a beautiful thing. But most people don't laugh when they're alone in public: not only are they seldom genuinely amused enough by anything to do so, but they are afraid of being thought insane.

Another salvo of grammar-mangling dissonance exploded a few yards away from the counter, where I was attempting to find some semblance of peace and sanity in the crossword puzzle.

The boy walked in to begin his shift and stopped at the counter.

"These bastards won't stop smiling at me," I said. "Every time I look up, somebody is smiling at me."

The boy laughed in my face.

"What's so funny?"

"Is that all you've got to complain about? It could be worse."

"I know. It's not a complaint that's likely to earn me much sympathy," I admitted.

I turned to the font of digital enlightenment at my fingertips, where distraction overlapped distraction in continual waves. It began with a search for the meaning of "linguistic materialism" and wound up in the gutter of Taylor Swift's love life.

"What have you been reading?" asked a customer I knew upon sight, as he purchased a book.

"Charles Willeford," I said.

"That's great, but what female authors have you been reading?"

"None, lately."

"You should read Laura Sweeney's new book."

"No thanks. Have you read Ivy Compton-Burnett?"

"I've never heard of her."

Despite the crush of bodies in the fiction aisle, I pulled open the stepladder and attempted to do some shelving, starting with the *G*'s.

Gissing, Kafka, Lawrence: What did these distinguished authors have in common? They had all produced a lot of great work, certainly, but surely their most important unifying quality was that they were all younger than me when they died. I had outlived Keats by almost a quarter of a century: that was a sobering thought. But let's leave poets out of this.

By the time he reached my age, Gissing had written twenty novels. By the time he reached my age, he was dead.

All these authors had written numerous books and I couldn't even write one. I had now lived longer than a lot of people who had achieved a lot more than I was ever going to achieve. Taking into consideration how much time I had already wasted and how much time realistically remained, and how much of that remaining time I was likely to waste, then that situation was unlikely to change. I had a lot of catching up to do. Even if I devoted every available remaining hour in unswerving devotion to this most unrequired and unrewarding task, it would still be impossible to ease the margin of defeat and offset the overwhelming backlog of lost time.

It was no longer possible to measure my own lack of progress by that of other late-blooming authors. One was supposed to take solace in the careers of Henry Miller, Raymond Chandler, Charles Bukowski, and other writers who didn't get started until they were in their late thirties or early forties, but I had now surpassed them all.

When I heard of an author's career taking off, and their *finally* producing the work for which they are now justly revered, the author was always at least five years younger than me. By which time most of them had also settled down and evolved in other aspects of their lives. It was bad enough to be ten years behind one's time when one was forty looking back at what one should have started doing when one was thirty, but when one was fifty looking back at what one could have done when one was forty, or thirty, it was much worse.

I had spent twenty-five years preparing to start, and it wasn't as if all that time hadn't been spent half-heartedly struggling with misbegotten fictioneering; it was just that I hadn't finished anything.

Well, that was something: a point from which to recede.

"Do you work here?" A customer called up to me.

"No. I'm just a compulsive book shelver."

My humor didn't receive its deserved appreciation. "What do you need?" I called after him as he walked off.

"No, it doesn't matter."

"Come back. Let me serve you."

Reluctantly, he returned and named a book by an obscure contemporary poet.

"It would be in poetry, did you look there?"

"I did, but somebody was standing in front of me."

I was certain we didn't carry it but returned to the counter and pretended to look it up on the computer. "We're out of it," I told him.

I was getting more tired, more tired than ever, of this routine. Twenty sales in the last hour according to the sales report. I couldn't move from behind the counter.

The energy required to interact (saying "thank you" does, in fact, consume energy), to operate the frequently malfunctioning credit card machine ("Take it out … Stick it in … Take it out … Slide it in …") and internet connection, and the strength of mind it took to endure being bludgeoned by innumerable involuntarily over-heard featherbrained conversations without losing my mind or temper had consumed far too much of my being.

Mona drifted in. She looked at books and after a few minutes I joined her.

"Jackson's doing really well," she said.

"Yes, he is."

"I'm just glad someone's happy."

"Same here. I just wish it wasn't him."

The mean-spirited quip was there for the taking and I helped myself to it, although it risked puncturing the mood as we stood together in the snug confines of the architecture section; I was getting a little tired of hearing about how well Jackson was doing, and I was beginning to wonder about the exact nature of Mona's interest in him.

This was her fourth lingering visit and every time I saw her she became more desirable. She was always alone when I saw her and her solitariness was sexy. As she stood close to me, exuding both frostiness and felinity, I could feel the electricity of need. At my advanced age the sensation of being desired had a powerful aphrodisiac effect. It was remarkable how attractive somebody could become when they found you attractive. Although there were concerns. She always wore tight pants and I worried that her legs might be blotchy, stubbly, or cellulite ridden. Such squeamish speculations, however, were offset by her pale, hairless, muscular arms, and when I looked at her delicate hands, I imagined them wrapped around my flagging manhood.

"I'm not coming in here anymore," she said, and handed over her card. It looked as if it had been in her wallet for a long time. "Call me up if you want to get coffee or something," she said. The "or something" part intrigued me.

"Is that Mute Books?" asked a flimsy-voiced young man on the other end of the line.

"Yes."

"Do you have yerba maté?"

"I think so, yes, I'm pretty sure." I seemed to remember seeing cans of the stuff in the kitchen, although I didn't know what it was.

"I'd like to know before I come down."

"I'll go and check," I said. I walked back to the café, with the telephone in one hand, leaned across the counter, and addressed the boy: "Somebody wants to know if you carry yerba maté. He's not coming down here until he knows for sure that you have it."

The boy seemed to find my exasperation hilarious.

"Yes, we have it," I informed the caller.

Ten greasy credit cards later, the phone rang again. Reluctantly, I answered it. "Do you carry yerba maté?" asked the caller.

"That's odd. Yes, we have it," I said, and wondered if a yerba maté convention was about to take place.

Numerous annoying questions and unwanted exchanges later, the phone rang again:

"Do you have yerba maté down there?"

"You're the third person that's asked about yerba maté tonight. Yes, we have it," I said, making no attempt to hide my irritation.

"Do you make yerba maté lattes?"

"What? I don't know. I don't make them personally. I'll have to walk back to the café and ask."

"Can you do that?"

"You'll have to wait a minute. It's busy down here," I said, the credit card machine making a ghastly beeping sound like a garbage truck backing up as another transaction went through.

"Eighteen dollars, please."

"No problem."

I didn't suggest there was a fucking problem.

"Are you fucking with me?" I asked the caller as I made my way through the fiction aisle, squeezing around texters, browsers and minglers.

Upon reaching the café, I slipped into the kitchen. The boy was leaning against the sink with the phone to his ear, chuckling to himself.

"You fucking prick!" I yelled and flung the store phone full force into the sink.

It had been a good prank but it had taken a lot out of me, and I had already had a lot taken out of me, and now I was taking more out of myself by overreacting, and the store phone was broken.

"I'm sorry," said the boy, as he came up to the counter. "Sometimes I forget that you're an adult."

"Take that back immediately. I'm not an adult. What a horrible thought." I didn't feel like one and I didn't feel that I looked like one.

When I got home I left the boy a voicemail: "Keep on pranking."

* * *

Counting the words, the hours, the pills, the minutes; checking the clock in the corner of the screen—acutely aware, while idly belaboring, that time is passing, running out … and this is how I have chosen to use it. I'm down to the wire, but the wire, a place of terminal hesitation, was reached a long time ago.

In a race against time, time will always win, and there's nowhere to run. I was still at the starting gate, floundering in the dust. A well-intentioned floundering, but nevertheless a floundering … foundering … undering. I was still in the same position I was in a quarter of a century ago.

I looked over the passage in which, according to the boy, I'd unjustly maligned Kelley Gimlet. It was a three-hundred-word scene that served several useful purposes and it contained a few lapidary lines that it would be a pity to delete. Maybe I could move them elsewhere. But cutting the scene would disturb the flow and something new would have to be added to fill in the narrative gaps. I couldn't bring myself to scratch it.

Doing anything produces too heightened an awareness of time already taken, and lost. All the wasted time comes rushing back and overwhelms the present. It never ends: this never ending, this never getting started. I was too distracted by what I'd already lost to proceed.

I concurred with an observation made by Jean Rhys toward the end of her days: "I wonder if it was right to give up so much of my life for writing. I don't think, after all, that my writing was worth it."

You don't have to write, you don't have to write, you don't have to write, I tell myself. But it makes no impression. It's unfortunate but having gotten this far, although it's not far enough, I can't stop.

But I had to stop what I wasn't doing and go to work.

As another well-intentioned afternoon died another unnatural death, I visited the LA Court website and tapped my case number into the designated window. No further developments had been documented. That, at least, was a relief.

* * *

A commotion in the doorway caught my attention. Bob McGilt, accompanied by a friend, was trying to make his way into the store unimpeded by adoration, but he was already surrounded. I caught sight of a receding jet-black hairline and an unexpectedly rich growth of immaculately sculpted facial hair, instinctively left my post behind the counter, and slid down the fiction aisle.

As McGilt, trailed by admirers, proceeded through the metaphysics and philosophy sections, I retreated further, into the staff restroom, where I anxiously considered my next move. The recent photographs hadn't lied: McGilt had put on weight. From the fleeting glimpse I'd caught of him, which was surely enough to confirm any unflattering impressions, he was getting fat. Indeed, he *was* fat.

On the previous occasion that McGilt had shown up, apparently, he had sat on the patio sipping tea for an hour. If he had already been served at the café and moved to the patio by the time I emerged from the restroom—allowing for a lot of stop-and-start action engendered by graciously sopping up the flattery of fawning devotees—it would be possible to return to the counter without being seen by him.

After five minutes, I peered out of the restroom door to make certain he wasn't in the corridor, and cautiously made my way back into the store. He was nowhere to be seen. "He left," said the disappointed barista. "He was getting too much attention."

A line in front of the counter awaited me, and I made my way toward it. McGilt's paunchy, pelican-throated, and laughably bewhiskered appearance afforded me some solace. The beard and mustache didn't suit him at all, and seemed a pitiful attempt at keeping up with the kids. I had aged better than him, I thought, as I rang up a three-legged ceramic pig figurine and some greeting cards for a patient customer. Following that mob scene, McGilt wouldn't be coming back in a hurry, I told myself.

I sat there, brooding over McGilt. Like many another musician, he had made the smart move of throwing himself a lifeline of excess to trade on for the rest of his career. He got all the transgression out of his system at an early age, knowing innately that he wouldn't be spreading it over the course of a lifetime—that when the right time rolled around he would reverse into the complete opposite of what he had once so brazenly pretended to be: he would sober up, straighten out, settle down, and become a clean-living family man with synthetic hair and a genuine paunch—and he would reap a ridiculous amount of credit for having once been a drug addict. That he'd really been one in the first place was open to question, although he certainly talked about it enough: the elephant in the room was that he never stopped talking about the elephant in the room.

How unoriginally damaged could one get, how formulaically fucked up? If one was going to be so predictable one could at least have the decency to keep it to oneself. Wasn't that what one was supposed to do when one was young, get fucked up? Now he expected to parlay his inability to handle drugs into some sort of credibility, as if it made him a hero. He had stopped taking drugs and found that beneath the camouflage of excess he was a regular Joe, albeit a very creative one. Good for him. Now he couldn't shut up about it.

Not that it was any of my business but that, at least, was my not entirely impartial take on it. The predictable timing of his trajectory irked me, mostly because I had gone about things differently. I hadn't reached early for the brass ring, and at this late stage it was too much of a stretch.

It seemed to me that one should maintain a certain degree of fidelity to the ideals, or even lack of ideals, of one's youth, and that McGilt had betrayed them. I had nothing against people changing, but why did it always have to be in the same obvious way?

It was all so dispiriting.

I sat there, eyeing the collectible books in the glass case against the wall. The signed first edition of Larry Clark's *Tulsa* would solve about a third of my problems. But I couldn't grab it; unfortunately, it wasn't in my nature.

"I have this recurring dream where I'm in the darkness and I turn a light on and it doesn't work, then I wake up and ..." Jolting me out of my futile meditations, the forlorn pest was standing in front of me yet again.

"I know," I said, spent. "We have this recurring conversation."

"This time it was different," he said.

I groaned, and he grinned. His dull-witted desperation was an unflappable and unstoppable force.

"The family dog came running at me in the darkness. It was a hostile dog in real life. I had an abusive childhood. That's why I'm always attracted to unavailable women. Because I had a mother who was unavailable. She wasn't there for me as a parent ..."

"I would imagine that most women are unavailable to you," I said. Life was beginning to repeat itself. It had been repeating itself for a long time. It was time to move on. For a long time it had been time to move on. But on to what?

Another Laura Sweeney book was placed in front of me.

You people have no taste whatsoever, do you? I said to myself.

Then a man walked up, holding a greeting card and smiling.

"Do you have Apple Pay?" he asked.

"No."

He slowly selected a credit card from a wallet phone case. I was sick of the sight of credit cards. I was sick of the thought of them.

"You don't have five dollars on you?"

"You do take cards, don't you?"

"What's wrong with cash?" I said. "Your purchase of this card is going to consume an entire minute of my life. I'm going to have to wait thirty seconds while you dig around in your wallet and choose which of your numerous credit cards to use for the purchase of a five-dollar birthday card when you could have had it ready when you came up here. It's going to take another thirty seconds to process the transaction, during which time you're going to stand there uncomfortably and fiddle around with your phone. If you had cash this transaction would only use up ten seconds of our time and we wouldn't have to endure this awkwardness. It's embarrassing, shameful really, not to have five dollars in cash on your person. I have no respect for somebody who uses a credit card to make a five-dollar purchase. Thanks to people like you we are becoming a cashless society, and it's at the expense of the disadvantaged. If you have no cash in your pockets how can you give money to a homeless person who might need a warm drink? But I don't suppose you give money to panhandlers. You probably don't even notice them as you glide by their encampments, insulated in your luxurious new vehicle. How are you going to buy vegetables from a street vendor, or drugs? But I don't suppose that factors into your e-life either. And what are you going to do if there's an earthquake? There'll be rogue taxi drivers driving around and they won't accept credit cards. You're not going to be able to get out of here, your credit cards will be useless. And they're a health hazard. I'm sick of handling filthy, greasy, chewed-on credit cards. I am sick of the sight of fucking credit cards. They ruin people's fucking lives."

I looked up. The customer was long gone. He had left the birthday card on the counter.

* * *

At least write one line this morning.

* * *

Following a moment of distraction that lasted two and a half hours, I crossed out the word "life" and replaced it with "things."

* * *

When I finally got Mitchell on the phone, he was running late for a tryst at his paramour's house in the hills.

"I should just give you the money back," he said.

"I beg your pardon?"

He always came through with the stuff; he could at least be depended upon for that: he bought it at an inflated price from somebody who had a prescription, and divided it between us. This agreeable arrangement had been running smoothly for several years and his efforts were deeply appreciated, but his paramour, Lyn Lamrock, had instituted a zero tolerance rule. Why he told her he took the stuff in the first place, I failed to understand.

"Yeah, my guy called me and I didn't go down there because I was over at Lyn's. I think he's pissed off with me because I didn't re-up; he might not call again," Mitchell harshly and heartlessly declared.

I had given him the money up front a week earlier, assuming he would pick the stuff up at the same time as he did every month. Now he was telling me that he hadn't re-upped because he had been too busy cuddling the woman he claimed to be repelled by.

"I'm on something resembling a roll with my literary exertions and I need them," I meekly pointed out. "What are you working on?" I added in an attempt to lighten the conversation by voicing an interest in something other than his ability to supply me with medication.

"I'm doing rewrites on the Adorno script. I'm going back and forth with a producer at Netflix."

"Netflix? I would have thought such subject matter might be a little too cerebral for them?"

"Well, I've had to make a few changes," said Mitchell, defensively.

"I've got creditors on my back," I said almost involuntarily, and began to tell him a little about my predicament.

"Yeah, I ran up $5,000 worth of debt but I paid it off," said Mitchell, canceling out my legitimate concerns with his own incomparable experiences. "I'm sorry but I've got to get out of here."

"I thought you were through with her," I ventured.

"I'm trying to do the sensible thing."

"What's sensible about it?"

He didn't have time to answer that question. "I'll call you tomorrow," he said. And I was left holding the bag, or rather, not holding the bag.

"The sensible thing," of course. I shouldn't have been surprised. Everybody was doing the sensible thing these days. If a mature relationship meant sticking with somebody you didn't like after you didn't want to have sex with them anymore, no thanks.

The poor bastard had placed me in the friendly position of encouraging him to break off his relationship. Then, without acknowledging any of his former ambivalence, he shamelessly backtracked, which made me look bad.

All of which would have been tolerable, but he wasn't making his customary effort to procure the medication that was vital to the discharging of my duties.

It was such a modest need, and it was sad to be deprived of it.

* * *

The sips of mercy slid down my throat, cool and calming.

I lay there staring up at the constellation of damp stains on the bathroom ceiling—the air bubbles, the blisters, the peeling paint.

The notion that I hadn't evolved was measured by conventional notions of development. I had yet to assume adult responsibilities. So what? Maybe I never would. Was it not an achievement of sorts to maintain fidelity to the values of one's youth, when one's vision is supposedly at its most pure? It must, at least, be a sort of success. It was, at least, the only sort of success I could make any claim on. Although it could have been achieved in finer style.

Pondering such thoughts, I lay in the bathtub, with one hand around a glass of whiskey and the other holding a book, slowly letting go and drifting into a brief nap.

An explosion roused me from my stupor. The hissing of silence was now cut through with clapping and crackling sounds from near and far. The sound of ignorance rumbled through the city. The people who celebrate things, who like to hear things explode, who view any possible occasion as an excuse to make noise were at it again, as always happened around the time of any public holiday.

Soapy water lapped against my chest. I released a yellowish stream into the gray water and got out of the bath.

* * *

As I walked in to begin my evening shift, Gilbert issued a formal grunt that served both to acknowledge my presence and put me in my place.

"Where can I buy a good second-hand fridge around here?" he was saying to the boy, who stood on the other side of the counter.

As he picked up his jacket and prepared to depart for a meditation class, Gilbert addressed me. "Is it really necessary to lecture customers about using credit cards?" he said softly. "This store *survives* by using credit cards. You are driving customers away from the store." The effort he was making to maintain evenness of tone was palpable.

I had anticipated having to answer this charge and had prepared a response in advance, tricky as it was to justify what had been a completely unwarranted harangue: "The guy gave me two cards that didn't go through, and then he gave me a lot of attitude. I can only take so much abuse. I'm sorry about that."

It was like being back in school. I was pushing fifty, for Mercy's sake, but I had brought this lowliness upon myself—not that being master of my own downfall provided much consolation.

Thankfully, the boy had walked off and hadn't witnessed the dressing down Gilbert had given me.

"Why does Gilbert need a fridge?" I asked the boy, a little later.

"He's got a new place."

"What?"

"He bought property in El Sereno."

"What?"

"His landlord sold the house in Silver Lake."

"So he bought a house? Just like that?"

"His parents paid for the down payment."

"That's nice. I know the way it goes," I said, not taking a deep breath. "How come I didn't hear about it? Not that it's any of my business."

"He feels guilty about it."

"Yes, that is tragic, a terrible burden. I should have offered my condolences."

It wasn't surprising that I didn't know about this recent develop-ment in Gilbert's relatively charmed life. Long ago, our friendship had deteriorated to the point that we no longer inquired after each other or exchanged pleasantries.

I decided not to let Gilbert's acquisition of property upset me. If I became incensed every time a friend suddenly bought a house, seemingly out of thin air, I'd be in a constant state of torment. It was fairly easy to predict this familiar scenario by now: the timing was always the same. Gilbert was making all the right moves in the right order: sobering up, buying into the business, buying a house. It could only be a matter of time before he found a nice girl to settle down with. At least he had the decency to feel guilty about his good fortune.

What disturbed me more was that the boy seemed to be on such cordial terms with Gilbert. When had they become so friendly?

* * *

You don't have to write. You don't have to write. You don't have to write.

I would like to dump my muse, or more accurately, I'd like to make a preemptive move before my muse finally loses her patience and dumps me.

This sense of purpose is a conceit, an affliction and a luxury, without which I wouldn't know what else to do with my time. I can't imagine prioritizing my days in any other way. After over two years of adhering to this routine, and all the preceding years that yielded nothing, it's bound to become wearisome.

It just takes too long.

Two years at three hours a day for five days a week amounts to 15 hours a week. That's 780 hours a year. That's 1,560 hours over the last two years: 65 straight days, or 195 eight-hour working days. Which, at the minimum wage rate of $15 an hour, should yield $23,400 in wages. In the unlikely event that *this thing* is ever finished, and in the even more unlikely event that it's published, it's unlikely that it will recoup that sum; it is unlikely that it will provide any remuneration at all.

As my powers—such as they are, such as they were—palpably dwindle and visibly dim, I feel myself losing interest in *this thing*. I lack the strength I once had, and my commitment diminishes in direct correlation to my waning abilities.

The spirit may be unwilling, but I have to finish it; I have to finish something while I still have a morsel of what I like to think I once had left in me, although this improbable goal seems further away every day.

The end, although in sight, is still a distant blur: it just keeps receding, sometimes fading from view, and when it reappears I don't like the look of it; while my own end, that other morbid undertaking, looms closer.

While I didn't do anything, failure could be endured, and to some extent indolence was a mechanism designed to forestall genuine failure. As long as I did nothing, I couldn't really complain about lack of appreciation. But neglect, after all the work I've put into *this thing*, will be the icing on the coffin.

Day after day, I drag myself to this tribunal of last resort, and catch sight of my aging reflection on a screen covered with mismatched verbiage, and rather than rise to the challenge of hacking it down, I add to the existing mess.

The slog, the endless bloody-minded, faint-hearted slog. Did I have to plumb these depths in order to have the privilege of reporting back? Just get it out of my system before I completely lose it. Get it over with, then I won't have to write anymore. Don't clog it up with any more unnecessary expansion, like this. Hack it down, for Mercy's sake, just hack it down.

Or give up.

To be within reach of one's goal at last, only to turn one's back on it, surely there must be some merit in that.

* * *

There were two messages awaiting me when I checked my email. They were both from Gilbert Blace: a name guaranteed to induce unease when I found it in my inbox on a Sunday night. The subject line, "Customer Service," triggered instant dread. Another scathing denunciation of my *people skills* surely lay in store, which was exactly what I didn't need. My nerves were already flayed from dealing with the public all day. Upon returning home, completely wrung out, I had gotten into bed, plunged my aching head into the thin pillow and drifted off for as long as possible, about twenty minutes. Then I just lay there, completely useless, until eventually I rose.

"Today my partner and I went to your bookstore and bought coffees. Then my partner went to buy a notebook from the book store—we spent a total of $40 (which should be irrelevant to how customers are treated?). Anyhow, my partner was deeply disrespected by the bookstore cashier. He did not take him seriously as a customer, refusing to engage respectfully and attentively with him when he asked him for assistance finding something. Additionally, his hyper-survailence of us made it feel like he thought we would steal something. Considering that your bookstore is located in a gentrifying area that has historically been inhabited by communities of color, I would hope that people of un-normative sexuality who are PAYING customers would be treated with more respect. We will not be returning to your store and will encourage other POC not to enter this white-dominated space where we are not treated as well as white customers."

I gave it a cursory skim. I was more interested in the second email that Gilbert had cc'd me on, which contained his response:

"Hi, I'm sorry you had a bad experience at my store today. I want to assure you that I would never employ a racist. The employee you encountered today will be rude to anybody when he's in a bad mood, regardless of race, appearance or age. These are not qualities one would prefer as the face of our customer relations on a busy day like a Sunday, but as he's been here since we opened and since he provides vital functions in the business, we put up with his all too frequent non-solicitousness and sometimes lack of common decency.

You're not by any means the first to be amazed by his poor customer skills, but I'd like you to believe me when i say that race is most certainly not a factor, he treats all races like crap when the mood is right. It is very frustrating, but the upside of not being a corporate organization is allowing for interactions with real humans and not the simulation of an interaction which you receive at many other businesses. Please feel free to come in and …"

A nauseous palpitating sensation gripped my stomach and incipient impotent rage began to swirl uncontrollably in my head.

Maybe I should have taken a few deep breaths. But I didn't.

"Hello …" Gilbert answered his phone in a soft and seductive way, as if he might have been expecting a Tinder caller.

"What the fuck have I done now?" I exploded in puerile bewailment.

"Sean," he said, soothingly.

But self-control wasn't an option: "Some idiot accuses me of being a racist and you take their side ... I bust my balls being gracious with customers all day, it's sapped every ounce of my energy being gracious to these cunts and at the end of the day I'm accused of being a racist, and you take their side ... I've got nothing left, I'm fried, useless, dead meat ... It was fucking relentless, and this is what I get at the end of the day, some cunt taking offense for no discernible reason and you telling me I'm useless!" As I spat the words out, I stormed around the room.

"Sean, read my email. I didn't say that. I had to placate them. If you read the email, you'll see I wasn't criticizing you. I said you performed 'vital functions' ..."

"What's this shit then? 'He treats all races like crap.' Who do I treat like crap? I knock myself out kowtowing to these people. I subdue myself to the point of nonexistence and I still catch shit from these idiots. I can't fucking win. I can't take the humiliation. I'm not cut out for this. I give up. I can't stand being around them, or you, with your fucking passive-aggressive disapprobation. I know you're trying to be a good person but you're going about it the wrong way. I'm quitting. That's it. It's not worth all the abuse ... You just put up with me because I've been here since the store opened?! It was thanks to me you got this job in the first place, because I was prepared to overlook *your* negative fucking qualities! ..." I was yelling so loudly now that my downstairs neighbor, the people on the next block, even the people in cars on the freeway could probably hear me.

But Gilbert couldn't hear me anymore. He had hung up.

I called him back four times to no avail, threw the phone across the room and flung myself onto the sofa.

A few minutes later the phone rang.

"Maybe you shouldn't work on Sundays," said Gilbert.

"I have no problem with Sundays. I have no problem with customers. I'm very discriminating about who I treat like shit …" The outburst had exhausted me, and I was quickly sinking into drained regret.

"So you'll be coming in tomorrow?"

"I don't know about that."

"It's tough. I know how it is. You have to deal with a lot of assholes on this job."

"Maybe you shouldn't have sent that email. I don't understand why you had to send it at all. You could have added some sort of commentary. It looks accusatory. How was I supposed to take it?"

"It's not the first time we've received complaints like this."

"I can't do any better. I'm already stretching myself and I'm still causing offense."

"We've known each other for a long time. I love you."

"Oh, for fuck's sake."

"I'm very aware that it's thanks to you I got this job."

"Yeah, that was a cheap shot …"

"So I'll see you tomorrow?"

"Yeah."

Lying on the sofa, stunned and drained, I cast my mind back over what had been a particularly demoralizing Sunday. There had been no time to read or think. I sat there, sucking it up as calmly as possible. A flamboyant young man, possibly still a teenager, had been prancing around the store, putting on a show of flagrant self-delight as he blatted brashly into his cell phone. I didn't draw his attention to any of the posters now plastered around the store that stated "Please Refrain from Cell Phone Conversation on These

Premises," which nobody heeded or noticed, for fear he'd take it personally.

He appeared in front of me, sucking a large purple smoothie from a straw. Despite my already being involved in a transaction, he demanded to know if the store carried notebooks. "Right behind you," I said, helpfully pointing them out—he was standing three feet in front of them—and returned to the tedium at hand. A few minutes later he was back at the counter, with a friend, presumably the author of the email, and placed a notebook in front of me. I could feel the laser-like intensity of his gaze drilling into me, and I shrank from it, sensing hostility. After weighing me up and considering the options, he then resorted to that reliable method of testing, or antagonizing, a bookseller.

"How are you today?"

I groaned.

"Doing good?"

He stared at me, as if expecting some kind of answer.

"Yeah, great."

This fucker looked witless enough to accuse me of being homophobic. A few weeks earlier, I had been accused of ageism; now apparently I was homophobic, or a racist.

I went back and read the letter of complaint more closely. It was mailed from a dot-edu address, which made perfect sense. A student was attempting to define themselves as a victim—oppressed to impress. "Refusing to engage respectfully and attentively ..." That was a good one. This brat, more than half my age, was coming on like a martinet, expecting their subordinates to snap to attention, whining about being ignored, then complaining about being the object of "hyper-survailence," and it had to be bigger than that, it had to be an attack on the group they considered themselves to be part of.

"I can't take the humiliation anymore!" I yelled into thick air. But of course I could.

"I'll quit. I'll return to hack work!"

But I couldn't: the meager payoffs wouldn't even amount to what I made at the store, and with all the effort involved in hustling for assignments it would take far too much out of me.

I read Gilbert's email again. At least he had defended me against the ludicrous charge of racism. I had been so ready to unload on him that I hadn't read it through closely enough. Now the fury of my overreaction had obliterated the original grievance, and I had foolishly given him an exaggerated version of how bent out of shape I got at the store on Sundays.

He had even said that he loved me, which made me queasy, but I did feel something resembling that overused sentiment toward him too. I was always attentive to his attitude toward me, and seemed to instinctively seek his negative attention. He was some-body whose opinion I valued.

Apologies were once again in order:

"I'm very sorry that I went off on you. Already in a bloody-minded humor I immediately took your reply to the letter of complaint as a personal attack. I now recognize that it was a neces-sary response to placate the insufferable. I remember the customers now. I pointed the notebooks out to them and didn't give them another look or thought until they were in front of me at the counter making a purchase and for some reason giving me the evil eye. The complaint, which has no foundation in reality, seems to be the expres-sion of some sort of myopic youthful identity politics stance. It's a pity that some people demand to be treated so delicately in this oversensi-tive day and age. In any event, I'm sorry that I unleashed such vitriol on you last night. You know I have great respect for you and the work you do. Don't bother responding to this. See you tomorrow ..."

I fixed myself a cocktail, lined up a Mendelssohn string quartet on the CD player, picked up a book, and sunk into a bubble bath.

But sedentary pleasures held no appeal. The delightful words of Ms. Pym fell flat. I was far too agitated and restless. I needed company, the fellowship of my fellow man, some sort of release.

I got out of the bath and began making phone calls. I called Jackson but he didn't pick up. He was probably avoiding me; he probably thought I wanted something from him; now that he was successful he probably thought everybody wanted something from him.

I called a few other people but none of them picked up. Perhaps they were all avoiding me. Perhaps they all thought I wanted something from them, which I did: company. The sound of a phone actually ringing was an echo from the distant past. Nobody called up just to chat anymore; these days the telephone was rarely used as a medium for keeping in touch.

I called Summer. Being from an older generation, my generation, she still sometimes used the telephone for its original purpose, which was how we made arrangements—and she answered.

"Hello, Sean. What's going on?"

"Nothing much, just seeing what you're up to."

"I'm meeting up with a friend," she said, cryptically.

"Who's that?" I asked, doltishly.

"Somebody I'm seeing," she said, rubbing in what she considered to be her good fortune.

"That's nice. How long has it been going on for?" Some quick calculations suggested it couldn't have been for longer than a month, since it had been about that long since we'd last seen each other.

"A couple of months," she said.

"Well, I was just calling up to see how you were doing."

"I'm doing well, thanks. How are you?"

"Great."

Not that I'd given it much thought, but I'd always assumed Summer was as satisfied with our arrangement as I was (on the rare occasions I'd invited her to spend the night, she had declined), but the presence of somebody new in her life seemed to have unloosened any mild resentment that might have built up toward me; even if she didn't want anything more from me, she could still resent me for not wanting more from her. Our longstanding unspoken arrangement of convenience was apparently over for the time being.

I moved on to the next candidate for the pleasure of my company. I telephoned the boy. He was also "seeing" somebody.

"She's a minor social media celebrity," he said. "She's a music supervisor ... She's worked on some big movies ... She's only twenty-nine ... She owns a house in Silver Lake." He sounded excited.

"I should have been a music supervisor," I muttered. "All the smoke that gets blown up Tarantino's music supervisor's ass owing to the obvious selections they use: I could do so much better than that. But I never tried. It's a highly competitive field."

"She's very knowledgeable," he said. "She knows a lot about jazz."

"What are you doing tonight?" I asked him.

"I'm seeing her."

"All right."

"By the way," he added, "I handed in my notice at Mute."

This didn't come as a huge surprise. He'd been threatening to quit for a while.

"Good for you," I said, with as much goodwill as I could manage. "What are you going to do instead?"

"I got a job as a personal assistant."

As was inevitably going to happen to somebody young, talented and attractive, the boy was being sucked into the city's cultural life. Even he, at half my age, was moving on.

That was it. My two conversations for the night. That would have to be enough.

I lay down on the sofa.

Then I called Mona up.

After some preliminary grabbing and groping, I pushed her against the wall and shoved my hand down the front of her pants. I buried my head in her long, lustrous black tresses and listened to her steady, tremulous breathing. All that darkness looked good in the dark, the black hair and black clothes. I looked down at her hand, that fair white hand I had long admired, as she rubbed my crotch. Looking down further, I was also aroused by the magnetic combination of toughness and femininity embodied by her motorcycle boots. With four fingers stuffed inside her, my sense of wonder was reawakened, but I wasn't getting much response. Her breathing became heavier and deeper after I placed a hand around her neck. Since she was taking her time about it, I unzipped my fly and placed that fair hand, marble white and laced with faint blue veins, around my flagging manhood; but her gentle touch failed to induce firmness. I thrust my hand down the back of her pants and brazenly squeezed her ass. My other hand pinched her nipple as I ground against her and sank my mouth into her neck. I yanked her pants down beneath her ass, turned her around, bent her over the back of the sofa and with my now serviceably tumescent prick pointing out of my fly, prepared to slip it in.

"Let's go into the bedroom," she said.

Once inside, she removed all her clothes. Her legs were neither blotchy, cellulite ridden, nor stubbly.

"Take your pants off," she said.

The clock on my bedside table read twelve thirty. After this was over I'd have to talk to her for at least twenty minutes. I could be asleep by 2 a.m. Five hours' sleep wouldn't be enough, but I could still put in a full morning of writing. The pills would help. The main problem was how to get her to leave. Between thrusts, I considered this difficulty. I could say I had to work in the morning, but she might still want to stay. And I would have to work tomorrow night. Facing Gilbert after tonight's unseemly display was a disturbing prospect. It pricked my conscience again and I got in another thrust, jamming into a pinpoint of sensation. I needed it. For fuck's sake, for the sake of the fuck, just enjoy it.

I turned her over and slowly pounded the shrine of her womanhood while tightly holding her waist and looking down at her ass. My eyes were wide with pleasure but my mind kept wandering. I'd shelled out fourteen dollars for her garden burger and she hadn't even thanked me ... or given me a blow job. I got in a vicious measured thrust. All this grinding was tiring. It didn't seem to be going anywhere. The act of love could become very repetitive and draining. The eruption with Gilbert had taken a lot out of me. Another wave of guilt and humiliation swept over me. I attempted to push it into the back of my mind. Another soggy thrust. She turned her head and looked up at me expectantly, invitingly. I felt myself wilting again. Getting a woman to leave after sharing such tender moments of intimacy was a tricky situation to negotiate. I could hint darkly at serious issues that stopped me from sleeping. Maybe I could tell her I had night sweats. I could even tell her the truth, that I was incapable of sharing a bed: *I don't do sleepovers. I have enough trouble sleeping on my own. What's the point, anyway? We've already cuddled.* I kept going as best I could, until it slipped out and I rolled off.

Neither of us had achieved congress.

"I don't care about coming," I said, breaking the tension.

We lay there chatting in a desultory manner for what seemed a sufficient amount of time.

"Have you seen Jackson lately?" she asked, adopting a line of conversation that caused my heart to sink.

"He's sopping up the gravy," I said, restoring the tension.

"I'm sorry ..."

"Enjoying the fruits of his success."

"He's doing really well, isn't he?"

"Yes."

After about ten minutes, she sat up. "I should get going," she said.

My heart sank even further. I felt disappointed, even a little put out, and wondered what I'd done, or hadn't done, to hasten her departure. And she had been so eager: We had met at a coffee shop. After an overpriced and disgusting meal, she had offered to drive me home and acquiesced when I invited her upstairs for a drink. The ease with which one thing led to another seemed magical now that she was leaving.

I lay in bed and watched her put her clothes back on. She looked good naked. Maybe I could get it up again. Forget it. What used to invigorate me now enervated me, and it was long past midnight.

* * *

Deletion feels so satisfying.

The boy had been right. It would be completely inappropriate to include that gratuitously mean-spirited line about Kelley Gimlet being the Hillary Clinton of rock and roll. It had to go.

(286)

It felt good to remove that page. It felt right. I had deliberated over it for a long time, but the simple act of deleting one page, which took half a second, was a more satisfying achievement than the hours on end that were spent writing it (and deliberating over deleting it).

In art as in life, too much time is wasted working up the courage to delete things.

* * *

"What's with these? Did Mike write a book?" I asked somewhat tentatively, surprised to see a stack of books bearing the authorial appellation of M. A. Supper behind the counter.

Gilbert replied cagily in the affirmative.

In the wake of our recent misunderstanding concerning the querulous teenager's groundless complaints, relations between Gilbert and myself were more strained than ever. I resented him for having brought such undeserved accusations to my attention without offering a personal disclaimer. But I had lost that battle when I lost my temper. A boundary had been crossed, and this faded friendship had already taken a lot of knocks. As usual, Gilbert had been very reasonable, very *fair*, and now he had even more of the upper hand.

"Pandemonium put it out," I remarked, having noticed the imprint of a thriving local press on the spine of Supper's book.

Mike Supper was a good friend of Gilbert's, a fellow twelve stepper and aspiring writer who often visited the store. I had no idea that he had written what appeared to be a short novel.

"How do you feel about switching your Sunday shift?" said Gilbert in a perfunctory manner as he turned his back on me and walked down from the counter.

"What do you mean?"

"Sunday nights instead of days," he said.

"Who's going to take the days?"

"Katy," he said, referring to one of the café girls.

This arrangement, apparently, had already been made. In the wake of our most recent blowout there was no point asking for an explanation or arguing about it. The services of somebody younger, more energetic, and less irascible were clearly required.

Now I would be working four nights a week. My social life would take even more of a hit. But at least I could write on Sundays.

"All right. What about this?" I said, returning to the subject of Mike Supper's book.

"I helped with that," said Gilbert.

"What do you mean? You're a literary agent now?"

"I'm exploring some possibilities," he said, as he walked off. "I can't do this all my life."

It hadn't occurred to me that Gilbert would ever quit his position at the bookstore. He had certainly been quiet about it. But he never told me anything anymore.

Maybe it shouldn't have come as such a surprise. He'd reached the summit here, and people did do that sort of thing—they moved on and took on new challenges.

Whereas the store had gotten too big for me; it had outgrown me.

I should have outgrown it, I moaned to myself as copies of *I Hate Dick* and *Milk the Internet* were placed in front of me on the counter.

Aaron walked in, shaking his head in horror as he scanned the rabble.

"Would you help me stage my death?" he asked upon his arrival at the counter.

"Sure. What do you need?"

"I want to do it Roman-style, but I don't have a bathtub."

"What's wrong with a bowl of warm water and a clean razor blade?"

"Too messy," said Aaron. "If I do it in the bath all they'll have to do, whoever it is that finds me, is drain the bath and carry the body out."

"Very thoughtful of you," I said. "No problem. You can use mine if you want."

"That would be the nicest thing anyone's ever done for me."

"That's what friends are for. Have you talked to Gilbert lately?"

"No. Why?"

"Nothing. I just wondered."

Aaron disappeared into the enturbulating mass, searching for a table to sit and draw at, and I was left to absorb the impact of Gilbert's alarming announcement.

Ten minutes into my shift and I couldn't put an act on anymore. The place had become unbearable, or was it me? I was older, crankier, more intolerant.

No, it was the place. Nowadays the store was more of a book-lined corridor leading to a café than an actual bookstore—and they were out in force this evening: the ululating dilettantes, the braying cacologists, the ready-made phrase spouters and the fake awe exaggerators, mutilating the air with sloppy diction and ersatz enthusiasm, dragging out their "Oh my Gods" from one end of the room to the other.

My ears were already ringing violently from the merry shrieking and high-speed drivel from high-pitched voices cawing and chainsawing into each other.

Hold it together ... hold it together ... stay sane, I told myself.

What happens when one no longer has the strength to tune out all the garbage anymore? One turns to the King. I tried to drown them out with *From Elvis in Memphis* (1969).

"What you want to play that shit for, man?" said a goateed white man as he headed for the door.

"I like it."

"What's the matter with you, dude? He's a racist fucker."

I could defend the music, and I could defend the man himself. But what was the point? It would only brand me as a racist in the mind of a fool.

It was all so dispiriting.

I couldn't possibly outlast Gilbert at this job and inherit the disconcerting mantle of being the store's longest-serving employee.

It would take a while for this most unwelcome development to sink in.

* * *

Every day, I satisfied myself that no immediate action regarding the debt situation needed to be taken. But I was continually worried about it. When this anxiety was eating away at me the entire time it was difficult not to mention it. But it only alienated people, so I kept it to myself.

I considered the possibility of raising money and coming to a settlement with Drago Lark, and drew a lot of blanks when it came to potential donors. I didn't feel comfortable approaching the few rich people I knew. It was an embarrassing mess that I'd gotten myself into. After agonizing for hours on end, I told myself that there was still plenty of time. But I wasn't entirely convinced.

I only had so much energy and it was being drained by practical problems: not from doing anything to fix them, only from worrying about them; and I was oppressed by that uneasiness peculiar to procrastination—an uneasiness that wouldn't lift until something definite was done to alleviate a pressing matter that required immediate action—and correspondingly, there was an abatement of the necessary urgency to proceed with my endeavors. In a realm of stifled suspense, where stasis was the status quo, I couldn't focus, couldn't strive. Sometimes it took all my strength just to remain awake.

There wasn't much point trying to write under such circumstances. But it was too late to stop now. If only for the sake of routine—the precious numbing comfort of routine—I pressed on, picking away at it like a carcass, limb by limb, draining the blood out of it, writing myself into a void.

By the time I'm done all that's left of *this thing* will be bare bones and dried blood. As barely and bloodlessly, picked away at like a carcass in a void, it keeps expanding.

Just hack it down, employ butchery, not surgery. Perfectionism is for the imperfect. Get it over with. If I don't finish *this thing*, the last three years of my life are going to have been a complete waste of time. Not that all the others weren't. But I will be able to say that I actualized myself. Great!

* * *

The low rumble of traffic, the steady sizzle of tinnitus, and the whirring of the table fan mingled in the dusty air. Medication and caffeine riled the waves of bleariness, turning the warm glow into noxious smog, weighing me down as I drove myself to the verge of giving up again.

I had no desire to emerge from this chemically insulated state, so here I remained, stabilizing my nervous system in the usual way. With all the urgent concerns that needed to be stifled, the aid of a certain medicine was more necessary than ever, and I was still both writing *and* editing in a medicated state.

Stale desperation: Could one be both stale and desperate at the same time? Yes, I had provided living proof. It was hard to believe I'd been at this for two hours. At what? I hadn't done anything. Even with the help of medication it was impossible to proceed with the required composure. I needed to re-up sooner than anticipated, and was too conscious of my depleting supply—down to seven pill-sized sessions—to appreciate what I still had at my disposal. I could start rationing it out, taking one pill a day instead of two, but then I wouldn't feel anything. And it was all about feeling something, or rather, not feeling anything.

* * *

Freedom ran out, the internet turned back on, and I paid my daily visit to the LA Court website. I tapped the accompanying case number, which by now I knew by heart, into the designated window, and was confronted with the following information:

XX/26/20XX PROOF OF SERVICE OF SUMMONS AND COMPLAINT FILED. SERVED TO (HANGLAND, SEAN) AN INDIVIDUAL. XX/26/20XX DECLARATION RE: DILIGENCE FILED.

Nothing had been received in the mail, nothing had been handed over, nothing had been left outside the door—yet they were claiming papers had been served two days ago, on which occasion I'd been home all day and would have heard any knocking on the door.

This was what I'd been warned about, and what I'd recklessly procrastinated about: the devious tactics of a debt-collection agency that I was powerless to deal with. Thrown into a queasy panic, I called the lawyer, Curt Sands—no reply—and set out on yet another internet trawl, reinforcing what I already knew: that bottom-dwelling debt collectors often deliberately avoided supplying proof of service in order to facilitate the practice of gouging defaulters whose debts they had bought at a pittance from credit card companies that had given up on extracting the funds.

I had thirty days to dispute the validity of the debt. If I did not dispute the debt within those thirty days, it would be assumed that it was valid. At which point, they could drain my bank account of its nonexistent funds or garnish my wages.

One alternative was to file a written response, send copies to their lawyers and to the court, and have them set a court date, which would probably take place in about a year's time. "Force them to prove their case ... Sometimes they don't have the paperwork," was the advice of one lawyer that I cold-called. "They won't show up," claimed another.

The prospect of a court date was daunting and fraught with complications, but it was something to consider, and I had a month to consider it. The other unappealing option was to come to a settlement with Drago Lark, but with insufficient funds and less than a month to pay out, that would be difficult, if not impossible.

"They could have a judgment against you in two weeks after that first thirty days is over," said yet another lawyer. "But usually it's going to take more like four to six weeks."

This lawyer's temporizing tactics were attractive, but could he be trusted? At the end of an exhausting afternoon of searching in vain for further cause for procrastination, a nap was necessary. *I've still got a month*, I told myself as I drifted off.

* * *

"We haven't had a real conversation in months. Every time I call up you can't talk because you're cuddling with your girlfriend or making her lunch."

Mitchell laughed it off. The convivial atmosphere of a mutual friend's birthday party at yet another newly opened local bar wasn't conducive to addressing the urgent matter of replenishing medicinal supplies, but I was far too preoccupied by the subject to keep silent about it. At the very least it could be built up to gradually while I inquired about the domestic arrangements that were proving to be such an obstacle to my needs.

"So you're buying in?" I said.

"What's the alternative?"

"Autonomy."

Mitchell chuckled knowingly, as if scoffing at such an unworldly notion.

"I didn't think that would be very convincing," I added.

"Autonomy, monotony—what am I going to do, man? I can't go on being broke and occasionally banging young girls forever."

"Why not?"

"People move on …"

"For fuck's sake … ." I reined it in. "The last time we spoke you seemed to think Lyn might be breaking up with you."

"That's because I backslid with the meds. That's over. She has zero tolerance for it."

"Which reminds me, what's up with the supplies?"

"Well, that might work out, and it might not."

Mitchell's attention was diverted by the presence of a slightly famous person whom he walked over to hug.

A woman I knew walked by, deliberately turning her head in order to avoid making eye contact with me. A few minutes later she was happily engaged in conversation with a middle-aged dullard who wasn't as fine a conversationalist as me, and wasn't even much younger than me.

"I could really use the stuff," I said to Mitchell when he returned from his confab with the minor celebrity. "I'm trying to write a fucking novel."

I had told him this enough times already but I could hardly expect him to recall a matter of such trifling insignificance.

"How far have you got?"

"It's hard to say. It will sound idiotic if I talk about it."

Speech was becoming painful: my tongue was getting sore from rubbing against the remains of another broken tooth.

"That's what I have in mind," said Mitchell.

"What?"

"A novel."

"I thought you said you couldn't get any work done because Lyn was always pestering you and making unreasonable demands on your body."

"It's getting easier," said Mitchell. "We've come to an understanding." He took out his phone and pulled up a photograph of himself and Lyn sitting by her swimming pool with Bob McGilt. "We've been hanging out. His wife's an old friend of Lyn's. They live on the next street. He's much nicer than I expected, very soft-spoken. He's looking at my script."

The possibilities for Mitchell were now endless, especially with McGilt as a neighbor. He wouldn't be letting go of that. And the great musician/actor/writer/director/artist/restaurateur (a vociferous proponent of "clean food") didn't do drugs or drink, although he never shut up about the glorious excesses of his youth—and this would certainly bolster Mitchell's budding temperance.

"I brought your name up," he said.

At some point I must have unwisely told Mitchell about my one-time friendship with McGilt. Now McGilt probably assumed that I was in the habit of dropping his name at every available opportunity. Naturally, when his name came up, which it did with annoying frequency, I sometimes lacked the strength of mind to resist mentioning that we had once been on friendly terms. He'd probably do the same with my name, if it was ever mentioned.

"And …" I said, with some trepidation.

"He asked if you were still writing."

"Great."

McGilt was everywhere. I dropped the subject.

"So you're moving in?" I said.

"Gradually moving things in, yeah. It's a slow process."

"Yes, I can imagine," I said, nodding in fake accord. "So it's a lifestyle choice?"

"I love her," he said, with a straight face, as if it were the most natural thing in the world for somebody who had always been inflexibly opposed to connubiality to suddenly, or rather, "gradually," throw his lot in with a woman of a certain age who just happened to be rich and well connected.

Not that it was any of my business but it was difficult to swallow my pride while I was biting my tongue and laughing bitterly at the same time. The options had been weighed and sacrifices had to be made, and one of those sacrifices was cutting out meds.

Another one bites the dust of the soft life. A dull and predictable pain sank in, but I couldn't say anything to nettle him, because, in the absence of any other source, I wanted him to continue providing me with medication.

I cast my gaze warily down the bar, observing the ravages of time, while avoiding the mirror. It was the sort of social gathering that caused one to reflect that maybe one had been in this town too long. There was a middle-aged man a few seats down whom I barely recognized. The last time I'd seen him he had been a pretty boy who fronted a band that was on the verge of success. That was at least twenty years ago. Now he looked like an aging adolescent, emptied by ambition, growing old without dignity in the land of permanent youth. Maybe I didn't look much better myself.

"What else is going on?" asked Mitchell, with unconcealed disinterest.

"What about your guy?" I said, in order to steer the conversation back on track.

"I'll hook you up with Jay. I'll call him up and set up an introduction. He hasn't returned my last few calls so I don't know. Come over for a swim next week."

And saying this, he walked off.

There was some cause for hope. As I sat there in the malt glow, staring at all the pretty bottles twinkling on the shelves, the attractive middle-aged redhead on the next barstool introduced herself to me.

"How do you know Lisa?" she asked, referring to the woman whose birthday was being celebrated.

"From around the way," I said. "How about you?"

"*We* know her from New York," she said. "*We* just moved here."

"That's nice," I said. "Where are you living?"

"*We* found a house in Silver Lake."

"Renting or buying?"

"*We* bought it."

"See you later." I slid off the barstool, left the bar, and walked home.

I had long considered my middle-aged bachelor friends to be my family, and this felt like one of them leaving the fold. Not that I'd ever exactly thought of Mitchell as a brother, but there were so few of us left and he had, at least, been a holdout. But eventually everybody, even the most seemingly case-hardened, ended up cutting a deal. One shouldn't expect people to remain the same and resent them out of self-hateful self-interest when they changed, but … there were many buts.

How could one produce honest work if one was in an opportunistic relationship? It made it easier to get work done when somebody was relieving the financial pressures, but wasn't the quality of the work weakened by such an (often tacit and uneasy) understanding? Sponging off one's spouse involved a massive amount of compromise, but for some the price of feigned desire and domestication on somebody else's terms was not too high.

On the other hand, there was a lot to be said for making a commitment to a partner whose stable and supportive presence allowed one to work in peace, and there were numerous examples of this in the history of literature: Wordsworth, Carlyle, Conrad, Joyce, Nabokov, among others who had sweet and understanding literary enablers.

Unfortunately, I'd never met anybody like that.

Patronage, of course, was an altogether more elegant form of sponging. Rilke, Duchamp, Pound—the list was endless (or used to be endless, as patronage seemed to have become a thing of the past). Unlike a needy partner who resented you if you didn't give them a certain amount of attention, one's patrons left one alone, although one probably had to make the right noises when called upon.

But I'd never met anyone like that either.

Then there was the academic crowd, the grants-and-residencies leeches. That was another world, and an even more impenetrable one—that I was ineligible for as I hadn't attended the right schools or been published in the right places.

With such thoughts occupying my mind, I walked home around the lake,[8] seeing the things that only I could see, thinking the thoughts that only I could think, and wondering if they were worth thinking anymore. I may have sold myself short, but at least I hadn't sold myself out. The opportunity simply hadn't availed itself.

* * *

"Pardon me for resorting to such a primeval form of communication," I said when the boy finally answered his phone. My two earlier messages hadn't been returned and I felt slightly humiliated about making another call. His unresponsiveness, I assumed, meant that he would be delivering a negative verdict upon the recent pages I'd sent along.

"Have you got any time this week?" I breezily inquired.

"I'd like to hang out but I'm going to Joshua Tree for a few days."

"With your girlfriend?"

"Yes."

"What did you think of the last batch?" I asked.

---

8. Yes, there is a lake. Perhaps I should have mentioned it earlier, as it might have added some much-needed local color. Echo Park Lake is usually thronged with walkers, runners, picnickers, sunbathers and anglers. The lakeside is inhabited by geese, ducks and scurrying rats, and it takes approximately twenty-three minutes to walk the perimeter. Key features include a gushing fountain, the Lady of the Lake statue, a closed-off rustic bridge leading to a small island of palm trees, and a boathouse from which swan-shaped pedal boats set sail. An annual blossoming of lotus flowers is celebrated by a festival every July. The northeast corner of the park, opposite the Angelus Temple (built by charismatic evangelist Aimee Semple McPherson in 1923), has in recent years turned into a makeshift homeless encampment, with many of the burgeoning dispossessed setting up tents. Other popular local attractions include Dodger Stadium, Elysian Park, and the secret stairways that link the hillside streets.

"The plot is hard to follow," he said, apathetically.

"What plot? What about the sex scene in media res? I thought you'd like that."

"You're going to be accused of sexism."

"If I'm lucky enough to be accused of anything. My main concern at this point is that I'm writing for a limited readership."

"That's fine. As Henry James said, 'Three thousand good readers is the most you can hope for.'"

"I mean a very limited readership. A readership of one: myself."

"Well, make it more accessible then."

"I've tried. This is the most accessible I can make it. It has no universal appeal, maybe no appeal whatsoever. The predicament of the protagonist is too singular. It alienates too many potential readers; people who might otherwise be sympathetic will see themselves as targets. There are too many targets, and when one shoots at targets one becomes a target oneself."

"Well, ease up on it then." The boy's attitude had become annoyingly noncommittal.

"It's not that simple. It's too late for that."

"I'll say this," said the boy, finally showing a little conviction, even if it was negative. "You have three or four characters that serve the same purpose."

"Yeah, what's that?" As if I couldn't tell where this was going.

"They've compromised themselves professionally or romantically or whatever; they've cut deals, whereas you ..."

"The protagonist," I said.

"Whatever," said the boy. "He has integrity—'perverted integrity' or 'perverse ambition' or whatever you call it. You're always measuring his failure and integrity against other people's success and supposed lack of integrity. A couple of those comparisons would be fine, but you compare yourself to almost everybody in this way, and it's kind of deceptive."

"You're confirming more of my misgivings," I said, with a heavy sigh.

"It's exhausting," he said.

"Well, yes, but I suppose you could say that's one of the themes."

"There's too much method on show for it to be enjoyable," said the boy. "It's too tight."

"That's what worries me," I said. "It has an airless quality that squeezes the life out of the work. I have to stop editing it, leave the looser passages as they are and space it out more."

"You know, Sean, your life isn't really that bad. You have a great apartment, good friends, a good job. You've exaggerated the negative aspects."

"It's not strictly autobiographical."

The boy snorted with derision.

"The problem … one of the problems," I said, "is that because the narrative takes place in a recognizable reality, people are going to assume it's strictly autobiographical, when, in fact, it's 95 percent fabrication. Some of these characters might have their origins in reality but they mutate into something completely fictive as the narrative proceeds. Still, I do feel uneasy about having pilloried this place and these people."

"The only person who's going to look bad is you," said the boy, helpfully.

"I hope you're right."

"You're never going to finish it."

"I know. What else is going on?"

"The record's coming out," he said, suddenly sounding enthusiastic. "I'm pleased with it. First a 45, then the album comes out in the spring. I'll be on the road a lot. Hopefully, it'll be heard. Some of the songs might get heard on shows ... TV shows. I'm friends with this woman who's a plugger, that's what she does and she wants to take me on. It'll get exposure. Then I won't have to work. Everyone else I know who's in this position doesn't have to work a job anymore."

He was the sort of bright young spark that influential people liked to help out; they wanted to be a part of his rise to the top. The years I'd thrown away still lay before him, and he was too smart to misuse them in the perversely fatalistic and fatally perverse manner that I had.

"So you've got it all figured out," I said.

"I'll give you a call when we get back from Joshua Tree."

He hung up. He wasn't expressing his disapproval so cautiously anymore. His initial interest in the work had dried up fairly quickly, and he didn't seem to mind if I knew about it—more cold water spilled on the embers of a dying venture, and our friendship, sadly, already fading.

* * *

"Mitchell said you'd be calling." A gravelly voice answered the phone. "I've only got about ten at the moment, so you'll have to mix it up with some other stuff."

"Eh ..."

"I don't go out for less than $200. All I've got is browns and yellows. How much d'you want to spend?"

"Two hundred."

"I can give you ten yellows and five browns."

"How about just $100 worth then? I only want yellows."

"How about nothing?" he said, grindingly.

"All right, make the rest up with the browns. What time's good for you?"

"Tomorrow at noon."

That was an inconvenient time of day. It would mean curtailing my session; I probably wouldn't get any writing done at all in the morning, and it was unlikely that I'd make it home in time to spend the afternoon writing. And I didn't want the other stuff; I only wanted one kind of pill, but in order to get it and adapt to this dealer's business practices I had to buy an equal amount of a different and stronger pill that I'd never taken before.

* * *

"Dinner time?" A dreadlocked stranger's grinning face leaned across the counter, breathing onto my slice of pizza.

"What about it?"

"Oh, I'm sorry. I didn't mean to interrupt."

"How else can such an intrusion possibly be interpreted? Just spreading good cheer, are you? I don't need your fucking commentary."

I couldn't even eat in peace. Inevitably, if I had something warm to eat, even if there hadn't been a sale in half an hour, I was going to be interrupted.

"Bon appétit," he said as he sauntered off.

There didn't seem to be much point in keeping up any semblance of politesse with the ruder sort of customer anymore. I kept my head down.

Penned in, but with the sheep crammed outside the pen, I sat there, bogged down in a blur, lost in thought, and thinking myself lost. Out of my peripheral vision, I only saw the incoming customers at cell-phone level, playing with their handheld gadgets as they filed in; and I heard them: the Like-ers, the Cool-ers, the Awesome-ers, the Oh-my-God-ers. I couldn't be bothered to catalog the interactions, the indignities, the trials and the humiliations anymore. It was more of the same, a lot more of the same.

Looking up, I found myself staring at the new Jackson Valvitcore book, *Fuck Fame*, on the display shelf of new hardbacks facing the counter. I hadn't realized it was already out. It was tastefully presented, as would be expected from such an esteemed press.

I walked across to the shelf and opened it to the first page, which contained one line: "I have decided to stop writing for a while."

So Jackson had added some final touches to the book, after all. I was confident that he would attempt to justify this act of blatant plagiarism with some quack postulations about how the essential uselessness of literature gave license to theft of this nature. The best thing, in the face of such shamelessness, would be to not mention it at all: that would really mystify him—although I was probably incapable of exercising such self-restraint. The main inconvenience was that I would now have to change the first line of my book.

I placed Jackson's book back on the shelf. Since I was standing there I did some quick arithmetic and calculated that out of thirty-five new hardcover novels, only four were written by white males. It was payback time. After having been in charge for centuries, now was the time for the straight white male to graciously defer. It occurred to me that my novel would stand a better chance of getting published if I turned the protagonist into a woman. That would certainly compensate for the lack of female characters and offset any charges of sexism. But all the name changing, pronoun flipping, and other narrative complications would require far too much work at this late stage.

It was all so dispiriting.

"Excuse me," I said to a young woman who was blocking the space between the fanzine rack and the front counter. I'd noticed her and her male companion when they had walked in a few minutes earlier, owing to their attractive surface appearances; they were probably models or actors.

"Why don't you go around that way," she said.

It took a few seconds to register that she was seriously suggesting I walk up one aisle and back down the next one in order to reach the front door a few yards away.

"D'you expect me to walk halfway around the store when you could move a couple of inches to let me get by?"

"Yes. Why don't you do that?" she said, and returned to browsing a book about the Ramones.

I returned to my post behind the counter and let this extraordinary exchange sink in. Even I couldn't absorb this degree of humiliation; I'd be seething about it for weeks. I had to stand up for myself, although I was somewhat concerned about her boyfriend, who was bigger than me.

I stepped down from the counter and addressed her.

"Get out of here. I own this store. Don't tell me how to act in my own store. Leave."

My ability to deliver this order with a level tone of voice, and without losing composure, surprised and pleased me, as did the ease with which my command was obeyed. Gliding through life owing to her temporarily desirable surface appearance, this woman wasn't used to being dealt with like an ordinary person, but the claim of ownership was a hard one to argue with.

Her boyfriend walked off and stood by the door, meekly waiting for her. His attitude indicated that he was used to her causing scenes of this kind. After an initial moment of hesitation, she followed him, with no further words exchanged between us. The few other people within hearing distance clucked among themselves in the immediate aftermath.

Ten minutes later I walked outside and found books scattered all over the pavement. The hateful shrew's parting gesture had been to upset the dollar cart.

I got down on the pavement and began picking up the filthy, splayed, unwanted books. This, I feared, was the fate that would befall my novel, even if it did get published. All this time and care had been invested in an enterprise that was doomed to failure. The sense that I had to make a contribution had finally been honored, but it was unlikely that anybody would care or even notice. All this work, all this preparation, just to have another book moldering on the shelf—to be picked up and put down, ignored, fleetingly despised, remaindered, forgotten, and left to die a squalid and premature death on the dollar cart. That was the life cycle of most books. This much, at least, I had learned from my work as a bookseller. All things considered, maybe it wouldn't be so bad if I could only get it published by a small press. A major press would probably demand a lot of changes before they even considered putting it out. Ultimately, I'd be lucky if I could get it published at all.

It was one of those awry, ill-starred nights populated by disturbing and disruptive people. Three young savages walked around the store taking photographs. As they filed down the aisle toward the front door, the one in front, a short, beefy individual in a pair of camouflage shorts, addressed me.

"How you doing, old man?" he said, as they walked out.

By the time his words had sunk in, it was too late, they had left. At the very least I could have asked him to repeat his words. But it wasn't as if I could deny the charge: I was old.

That made for two "Did you actually say that?" moments in the space of an hour, and one act of blatant plagiarism.

Scum … scum … I was surrounded by scum.

A teenager opened the front door, waved a cell phone frantically, and yelled at me: "What's the wifey called?!"

"What?" I couldn't hear him clearly.

"The Wi-Fi code?!"

"It's up at the café counter at the other end of the room."

"You're a faggot, dude!"

That made for three "Did you actually say that?" moments in the space of an hour.

As I was closing up a young woman came in.

"Do you have the new Valvitcore?" she asked.

Jackson had become so popular that his readers now referred to him on a last-name basis.

It was all so deeply dispiriting.

* * *

When I got home, there was an incoming call from Jay, but no message. I called him back.

"Hey, man, those brown ones, cut them into thirds. They're very strong," he rasped.

"OK. Thanks."

"And don't drive on them."

At first I was touched that he would go to the trouble of making a personal call to offer this thoughtful advice. Maybe he wasn't as cold and sour as he had first appeared. Then it dawned on me that the call wasn't entirely motivated by selfless concern: he was worried that the trail would lead back to him if one of his customers died. The president had recently been recommending the death sentence for drug dealers. There was an "epidemic" on, and in some states, not California yet, there were already laws in place for arresting dealers if their customers overdosed.

* * *

That was a pointless episode, and I have no intention of following through with it. It adds nothing.

Might as well delete it.

* * *

I waited to feel something, to feel nothing, and I didn't feel any-thing—no warmth, no glow, no flow—only the undesirable aftereffects.

I was beginning to dread entering that once-comfortable state. It was wise to take breaks from medicating, and I hadn't been taking any breaks. Rather than allowing me to sit in one place and focus on my redemptionless narrative for three hours, it induced a jagged bleariness, a heavy weightlessness, completely unsuited to the purpose of clearheaded literary endeavor. I could feel the vitality draining out of me as the pills dissolved in my system, generating a sludge that had to be waded through in order to get anything done—a high-voltage grogginess that gave rise to the lowering of standards and found its equivalent in the turgid prose I churned out.

Drowsified in bottomless torpor, it was a struggle to construct a sentence. The critical faculties could be subdued but they could also be wiped out. A creative tool should open one up, not close one down, and this creative tool had shut me down. The building up of resistance, diminishing of beneficial impact, supply difficulties, strain of expenditure, the need to finish *this thing*: all of these factors led me to believe that this stuff had become more of an obstacle than an enabler, and that the time had finally come to cut it out.

But it was hard to break with tradition, and life was too stark and too fragile to endure without it, especially with debt problems preying on my mind.

I nibbled off another bitter sliver and plunged into an even more rancorous stupor.

* * *

The computer keys were hot to the touch and the text was turning blue. The place felt shaky and combustible, as if the cumulative impact of day after day of relentless stultifying heat might result in a long-overdue major earthquake or other force of nature that would cause this rickety structure to collapse and destroy this work in progress, along with everything else.

With only a table fan trained on me, I stroked the mark on the edge of the desk where, for years, my elbow had rested, gently scarring the wood. The vitality I had once brought to this increasingly morbid undertaking was fading. It was getting stale; it had been stale to begin with, and now it had passed beyond staleness into some other realm of belletristic putrefaction. It was overpowering: the mephitic stench of rotting prose, even as I attempted to pump life into its bloated corpse.

* * *

I felt nothing, then I felt groggy. So fleeting a reprieve, then right on time the dip into murky irritation. It was a race to get anything done before I became ensludged and incapacitated. After taking this stuff for so long, without any days off, it was having a dulling rather than a sharpening effect. Toxicity outweighed therapeutic value, but I kept taking it because it kept me sitting here, which was about the only benefit it continued to provide. Other than killing the discomfort caused by not taking them, there was nothing to be gained from these pills anymore; all they did was muddy the mind.

What kind of fuel was this, that slowed one down, that induced physical, mental and emotional constipation? It was foolish to assume that this stuff would always have the desired effect. Why should it?

The amount of time that had already been lost in this claustrophobic sprawl was irrelevant: the rest of it needed to be dispatched as swiftly as possible. I was writing in order to take drugs rather than taking drugs in order to write. Which seemed as good a reason as any for engaging in literary activity. But the only way to finish *this thing* was to stop medicating and give it a straight, hard edit.

This is what happens: things stop working. That's when the drug memoirists go to work: never when the drugs are working for them, only when they cease to be useful and fun. That's when the "struggle" begins.

But if I stopped medicating, I would never stoop so low as to write about it. There was nothing more desperate, boring or played-out than writing about drugs.

* * *

"I'm sorry," said Gilbert.

So this was how they operated. They didn't even pay you the courtesy of contacting you directly. Of course they didn't: you had to endure the further indignity of finding out about it from your boss. I was shocked, and I had no rehearsed explanation.

Gilbert seemed to be embarrassed for me: notifying an ex-friend and current employee that their already modest wages were going to be cut a further 25 percent in order to pay off a debt-collection agency was a sordid matter and required some sensitivity from the bearer of such bleak tidings.

"Those debts are from years ago. Student loans," I stammered out, unconvincingly.

Gilbert expressed his sorrow again. He put a lot of feeling into that "sorry," for the instant it took him to utter it, and then he left with a beautiful woman who had been waiting for him in front of the counter.

It didn't make sense that a default judgment had been issued against me when the papers were only served two weeks ago. Every lawyer I had spoken with had clearly stated that one was given at least thirty days between the serving of papers and a default judgment being issued, and other sources had confirmed this.

I was stuck at the store in a mystified and maddened state of suspension. I couldn't consult anybody about it now. It seemed, however, that it was official. The store had been notified—and, humiliatingly, Gilbert knew all about it: a quarter of my income would be going to a debt collector every month.

A stack of children's books was slammed down in front of me. There was no time to think.

"Will you wrap *The Runaway Bunny* and *Little Fur Family*?" asked the woman on the other side of the counter.

"Together or separately?" I asked with unconcealed displeasure.

"Separately. It's just that kids have birthday parties together these days and you have to bring two gifts."

At least she had the decency to offer an explanation.

"Don't watch," I said.

"Can you give it some flair?" she said.

She stood at the counter, fiddling with her cell phone while I wrapped the books and poured all my frustration into tying the pink bow. With a hideous grimace, I handed them back.

Why were my wages being garnished when I was supposed to be given a month after the papers were served to prevent this from happening? This baffling question kept spinning through my head, and it wasn't likely to let up until it was answered. Obviously, I'd been misinformed. Debt collectors were known for their cruel and devious ways, and lawyers were notoriously unscrupulous—perhaps they were even in league with each other. But it was clearly stated on the court-case document that papers were served only two weeks ago, which meant that I still had another two weeks, at least, to forestall a default judgment: time in which to go bankrupt, which I should have done when I initially defaulted on the credit cards, years ago.

"Do you guys have any books by Laura Sweeney?" The voice of another helpless customer bleated into my ear.

I couldn't bring myself to look into her face. "Under *S* in fiction," I groaned, and pointed to the relevant section.

With teeming brain and shaking hand I reached for the calculator and started running the numbers. Twenty-five percent of my wages would automatically be deducted until the debt was repaid. That meant ...

"How much is this?" The customer had returned, bearing a copy of *Conversations with Beautiful People*.

"There's a price on the back. Can't you see I'm trying to think?"

The customer looked at me with contempt and walked out in high dudgeon, leaving the book on the counter.

It would take at least two and a half years to repay the debt by means of wage garnishment. It was hardly worth holding on to the job. But what else could I do? What else was I capable of doing?

Perhaps there was a way around it, but I couldn't do anything about it now. Calling a lawyer would have to wait until the morning.

A man entered the store and walked straight up to the counter. "I'm looking for something," he said.

"You're not looking for it," I said.

"I'm sorry," he said.

"You're not looking for it," I repeated. "You walked straight in and asked me to look for it. What is it?"

"Don't worry about it," he said, and walked back out.

If I'd cut a deal with the debt collectors, I might have gotten off with paying half as much, or less. Or I could have hired a lawyer and faced a court date that the plaintiffs wouldn't have showed up for. Most sensibly of all, I could have gone bankrupt. I had intended to deal with it, but I had continued to weigh the options, and all those options cost money—and that consideration, compounded by a predisposition for procrastination, had been responsible for the delay.

A friendly, open-faced young fellow appeared at the counter.

"Do you guys have Hermann Hesse?"

"Do we *have* him? Yes, he's over there, sitting in the café, looking at Facebook on his laptop."

"What?"

"What does Hermann Hesse write?"

"Novels."

"So where would you expect to find his novels?"

"I'm not sure, I've never been here before. In the novels section?"

"Exactly. So why don't you walk ten feet over there to the fiction section, which is clearly indicated, underneath the sign with the big letters on it that spell out FICTION, and look for him there."

"Is this like some sort of joke?"

"Yes, it's a massive joke. The world, life and everything. Try to remember that. It will help enormously as you make your way through life. And can you stop saying 'like,' you're over the age of twelve."

He just stood there, gaping in horror.

"What are you staring at? This isn't a fucking zoo. You want a book, go and get it. Do I have to lead you by your prick? It's right under your prick, level with your crotch in the shelf. Walk ten feet in that direction, unzip your fly, pull your prick out, stick it into the shelf, and you will be thrusting it between *Siddhartha* and *The Glass Bead Game.*"

"Go fuck yourself," he said. It was the "Go fuck yourself" of a decent man who wasn't used to telling people to go fuck themselves. And I was fucked. I had fucked myself.

How was I going to get through this night of suspense and inchoate anger, with an answer I didn't want to hear undoubtedly awaiting me in the morning? Fresh stabs of anxiety, suffused with regret, cut into me every few seconds as I contemplated how I had mishandled the burden of debt. I should at least have filed the written response: that would have bought me some time.

Another customer appeared: another simpering smile, another grating voice.

"D'you have a specific section for philosophy?" he asked.

"No, we have an unspecific section for it. Would you like me to escort you to it? Obviously, I've got nothing better to do than answer questions you're too stupid or lazy to figure out for yourself. D'you think that I—tired and beaten down by the demands of the likes of you and life itself—that I don't already have enough to do, that I have time to save you who have sauntered in here fresh and alert, without a worry in the world, the trouble of doing something you could easily do yourself if you possessed the wherewithal? Here, let me show you."

I got up from behind the counter. A man was standing in front of it, lost in a world of texting. "Why don't you just stand in the middle of the floor texting, blocking everyone else's way, you useless you ... Get out of the way!" I barged past him, almost knocking him over, reveling in the agitation. There was no point in holding back anymore.

"What if every single person that walked in showed a similar lack of self-reliance and had to be escorted to the book they wanted? I can't take it anymore. Just look, just fucking look!"

But the customer who had politely inquired after the whereabouts of the philosophy section, along with everyone else within hearing range, which amounted to every other person in the store, was standing back in horror.

"Here, philosophy, you want philosophy?" I started pulling books off the shelves and throwing them on the floor.

It felt good. So I kept going.

"Just fucking look. What's the point of having eyes if you're not going to look?! You too. What the fuck are you all gawking at? Haven't you ever seen anybody lose their shit before?! Just get the fuck out of here! Get out of here. All of you, get the fuck out of here! Get out ... out ... out!"

I started throwing books at the customers.

"Go away ... just go away ... for fuck's sakes ... away!"

A woman standing a few yards away, at a safe distance, was filming me on her cell phone. Why not go all the way? Fuck it. I ran across the room, grabbed the cell phone out of her hand and smashed it on the floor. It felt good.

"Get out of here, all of you, just fucking get out of here. Get out, out, out, just get the fuck out. Leave!!!"

There were books all over the floor—Kant, Kierkegaard, Locke, Montaigne, Nietzsche—the wisdom of the ages scattered in rage and sadness. I left them there and returned to my post behind the counter. The fuckers, the fucking fuckers, they had finally succeeded in driving me mad. *The Fuckers*, yes, that was it, that was my title! At last. I couldn't go wrong with that. It would sell. Yes, it would sell. Forget it. It sounded too much like Jackson's book ... the fucker.

After a few minutes of sitting behind the counter, heaving with emotion, my shaking and panting began to subside.

"Are you OK?" Somebody I vaguely recognized was inquiring after my well-being.

I was touched that somebody cared enough to ask. It was Alicia, the maternal young barista. I replied in the affirmative, although there was no way of concealing the shame and embarrassment that were rapidly unmanning me.

Although far from calm, I returned to the shelves, keeping my head down, and began sheepishly picking books up from the floor, along with the pair of scissors I'd also flung across the room in the midst of the frenzy.

As I was crouched on the floor, exhausted, a woman entered the store and stood over me.

"Do you work here?" she asked.

Since I wasn't sure anymore, I didn't answer that question. "What do you need?" I said.

"Do you guys have a restroom I could use?"

I was still crouched there twenty minutes later, reshelving the books, when Gilbert appeared. He looked down at me with disgust and pity, maybe even disappointment.

"Just go home, Sean," he said very calmly.

* * *

At four in the morning I was jerked awake with an electrifying jolt of shame and dread. With the bedtime cocktails no longer clouding my judgment, an acute awareness of the previous night's misbehavior was quickly sinking in. How could I justify such a loss of self-control in public? It was one thing to have tantrums in the privacy of one's home but this was no way for a middle-aged man to be conducting himself. Mortification was compounded by my powerlessness in the face of malevolent forces that were intent upon stripping me of my meager livelihood.

I took a little white pill but it didn't have the desired soporific effect. I just lay there, drowsing in and out of semislumber, gently pulling on my knob in an unsuccessful attempt to soothe the surging and spiraling bleakness of an uncertain future.

At 7 a.m. I rose, feeling like the hapless victim of an elaborate self-defeating plot that I had unwittingly perpetrated against myself, and exuding a morbid effluvia from which all but the most kindred souls were bound to recoil.

Forgoing my usual morning ablutions and apotropaic litanizing, I started looking up the numbers of New York consumer debt attorneys online. Lawyers on the East Coast, three hours ahead, were already at work and ready to field inquiries.

I called one up at random, a Mr. Firmlayer, and explained my predicament to him.

"There's not much you can do about that," he said.

"Not much?"

"Nothing."

"But the papers were only served two weeks ago. Or so they claim. I never saw them."

"The date reflects when they were filed, not when they were served. They could have been served two- or three-weeks earlier than it states on the court's website. What matters is the date that they served the papers. Sometimes there's a two or three week gap between serving the papers and filing proof of service. You could have checked with the courthouse to discover exactly when they were served."

"But that's so devious."

"It is, but it's standard procedure for debt collectors."

"But I never saw any papers in the first place. Could I ... we ... challenge, countersue them for not filing papers?"

"You could but it would be very hard to prove. They will claim that they left the papers in your mailbox, and the court won't necessarily believe you when you claim that you didn't receive them. And if you lose, you will have to pay their court costs."

"But it would buy more time," I said, and considered all the time I had already bought, and how much it had cost me. "Is there any way to reverse the ruling?"

"Unfortunately not," he said. I found myself heartened by the vague note of sympathy in his voice.

It was futile to seek solutions: there weren't any; and I couldn't take up any more of Mr. Firmlayer's time when I wasn't paying for it.

I got back into bed, lay on my side, and began to berate myself. It was dangerous not to have dealt with such a pressing matter in a timely manner. I had still been making my mind up about exactly how to go about it. That was no excuse. Out of laziness and unwilling-ness to confront such an ugly matter, I had taken too much comfort in false hopes rather than probing more deeply into the more inconvenient complexities of my predicament. I should have filed for bankruptcy years ago. All the things I had been telling myself to do all along returned to torment me with fresh poignancy. I lay there until I couldn't lie there any longer, then I clambered blearily out of bed and made for the telephone again.

As a further desperate last resort, I called Curt Sands, the lawyer responsible for providing me with the most perilously inadequate information. Why hadn't he told me about the discrepancy between serving and filing papers? Surely that was something I needed to know about. But I hadn't retained his services. All he'd done was offer free advice over the phone, and such advice was free for a reason.

Sands didn't answer his phone. I returned to the computer and began combing through the online debtor forums. Despite the extensive research I had already conducted, there was still a lot I had missed. Inundated with information, I hadn't been able to decide how best to proceed, but all that research should have led to some action.

I was taking solace in the crossword by the time the anticipated email from Gilbert arrived: "I know you've had a hard time recently but there's no excuse for attacking customers and destroying store property. I'm sorry but you've left us with no alternative. We can't keep you on after this. If you need references for other employment, we'll provide them. Thanks for everything you've done for the store." This insincere expression of gratitude heartened me: I was so easily heartened.

Compared to nothing, my wages, even minus 25 percent, now seemed bountiful. It had been foolish of me to blow my top. Surely I could find a way to blame somebody else for my misbehavior. Now that I came to obsess about it, Gilbert could have broken it to me more gently: he could have informed me about the wage garnishment when he first learned about it, presumably that afternoon, and given me a chance to let the news sink in, rather than thrust it upon me the moment I arrived at the store; he'd never been slow to email me when it came to complaining about some minor wrongdoing, but when it was information I could have benefited from being notified about in advance, he held his peace. Perhaps he preferred to deliver the news personally in order to inflict maximum discomfort. If the facts had been allowed to settle in before I got to the store, I wouldn't have blown my top. Yes, it was Gilbert's fault.

Now what? Now that I no longer had any wages to garnish, what could the debt collectors do? Then it struck me: What about my bank account? I checked online and found that it hadn't been frozen yet. But as soon as they found out I was no longer employed, if not sooner, they'd be putting a levy on it. The little it contained should be withdrawn as soon as possible. Therefore, with the intention of emptying my bank account, I walked downtown. Fired from a bookstore position and embarking on a fresh start at my advanced age: It was all so dispiriting that I almost felt elated.

After emptying my bank account, a celebratory drink was in order.

As I approached the Sterling Hotel I noticed that the scaffolding that had been growing around the adjacent buildings for the last year was now surrounding the hotel, and the entrance was boarded up. Remodeling was clearly in progress. It was probably being transformed into a boutique hotel. The last good bar in Los Angeles had closed its doors. There was nowhere left to go but home.

* * *

At least now I could focus entirely on writing.

* * *

The last ant of summer crawled across the desk. I looked down at my hand. A gnawed knuckle was all I had to show for two hours of staring at words blurring into each other on a page. I couldn't envisage ever finishing *this thing*. But I had to. Then I could return to other work: journalism, if possible, which it probably wasn't, or something outside myself—"A touch of the strenuous life," as Michel Leiris said before setting out on a two-year ethnographic expedition to Africa. That would be refreshing. But he was twenty years younger than me at the time, and a millionaire.

Now that there were no wages to garnish and no bank account to drain, my creditors had started sending me letters again. I threw them straight into the trash, unopened.

At least I would never have to handle another three-legged ceramic pig figurine. But what could I do instead? I could collect unemployment for a while, and I could sell things (no longer could the luxury of medication be afforded, which was perhaps a good thing). I was too embarrassed to go anywhere near the bookstore now that my dismissal and the disgraceful behavior that precipitated it must be public knowledge. Let it settle. It wouldn't be so raw in a month or two. Meanwhile, eBay beckoned.

* * *

Now that the end was in sight, I kept dragging it out. Rather than putting an end to it, I kept refining, supplementing, and running word checks to make sure I hadn't overused certain words.[9] I recoiled[10] from the obligation of putting an end to *the process*. Maybe it would be better to go out on a positive note and offer some hope, although I refused to conclude with a deflating compromise like Orwell's bookseller protagonist in *Keep the Aspidistra Flying*, Gordon, who ended up embracing all the values he'd defiantly opposed throughout the entire book. Conversely, I couldn't bring myself to revise or even reread the shamelessly calculated denouement. Such melodramatics were obnoxious and embarrassing but unfortunately necessary if the work was to be regarded as a real novel. But I did feel deflated, and the source of this deflation was at least partly attributable to the suspicion that when I was finally done with *this thing*, I wasn't going to do anything about getting it published—that three years of disciplined endeavor would be filed away and forgotten, not only because I couldn't face dealing with the struggles of trying to get it published, but also because I felt more than a little uneasy about having maligned certain people and certain places.

* * *

9. Two hours were spent using the Find and Replace feature to conduct searches for "endless," "constant," and variants thereof, as a result of having suspected an overreliance on those words. These lexical apprehensions turned out to be well founded: on one occasion "endless" was used twice in the same short paragraph. Altogether, there were more than twenty "endlesses," and about the same number of "constants." There are now eight or nine of each. (One wonders if Faulkner would have run up so many "indomitables" and "myriads" if he had been able to carry out a word-repetition check, although it's hard to imagine him doing anything so methodical.) The word "browse" appears seventeen times: there's not much that can be done about that.

10. The word "recoil" appears too often throughout the text: on eight occasions at present. Some of these "recoils" can be replaced with "balks," but there are also too many balks, which also need to be switched around. "Quail," "shrink," "demur": some of these words will need to be implemented.

A bildungsroman that has been percolating for so long that it has become bitter and stale; a textbook example of the self-conscious novel as a failure of the imagination; a work of narcissism, hypocrisy and betrayal? Yes, *this thing* was all of those things, and more. The warm glow created by low-maintenance substance bribery was one of self-delusion, and it had facilitated the suspension of moral judgment. Maybe it was a good thing that the characters were so undeveloped, and at least there were no plot holes, because there was no plot. Most worrying, perhaps, was the hostility extended toward the reader, who would doubtless recognize him- or herself among the various crudely caricatured types.

There was no escaping the fact that I was the jaundiced dissembler who had thought these thoughts, who had taken the time to articulate them, and was now hoping to fob them off on others. It deepened some doubts I had about my own character, that maybe I wasn't a good person.

No amount of self-deprecation could save me now. Self-deprecation was a disingenuous safety valve, a hustle, a hollow hustle. The absurdity of assuming that anybody should care about what one did required a healthy degree of self-deprecation from any thoughtful or honorable person, but one didn't want to overdo it. Self-deprecation was the residue of self-confidence. One was as self-deprecatory as one could afford to be. But there came a point when one couldn't afford it anymore, and by then, usually, it was too late—for self-deprecation, among other things.

Pondering these vexations, I lay in the bathtub with a glass of tequila and soda (I had switched to tequila—apart from its obvious health benefits it was delicious and had less hangover potential).

Was this piece of overwrought middle-aged juvenilia something I'd want to read? Frankly, no. It would probably annoy me.

It was just a hint of what might have been.

It could have been much better.

Or could it? Maybe this was all I was capable of.

Who am I kidding? This is all I'm capable of.

Unfortunately, I can't pretend that I didn't give it my all. And I can tarry with it no longer. It feels done—unsatisfactory, but done—and all the flourishes I'd anticipated will have to be left undone.

There won't be any more. And there isn't time.

No more time, anymore.

This, however misguidedly, is how I have chosen to spend my time. And even now, in what should be the aftermath, it still feels like preparation, as if I haven't started yet.

Has it been a useful, defensible way to spend my time?

It has not.

Has it been a useful investment of a lifetime?

No. If I could do it all again, I'd do things very differently. I'd do something for other people.

The silence sizzled, the dissolving soap bubbles floated listlessly, the glass was emptied of its remaining drops, the plug was pulled, and I watched the tiny tornado funnel of draining water cast its shifting shadows from one plug hole to the next, until I was left naked in the empty bathtub with some Chopin playing softly in the next room.

* * *

After selling off all the collectible books I could bring myself to part with, I walked down to Mute one evening, laden down with three bags of leftover books, many of which had been acquired during my years there as an employee. (I found it hard to let go of any book that I'd read from cover to cover. As well as compulsiveness, there was an element of narcissism involved in this desire for possession—because I had turned those pages and left my mark on them, as they had left their mark on me, I couldn't bring myself to part with them).

Banners on the sides of a recently erected loft complex that resembled an orange-and-gray cheese grater read: "Live Loft to The Fullest" and "If You Lived Here … You'd Be Home By Now." New dining and drinking options abounded. A shiny new meatless burger joint looked like something that had landed from another planet. Beside it stood a high-end sneaker emporium, with shoes arranged on stands like priceless objets d'art. The gentrifiers were now being gentrified. The artisanal (art-is-anal) bakery that replaced the yoga studio was now an eatery that specialized in toast. Customers stood in line waiting to pay fourteen dollars for avocado toast, which, judging from the alfresco dinners on display, consisted of a few slices of avocado spread on gluten-free toast with pink sauce squirted artistically across it.

An unsightly mercantile disease of new apartment blocks and retail outlets, all steel and glass, crawled down the avenue in various stages of construction. Now that every single place had become a bloated parody or sanitized version of its former self, the bookstore, at seven years old, had become one of the more venerable and long-standing establishments in the neighborhood.

I timed my visit for one of the evenings that Gilbert didn't work, but when I walked in he was sitting behind the counter, and he saw me before I had time to turn around.

He greeted me warmly, making no reference to our last encounter, two months earlier.

"I hear you're writing a book," he said as he sorted through the bags.

"Bad news travels fast," I said.

"Can I take a look at it?"

"I don't know about that," I said. "It's still a work in progress."

"I might be able to help," he said.

"I'm somewhat apprehensive about showing it to anybody I know but eager to have it appraised by influential strangers," I said, as an obvious dilemma presented itself.

"I just sold a novel to City Lights and I've got another one that's being read at Prolix. I'm not going to be here much longer," he said.

"So you're becoming a full-time agent? That's great," I said. The possibility of removing any unflattering passages about Gilbert was already racing through my mind. But his presence was so crucial to the general shapelessness of the work that it would be impossible to completely lose it or tone it down.

"It's up to you, but I'd be happy to shop it around," he said.

Wonderful: now I knew an up-and-coming literary agent who was willing to go to the wall for me and he was the one person I'd stitched up most acrimoniously in the book.

"That's very kind of you," I said.

And it was. But how could I show it to him when he was the "character" I was most afraid about having thrown under the bus?

In any event, I had to return to the beginning now: it was the weakest part. Back in the halcyon days of hackdom, one of my editors often admonished me for "burying the lede," and I was still guilty of it now. It should start with a bang, maybe a sex scene. I didn't have it in me to write another one, but perhaps I could place the episode with Mona at the beginning. Either way, some passages could be shifted around. I could piss around with *this thing* until the end of time, but at some point one had to stick a fork in it, preferably before it became overcooked.

I stood behind the counter while Gilbert combed through the bags, and it felt like a comfort zone, a pleasant relief from everywhere else.

I hadn't expected to fetch much for those books, but Gilbert paid me generously.

"Well, whenever you're ready," he said, having repeated his offer to take a look at my *work in progress*.

"Thanks," I mumbled.

* * *

From the other side of the street the welcoming lights of the bookstore shone out like a magnetic beacon amid the plague of vapid nightlife. It looked cozy and peaceful in there—a precious sanctuary and a valuable resource, the last old-world cultural outpost for miles around. All those nights spent reading and listening to music among the regulars: it hadn't been so wretched; it hadn't been wretched at all. At the time, perhaps, I had tended to focus a little too much on the negative aspects of the job, but it was an honorable and timeless profession, and it had given me a useful purpose. I missed those nights now. Could I ask for my old job back? That wasn't going to happen. I'd keep collecting unemployment for as long as I could, sell things, and hope to get this thing published. What a joke. And under no circumstances would I go out on a positive note. That was out of the question.

* * *

Why is it that the last chapter of a novel is usually the shortest chapter? This one won't be. Then again, fuck it, I'm tired.

ABOUT THE AUTHOR

John Tottenham is the author of four volumes of poetry: *The Inertia Variations* (2004 & 2010), *Antiepithalamia & Other Poems of Regret and Resentment* (2012), *The Hate Poems* (2018), and *Fresh Failure* (2023). A unique purveyor of "magnanimous misanthropy" and "magical cynicism," Tottenham has been described as "Los Angeles' foremost poète maudit." His long-standing column in *Artillery* is widely read, and his paintings and drawings have been exhibited in solo shows at galleries in Los Angeles and New York. *Service* is his first novel.